OFF
THE
CHART

A TAKING RISKS NOVEL

SANDY PARKS

Other books by Sandy Parks

Romantic Thrillers

Hawker Incorporated Series:
REPOSSESSED
OUTFOXED

Taking Risks Series:
UNDER THE RADAR
OFF THE CHART

Science Fiction Thrillers

Infinity Solution Series:
TO DIE AGAIN (INFINITAS SQUAD NOVEL)
TO KILL AGAIN (SOLDIERS OF THE UMBRA NOVEL)
TO CONSPIRE AGAIN (INFINITAS SQUAD NOVEL)

*To friends and critique partners
Sharon Calvin, Laurie Cooper, and Julie Moffett.
May our days of plotting wicked situations in which to place our
characters, building obstacles to test their mettle, and inventing
glorious situations to create laugh-out-loud humor never end.*

OFF
THE
CHART

CHAPTER ONE

Africa

Mobile. Tactical. Tiny.

Joni Bell manipulated a drone, no bigger than a dinner plate, over the African bushveld toward tents of a makeshift camp. Bushwillow leaves ruffled in a breeze that masked the slight buzz of the eye in the sky but did nothing to halt the drips of sweat running toward her eyes.

Doubt inched into her mind. She had one chance. *Focus.*

Four men in fatigues, with enough weapons to remove her as a problem, came into view on her phone attached to the drone's command console and controller. She guided the craft past an all-terrain vehicle and over the broad spread of a knob thorn tree where the men huddled. One knelt and motioned at the screen of an electronic tablet. She zoomed the lens to see they studied a satellite view. The limit of her zoom and moving leaves and twigs of the tree made what they were studying unclear.

Her minimal covert field training had the potential to kill her, but one man, one who offered hope for a fulfilling future, believed in her natural skills. *Prove him right.* Her success and his life depended on it.

A civilian, dressed in the light green shirt and olive khakis often worn by professional trackers, approached the others. One more advantage for the enemy. The kneeling man rose and addressed him. They hunched over the tablet, discussing something on it.

A tap on her phone directed the hovering drone past the protective edge of the tree canopy. Her focus zeroed in on the tablet display.

A low-battery warning flashed. She tapped it off. Another second and she'd learn the exact target.

The tracker pointed at tangled brush on this piece of savanna. The leader shifted, covering the tablet with his arm. The tracker then swept his arm around to indicate something behind them. The other men looked where he directed. One soldier glanced up. He yelled and pointed skyward, directly at the camera.

Crap.

The actual target wasn't clear, but a prominent landmark had stood out on the leader's tablet—an isolated runway with a unique configuration.

Joni whisked the drone off in a nebulous direction and set it to continue on that heading if the signal was lost. She disconnected her phone and stashed the console out of sight. She grabbed her day pack and hustled to create distance from the men.

They had a vehicle advantage.

She was on foot. But they had to figure out in which 360-degree direction she had escaped in a large, wild countryside.

Stones lined a dry gully ahead. The V cut provided cover and aimed away from the dirt road the men used. Minutes passed, and with each one her chance of successful evasion increased.

The rattle of a fast-moving vehicle over rough road sounded in the distance. Were they following the drone? If so, it wouldn't be long until it ran out of power. Before then, the auto-land feature should cut in. She'd disabled the auto return so it wouldn't come back to its starting GPS and pinpoint her location. Hours spent flying recreational drones with her nephew had helped, but one major difference existed. This time she used an advanced drone and played for people's lives.

Her heavy breathing, mixed with the constant chatter of grasshoppers, made it impossible to tell if the vehicle moved closer. She scrambled over slabs of grayish rock and up the red clay sides of the gully.

Sweat dribbled down her back. Dry, wild grass crunched under her feet. She headed toward softer soil only to see the hardened impression of a paw. A big one.

Rain last night had softened the ground while the night hunters prowled. Now the day's sun was well on the way to hardening their tracks. She dug out her meager handgun and shoved it into her belt behind her back. Best to be prepared for the nonhuman dangers as well.

She hid behind a copse of mopane brush and stopped to listen. The damn chirps of birds in nearby grass masked other sounds. Scare the birds and they'd swarm, alerting the men. In the back of her mind, a warning rose about cheetahs hunting during the day and the birdlike chirping communications they made. Great. Did they eat people?

The air seemed oddly quiet of man-made noise. The truck had stopped. Where?

With soft steps, she set out, only to hear an engine start up. They had paused to track and were moving again…in her direction.

The engine strained as the driver maneuvered over uneven terrain, but the 4x4 progressed steadily. She headed behind and up a hill in an area difficult for vehicles to traverse. At her next pause, the vehicle noise had silenced. Likely she had forced them to proceed on foot.

That gained her time, but not much. The moves she made in the next minutes held the key to survival. She longed for Ian Taljaard at her side. His wisdom of the African wild could guide her steps, give her strength. How would he slip away from these men?

His answer whispered in her head. *Become one with the land.*

Yeah, right. Easy for Ian, Zimbabwean wildlife rancher and former British SAS. The African bush was his playground. His childhood pet likely had sported a mane and roared. What she wanted was a helicopter to fly out of trouble.

Not far away, the grassy patches became heavily dotted with trees and entangling brush. That added cover would work to her advantage. She tapped out a quick text message on her phone, highlighting her discovery. A least the message made it out, even if she didn't.

She took a direct path toward the thicker foliage on the flats…and so did the men. They made little attempt to hide their movement as they pressed closer. Cocky bastards. Her hands shook. No help would be coming. She alone had to succeed.

Joni's feet scrambled in conjunction with her mind. Step quick and careful. She had no way to outrun these men, and turning to fight with their weaponry shouted lousy odds. Still, she was relatively sure they had yet to see her. Her chance of escape rested on whether or not the tracker had stayed with them.

Past a large tree ahead, the ground grew rough. She leaped over a small mound into a huge rut. Soft soil shifted under her feet. A stench overwhelmed her.

Shit. Literally. She'd landed in a rhino midden, a communal dung heap. Shade from the tree kept piles of dung soft, and from the pungent odor—fresh.

A quick check revealed the horned, tanklike animals must be scouring a different pasture. She lifted a foot to climb out, but stopped. Ian had taught her the best places to hide were where no one wanted to go.

A dung beetle rolled a compacted prize many times its size out of the long rut. The piles of poop in and around the depression offered opportunity if she chose to take it. Her insides threatened to retch.

In an eerily calm moment of clarity and with no time to waste, she yanked a handkerchief out of her pack and propped herself against the short back wall of the rutted depression. Cool moisture of the mound seeped through her pants. No time for second-guessing her decision.

Joni covered her legs with intact chunks of grass-ridden scat. Her mind, in a strange attempt to avoid thinking about the odors, classified the poop as from grazing white rhinos. Perhaps Mr. Lemmon had been right about her needing a vacation. She was losing it, becoming certifiable. Likely headed for downtime in a locked ward.

Dry ground litter crunched under boots in the direction of the big tree. She put the cloth over her face, folded one arm over it, and then loaded on pellets and muck with the other arm. Once done, she worked her free hand and arm into the slimier mass. At any moment, the men should pass her position.

Although muffled, sounds of the living bushveld came through the load of dung. The men had gone silent. No footsteps, no voices, no weapons jostling…just dang crickets chirping away. Breath became hard to draw. Panic welled, and she fought it down.

Then a faint sound reached her ears. Not sharp or heavy enough to be from firearms. Her gut clenched on recognition of the electronic clicks of a digital camera and then all-out laughter.

Defeated, she flung down the dung-slick arm covering her face and lifted off the handkerchief. One of the men leaned over the midden. To his credit, he didn't laugh. Instead, he straightened and pointed into the air. High above them floated a dull bluish-gray drone, bigger and meaner looking than the one she'd used.

"You're not the only one who plays with toys, Bell."

The humiliating failure left her strength gone, along with hope to rescue Ian. Her throat swelled closed. Each rancid, disgusting breath of air took effort.

No one would ever know if Ian had survived the last mission or sat inside the hellish confines of a Zimbabwean intelligence cell. She'd lost her opportunity to find out.

"No second chances, I assume?"

The soldier shook his head.

"Any possibility I passed?"

"I merely offer a report." He chuckled and pointed at the camera. "Mr. Lemmon is the final judge."

Zimbabwe

The jolting of the pickup on the potted dirt road threatened to tear open the bandage on Ian's side. He refused to slow.

"You can't keep up this pace or I'll be restitching that side." His passenger, Dr. Tambare, firmly gripped the window jamb and didn't share Ian's urgency. Beads of sweat ran down the man's dark face.

"We both know every second counts."

"What's done is done. You can't change that."

"The hell I can't. These people are family to me." A voice in his mind whispered *you're responsible*.

"We don't know what happened."

"No, but I intend to find out."

Bright geometric designs adorned the block wall at the entrance of Chief Zwide's Ndebele kraal. Thatched roofs covered the painted concrete-block houses and huts of her extended family. A wind whipped the shirts and skirts of gathered tribe members.

The chief's sister, Sibongile, had placed a marker for Ian,

indicating no threats to him lingered in the area. He risked a bold entry and pulled up to the narrow foot gate into the clan living area. He bounded out with the doctor on his heels. Ian dashed past the elder manning the gate without pausing for the appropriate welcome. Nothing about what had happened was appropriate.

"Mana!" The elder shouted.

Ian ignored the command to stop until he realized the doctor wasn't behind him. The gatekeeper had used his body to block the stranger from entering the kraal.

Tambare patted his chest. *"Udokotela."*

The elder scowled with the ferocity of his Zulu forefathers.

Ian, who'd grown up around the tribe, returned to the entrance. "Dr. Tambare is here to help."

"Shona have done this to Chief Zwide."

"Tambare has no more control over this country's corrupt leaders than you do. Sibongile requested his help. The doctor has cured people of this kraal in the past."

The old man didn't budge. "The *sangoma* will heal."

And when the herb doctor's cures didn't work, tribe members arrived at hospitals in dire condition. Ian placed no confidence in the superstitious *sangoma*, who less than a week ago had betrayed Ian and his godson, Sipho, while under the chief's watch.

A commanding voice carried over the din of concerned chatter and wailing. The gatekeeper nodded and stepped back. Ian turned toward the speaker. The *sangoma*, or witch doctor, as Joni had called him, glared long and hard at Ian before stalking away.

New urgency enveloped him. The herb doctor had given up, and that didn't bode well for Chief Zwide.

Pandemonium ruled her small house. Scents filled the air, and talismans were tagged on the doorjamb and walls. So many people packed the space, entry proved difficult. He waded in, the only white face, yet accepted as family.

Women wailed and men whispered. Ian cleared out all but a few family, making room for the doctor. The chief's sister moved back from the low bed, revealing a bloody leg stretched out across the dirty blanket on which the chief had been carried inside. Stunned, Ian forced his limbs to move forward until he stopped beside the unconscious woman.

Swollen cheeks, a missing tooth, and deep cuts marred the young face of Chief Zwide—the educated teacher, the beautiful woman who had so proudly agreed to guide the tribe in these turbulent times. New to a job traditionally held by a man, leadership had been a challenge since the first day.

Ian stood to one side of the bed and Doc Tambare the other. Doc checked her vitals before examining the purple discolorations and cuts along her leg, likely broken, as was the arm next to Ian.

Sibongile, tugged on his shirt, her eyes swollen with tears. "Please, help her."

"Where did this happen?"

"On road from Bulawayo."

Chief Zwide taught in the city. Everyone knew her schedule. "Who found her?"

"Jabu. He put her in car. Drove to kraal."

Anger bled in Ian's stomach. Signs were clear that more than one person had forced the chief to stop. The beating had likely included batons or pipes or something able to enact swift, painful damage. Her face, on the other hand, had been punched or kicked. Not a hard thing to do once your victim hit the ground. Cowards. He prayed the men hadn't carried the attack further.

Doc looked up at him and gave the slightest shake of his head. "Sibongile, get men in here. We must take her to hospital."

The chief's sister slipped away while Doc did his best to stabilize the chief's limbs. In no time, a group of six lifted the chief using the blanket as a stretcher. Sibongile collected sleeping mats and ran behind them.

Ian nestled the chief into the truck bed on top of the mats. The ride would be rough, but they had little choice.

With resolve, and rightly a touch a fear, Ian jumped down. "You ride in back, Doc. I'll drive."

Doc stood in his way. "You're not going."

"The hell I'm not." Ian brushed past and climbed into the cab.

Doc reached in across Ian and snatched the keys. "If you want the best for Chief Zwide, stay away. The CIO is looking for you."

"At the moment, I don't give a damn about them." The Central Intelligence Organization and its chief operative, Kagona, were likely behind this, but getting even would have to wait.

"It doesn't matter what you think. You care about the chief. If I'm seen with you, I'll not be able to work in hospital. Then who will take care of her?"

Doc's words struck home. In the last weeks, being a friend of Ian's had become risky. Begrudgingly, Ian slid out. Several men clambered onto the truck to ride with the chief, and Sibongile secured a place in the cab. In seconds, Doc had the pickup rolling down the road. He dodged potholes but moved swiftly.

Ian stood on the road and stared at the cloud of dust rising in the distance. Had his years of helping the tribe come to hurt them? Layers of guilt weighed heavily. His hand pressed against a throbbing in his injured side.

He propped his exhausted body and soul against the entrance wall until the last signs of the vehicle disappeared. The clan dispersed, slipping deeper into the kraal. No one offered Ian a welcome.

An intentional scuff of stone came from the roadway. A scrawny teen, edging toward manhood, trailed a hand along the wall.

"Chief Zwide be okay?" Jabu paused before Ian, looking dazed by events.

A resident of a neighboring kraal, and member of the ruling party's youth brigade that snitched on fellow tribesmen, he often did local odd jobs to suit government purposes, leaving the chief's kraal members wary of him. Lines where tears had cut across dust marked his face. He cared.

"Maybe. Sibongile claims you brought the chief here?"

The youth nodded.

"I didn't know you could drive."

A half smile blossomed. "First time. Easy."

Ian noted the chief's battered Mercedes parked at an odd angle not far from the kraal. Perhaps not so easy. "Care to tell me what happened?"

Jabu's face drooped. He looked away. A shiver shook his thin body. Something or someone scared him.

Ian decided to speak in Ndebele and use a softer approach. "You made the right choice to bring Chief Zwide home. She will owe you much gratitude for your actions."

Tears again ran down Jabu's cheeks. He glanced everywhere but at Ian. "What happen to chief my fault."

"None of this is your fault. But I suspect you know who did this."

"They make me come with them."

"Who are they?"

"Same men who talk to me night after Chief Zwide's coronation."

The news disturbed Ian. The coronation had taken place less than a week ago. "What did these men want? Were they with the CIO?"

Jabu shrugged, likely not familiar with the intelligence organization acronym or whom these men represented. "They asked if Chief Zwide go to Bulawayo day after coronation." Jabu's brigade had worked the roadblock that day heading into the city. "I tell them she goes to city on school days to teach."

Except the day after her coronation and extended celebrations, Chief Zwide had planned a day off, and thus had no reason to go to the city…but she'd gone anyway, later in the morning. She'd smuggled Ian and Joni into the city of Bulawayo under the noses of state intelligence in order to rescue Sipho, who had been snatched from the kraal during the night. Kagona and his CIO knew Ian had been there. Had they set out to teach a lesson to those who aided him?

"What did they ask today?"

"Nothing." Jabu choked up and started to cry hard. Ian slid an arm around his shoulder. "They take me to the road. I not know what they want. Men stop Chief Zwide. Pull her from car. They ask about you."

Ian's nightmares were coming true.

"Chief shake her head. Men hit her. They ask again. Chief say nothing." Jabu tried unsuccessfully to wipe his tears. "One man say she make Mr. Kagona unhappy."

Kagona had declared war. His men brought Jabu to the scene to pass along a message. Kagona wanted Ian to hear the tale and see the results. More stood to be hurt unless he stopped the bloody son of a bitch.

The future promised a heavy toll on all sides, but Ian planned to fight, even as his resources and network dwindled. The only question was…could he survive the cost?

CHAPTER TWO

Hoedspruit Air Force Base, South Africa

Joni sat in a dim briefing room inside the project office where she flight tested Taz, a one-man Special Forces copter. The Americans had infused funding into the South African development project and she'd been hired as a token of cooperation between the two countries. That relationship had come back to haunt both her and the project office.

The briefing room chair seemed harder than the tattered vinyl padding promised. Still, it was a place for Joni to plant her beleaguered body. The cheap floor tiles cooled her bare feet. No matter how old and worn the building, no one would allow her boots inside. She'd hosed down outside from head to toe to remove dung stuck on her clothes and hair and had nearly dried, but a fierce stench hung on.

Mr. Lemmon, a middle-aged American CIA officer visiting the project for the last week, paced a safe distance in front of her with his arms by his side and no discernible expression on his face. She rather begrudged the fact that he used this room where typically her fellow pilot and team members briefed. The project had been disrupted ever since Lemmon's arrival.

He stopped pacing. Wisdom dictated she let him speak first.

He reached under a nearby table and brought out the drone she'd thought lost. He planted it on the table. "This is an expensive and state-of-the-art piece of equipment. Results indicate you didn't have time to familiarize yourself with all its particulars."

She barely had time to learn how to turn it on and off, and he knew it. She remained silent.

"Your failures were many, Miss Bell."

"My mission was to figure out the men's intended target. That, I accomplished."

"And whom did you inform?"

"I texted the info to you."

"Really? Perhaps you should check."

Joni slid her satellite phone from a slimy pocket. After pressing her thumbprint to unlock it, the screen displayed the last text. *Not delivered* shone in red. *Try again?*

Mr. Lemmon chuckled as though the entire exercise had been one big joke. "Once those men picked up your position, they used a drone above you to jam any signals. That is something you should've expected. Next time get your message off sooner."

Who knew? "Kagona and his CIO won't be that sophisticated."

"There's no replacement for time and training. Learning a few tricks can be dangerous without the knowledge behind it. Did you notice your drone running low on power?"

"The stakes were high. I figured it better to lose the drone and obtain the information. Once discovered, I sent it off to draw the men away."

"Your model has a return-home function. If power gets low, or the unit loses a signal, it flies at a set height back to the GPS location from which it launched."

"I disabled the function."

"You have much to learn about the latest drone capabilities."

"What do you mean?"

"The men hacked your drone signal and reprogrammed the return command."

"I thought those transmissions weren't hackable."

Lemmon simply raised his brows.

Great. Outed by a faithful buzzkill. "Is there a way to outsmart the return function?"

"Of course." He let her ignorance sink in before continuing. "You requested a few days of crash training before, or if, I send you back to Zimbabwe. It's impossible to learn everything, as you can see."

Yeah, after today, her limitations were pretty damn clear. "You counted on me failing."

"My tests are not designed for success."

"So what now? Do you expect I'll share intel so one of your operatives can contact Taljaard? It won't work. No matter what I tell you, he won't trust anyone but me."

"After the results of your last mission to Zimbabwe, I wouldn't expect less."

"So, why this test? Why not just give me some training and let me go?"

"Because it wouldn't be enough for you. You seem to think I manipulate your world, that you have no control."

"That pretty much sums up my relationship with you."

"Is that so unacceptable for a novice like you?"

"I'm not asking to be the big chief. I'm asking to be fully briefed on all aspects so I can do my job."

"Seems to me you've been quite effective on my assignments."

"No thanks to you."

"Come now, Miss Bell. I'm not the only one not to share all. What about Taljaard? Did he give you every last detail last week when you undertook the rescue of the Zimbabwean finance minister's son? Did he brief you on Kagona, or explain his situation when you arrived in Zimbabwe?"

Ian had revealed damn little. Lemmon, his observational skills in full force, caught her unintentional fidget and cocked his know-it-all head.

"He's different," she countered.

"Is he? If you'd known more about the boy's rescue offensive, Kagona would've extracted the details from you. The mission would have failed. In the end, you succeeded despite knowing only part of the pertinent information."

"You could've saved me a good deal of grief."

"Do you want to control all the pieces to the puzzle? Be the one who makes the decisions? Do you think that will make life easier?"

Not much she could say to such an off-base assessment.

"You have good instincts, combined with survival techniques learned in military training. They've served you well so far, but—"

"—I'm not a spy, or Special Forces soldier."

"You're a damn good helicopter pilot, Miss Bell. A student might get the feel for flying long before she ever understands the nuances necessary for safe flight. My field is no different. It takes a while to absorb all the possible variables. But—"

"You're good with those negatives." A distinct grumpiness worked its way into her psyche.

He gave his head a shake. "For your own protection, I want you to be aware of your limitations. Today's lesson might save your life someday."

"Don't count me out yet. I still have a few tricks up my sleeve."

Lemmon studied her face, looking for weaknesses she expected were imprinted across her forehead. "Interesting. Overconfidence is not one of your listed personality traits. Taljaard has had quite an effect on you."

"He saved my life."

A mere week ago Ian had stood up to Kagona, who wanted

nothing better than to see him suffer. Was he even alive? Over and over her memory played out the gunshot in the distance when Ian had run interference for her and the boy's escape.

The *boy*. Ever since returning to base, she'd followed Lemmon's tack and for security reasons had referred to Minister Mukono's son, Sipho, as *the boy*. She'd tried to distance her mind from the overwhelming emotions projected from his hopeful eyes, but he wasn't just any eight-year-old child. His innocence and trust of her had reached deep into her soul and healed her outlook on kids. She sought to succeed for Sipho, too.

Lemmon shrugged. "Okay, Miss Bell. You're in charge of making contact with Taljaard, and when you do, reestablish communications with me. I'll get you in the country, but it will cost."

"You've made that quite clear."

"The South African government has given this action their blessing. Likely because the president is a friend of Mukono, but they are curious as to what their neighbor is planning. So, I'll expect you and Taljaard to help us ascertain the status of Operation Chitima, whatever the hell it is. We can't let Minister Mukono's intelligence on it go to waste."

"Sounds fair, as long as you'll aid Taljaard in finding Mukono and figuring a way to free him from Kagona's jail. Sipho needs his father."

Lemmon leaned onto the briefing table where she sat. "Be careful what you ask for, Miss Bell. You might not like the consequences." He walked to the doorway before looking back. "Your flight leaves early. I strongly suggest a shower." He crinkled his nose. "Perhaps two."

"Wait. One last thing. I want to know more about those drones."

He stared at her for a long moment as though discovering something about her he didn't already know. Her skin prickled when his mouth quirked up in satisfaction. "Arranged in one hour. The instructor requested you wear clean clothes. Even experts have their limitations." He and his know-it-all expression disappeared. "Taz's hangar," floated down the hallway.

Joni tossed her phone on the table and lifted dirt-streaked hands. Dung was embedded under her nails, and her clothes belonged in a waste burner. Still, she'd endured worse.

The drone sat there, a stark reminder of failure. Could she act alone and succeed? Given a chance, yes. She'd done it two years ago in the Colombian jungle, yet Lemmon still refused to fully admit the fact. Why? What was so damn wrong with a pat on the back, a job well done, or kudos for saving someone's life?

Asshole.

So why was she going back to Zimbabwe? To prove something to Lemmon? Or to Ian? Or to herself? Or because Ian offered hope for something more in her life?

Uncomfortable contemplating her motives, she rose and leaned onto the table. She had nothing to prove. If Ian lived, she would find him.

The tough part would be convincing him to do Lemmon's bidding before receiving assistance with freeing Sipho's father. A delay in finding Mukono, a prisoner tucked away by the CIO, could cost the man his life.

She flicked a finger at a propeller on the drone. Thinking of the CIO roiled her stomach. The scar along Kagona's arm, his deep, jarring voice, and his unholy, confident smirk haunted her nightmares. He had thrilled at his power in the death of a man ripped apart while alive.

Kagona had a score to settle with Ian and would use Minister Mukono as a carrot to draw him in.

Eastgate Airport, South Africa

Joni loitered outside in a garden area at the small civilian airport adjacent to the air base in Hoedspruit. A lizard leaped from a tall tree trunk onto a giant sago palm and disappeared. Likely it had spotted a predator and sought camouflage and cover. A better tactic than her quick haircut and color change, and seeking cover wasn't an option for her.

Mr. Lemmon had created a fake name and South African passport for her with enough travel stamps to make it appear legitimate. To cover her American accent, she'd practiced speaking with a British one, claiming her mother had married an Afrikaner. The effort made her head spin. Her last attempt at impersonating another nationality hadn't ended well. She'd been lucky to retain all her body parts.

The distant burr of props indicated her plane had arrived. After passengers deplaned, the commuter would be ready to board in a short time. She stuffed the passport into a pocket on her hiking pants and snatched up her day pack, filled with equipment disguised to pass through X-ray machines and containing enough touristy things to make her trip to see the famed Victoria Falls believable. CIO Chief Kagona would hardly expect a woman who had just fled for her life to eagerly return days later.

His mistake…and she planned to help him make more in the coming days.

Inside, the terminal was small but modernized. Tired tourists loitered about with dusty day packs and expensive cameras after sightseeing tours at nearby Kruger National Park.

A television showed news clips of a protest in Harare, the capital of neighboring Zimbabwe. At the bottom of the news screen, a message ran declaring the opposition political party to the ruling Zanu-PF was stirring up trouble before the African Union ministers' meeting there later this week. A protester held a sign with CLEAN UP CORRUPTION in bold print. Another read FREE MUKONO.

Hope swelled. People were rallying in support of Sipho's

imprisoned father. Her hand went to a bulge in her leg pocket where she'd secured the red braid Sipho had given her for good luck. The chances he'd see his father again were slim, but they'd be zero if she and Ian didn't try.

The videographer panned the protesters and then faded back to a wider view. Above the crowd, she caught sight of a drone. Kagona's new toy? The government watched…more precisely the CIO.

His name brought a chill. She shifted her pack onto a shoulder and foolishly looked for a familiar face in the protest crowd. Ian, maybe, or his friend Thabo?

A presence hovered behind her.

"Think Taljaard is involved with that?" an Afrikaans voice asked.

Bram Kriegler, a fellow chopper pilot, caught her surprise in the screen's reflection. She faced a man thinner and cockier than Ian, but about the same height. "What are you doing here?"

"Going on holiday." Dressed in long khakis and hiking boots, he gave his signature impish grin before shifting his stuffed day pack to his other shoulder.

A sneaky, low-down suspicion of Lemmon's involvement rose. "Dare I ask where you're headed?"

"Same place as you, *bokkie*."

In stunned disbelief, she didn't move. Only thoughts of ways to strangle Lemmon filled her mind. She grabbed Bram's arm and with a quick tug directed him to a quiet corner.

"You can't come along. This isn't some action-packed game. It's serious business."

"Quite serious, I'd say. You nearly didn't make it home from your last trip."

But she had. "I survived because of Taljaard. Now he needs my help."

"You paid him back by saving that boy."

Seems everyone at the project office but her had known

about Minister Mukono's son. "His name is Sipho, and it's not like that."

"Then what's it like?"

"This isn't the time, Bram."

He shrugged his acceptance. "Okay, not my business. Although I'm still not clear on why Lemmon is sending you back to Zimbabwe."

Guilt rose at closing a colleague—and her only real friend in South Africa—out of this crazy mission. But she had no choice. Last week she'd flown Taz, a Special Forces craft being developed by her project office, covertly into Zimbabwe. While there, someone from her office had betrayed her presence to Zimbabwean intelligence. Neither she nor Lemmon had determined whom the traitor might be.

As much as her head found it nearly impossible to imagine Bram was willing to betray her, that left work friends on a suspects list. Which left her puzzled as to why Lemmon had risked sending Bram along. Or had he?

She dug a phone from her pack and punched in the memorized number for Lemmon. Bram observed her actions with blatant curiosity.

The ringing stopped. Someone had answered. "What is Bram doing here?"

"Accompanying you," Lemmon answered.

"This mission has nothing to do with the project office. There is no reason for his presence." The comment raised a wry grin from Bram.

"A tourist couple entering the country will gain less scrutiny than a single woman."

She moved away from Bram and whispered, "Hogwash. You don't think I can do this alone."

Lemmon sighed. "I have complete faith in you."

"I can't put Taljaard at risk with someone from the project office along."

"Bram is only tasked to accompany you across the border."

"You'd no right to involve him. He's an adventurer, doing this to have stories to share with his buds at the bar. How could you say yes to him?"

"Make the best of it…and watch your back." The connection clicked off.

She stared at the phone in disbelief at the brush-off before numbly slipping it into a pocket. None of Lemmon's actions made sense, and that triggered her personal radar. He never did anything not in his convoluted CIA plans. Bram was here for a reason. To help her succeed or to prevent it?

An announcement for boarding sounded over the speakers. People lined up to have luggage hand searched before walking out to the tarmac and plane. Low-tech for a tiny airport.

Bram studied her as she rejoined him. "Get everything worked out?"

"Don't take this personally, but to be honest, I'm not sure why Lemmon sent you and even more surprised Obergen let you come."

"Our boss doesn't know."

She shook her head at his brazen move. "I'd suggest you don't risk your job. I'm perfectly capable of handling things."

"Now you're aiming at my man card."

"It's not you." Jeez, could she sound any lamer? "It's simply your help is overkill."

"Maybe. Maybe not." In a rather intimate gesture for casual friends, he brushed her short hair back over an ear. "But I know you still have a yellowing bruise under the makeup on your face. If I can keep that from happening again, I will. The CIO is looking for woman of your age and size traveling alone. I'm along to complicate the picture."

And complicate things he did.

She let her hair fall loose against her cheek. "The fewer people that know I'm going there the better. I told the office I was taking a week off. But with you gone—"

"I called in sick."

"Oh, yeah, no one will see through that excuse." Life promised to grow difficult if the wrong person figured out where the two project pilots had gone.

"Accept it. You're stuck with me until I put you on the train to Bulawayo. Whether you believe it or not, I take your safety seriously." He brushed past her. "Your boot's untied."

An errant lace stretched the gap between her new hiking boots. Irked, she whipped the stiff laces into a double bow before hustling after Bram, certain in the next few days she'd learn where her companion's true loyalties lay.

CHAPTER THREE

Zimbabwe

A grove of trees near the Goromonzi Police Camp, about forty miles east from the capital, Harare, offered few comforts for Ian's extended surveillance. Off and on for days, he'd tucked his six feet four inches away in the branches, watching for a glimpse of Edward Mukono or at least some clue as to where Kagona might be hiding him.

So far, no sign of his friend. That made Ian restless, grumpy, and consigned to shutting down this surveillance and coming up with a better idea to rescue Sipho's father.

Sweat dripped off his face and ran down his back under his shirt. The trees offered shade, but the humidity reached new highs as storm clouds gathered overhead. He smelled rain in the dusty air but saw no drops.

A rustle of leaves and chattering nearby made him smile. His daily companions had returned. Two vervet monkeys dropped down from up above and sat nearby. He made a quick survey of his equipment, making sure everything was securely attached to him or the tree. A hunt for food and water drove these creatures. His continued presence made him less threatening and a target of their curiosity.

He kept a wary eye on a third monkey, which worked her way behind him, a baby clinging to her tummy. The baby's face still had a pinkish color. The mother poked his body, looking for anything tempting.

Human voices and a clunk of metal shifted his attention. He raised his binoculars. During his distraction, two men had exited the building and climbed into a vehicle. The starter churned, then died. The men tried again, to a less enthusiastic response from the vehicle. For an organization of secret police feared by the citizens, their equipment suffered a lack of funding like the rest of Zim's infrastructure.

The men climbed out, swearing in Shona. Satisfaction brought a grin to his face.

Velcro on Ian's leg pocket ripped open. Before he could reach down, the black-faced monkey had slipped out an energy bar. He grabbed for the bar, but the monkey jerked back. His companion snatched the food from the other's hand. In the struggle, the bar flew from their fingers and headed for the ground.

One of the men looked directly at the trees. Sunlight glinted off the shiny wrapper as it plunked to the ground. Ian saw it and assumed the man did, too. He said something to his companion and pointed toward the trees.

Shit. Ian tucked his binoculars away and blended into his perch. A monkey decided to examine the rest of Ian's clothing and starting tugging on every pocket and loose piece.

One man opened the hood of the vehicle, but the other started toward the trees.

The mother chattered to the other monkeys. One continued its assault on Ian's clothing, while the other scampered down the trunk to retrieve the bar. The approaching man stopped, shook his head and turned back.

Ian breathed a sigh of relief and shook off the monkey clutching his leg. The creature backed off and headed down the tree to the join his mate. The monkey below had removed the energy bar and carefully examined it, pulling it apart and tasting small pieces. It let the wrapper drop, which his mate quickly snatched up.

The monkey licked the wrapper, shifting it around in its hands and making sure to glean every morsel. Ian prayed the men didn't notice the writing on the label. The bar wasn't sold in Zimbabwe. He'd found it in a stash of supplies kept by his longtime friend and tour chopper pilot, Mad Mike. Another reminder of how Ian's operations had affected his friends. Mike hadn't returned to Zim since Sipho's escape.

Ian retrieved his binoculars. The men at the vehicle messed with the battery, brushing away dust from the terminal leads. After some discussion, one man pointed at a nearby spigot on a pipe sticking out of the ground near the building. The other collected a rag from the back of the vehicle and dampened it. He cleaned the battery surface as the other pried open the ports to check water levels.

The monkey with the wrapper watched their action with interest but homed in on the dripping spigot. Ian froze. These little guys relished water. With no rivers nearby, and the nearest reservoir a block away, this spigot offered a safe alternative to being away from the protection of the trees.

With wrapper in hand, the monkey moved toward the spigot not ten feet from the men. CIO officers represented the cream of the police crop. They'd wonder where a monkey in this isolated area would have secured the food, and start investigating.

The monkey licked a drip, then dropped the wrapper to hang on the spigot for a long drink. A light gust from an incoming rain cloud rolled the wrapper slowly toward the vehicle. It stopped faceup.

The monkey hung upside down and watched the wrapper.

Pick it up, little guy. Bring it home.

The breeze rolled it closer until it hit the packed dirt of the parking area behind the men. The monkey returned to drinking. Another waft of wind rolled the wrapper against a man's boot. Ian had ceased breathing. The man shook his foot, and the paper lodged against the front wheel.

Crikey.

One man sat in the driver's seat and cranked the vehicle. The engine started up. His friend dropped the hood in place. He glanced down at the wrapper, then over to the monkey. He shouted something at the creature, which ignored him. The officer climbed into the vehicle and seconds later drove away.

The wrapper blew across the lot and perched against a shrub. Ian would collect it after dark when he shut down surveillance…for good. He'd planned two days and given it three.

A successful rescue of Mukono meant uncovering where Kagona had hidden him away. He needed to force the CIO to move the finance minister and hopefully expose his location. Of course, that meant more eyes on all the possible places he could be detained. Not so easily done. Whatever the solution, Ian required help. Lots of it.

The American CIA offered Ian the best opportunity for assistance, only it came with a problem…Joni Bell. She knew more about him than any American operative he'd ever encountered. Falling for her had been stupid and unprofessional, but impossible to fight. Bloody hell, the heat of her body, the dusty, sweaty smell of battle clinging to her skin, and her damn wit and courage had messed with his head and heart for the last week.

If he asked for CIA help, Lemmon would use his best resource for the job. Joni knew the situation *intimately*, thanks to Ian. The CIA would send her back, and while he'd love holding her again, allowing her within Kagona's reach wasn't in his game plan.

Joni thrived in the air. She'd taken control, remained steady under fire, and stolen Kagona's chopper. He closed his eyes and recalled the whine of a helicopter starting up and the *whop* of blades. On the ground, she required training but had the attitude and smarts to learn fast. He'd fallen for that attitude of getting the job done and still finding humor in the process. Teamwork meant something to her, and damn if he didn't like being at her side.

An arriving 4x4 redirected his thoughts. The well-dusted vehicle had seen some rough terrain. Mud splatters had caked to the fenders and lower parts of the body. The driver and another Ian recognized as Kagona's right-hand man, Chaipa, slowly stood. He stretched his legs as if he'd spent hours sitting.

The two tugged a cuffed man from the vehicle. He staggered, but Chaipa kept him on his feet. Ian recognized the unlucky soul—a reporter working for the Africa News Beacon. Guess the fellow wasn't airing stories the way the ruling party wanted.

And that raised a curious question. What story was the man covering in a place that would take him out on rugged terrain and put the CIO on his case? Where was the rest of his crew?

As the men hustled the reporter inside, they took the answers with them. At least the man had some hope of being eventually released. Broadcast companies reported when employees went missing or were imprisoned.

Lucky man. Ian had no expectations of a rescue if he ever fell into Kagona's hands again.

Victoria Falls, Zimbabwe

The colossal vibration of Victoria Falls shook Bram to his core. Spray rained onto the ponchos he and Joni had rented, soaking everything on top and a good amount underneath. The sheer volume of the falls pounded the earth, and its thunder made casual conversation a challenge. But he had little desire for talk as the power flooded his spirit and strengthened him for the tasks ahead. The first—manipulating Joni to his will.

She'd snapped a healthy number of photos, making sure on occasion to capture a stranger who had been following them at a distance and keeping tabs on their progress. Dressed in dull street clothes, the man's initial appearance after arrival in the Zimbabwe terminal had given away that he was more than a simple con artist. Bram couldn't be sure when she had noticed the tail, but somewhere the man had given himself away.

Part of Joni's success was her sharp observation skills. Bram counted on them to find Taljaard, but had to be wary of them not to betray his own intents. The challenge brought a quirk to his lips.

True to her talents, Joni caught his expression and shot him a questioning glance.

He rested a hand on her shoulder. "Amid all the bad, I'm glad to see the falls work their spiritual magic on you. Don't worry, we'll find this Taljaard of yours."

"Mine?" An uneasy look swept her face. "That's just it. I'm not so sure he is. His life mission is tied to seeing the animals and this country survive. That's not something I'm capable of changing. I'm not even sure I want to."

"But you're here to find out?"

"It's a question I have to answer—that is, if I can find him alive." The tip of her chin, the way her gaze penetrated deep inside him, raised pangs of jealousy. She'd fallen hard for Taljaard, and he was bloody lucky to have a woman risk so much for him. If the man felt the same way about Joni, Kagona would gleefully use that against him.

"Hey." He put an arm around her shoulders. "You wouldn't be here if you didn't believe he was alive. You'll get your answers, and I'll help where I can."

"You already have."

"Didn't seem like much. You sailed so smoothly through customs, my presence wasn't needed." He layered in a little guilt and debated how long until Joni caved in and told him about the man tailing them. To lose the guy would require his help, and he had plenty to offer.

They continued in silence along the trail edging the falls. Water from the broad Zambezi River plunged over one side of a mile-long crack in the earth. Once the water hit bottom, the opposing cliff walls channeled it into roaring rapids along a narrow river channel. Joni kept her expression blank, her mind surely debating all the possible choices she faced. He hung back to give her space to make the right decision…the only decision.

By the time they reached the end of the trail along the crevasse, they had two choices—one, to head away from the falls toward the park entrance and toilets, and the other to backtrack along the falls. Instead, Joni walked out over uneven ground to the very edge of the cliff across from the falls. Where most people crouched down on all fours to peer into the crevasse, she stood tall and immobile.

He waited, patience being one of his well-hidden virtues. Eventually, she returned to his side and flicked back through several photos on her camera. "Check this out."

The not particularly well-framed photo showed rising mist nearly obliterating the falls. In one corner, a man in a loose gray shirt and khakis stood. "I've seen better landscape shots, but I'm assuming the attraction is your human subject."

"He picked me up back at the airport."

"Outside?"

"Inside." She planted a hand to her shade her eyes and turned to face the falls again, taking in the man's position on the way. "He's stayed well away so far. Never been close enough to overhear our conversations. Honestly, after what Kagona did to me, I believed the CIO wouldn't expect me back."

"Maybe they're not taking chances. This guy is likely a cheap hire attached to watch every white woman of your build and age entering the country. He'll get bored with us after we make it perfectly clear we're simply tourists." He set his hands on her hips and tugged her closer to bring home his point. "He'll probably report back in an hour or two that you're no threat."

"And if he doesn't?"

"We'll help accelerate the process."

"I can see you have something in mind." Joni stepped back to put the camera away. "What if I'm wrong and he's really interested in you?"

Bram grinned at how she'd just made his job easier. "There's one way to find out. Head back toward the entrance. Stop in at the toilets. I'll linger behind and see if he stays with me or follows you."

Joni casually pointed up the trail to the entrance, and Bram indicated he wanted to watch the falls a bit longer. After a quick peck on his cheek, she meandered away. A baboon with a baby on her back followed, trotting along the trail.

Bram's cheek tingled where she'd planted that casual kiss—a trusting one, and one between friends, the few of which he could count on one hand. Once she'd moved out of sight, he leaned up against a young tree sprouting from between a wide crack in the rock beneath his feet. His fingers, tucked in a pocket, played with a packet hardly bigger than a matchbook.

The man in gray wandered closer along the trail. The little packet weighed heavily in Bram's fingers. He slid it out and stuffed it where two branches created a tight V. Not looking back, he shoved his hands into his pockets and strolled after Joni, trying not to let his feelings for her change his mind.

CHAPTER FOUR

Against her better judgment, considering prior encounters with the Zambezi River, Joni settled in on a booze boat about a half mile above the mighty falls. Built for twenty people but carrying ten, the single open deck covered by a stiff canvas awning offered plenty of room between passengers for animal viewing and private conversations.

Bram snagged two chairs on the port side, where they could sit shoulder to shoulder and face out to the water. "Just sit back and relax." Soon they each had a Zambezi beer in hand and wind in their hair as the boat pulled away from shore.

He tapped Joni on the arm. "Wave good-bye to our *friend*."

Their tail with the gray shirt was waiting down the road with a bike. "You'd think he'd have given up on us by now," she said.

"That's why we're helping him along."

With a plan Bram had suggested and set about executing. Relaxing was the last thing she planned to do cruising on a river laden with crocs. Water splashed against the hull as the boat puttered along the broad, braided upper Zambezi and left the rising mist of the falls behind.

Bram leaned to the edge of the boat when it slowed and began to circle. "Check that out."

Beady eyes, belonging to a float of crocodiles, protruded above the river surface. She shivered. "I've seen enough crocs to last a lifetime." And remembered hearing them rip a person apart. The stench of fresh blood, body fluids, and sweat, mixed with wet sandy earth sticking to her skin, came back in vivid detail.

"Good." He sipped his beer. "Then you can check out the hippos instead."

He pointed ahead to where a hippo and her calf came into view, playing near a flat rock island in the river. Her pulse leaped. A flashback brought darkness, the beat of rotors, and the sight of Ian launching Mad Mike inside the chopper.

Bram waved a hand before her eyes. "Hey, you still in this world?"

"Sorry." She lifted the Zambezi beer and took a long draw. With the bottle, she pointed across the water. "See that island?"

"Not much to see. At least the others have trees."

She gave him a half smile. "I rescued an ornery one-legged man there from under Kagona's nose." Yeah, the CIO probably had her photo posted on their dartboards. Coming back to the scene of the crime rated right up there with bungee jumping over the croc-infested Zambezi. Incredibly stupid...or ballsy smart. At the moment, she hadn't decided which one.

"Holy shit, *bokkie*." Bram leaned in closer, clearly hopeful of hearing more of the story. "No wonder the man hates you. Maybe you should have told me about this before I came along."

"Maybe you should have told me you were coming. The smart thing for you to do is leave quickly, before he slaps us both in prison."

"That's what I like about you, a sense of humor." He sat back and fondled his beer. "I may have wanted to see you splattered in pieces on the tarmac when you first waltzed into my project office, but I've become a bit fond of you since then. You need my help, and that's why I'm here."

"Your office? Have you forgotten Obergen's daily lecture that developing a Taz prototype is a team effort?"

"Like I said, before you arrived, I had a different view on things. Now, flying Taz is *our* project." He confidently stretched his arm across the back of her chair. Still, he had a hint of humor in his tone, saying he enjoyed goading her far too much.

"How did you convince Lemmon to let you come?"

"I didn't. He came to me."

His answer left her confused, if not further irritated. Evidently Lemmon had planned on sending Bram from the start. Everything about being in Zimbabwe with him felt wrong. This country was Ian's territory. Bringing another man here seemed nothing less than sacrilegious.

The sun dipped lower in the sky, but not fast enough. The train didn't leave for Bulawayo for well over an hour, and she didn't wish to show too early or with the man in gray in tow. In this small town, it wouldn't take much detective work to figure out the way she'd escaped Victoria Falls.

A small, metal, flat-bottom boat matched their speed and pulled alongside. A crewman tossed bumpers over the edge along with a line to secure the boats together.

"Time for a change of venue." Bram headed for the small boat.

Joni grabbed her day pack and followed, thinking how surprised their tail waiting back at the dock would be when they didn't disembark. Or would he?

Heart heavy and radar on high alert, the image of Bram placing something in a sapling back at Victoria Falls remained front and center in her mind. Trust was a relative thing, and hers was lacking when it came to Lemmon, Bram, and this mission to Zimbabwe.

Experience had taught her to be patient, let events play out to expose the unknowns, and while doing so, watch her back. A difficult task when a friend like Bram was at the center of the action. Whatever Lemmon had in mind this time, she'd rise above the circumstances and put the pieces of his puzzle together. No more being blind to events.

Their new captain headed the smaller boat upriver before rounding one of the islands and turning downstream. They stopped at a dock and unloaded with no more response than a nod from their captain, who accepted payment from Bram.

"I'd ask Lemmon for reimbursement," she said as he stuffed a money clip back in his pocket. "Your *vacation* is getting expensive."

"Lemmon gave me an allowance before I left…just in case. Said he didn't want you spending the money meant for Taljaard, if anything came up."

That Bram apparently had inside knowledge of what she'd brought for Ian rather pissed her off. Irritation swirled with the dust as they hiked toward the historic Victoria Falls Hotel and the train station next to it.

Bram glanced at his watch, one that appeared to have more functions than simply telling time. "You've about an hour till the train departs. The sun should be down by then."

"The darker the better. When's the booze boat return to dock?"

"After sunset. Hopefully the train is on time and you can board before our tail discovers we're not on the boat."

The short walk passed in silence, while she picked up the pace and kept a watch over her shoulder. Misty smoke rising in the distance from the falls gained a fiery hue from the sunset. They strolled past warthogs rooting for grubs on the hotel's front lawn. The animals' presence gave the early-1900s British colonial architecture a distinctly African setting. The resort, situated in its perfect location overlooking a natural wonder of the world, had weathered several changes in government over the last century. It likely would survive more decades. Would she?

Bram pulled her aside before they reached the station on the other side of the hotel. "Beer might be a pilot staple, but you need food for the train. I admit my stomach is focused on a decent sandwich, too."

"I've energy bars."

"I said food. Save the bars. The way Taljaard treats you, you'll need them for later."

She frowned after Bram as he strode into the hotel, leaving her nerves on edge. The last thing she wanted was to parade in after him. She found a shadow on a low rock wall and sat, watching locals and a few tourists straggle past to the station.

After fifteen minutes, he returned with paper-wrapped food.

"Time's tight." Her irritation at the delay came through. "I'll get my ticket, then we'll divide up the food."

A train sat on the tracks adjacent the small-town station. Hooked together were well-worn general seating cars and a number of red-and-tan sleeper cars emblazoned with NRZ. This one and only train to Bulawayo, the nearest city to where Ian grew up, arrived in the morning and left at night. People, mostly locals, waited to board. For a once-a-day train, the line at the ticket window was short.

Bram loitered, peering into a sleeping car, when she reached the ticket window. "Bulawayo, please."

"General coach is full up. All we have left are two person coupés."

"I'll pay extra for a private coupé." Two tickets would come in handy if her suspicions about Bram were right. She handed over her passport. "It is in one of the historic cars, I hope."

The ticket agent opened her passport and smiled. "Of course, Miss Evans. Tourists like the private cars. Built back in the fifties. A fine piece of history. Be aware the cars are a bit tired. Ask the porter onboard for clean sheets. It helps spiff up the compartment."

He handed over the tickets. "Boarding in five minutes."

The sun had finally set, and only meager lighting brightened the cement train platform. She corralled Bram near the rail coaches.

He handed her a bag with food. "This should hold you over till lunch."

"I do believe breakfast comes in between."

"You'll find an extra scone in there. This train is notoriously late."

"How late?"

"It's scheduled in Bulawayo at eight in the morning. Could be nine, or ten, or on a bad day two in the afternoon."

"I should have taken the bus. It would be faster."

"Be patient. Lemmon warned me against being tempted to let you take one. Said buses can be overcrowded, frequently late. Also claimed with elections upcoming and in a region unfriendly to the current regime, buses will be under more scrutiny than the train. Checkpoints can be unpredictable. Authorities know who gets on and off the train, and where, so they tend to be less concerned with it."

Bram's explanation seemed well rehearsed. Too bad the shadows didn't show more of his expressions.

"Lemmon gave you a lot of details for a quick escort job."

"He knows you well. Said you can be quite persuasive."

"Persuasive?"

"Actually he said bullheaded, but I thought the other sounded better."

The call to board was announced. People bustled past them.

Bram walked her toward the first-class car, whose battered appearance showed its age and lack of maintenance. "Honestly," he said. "I'm not here simply because you're a friend. The CIA is running this show with South Africa's blessing and assistance. I figure the least I can do is represent my country, if only in a small gesture. So, allow me to finish my job."

Joni understood the motivation behind his rather honest confession. She climbed onboard, stepping into a space reminiscent of a well-used Agatha Christie's Orient Express.

Bram followed.

"Are you going to fasten my seat belt, too?"

"Don't think this historic lady has any." He fingered an etched and overlapping RR on a car window, representing the old Rhodesian Railways logo from when the cars were built. "Just escorting you to your berth."

She slid open the door. A single weak light glimmered in the compartment. Tiny, compact, and at best rather tired in appearance, the coupé retained evidence of the heyday of train travel. The once highly polished wood wore a well-used luster, and the wooden bunks showed a sturdy build. On the other hand, the metal had tarnished enough to remove any gleam, and the vinyl cushions were torn.

Joni dropped her pack on a bunk. A stuffy smell permeated the air. She fiddled with the window until it opened. Fresh air flooded into the compartment. Outside a yellow light cast an eerie glow on the platform and train. She watched a conductor walk along the car. He passed a figure standing just outside the lit circle. Even in darkness, the characteristics of the man in gray stood out.

Not much of a stealthy tail. Bram misjudged her skills.

He picked up her unease and looked over her shoulder. The man moved deeper into shadow.

"It's him," she whispered. "Think you can make it off the train without being seen?"

"Don't underestimate your fellow pilot. Although what concerns me is who may be waiting at the station on the other end. Somebody needs to tell Lemmon when you get nicked."

"Your confidence in me is astounding."

"Telling it as I see it."

And likely exactly how he planned it.

"Going with me isn't in the plan. Ian won't approach with anyone else around."

"Taljaard will never know. I'll stay out of the way."

"Taljaard always knows. He has a network of friends."

"Once we get to Bulawayo, I'll go my own way. If our tail or his like follow, I'll distract them so you can slip away."

"Isn't that what you were going to do here?"

He moved back and sat on the end of the bunk. "I'm not the one on Kagona's persona non grata list." Bram offered no real protection should Kagona decide to double-check on women riding the train. "So do I stay or go?"

He had brass balls to leave the decision up to her and pretend she controlled the situation. Her spirit grew heavy as the person she'd considered a friend fell into her predicted ploys. Was he morphing from friend to foe, or had she misread his intentions?

The conductor stuck his head into the berth. "Tickets?"

Bram's hand slid along the vinyl seat to his pocket, but he waited to see what Joni decided. She reached to her pack and drew out two tickets for the private coupé. Bram raised his brows in surprise.

A smile crept to her lips, letting him know she had suspected he'd stay.

The conductor spoke a few pleasantries and mentioned the extra cost for the linens that would be brought by later. The train jolted and wheels creaked. The coach started moving.

Without a word, Bram propped his day pack on the lower bunk against the doorway wall and settled back. The swaying of the car forced Joni to sit on the bunk by the window.

She stared out into the night. The compartment light flickered. Later she would dig out a small flashlight tucked in her pack. But for the moment, she studied the reflections in the train window, in particular the one of Bram behind her as he furtively moved something from his front pocket and slipped it into his pack.

Ian's backside had grown stiff. The monkeys keeping him

company had long disappeared and hunkered down for the night, leaving his stomach complaining over a lost meal. The night shift at the police camp had arrived and, as evening settled in, the last of the daytime shift departed. He waited until darkness was in full swing before dropping from the tree, skirting the parking area, and snatching up his errant energy bar wrapper.

He kept to the shadows on the mile hike to his rendezvous. An approaching vehicle sounded in the distance. It paused under a lone tree by the road. Seconds later, Ian slid into an old but well-maintained Land Rover.

Zamani eyed him carefully. "Learn anything new?"

"Not much." The question foremost in his mind had trouble working past emotions and forming on his tongue. "The chief?"

"Alive, but not well. She is sleeping." Zamani shifted into gear. "Chief Zwide is young."

A similar sentiment used for so many people who had not survived in the last fifteen years, when violence flared up on new whims of the government. Ian shoved the thoughts away, knowing if he dwelled in one place his effectiveness would be gone.

His nose detected the smell of fresh bread. His longtime friend understood his ravenous appetite. Ian grabbed for a cloth bag between the seats and tore a hunk off a loaf. "Thank your wife for me."

"I tell her it is for me. You charm her heart, but she worry I'm not safe around you." Zamani's lips had thinned to a line.

"She's right, but you're too pigheaded to stay away." Ian devoured the bread while digging out cheese.

"I fight for my children. My country. Some days we win. Some we lose. Sipho will grow up and understand."

"Understanding is not good enough. I'm not giving up. Kagona has his father imprisoned somewhere. I'll find him."

Zamani sighed in resignation, believing his advice fell on deaf ears. "You cannot save the world."

"I can make a dent."

"You already have…at expense of your life. I have wife and two children. You have…what do you have, *mngane*?"

Zamani had called him *mngane*—friend—since their first adventure together. "I've friends like you."

"Ah, but granted…only friends."

Zamani's sentiment had held true until Joni had come along to remind Ian what he was missing. Yet circumstances made it clear he had no possibility of working her into his life.

"I've no time for attachments." Ian tossed a chunk of cheese into his mouth. "Zimbabwe needs help. At least until voters get smart enough to find leaders who won't rob them blind."

"Zim has lived in turmoil for thousand years. You cannot stop it. Nudge it, maybe, but change happens slowly. It may not be complete in my lifetime or yours."

"That's rather pessimistic. So why are you involved in helping to fight corruption?"

"Nudging is good." Zamani grinned. "I still have life and someone who shares my hopes and dreams. Who do you have?"

"I'm doing okay."

"What about Miss Joni? You've not been same since she left."

"Doesn't matter."

Zamani slowly shook his head. "Where is my friend who loves laughter and games…cherishes friendships?"

"He's older and wiser." And sadly more cynical.

"When a soul is happy, it gives more to the world."

"I don't need a lecture." Ian took his last bite and brushed his hands together. "We've work to do."

"I only hope to see you smile again."

"I'll do that once Mukono is set free. What's happened in Harare since I've been parked in that tree?"

"Demonstrations." The upturn in Zamani's voice indicated

he was pleased by the actions. "Pushed by someone targeting release of Mukono."

"Likely the American CIA, hoping it will encourage me to make contact again."

"Why haven't you?"

Ian stared ahead into the night. "We both know who'll they'll send to help."

"You can't be sure."

"Mr. Lemmon is not stupid. He'll know she's worked under my skin. They'll use her to make sure I cooperate, put their desires first."

"Is that so bad? They do not like the president. Neither do we."

"The CIA's agenda is rarely clear." Ian had accepted that fact the first time he requested help. "My focus is Mukono first, then taking Kagona and his CIO brutes down. The president isn't even on our radar. That's for the people to choose."

"If the Americans act in Harare to support Mukono, then they show you good faith."

"I will not fall to Lemmon's temptations."

Zamani looked toward him. "Would seeing Miss Joni again be so bad?"

"It's too dangerous."

"For you or her?"

Ian had no intention of answering that for Zamani, or even for himself. "She detests being used by Lemmon, and that's exactly what he would do."

"So you say, but Kagona does not like protests. His men are pressuring organizers."

"Good. No better way to force him to do something. Every move he makes reveals a clue to Mukono's whereabouts. That will help us."

Zamani stopped at a crossroad. "Where to?"

"Harare."

"There will be roadblocks."

Ian patted his friend on the shoulder. "No one knows better how to work around them than you."

"What's the plan? Assist in the background at the protests?"

"The Beacon."

"What do you need from a news bureau?"

"Nothing. They need something from me."

CHAPTER FIVE

The train swayed back and forth, not in a calm way promoting sleep, but in more erratic jolts that left Bram wondering if the wheels might leave the track. While he dozed on the lower bunk, Joni had stretched out on the upper one. Bram's tiny security light reflected just enough on the window to catch her staring out into the darkness. She'd been that way for a good part of the night.

This time she caught his scrutiny and glanced down at his reflection in the window.

He stretched and sat up. "You get any shut-eye, *bokkie*?"

She dropped down to the floor and perched on the lower bunk. "Too much on my mind." She leaned back against the window.

Bram knew exactly who occupied those thoughts. "Why are you so eager to get involved in the political quagmire of this country?"

Joni guffawed and looked away.

Yep, she had it bad for Taljaard. Unfortunate. Falling for someone in this business had tragedy written all over it. "Surely spending three days with a man who nearly got you killed isn't the only reason for coming back?"

"There's a young boy expecting me to do something…anything to give his father a chance to survive."

"The boy you flew out of Zimbabwe days ago? Finance Minister Mukono's son?" Her suspicious glare said he'd regained her attention. "Lemmon gave me meager details. Why's he so important to the CIO?"

Joni hesitated, surely deciding what to reveal that wouldn't impact her mission ahead. "Sipho has a photographic memory. He memorized sensitive financial data his father had collected."

"Must be bloody sensitive to have the state security agency after him."

"It's not so simple. Just because he can recall the data, doesn't mean he will. That's why we have to rescue his father, and there is only one man I know capable of doing that."

"Who you're not even sure is alive."

"Don't remind me." The train rocked Joni back against the window glass.

Something about her reached past his cynicism. "If Mr. Lemmon hasn't heard about his demise, then it's likely he's alive."

"Yet Ian hasn't made contact."

"You're the one claiming Taljaard won't risk connections he doesn't believe secure. You even dropped the rescued boy off somewhere before returning to base at Hoedspruit. Was that his decision or yours?"

She hesitated. "Ian's."

"Evidently he doesn't trust Lemmon, either."

"He thought it best for Sipho, but at least you can understand why explaining your presence is going to be difficult. Ian is likely to stash you somewhere until we've accomplished our mission."

"I'm not so easily dispatched. Besides, if you're taking on this Kagona guy, you'll need all the help you can get."

She attempted to read the truth behind his eyes. Clearly she didn't trust him. Smart girl. He'd believe the same if he trod in her shoes.

The appearance of a few scattered lights indicated another small town ahead. Brakes screeched. Bram rose and leaned a hand above the window for balance. The trained slowed and pulled to a stop near a dim light on a pole.

He shifted to watch two shadowy people on the platform. "Pack your stuff."

Joni caught the urgency in his tone and acted without question. She stuffed the remnants of the food into her pack and put on her boots. "Police?"

"Two men. Plainclothes. Showing badges to the conductor on the platform."

"Think they're coming for us?"

"No way to know." This action didn't jibe with his expectations. If he'd been alone, the berth would be empty when the men showed up, but with Joni in tow, the dynamics changed. He understood a bit of what Taljaard must have experienced on her last trip.

Joni propped her pack behind her back and pulled out her phone. On it, she brought up a book—a damn thriller by the look of the cover.

He stretched out across the rest of the berth and let his feet hang out on the floor. He slipped his hands behind his head and closed his eyes.

Footsteps sounded in the corridor. They came closer to their compartment before stopping. Feet shuffled. Voices whispered.

A dreaded knock shook their door. Bram considered rising to open it, but the old lock no longer engaged, a concept those outside must have realized as the door slid open. Bram opened his eyes and looked up as a white man entered. A second, black man waited in the corridor. The conductor passed in an electric lantern to brighten the room.

"Passports."

For a moment he sensed Joni might argue, but she dug hers out. Bram sat up, eyeing the men, as he unzipped an outside pocket on his pack. The men's body language didn't display the power swagger of a CIO crew. Nor was a mixed-race team common anymore in the agency. Bram took his time to size up their clothes, their stature, and anything that might identify their true intentions before sliding his passport out and handing it over.

The man in charge flipped each open and looked from the photos to their faces. "Mr. Kriegler. Miss Evans. You must come with us."

Bram caught the flash of concern on Joni's face. Had the use of her fake name set her off balance? She rightly feared the CIO, but he had to keep her from doing something stupid and getting hurt before they found Taljaard.

He stood, towering over the intruder by a good six inches. "Might I ask why?"

The man he addressed stared at him silently, as though assessing how Bram would react to an accusation. "You, Mr. Kriegler, are wanted for questioning."

"Me?" He stopped himself from glancing at Joni as though these men had snagged the wrong culprit.

"Please step outside the compartment."

"Questioning about what?"

"We can discuss the matter once off the coach, sir."

Joni shouldered her pack. He suspected she didn't want to be separated from the disguised spook toys Lemmon had sent along, which likely would end up in the hands of these men, whoever they were. They had no reason to target him, but scams were abundant in African countries and he didn't care to fall prey to one.

"I'd like to see your badges and know what is going on before I move one inch."

The men glanced at one another but complied with Bram's request. He'd seen enough Zimbabwean police and CIO badges to recognize these as genuine, or at least quality fakes.

Confused and still trying to peg what or who these men represented, Bram nodded his acceptance. "You said you had questions. What about?"

"Poaching in Hwange National Park. It seems, Mr. Kriegler, on your last visit to Zimbabwe you took not only your allotted leopard, you participated in a raid on a den of bat-eared foxes inside the park perimeter."

Bram's jaw dropped open. The claim had no merit. Hunting—at least animals—was not on his list of leisure activities.

"Gee, *dear*. I didn't know you were a sportsman." Joni's sarcasm nearly made him laugh.

"Neither did I."

The men backed out of the compartment and signaled them to follow. They had little choice. Arguing the case here would do no good. Bram snatched up his pack and fell in behind the spokesman. The second officer made no attempt to put handcuffs on Joni. She followed and he brought up the rear. The conductor appeared relieved when they stepped to the platform.

Barely a dozen steps away, the train started off.

"This way." The second officer led them past shadowy trees to a dirt road where a small tourist-like van waited. Not exactly the kind of transportation used by bandits. Bram had not seen a station sign and had no idea where they'd stopped.

A driver waited at the van and signaled Joni into the middle seat. The second officer, whose features read of concern, motioned Bram to put his hands behind his back. They didn't trust him, any more than he trusted them.

Bram glanced around, contemplating action, but with Joni along he had no choice except to comply. Once bound, the men stuffed him into the seat next to her and looped a seat belt through his cuffs, then pulled the belt down through the cushion. If things turned rotten, he'd be in no position to help.

The second officer then signaled Joni to put on her seat belt. Once done he asked her to extend her hands.

Lines edged her face. She glared at Bram with nothing short of vehemence. The man cuffed one wrist and hooked the remaining end through the seat belt across her lap before clasping it onto her free wrist. Surprisingly not all that secure.

"All snug." The man patted her shoulder before taking the third row behind Bram. His foot landed on the belt, snugging Bram's cuffs up against the seat. The spokesman sat up front.

The rubber mats and interior of the van were clean, but worn, like much of the country, as people did their best with the limited resources. The van showed no signs of the traditional trappings of a police vehicle. No protective divider for the driver, no radios, no weapons, no visible lights, nothing to say they belonged to any enforcement group, except the handcuffs.

The men drove off into the night, speaking quietly, apparently unhappy about the situation. If he had to guess, taking him and Joni from the train had taken longer than planned. The driver wasted no time on the road filled with potholes and uneven patches. It was almost as though they raced the train.

"Where are we going?" Joni asked.

"Bulawayo."

"Why not wait to take us off the train there?"

The spokesman looked back over his shoulder, first at Joni, and then at Bram. In the dim light of the vehicle, a grin spread across his face, but he kept silent.

Talk wasn't necessary. Bram had already started piecing together facts. These men weren't CIO—they waited in Bulawayo at the train station. And considering he and Joni remained cuffed and their captors offered no explanation, they likely were not Taljaard's men, either. So what was their agenda, and how did he and Joni fit into it?

Exhaustion racked Joni's body. Anxiety, plus the constant change from good roads to back roads, wore her down. Bram, on the other hand, even in his uncomfortable position, succeeded in catching short naps. If he understood Kagona's threat, those eyes would be wide-open.

Perhaps they were now, if she could see them under the blindfolds the men had put on them more than an hour ago. From the washboard under the tires, thirty of those minutes had been off the main roads.

The vehicle slowed. Twigs and gravel snapped under the tires. Seconds after they stopped, her seat belt popped off and they dragged her from the car.

"Where are you going with her?" Bram shouted. His concern reflected her own.

The men slid shut the van door and left the driver there to guard Bram. With a hand under her armpits, two men half lifted, half tugged her along. Up a few steps and over a threshold, they entered a cool place. Soon they pressed her shoulders down and she sat in a chair. The blindfold came off.

She blinked at the morning light coming in from open windows. Her eyes watered. It took a minute for them to clear and the rustic house to shift into focus. Small and single story, it had the trappings of an old Dutch farmhouse—a steeply pitched thatched roof, brick and plaster walls, and long windows.

The men stood back, a heated discussion underway. Whatever the problem, she needed answers.

"Mr. Kriegler isn't a hunter. He's had one vacation in the past year, diving with sharks in Cape Town."

The man who had first spoken to them on the train pulled up a chair. Odd, he took away his advantage to hover over her. A posture to gain her trust?

"Tell us more about Mr. Kriegler."

Joni hesitated, unable to read the situation. Lemmon's idea of having a second person along to deflect suspicion on her hadn't worked. It simply gave Kagona another person to torture to obtain her, or Ian's, cooperation. "Who's asking?"

Perturbed, the man sat back. "We hadn't expected you to bring anyone else along."

"Why wouldn't I travel with my boyfriend?"

The men frowned at one another.

"Neither Mr. Kriegler nor I have done anything wrong," she added. "At this point, I think it's best if I don't say anything more."

"That won't help either of us, Miss Evans. Although I do believe your real name is Joni Bell."

Only a limited group of people knew her name. The CIO topped the list.

The man before her smiled. "Yes, I see you want answers. So do we." He reached for her handcuffs and unlocked them. "Mike indicated you would return alone."

"Mike?" She rubbed at her wrists.

"You probably know him better as Mad Mike. He's yet to return to Zim since last week and has been unable to make contact with Taljaard. That leaves him rather concerned. We've tried to help, but none of us have been able to determine his mate's whereabouts."

"What makes you believe I know this Mad Mike or Taljaard?"

"He told us to treat his missy well. He is counting on you to find Taljaard for him."

Missy rang in her ears. Mad Mike's nickname for her. Her initial excitement turned to suspicion. "Why the handcuffs?"

"Because of your friend, and because Mike suggested you were a bit feisty."

She couldn't help but smile, imagining Mad Mike explaining just how much trouble she could create. Still. "There is no way he'd know I was on that train."

"He suspected you'd be tough to convince. He contacted a rather dour, no"—the man snapped his fingers together—"sour individual back at your project office in South Africa. The person passed along your travel plan to Bulawayo."

Lemmon? How many more ways would he sabotage her mission? "If that were true, why weren't you informed about Mr. Kriegler?"

"That's what has us concerned. Care to elaborate further on your relationship?"

Her lack of training in spook skills landed front and center, with no idea how to read truth or lies in this situation. How had Mike heard she'd made it safely back to South Africa if he hadn't talked to Ian? Those two were longtime comrades. Surely they had a way to contact one another…unless Ian was in trouble.

She studied the faces of the men. Nothing she'd seen to date indicated they lied. Instinct, likely faulty, said to trust them.

"I had no idea Kriegler was coming along until he showed up at the airport for the flight here."

"Do you trust him?"

Ah, the man hit the crux of her problem. "He's a coworker. Supposedly sent along to provide cover for me entering the country. The powers that be decided the CIO would be looking for a woman traveling alone."

"And?"

Nothing like throwing a friend under the bus. "Honestly, I don't trust anyone in my office. It's proven to have leaks."

Her interrogator nodded at the other, and the man left the room.

"Wait. What are you going to do with him?"

"We plan to hold onto him until you've made contact."

"How altruistic. Are you blackmailing me for his life?"

"On the contrary. We're keeping him safe from Taljaard."

"Ian?"

"Mike warned us Taljaard was taken with you. He has quite an invincible reputation among us. No saying what he might do if your *mate* shows up. Unless you wish to risk Kriegler's health."

"Ian would never hurt him."

"Perhaps, but it will also ensure Taljaard isn't put at further risk."

"Further?"

The man took a deep breath. "The CIO was waiting for your train in Bulawayo."

The confirmation hit hard. The mole at work again, or did their tail back at Vic Falls represent a greater threat than she suspected? "Does the CIO regularly check out passengers?"

"No doubt they receive names of everyone who travels the train. But this morning my man discovered at least three operatives at the station. I'd say they were aware you were onboard."

"You took a risk taking us off early."

"Losing you to the CIO would perturb Mike. He is a strong ally in our fight to keep Zimbabwe above water. And forgive me for not introducing myself earlier. I go by John."

Real or an alias, at least she had a tag for the man. Her name floated in the door from a distance outside—Bram calling out for her. Guilt swirled. His offer of protection wasn't working out too well. Staying put with these men would keep him out of trouble. "Is he going to be all right?"

"I've learned never to underestimate any man. We will detain him for as long as you like."

She sat back in the chair and considered the various possibilities her new friends offered. "I'll need transportation to town. A cycle or scooter would be best. One I can easily hide."

"No problem."

One of the men who'd taken Bram away returned and positioned himself by the door.

Joni shifted her attention to him. "Is Kriegler okay?"

"Yes, ma'am. Unhappy but okay."

"He eats a lot."

The man chuckled and looked back outside.

"Anything else, Miss Bell?" John asked. "So far your list is rather short."

Meeting these men had changed her game plan. Contact with Mike if he'd returned to Zim had been her first step. Instead he'd placed his hopes on her.

Step two fared no better. "I'd planned to stop by an Ndebele village, but the CIO knows I've been there before. When I don't show up at the train station, they'll check out the kraal."

The man standing at the door turned with a worried look on his face. "Chief Zwide's kraal?"

"Yes."

The men looked at each other. The big black man wrung his hands and stepped close. "The chief is in hospital."

Joni rose slowly to her feet, doubtful the cause was accidental. "Is she okay?"

"No one knows. Everyone in town is talking about the attack. A boy saw her beaten by men."

Kagona's thugs. He had started wiping out those known to help Ian. Her presence at the kraal would only further threaten them.

She faced John. "I could also use whatever knowledge you have on Taljaard. He's from Bulawayo. Where are his old haunts, the places where people know him? He must have a network of friends to have evaded the CIO for all these years. If Kagona hasn't destroyed them all, perhaps one of them will let him know I'm in town."

"Can you be sure he isn't already in CIO hands?"

"When was the chief attacked?"

"Yesterday."

She closed her eyes. All the worry, the personal condemnations for leaving him behind, lifted off her shoulders. "Ian's alive and free."

Kagona had more pressing matters than cleaning up the chaff of Ian's legacy if he were dead. Ian thrived as a viable threat to

Kagona, and the CIO leader sought to force him into a confrontation.

"If you show up in town, there is no guarantee you'll not end up like Chief Zwide."

"It's a risk I have to take. I plan to make my exposure quick and then disappear."

"And where will you go?"

"The one place Ian will know where to find me."

CHAPTER SIX

Harare, Capital of Zimbabwe

Ian stood under a tree, pushing away sadness filling his heart. The grass under his feet had given way to weeds and red earth, and pieces of trash littered the ground. This meet had risk, but considering the situation, the other party had as much at stake.

The trees that had filled the cemetery suffered a similar fate to the grass—neglect. Many had been cut and the lumber stored in a former memorial chapel. The cleared view made it possible to notice a car, which had slowed and circled the large cemetery more than once.

Only one person had alighted from the small vehicle. Ian focused away as his visitor approached, offering confidence that he believed the location secure. Ian's greatest risk was others accompanying her, whether intentional or not.

Footsteps stopped under the edge of the tree canopy. The visitor preferred the comfort of shade. "This is a curious place to meet, Mister...I'm afraid no name was attached to your message."

Ian turned and gave a measured but polite smile. "Purposefully,

Mrs. Chipunza. I wish to remain a confidential source. As a reporter, I'm sure you understand." Ian held no expectations of any confidentiality, but played the game.

"I'm not a novice reporter."

"You attended university in Harare, reported for the South Africa Broadcasting Corporation before going to the Africa News Beacon, and I've seen your work in CNN's *Inside Africa*."

"So you have an advantage. Without knowing who you are, any story I write would have no credibility. But then, I don't believe you have any intention of providing fodder for a headline."

"I'm more interested in a story your bureau is working on in Zimbabwe."

"I'm sure you understand that would be confidential."

"Then why did you come, Mrs. Chipunza?"

Her face blanked and arms tightened about her waist. She took a few steps before looking at him. "Your message asked if I'd recently contacted the other reporter in the bureau."

"Have you?"

"I've tried. There are many areas where phone signals have trouble reaching."

"I can imagine he also failed to report in at an arranged time." He rubbed his thumb across a small, flat stone he held in his fingers.

"What do you know about the situation?"

"Now we've come to the part of the negotiations where there must be a little give-and-take."

Uncomfortable, she moved toward the trunk and leaned a hand against the bark. "I won't give in on my principles."

"Funny, I feel the same way." He gestured toward the tree. "I wouldn't lean back on that. Ants."

She quickly straightened and removed her hand. "I'm not sure where you expect me to start, Mister..."

"Jones." Time for him to give a little. "At his last sighting, your reporter had no crew with him. Did his cameraman also fail to report?"

Consternation flashed across her face. "Our reporter shoots his own photos, but he took a videographer with him."

"Care to tell me what story he was covering when he disappeared?"

The line of her jaw grew taut and she looked away, finding a tilting headstone nearby much too fascinating. Something scared her—a surprise for a reporter whose articles typically supported the current government, even if they included the opposition's view. "I'm not able to reveal that information. You must understand. While we independently report on stories, our bureau maintains a working relationship with the information ministry."

"A ministry that might take exception to reporting on a sensitive story with international implications? Particularly a story that takes a reporter into far-out places where the roads can be rough, dirty, and difficult to navigate."

Her focus shifted back to Ian. "You've seen him?"

Her confirmation said his guesses aimed in the right direction. "Knowledge of the angle of his investigation might stimulate my recall of where I last saw him."

She opened her mouth to protest, then closed it. "The where is doable, not so the what."

"That seems a good place to start." He waited. The next offer of information must come from her side.

"What are you hoping to gain with this knowledge?" Her evasive question indicated she still hoped to get more than she'd reveal. Fat chance.

"It's personal. I've no plans to steal your bureau's story."

She stared down at her sandal-covered feet before tipping her head at Ian. "He's investigating a lead in northern Zimbabwe."

"Ah, so that's why I saw your reporter in the *central* part of the country."

Anger flashed in her eyes. "No need to be insulting, Mr. Jones."

"I'm not inhuman, Mrs. Chipunza, but I believe your reporter has a young wife and family who care about him. His safety might well be dependent upon an answer. To me that trumps the need to cover your arse or protect your sources. The sooner you act to rescue your reporter and crew, the better their chance for survival."

"Why are you concerned about a Beacon reporter? Every day people suffer hardships in this country."

"And your job should be exposing the problems creating them. Isn't that why you went into journalism? Or was it to support your ideals, or for fame, or, God help us all, for greed, like half the politicians in this country?"

"You've not answered my question." Anger seethed behind her answer.

"Because I've fought for years to help the people of this country help themselves. When I see an injustice, it's hard not to get involved." And because inevitably one injustice usually related to another, and piecing together the puzzle of what had the CIO riled might well lead back to Mukono.

He tried another tactic. "What if you were missing and I was speaking to your reporter, insisting you were in grave danger? What would you want him to reveal?"

"Are they in danger?" She adjusted the large purse over her shoulder, likely holding paper or an electronic notepad.

"I can only speak for the reporter. Considering where I saw him, his well-being is at stake."

A grim smile arose. "My hands are tied. The what and where of his story are intertwined. If I reveal one, the other is exposed."

Ian shrugged. "So be it, then. My conscious is clear." He walked away. Each footstep heavy, but he'd gained a better idea how deeply ingrained the hand of the government was in the news media. He'd done his duty…made an attempt to right a wrong.

The ground crunched beneath the feet of Mrs. Chipunza, hurrying after him.

"Wait, Mr. Jones." The sun and humidity added a moist flush to her dark skin as she faced him. "He'd been digging into stories about the financial impact of China on the economy. Over the last year they've been actively developing—"

A cell phone buzzed loudly in her purse. She dug it out. "A moment, please." She stepped away to take the call.

Ian studied her actions. Her chin rose, and she listened intently. Important news? She spoke a sentence, likely asking a question. Slowly her shoulders sagged and a hand rubbed at her forehead. A minute later, she secured the phone back in her purse and walked back to him.

"I'm afraid that's all I can say, Mr. Jones. I've business to attend to."

"More important than your colleague?"

"His welfare is of utmost concern to me, but I can't discuss his situation more at this time."

He crossed his arms, rather curious about the implications of her quick change of heart. "So you have no further questions for me?"

She tipped her head, and that journalistic curiosity showed in her expression. "I have one—perhaps you will answer. Why did you choose this location?"

He opened his hand to reveal the flat stone. "I have a childhood friend whose husband is not free to bury her remains, or return them to her tribe. Her spirit is destined to wander, unable to rejoin her people." The beautiful, trusting face of Sipho's mother, Nomathemba, rose from memory. "I work every day to see justice done, so someday, in accordance with her tribal tradition, I can drop this stone on her grave and bring peace to those who loved her. Meeting you here reminds me of my goal."

Mrs. Chipunza shifted on her feet and repositioned the purse on her shoulder. "Good day to you, Mr. Jones." Clearly uncomfortable, she walked away.

Ian loitered in the cemetery in sight of the Beacon reporter, but his thoughts stayed on Nomathemba. He'd grown up around her tribe and she'd played on his family's wildlife reserve, both trusting in one another as the best of friends. Later, as the wife of powerful Finance Minister Mukono, she had trusted her son to Ian's hands and convinced her husband to accept him into their circle of friends. She'd coaxed out the conscience in her husband, who garnered disapproval from his corrupt political compatriots.

Ian crushed his fist around the stone. That simple crime of the heart had signed her death warrant.

The reporter's car drove away.

A quick call brought up Zamani. "Don't lose her." He strode toward his vehicle.

"No problem, *mngane*. I'll call you when she lands."

Mrs. Chipunza's sudden decision not to give him more information meant one thing—the cameraman had made contact. The CIO had likely destroyed his equipment, taken his phone, and left him stranded. If the condition of the CIO's dirt-covered vehicle at the police camp was any indication of road conditions where he was stranded, she'd need a 4x4 to retrieve him.

As a person comfortable in sandals and a shift, Chipunza would send someone else to make the rough journey. It hardly mattered. Ian planned to be on the tail of whoever headed to northern Zimbabwe in the rescue vehicle. In the meantime, he had a few calls to make.

CIO Headquarters

The flat screen on Kagona's office wall showed President Jacob

Tangwerai speaking at a press conference, basking in the spotlight of positive coverage for sponsoring the African Union minister's meeting in Harare in three days. Three fucking days. Ironically, the group planned to focus on mineral resources.

The timing couldn't be more…awkward, and if the protests continued, problematic. Even more dangerous, the president had allowed a large number of foreign press into Zimbabwe to cover the meeting. Kagona's men were stretched thin covering their movements. If one caught news of the dealings up north, hell would break loose. While he'd like to see the president gone and secretly worked to that end, his own position until that time relied on doing the leader's bidding.

Kagona's secretary opened the door and announced his operative who was leading the charge to find Taljaard. Kagona muted the volume, anxious for positive news. Taljaard had gone deep underground since Victoria Falls, where he'd snatched back Finance Minister Mukono's son.

Kagona sat back in his desk chair and scratched at the damn bandage encircling his head and holding his injured jaw in place. "The news had better be good," he grit out between his teeth. The frown the man wore didn't bode well.

"Joni Bell wasn't on the train when it reached Bulawayo."

Kagona stiffened, letting the unexpected announcement settle in. "What did the conductor say?"

"She and a companion were taken off by two men at an earlier stop. The conductor thought they were CIO or police, because they showed badges. Bell appeared surprised at the encounter and checked their badges."

"An act or possibly some other force at play?"

"I'm not sure, sir."

"Descriptions?"

"The conductor claimed the woman had a tanned complexion, dark brown hair cut to below her chin, and was short in stature. It's different than the photos we have from your prior interrogation of her. Airport tapes offer no clear views of the woman's face to compare for positive ID. Are you sure it is Bell, sir?"

Kagona asked himself that very question. Could he trust the source of his intel? To date it had been correct, but sketchy and at times too late to be of any use. And now the woman they tailed had made an unexpected move.

"All indications say she is back in the country."

"If so, she's using a South African passport under the name Sarah Evans."

"Only the American CIA could equip her with a fake passport so quickly." Kagona didn't care for the many implications of a quick return. Certainly not one he anticipated. If it hadn't been for his mole, they'd have been caught off guard…again.

"Her companion?"

"An Afrikaner named Bram Kriegler. We have a brief dossier on him. He's a pilot for a South African development company flight testing helicopters. We are attempting to uncover more details on him."

Kagona absently nodded. His mind considered the implications, unable to decide if Kriegler's presence at the woman's side created a problem or an opportunity.

"You're not surprised she brought another pilot with her, sir?"

"Surprises should only be brief moments while considering how to manipulate the situation for your gain. What preparations have you taken in Bulawayo to find her?"

"My men are spread out across town."

"I want her found and Taljaard in my prison. You know what to do?"

"Yes, sir."

On the way out the door, the man shuffled past Chaipa, Kagona's top field operative and protégé, who stood in the doorway with a frown on his face. With Operation Chitima about to reach its apex, Kagona expected difficult days ahead.

He waved him in. Chaipa shut the door.

"By the look on your face, I'm assuming the news isn't good?"

"The crowds in Harare have learned the Beacon reporter is missing."

Kagona smashed his fist onto the table and then straightened. "I figured we'd have another twelve hours before the news leaked. The cameraman knew better than to talk to anyone."

"I don't believe he is the leak. The security team reported he walked into the park ranger post at Mkanga Bridge barely three hours ago. The only phone there is controlled by our man."

"Did you monitor his call?"

"We have a recording. He simply asked his office to come for him. He said nothing of who took the reporter or what happened to him."

"Reporters aren't stupid. The military may have stopped their vehicle and taken the reporter, but his colleagues will figure we have him. At least they have no proof. We need time to devise a cover story before the news hits the streets."

Chaipa hesitated. "There is no time, sir. Protesters in Harare are speaking new chants. They've heard about the reporter. They are saying he discovered the truth about why you jailed Minister Mukono. They demand to see both men."

"Let them demand. Stick to the story that Mukono has fled with the money. The cameraman knows better than to talk. He has four children. All they have are rumors about the reporter and Mukono."

"What about President Tangwerai? He will hear the reports and demand an explanation. What will you tell him?"

"I'll think of something. The shipment will soon be underway. By then I'll have Taljaard, the biggest troublemaker, secured."

"What about the protesters?"

"We need to silence their claims before the African Union meeting. Give me time to figure out a way." Kagona came out from behind his desk. "For now, our focus must be on successfully launching Chitima. Is all ready for our special visitors in the morning?"

"All is on schedule. Transportation is set for final inspection."

"Good. Don't let your guard down. Our enemies are smart. We must prove to be smarter."

Chaipa nodded and then disappeared out the door. A speaker beeped on the desk, along with a voice saying President Tangwerai was on the phone.

Kagona took his time formulating excuses and figuring out how to aim the president toward the positives they would accomplish in the next forty-eight hours.

CHAPTER SEVEN

Bulawayo

One thing about the start of rainy season—it also heralded summer and hot, humid weather, which encouraged casual dress. A good number of the men in the bar wore shorts and collared pullovers, and the women cotton shifts, shorts, or simple lightweight dresses, and most everyone sported sandals. Joni dressed tastefully in a navy stretch knit dress impossible to wrinkle when rolled up tightly in her pack, and sandals with just enough bling to be feminine.

She made a quick sweep of the room. Most of the ten or so people present were tourists escaping the heat after a long day. An older gentleman closer in age to Mad Mike sat alone at the bar playing a board game. Mike's compadres claimed he and Ian hung out in the same places for years, until Ian's actions relegated him to underground movements.

The bartender moved a piece on the man's board before shifting away to refresh a drink for a patron farther down the bar. She noted the exits and looked for threats before sliding onto a bar stool a few spaces down from the older gentleman.

She placed a palm-size purse on the bar and fingered a gold

earring as though debating what drink to order. Used to longer hair parted on the side and easily pulled back in a ponytail, she fought the urge to sweep back the annoying locks dropping across part of an eye. Lemmon had suggested a different look for her return. Rich dark brown hair cut in a stylish wedge curved under her chin and long bangs hung over her brows. Her skin had been chemically tanned from head to foot. No more signature red hair and pale face, well photographed by the enemy last time she'd dropped into the country. Would Ian even recognize her?

A memory of his lips sliding up her neck to behind her ear gave her a quick answer. He'd see her coming a mile away, no matter what had been done to alter her appearance.

The confidence helped her smile up at the bartender, who moved her way. A middle-aged white gentleman—she guessed in his forties. "A sundowner for you, miss?"

"Wine. Pinotage if you have it."

"You must be South African." He smiled and snatched a glass. Whether he hoped for conversation or to use her to draw in other customers, he filled her glass fuller than the drinks he'd poured for the couple across the room.

He placed a napkin and then the glass before her. "Are you staying in the hotel?"

A predictable question, but she swore there was more behind it than whether he could charge the drink to her room. "It's a nice place, but no. Please run me a tab."

"No problem." He closed up the wine bottle and wiped the counter but hovered close enough to talk. "Waiting for someone?"

She leaned close as though to keep the conversation semiprivate. "Actually looking for a friend of my father's. My dad recently passed." She glanced down and played with the edge of the cocktail napkin. "Thought maybe his friend would like to know."

The bartender leaned in closer. "I know a lot of folks around town. Been working here for twenty years. I'd be glad to help."

"Thanks." She offered a weak smile as though the death had taken a toll. "I haven't seen him in a while, but he used to sit in here and drum up business. Crazy old codger. Used to call me missy."

The man's features blanked, not really frowning nor smiling, but assessing every inch of her being.

"This may seem a bit silly," she continued, "but I can't even tell you his name. I always called him Mad Mike."

She tasted her wine as the bartender moved away to fill a waiter's order. He then spent an excessive amount of time doing busywork, taking and making phone calls before working back down in her direction.

"Can you tell me anything more about this Mike? I've a couple of gentlemen in mind, but anything you add could help."

She offered a polite laugh. "He would get a kick out of you calling him a gentleman. He flew helicopter tours out of Bulawayo for tourists. Been doing it for years. I clearly remember going up with him. I'm worried with hard times maybe he left the area."

"I know the guy you're talking about. Haven't seen him for a while, though. But I'll ask around. Tell me where you're staying, and I'll pass it along."

Fat chance she'd give out that info. "This will work better." She removed a blank business card from her purse with writing on it. "This is what he can use to get hold of me."

She fished out cash from her purse, but the bartender held up his hand. "I'll carry your bill over till tomorrow. If I can find your Mad Mike, he'll want to pay."

The bartender slid down the bar to continue his game with the older gent and left her to finish the drink alone. Odd, but years had passed since she'd drunk alone, without a friend…without somebody. Hell, she hardly drank at all now. A testament to the number of friends and lovers she had.

Ha, lovers. Years had passed until—she fiddled with the cocktail napkin—until a few captured hours only days ago.

A chill breezed down her arms. She ran a hand along one to warm up only to realize the room bordered on hot. Hot, like in Ian's arms, his rough hands skimming down her back, along her legs—

Heat burned onto her face. She downed a gulp of cool wine. Would he find her? Did he want to? Was what they shared real or simply the aphrodisiac aftermath of a near-death experience?

Ian had never seen her in a dress. Heck, he'd never seen her in makeup. Her outfit during their time together had been tattered, torn, and bloodied, and paired with camo face paint. Yeah, she'd left an impression, all right.

A mere sip remained in her glass and she'd yet to toast to this risky venture. She smiled up at glassy eyes staring down at her from behind the bar. Her father once claimed the quiet friends were the ones you needed to watch.

She lifted her glass and winked at the stuffed buffalo head. The last drops of wine slid down her throat.

Five minutes later she left and began the process of losing the man who had followed her out of the hotel.

Bram sat on the cold floor of a windowless cement cellar tucked under the little house. A single low-watt bulb in the ceiling had been left on. A good sign his captors tended more toward the friendly side.

Musty and dusty, spiders made their homes in the corners, old rags littered the floor, and odd, useless clutter lined one side. Shelves held meager jarred goods, likely canned by the homeowner. Small baskets were filled with potatoes, carrots, and other tubers. He'd searched them all. Best to know one's dungeon inside out.

Joni's new *friends* had moved his handcuffs from behind him to the front, in exchange for another set added around his ankles. At least his hands were free to eat. He'd considered greeting the next visitor at the door, but wanted to take the nicer approach first, since their actions had not yet appeared life threatening. He had as much to learn from them as they had from him.

He stuffed the last bit of bread into his mouth. They fed him well. When the man who'd cuffed him dropped off the tray without a word, Bram had asked to talk with his partner. Not knowing who these men were left him at a disadvantage, one he desired to quickly correct.

The door opened and the Caucasian entered. He pulled up a stool and sat across from Bram. "You don't seem like a bad sort, but we can't have you interfering with your lady friend."

"Is she okay?"

"You mean Joni?" The man gave a smug smile. "Oh, I'm sorry, guess I should say Sarah—that's the name on her passport."

Had they coerced her real name from her?

"Don't worry. She's perfectly fine. Told us you came along as an escort. Not exactly a welcome one. Rather worrisome, that last part, as we are growing quite fond of her."

"You better not have touched her."

"Only to assist in her needs. Which makes me curious as to your role. How do you know Miss Bell?"

"Bell? You mean Sarah. She's a workmate, but then I suspect she's already told you that."

"Yes, she described her surprise when you arrived at the airport."

"Her boss wasn't forthcoming about his plans. She's a bit of a loner. He rightly predicted she wouldn't care for assistance."

"And why were you chosen for escort duty, Mr. Kriegler? She neglected to mention you had any special talents. Or perhaps she's not aware of them?"

"The only special talent I have seems to be getting in trouble when I'm supposed to be assisting."

"Is that so? My friend has taken a close look at your day pack. You chose interesting things to bring along." He reached into the pack and brought out a cloth-wrapped object. "A state-of-the-art nightscope."

"Big cats hunt at night. Wouldn't want to miss them."

The man replaced the scope and lifted out a long object. "A camera with an amazing distance lens."

"Never know when you'll catch that once-in-a-lifetime wildlife shot."

"Hmm. An interesting pack of oversize playing cards. Rather elongated and with little propeller impressions on several. I'm sure they easily punch out. Rather clever disguise. Had my partner searching for the motors." He held up a travel hair dryer. "Your short hair hardly requires styling."

"I was carrying that for Sarah."

"Unique items for an escort, nonetheless."

"Not much different than I suspect you found in her pack."

"In the spirit of working toward similar goals, we thought searching hers a bit crass."

"What? Do I lack her charm?"

"Your charisma is lost on me, Mr. Kriegler. You were not supposed to be here. That makes us curious to know why."

Bram wanted a few answers of his own. "How did you know Sarah was on the train?"

"Come now, we can't share all our secrets with you."

Bram didn't like unexpected players in his game. Lemmon had made no mention of these guys. Ignorance or on purpose?

"My day pack is full of stuff for Sarah. I'm her mule as well as escort. Was supposed to give it to her when we got to Bulawayo. Your interruption precluded that."

"I see. And she is trained on this particular equipment?"

"I heard she's a decent photographer, if that's what you mean."

His interrogator reached into his pocket and pulled out Bram's watch. "I removed this from your wrist. The band is much too large for her small wrists. What did you plan to do with it?"

"Tell time?"

The man had the balls to chuckle. "We still haven't discovered all its functions. Until then, sit tight." Slowly he dropped items back into Bram's pack. "I believe we've been more than cordial, and you, Mr. Kriegler, have been less than forthcoming. I suggest you lie facedown."

Bram had debated the moment to act. Evidently his interrogator had chosen it for him. Before he could move, a shuffle sounded near the door. A pistol aimed at his heart. He suspected the man behind it fully capable of inflicting a fatal shot.

His interrogator dangled a piece of chain. "Facedown as I requested, if you want to live until your friend returns."

"Sarah's gone?" He stretched out on his stomach, irritated at his situation. How far of a head start did she have? The man set a foot on his neck and pressed hard. He undid a cuff on Bram's wrist and pulled his arms to his back, where he refastened them…tightly. With a piece of chain, he hog-tied his feet and hands together. Damn inconvenient.

The second man put his weapon away and disappeared.

The interrogator shouldered Bram's pack. "Sleep well, Mr. Kriegler. I'm sure she'll be back in a few days. Perhaps then the man she is going to meet will advise her on what to do with you."

He walked to the cellar door before turning back and

smiling. "Don't get your hopes up, though. I don't believe Mr. Taljaard is going to like you much."

Harare

The capital, the big city that wanted to be…could be…if only. Ian shoved aside the thoughts and waited in a dusty SUV parked curbside on a back street. The sun headed down. Shadows deepened. Lights sprang up on a few tall buildings.

At first glance, the city had the hallmarks of a thriving capital morphing to nightlife. A closer look pointed out the deficiencies that dragged Zimbabwe to the bottom of the economic scale. In particular, the portion of the city that remained dark. With rolling blackouts, eating by candlelight had become a necessity in the country instead of a romantic pleasure.

Mrs. Chipunza had returned to her tiny bureau office. No light shone from the building or lit streetlights. Other occupants had long left, smart enough to get off the streets before they became dark and dangerous. She emerged and headed toward her vehicle.

Ian tapped quick dial on his phone. "You awake, Z? Time to take an evening drive."

"Right here, *mngane*."

Ian smiled at the nicknames they used on unsecure phones or among strangers. As situations increased in deadly unknowns, having his closest friends, Zamani or Thabo, at his side felt oddly reassuring.

Chipunza drove a circuitous route to a hole-in-the-wall eatery at the capital fringe. This time Zamani parked in a Land Rover in sight of the door and Ian was relegated to watch the rear. Night had fully engulfed the city.

"Hey, *mngane*. Two visitors arriving in a 4x4."

"The rescue team, I presume." Ian predicted a long

surveillance ahead if he wanted to find the cameraman and get a clue as to what he was covering. If smart, these men would wait for sunrise to start their journey. Traveling northern back roads during the day was wrought with challenges. At night it would take guts or desperation.

Ian pictured a night cuddling the steering wheel while the men slept in their beds. At least that would give him plenty of time to reflect on why he drove himself and those around him to extremes.

Zamani's advice to slow down and find a life held merit, except for one small detail. Time was running out for Sipho's father. Mukono had dug up unusual activity in the mining ministry accounts belonging to his political cronies. Accounts beyond the typical ones where the politically privileged stashed their unsanctioned retirements.

Curious, but unable to further trace the accounts, Mukono gave Ian information on several in hopes he could find someone with enough means to unravel the mystery. Ian passed the information to the American CIA, where the money trail produced more questions than answers. One thing became certain, though. Foreign entities were receiving money from a Zimbabwean government account that people at the top wanted to keep secret. Something big was happening…now.

Kagona had hoped to stem the leaks by having Mukono disappear into a CIO cell until they could obtain his records. With his wife and son threatened, no doubt he'd reveal what information he'd leaked and to whom. But plans went awry.

Mukono's wife died when they snatched the minister, his notes were destroyed before they could be examined, and Ian had ended up with his son. Kagona had believed knowledge of the accounts was safe, until he discovered Mukono's unique kid had memorized names and numbers and could pass them along. That's when Ian asked the CIA for help to safely extract Sipho from the country.

His lips curved at the surprising result. They'd sent Joni in some developmental Special Forces craft. She'd arrived assuming the *information* was a stack of papers or electronic storage. The CIA had lied to her, the one resource they knew capable of pulling off the job. Her resourcefulness had burrowed a path straight to his heart.

Damn. He picked up the phone and hit call. "You playing games or doing your job, Z?" He sounded grumpy.

"Nothing exciting around here. You lonely, *mngane?*"

Crikey, his friend read him well. "Just impatient."

"That's not like you."

"I don't care to discuss my psych state with you." A beep came from his phone. "Hang in there."

He hung up and answered an incoming call from Thabo back in Bulawayo. "Yo."

"Hope you're not having too much fun off visiting friends."

He froze. Thabo had used their phrase for a problem. "Miss me?"

"Naw, busy working for a night's meal. Aunt Missy stopped by unexpectedly while I was away. Stayed for a quick chat with Oscar, then disappeared."

The thud in his chest sent his mind in a whirl. Joni had shown up in Bulawayo at a bar he and Mike used to frequent. How many times had a few drinks and a lonely night led to a one-way conversation with the water buffalo head hanging behind the bar? Oscar never had a bad thing to say.

"Sorry I missed her." A flash of moist lips, bare skin, and hot breaths against his neck tightened his body. "Did she head home?"

"Still in town. Staying with a friend, I believe. Do you want me to invite her over?"

His phone beeped again, but he ignored it. Why did everything happen at once?

"It's not necessary. I'll ring you back when I get home." He tapped off the call and took a long breath. His pulse pounded at the news. A thousand memories of their few special hours together in the barn ate at his soul.

His phone vibrated. This time he answered.

"You on the moon, *mngane*? Your friend's left. I'm a block away. Take two right turns."

Crap. He gunned the engine and sped off in pursuit.

Joni had taken a foolish risk coming back. Damn the CIA. Lemmon had no right to endanger her life.

Ian considered a dozen scenarios as he and Zamani kept the 4x4 in sight. The men drove north of Harare. He had a decision to make—follow these men when they set out for the cameraman and uncover what secret scheme the government had underway, or find Joni, keep her out of Kagona's hands, and learn what the Americans expected of him?

Ian punched Z's number.

"Yebo, mngane."

"We need to talk."

CHAPTER EIGHT

Bulawayo

The air hung sticky around the little farmhouse where Mr. Kriegler had been tucked safely into the basement for the night. Much-needed rain threatened. John sat at a rickety table that barely fit two people and watched his companion Fadziso pinch off a hunk of corn *sadza* and roll it in his palm. Once satisfied with its shape, he dipped the porridge ball in a spicy red relish of tomato, pepper, and onion.

John finished off the rest of his peanut butter stew and pushed the bowl away. The phone on the table buzzed. He checked the name. "You missed a cloudy sunset," he answered.

"Counting on you to savor it for me. How's my girl doing? Did she make it to see you okay?"

"Had a small snag with that."

Mad Mike went silent for a second while digesting the news. "Didn't get mugged or anything, did she?"

"No, just had company along on the trip. A last-minute thing, I guess. Nice fellow. Staying with us this evening. Doing some work downstairs." Mad Mike would know exactly where they had stashed Mr. Kriegler.

"Where is she now?"

"Out trying to find an old friend."

"Splendid. She's a social gal. Hope she finds everyone well."

He could hear Mad Mike's concern about his friend Taljaard. Word was he'd been injured. Then nothing else circulated. They all worried he'd run into problems. The man had a reputation for helping out Ndebele, Shona, or anyone who had conflicts with the government.

"I'm sure I'll hear all about her visit when she gets back."

Fadziso wielded a wood spoon. "Tell him I have his cycle fixed up. Needs paint, but looks smart."

"Sounds like my Shona friend speaking." Mike had overheard Fadziso's comment. "Feed him well. He's the only one I let touch my machines."

Fadziso grinned. Bits of yellow stuck to his mouth.

"He's stuffing mac and cheese into his face as we speak." Whether working on Mike's helo or a tiny scooter, mechanical things fell under Fadziso's spell.

John rose and carried his bowl into the kitchen. With Mike's sudden departure under circumstances that put anyone associated with him at risk, John had taken refuge with Fadziso back at his little farmhouse he'd bought off a relative, who'd claimed it under land redistribution. "Any idea when you'll be back?"

"I'm searching for an old friend, too. Not an easy guy to catch, but his family needs him. Don't know how long that will take. You don't need me anyway, with a visitor to entertain."

"Thanks for reminding me. We're looking forward to playing with the toys our unexpected visitor brought."

John reached for the watch he'd laid on a wood chest in the kitchen…only it was gone. Perhaps he'd moved it elsewhere. He looked around.

"You still there?" Mike asked.

A rumble came from outside. It took a second for the sound to register in John's mind.

"Duzvi!" Fadziso lunged to his feet and flew out the door.

John dropped the phone to the counter and ran for the barn, where Fadziso had been rebuilding Mike's motorcycle. Down the drive near the road, a cycle motor accelerated.

John sprinted to the van. He shoved the key in the ignition, but nothing happened. "Bloody hell."

He dashed back inside the house. Moist breeze blew in through an open window in the back room where Fadziso had been going through Kriegler's pack. Nothing remained on the low table where he'd been working.

Fadziso's footsteps pounded into the house. "Kriegler is gone. He laid the cuffs and chain out nice and neat in cellar. He's laughing at us."

And at the moment there was damn little they could do about it. They had no contact number to warn Joni in Bulawayo. Following Kriegler blindly into town could be a trap for them all.

"Nothing we can do until we get the van fixed." John stormed back to the kitchen and rummaged for flashlights.

Ten minutes later, Fadziso wiped his hands on a rag and clicked off the flashlight on his cap. "Easy things are reconnected. The next might take a while."

"How long?"

"With right tools and in good light…an hour."

"Without those things?"

"Maybe two." Fadziso had spent a month playing with Mike's motorcycle. Finding vehicle parts had grown into a sport. "Enough time to give our visitor a solid lead."

John paced. No solutions sprang to mind. "He stole back his stuff while we ate."

"What do think he has planned?"

"No way to know." Mad Mike was going to be royally

ticked. "But I can tell you one thing, I'm no novice at restraints. Kriegler is a lot more than an office mate."

Fadziso tossed his rag onto the open hood. "Miss Bell better watch her back."

"Bloody hell. She doesn't stand a chance."

Mad Mike's quaint little cottage tucked away on a back road seemed out of character for an old codger with one leg and a crusty demeanor. Sure, he had a dirt front yard, but the metal roof was in good repair and the whitewashed wood gave it a lived-in look…at least it had on her one daytime view from a vehicle last week. Tonight she nearly drove past the cottage, which sat lifeless in the dark.

Joni tucked her scooter into a spot in back that showed signs of sheltering a larger bike from prying eyes. She had changed from a dress to practical wear back at the hotel, where the front desk had held onto her stuffed day pack while she visited the bar. Her ears rang from the hour it took to lose anyone following her scooter before she'd doubled back to Mike's place.

A pocket light guided her over unfamiliar ground. She moved with cautious steps around to the back of the cottage. Experience had taught her Mike left nothing to chance. He counted on trouble, thus planned for it. An unexpected visitor, like her, meant trouble.

Crazy as Mike might seem, he had a green thumb. On the back porch, a potted succulent sat on each side of the door. One had star-shaped yellow flowers with tiger stripes. The other was a campfire plant, like she grew at her apartment. The thick propeller-like leaves were fitting for a chopper pilot. Both plants preferred dry soil and underwatering. Perfect for someone with an unpredictable schedule.

She shifted the campfire plant aside in order to shine the light around the frame. With no visible house lock, Mike would have rigged something to discourage people from messing with his stuff. Her eye caught a slight shadow. She kneeled to inspect the spot. Something breached the gap between the door and the jamb. The narrow space required a credit card. Too bad she didn't have one.

What if Mike came home without one? Did he hide a substitute under the potted plant? Close inspection of the plants revealed a thin piece of metal, with a little notch in it, stuck into the soil near a stalk.

The metal easily slid into the space under the obstruction. After moving the piece to a few positions, the notch caught and released a spring. Still uncertain of the function, she flattened herself against the cottage wall and opened the latch. She slowly pushed the door wide and counted to ten. Nothing happened.

A quick reconnaissance noted a tiny canister mounted above the door and angled toward the person entering. "Tricky, Mike. What's in it? Mace? Pepper spray?"

If the CIO had checked out his place after the adventure she, Mike, and Ian had had in Victoria Falls last week, nothing gave away their presence. An eerie quiet hung over the interior, reminding her she was an uninvited guest. Night birds' songs drifted inside, and tree leaves rustled. With care, she closed the door, dropped down a latch, and added a safety lock.

She bypassed a light switch and maneuvered around a relatively tidy main room that sat between a kitchen on one wall and a bedroom and bath along the other. Two cupboards and a counter with a sink made up the kitchen wall. She slid her day pack off and onto the counter. Past it, a well-used kerosene lamp sat on a wood tabletop mounted on a battered metal fuel barrel. Dining at its best. A fire starter lay next to the lamp. Once a good glow filled the cottage, she turned off her light and secured it in a leg pocket.

A quick survey exposed no further booby traps, at least no obvious ones. In the narrow bedroom, a blanket had been thrown up over the pillow. Mike had expected to return the day he left.

Hunger drove her back toward the kitchen. On the way she flicked the overhead light switch, to no response. Rolling blackouts. The quiet in the cottage made sense.

A scout of the cupboards uncovered canned goods, moldy bread, crackers, jam, cheese, dried figs, honey, and green bottles of beer. Enough food to feed her for a few days while she hunted for Ian. She expected a short stay. The man at the bar knew something.

After a meal of crackers and cheese and a slightly cool beer she rescued from the silent small fridge, she settled on a sofa just large enough for a man to stretch out. Mike had no computer or television, only a stack of books on a low table and a wood box to the side that held magazines. Some were stuffed in haphazardly and two others were tightly rolled.

She snatched up a month-old hunting magazine. Then a health magazine touting How to Get Six-Pack Abs. "Yeah, I ought to check that one out." She tossed them on the couch and reached for a rolled magazine. The loose pages were tucked to the inside, and a string held it together.

She slid off the string. The magazine was two years old. *Strange.*

A few odd clicks indicated the electricity had come on. The small fridge purred. She checked her watch. Eleven p.m. The rolling brown out had ended.

Curious about what produced the nearby clicks, she examined Mike's place with a more critical eye. He had equipment hidden from the casual observer. No surprise there. The wily guy camouflaged his helicopter to keep vandals away.

Mad Mike and Ian's father had belonged to an elite team of Special Forces soldiers who operated back in the days when the country had been called Rhodesia.

Her last adventure with Ian and Mike had shown their survival and tracking skills came not from fancy equipment, but from knowledge and spirit within. They loved this country. While a change in government had been in the stars for the right reasons, not all the changes had proved positive for a country unable to avoid corruption.

A tiny beep emanated from the low coffee table. A thin drawer beneath it held a long-handled flashlight. She set the light on the table and reached back inside. The drawer was empty.

She slid her fingers along the underside of the table where the drawer fit. They played over a rectangular object taped in place. Likely a phone. She left it alone.

Personal protection ranked high on everyone's list when living in an uncertain country. Mike was in his sixties and walked with a limp because of a war injury. He seemed to have a proverbial target on his back. However, pity the poor miscreants who pictured him as easy pickings.

In a tall canister by the door sat an old-fashioned umbrella with a long, stiff handle. A cane next to the umbrella had a shiny brass derby handle, which could inflict pain if swung properly. The drawers in the kitchen held an array of knives, more than he'd need to prepare meals for one person. A long, thin ice pick rolled to the front in another. Who needed one today? His fridge didn't have a freezer. She set it on the counter behind an empty soda can.

In the bathroom, a little cabinet by the sink held shaving cream, razors, and hair spray. Mike didn't seem the stylish hair type. Heck, his was thinning in too many places to style. A one-flick lighter lay next to the hair spray. Dangerous.

She crossed her arms and leaned back against the doorjamb. Even though a stranger to Mike's place, every touch reminded her of the endearing—although cautious—old codger. Ian and Mike probably had shared a few good beers here together.

If so, Mike left few signs behind. A purposeful move to protect friends or a necessary lifestyle he'd adopted through adversity?

Few personal things lay about his place. In the bedroom, a single four-by-six frame sat on a small dresser. A faded photo of a woman in a park smiled up.

Feeling every bit a voyeur, but unapologetic for it, Joni carried the frame back to the main room for better light. The photo had yellowed, and the colors faded from vivid to pastel. The hair and dress suggested the 1970s or even eighties. The woman had a twinkle in her eyes and a mischievous grin. Not a plain Jane or a stark beauty, but her composure radiated a certain sex appeal, just the type to wrap Mike around her little finger.

As the only visible photo in the cottage, Mike clearly treasured it.

"Someone once tamed your crazy ways, Mike…or at least loved them."

What if Kagona prevented him from ever returning? She placed the frame facedown and worked off the backing. A name in flowing cursive had been penned on the back, but fading ink left it unreadable.

Photo in hand, she settled onto the couch. No matter how many different ways she tilted the back, the name escaped her.

She swung her feet up on the old couch and stretched out. Was this the life that awaited Ian if he stayed in Zimbabwe: a tiny cottage without personal touches, a photo of her near his bed, and memories to sustain him? Would his warmth go unshared? His touch be merely that of cold sheets beside him?

The long day and food produced a yawn. She secured the photo and then slung a crocheted blanket over her shoulders and curled her legs up. The only thing missing…strong arms to draw her into a protective clutch.

Was Ian the real reason she'd returned, or had it more to do with shoring up her own self-confidence? Face reality, girl. Ian might be pissed she'd come back. Her lack of field skills had put him and Mike at risk. Had her one-night stand with Ian resulted from their near-death experiences? Had she fallen for her rescuer?

Shame rose at the doubts. He'd risked everything for her. Or had it been for Sipho?

She shoved away truths that revealed her inadequacy. Plain and simple, she'd come to find answers about a boy's father. About her life. About Ian's. With closed eyes, she pictured his cocky smile, his self-assurance, and his dogged pursuit of the enemy.

By the time she awoke with nightmares dogging her memories, hours had passed. She sat up and rubbed her face. What if Ian didn't show in the next few days? How long could she stay here unnoticed? How many days could she return to the bar before the CIO caught her or followed her here?

She considered brushing her teeth but decided to forgo anything more than a pee before turning out the light and hoping for more sleep and a productive day in the morning. The floor creaked under her boots, creating spooky music on the way to the bathroom. Maybe she'd let the lamp burn through the night.

With the basics complete, she zipped her pants and turned on the sink spigot to wash. Nothing came out. Her swear cut off in midstream.

A screech of wood being pried and splintered came from the living area. She partially closed the door of the closet-size bathroom and peeked out. Wood under stress groaned at the kitchen window. Someone knew to avoid the door.

Her hands shook. The tiny toilet window provided air, but no escape. She peered out the door again. A shadow appeared through the kitchen window as it slowly opened. She slid back to the corner where Mike stored his mop and broom.

Both had sturdy wood handles. But the shredded bristles and limp mop head would add an awkward element to a fight. *Unless.* With two easy twists, she screwed the mop head off.

Mike had sharpened the pole beneath it to a point. Another case of planning ahead?

Footsteps dropped to the floor. Certainly Ian wouldn't pry open Mike's window when he could use the door?

She peered out, the mop spear in hand. A lean face with dark complexion protruded from a shirt hanging loose over long pants. A second look revealed no familiar features of Ian's friends or even her new acquaintance Fadziso. This could be Kagona's man or simply a looter creating havoc for the locals.

The man moved about as though assessing items for easy sale. Her pack sat on the kitchen counter not far from the window, but for the minute he ignored it. Made sense. He planned to snatch it on the way out. Instead, the table drew his attention. He scooped up the keys to her scooter.

Her blood chilled. She'd be out of commission without wheels.

As though aware someone watched, he turned and stared at the bathroom door. A wicked smile rose on his face. Confident bastard. He'd scouted the cottage and knew she stayed here…alone.

A sense of injustice riled her up. He didn't work for Kagona. He worked for himself.

The fear shaking her hands refocused into stopping this common thief from destroying everything she'd risked. Letting out a war whoop, she barreled out with the sharpened mop staff pointed at his midsection. His eyes widened in surprise, then flashed to a kitchen drawer.

Go for it, creep. She drove at him via the kitchen to keep him from reaching the knives. In response, he snatched up the kerosene lamp and backed up, keys still in hand. She caught up to him before he reached the door.

"Drop the keys." She jabbed the mop handle toward him with its pointed end threatening.

A brash grin blossomed on his face. He held the lamp high and dared her to skewer him while he escaped.

Call her a coward, but stabbing a fleeing man or burning down Mike's place if he dropped the lamp didn't rate in her game plan…and damned if the bastard didn't fully realize it.

He swung open the door and stepped outside. Overconfident, he turned back in victory and dangled the scooter keys.

"Prick." In total indignation, she yanked the fine trip wire attached to the cylinder perched above the doorframe.

Pepper spray foamed crimson on the man's face. Grin gone, he staggered back, his fingers releasing the lamp. Joni abandoned the mop and lunged after the lantern. The foam-slimed glass and ceramic slipped through her fingers, but she softened the fall and it landed unbroken.

The thief frantically clutched at his face. With agonizing screams, he retreated. Through eyes watering from the spray's pungent smell, she glimpsed light gleaming off keys falling from his hands. They disappeared into wild grass and dust.

The man tore off his shirt and wiped at the spray stuck to his face. His form faded into the night-shrouded yard, but his labored breathing and cries of pain echoed in the air.

Her fingers sizzled from touching the contaminated lamp and her arm burned where it had brushed against pepper oils on the doorjamb. She flicked on the one overhead light and ran for the kitchen sink. No water came out of the faucet. A frantic urgency pushed to cleanse her burning skin. *Calm and think, girl.*

Her save-the-planet college roommate had been sprayed more than once. The girl bragged she wore gloves and had decontamination stuff with her on protests. A little late for gloves, but Joni remembered the dish soap and water mixture her bohemian friend prepared.

She grabbed the soap container by the sink and snatched up the mop handle. Needing to stop the burning drove her out to the side yard. A watering bucket sat against the well house near the parked scooter. After adding a liberal amount of soap in the bucket, she dunked her arms up to her elbows, again and again.

After much of the spray's oily sheen had been washed away, her skin still burned. She clawed at the ground, letting the dusty clay cover her hands and hopefully soak the remaining oil from her pores. Another rinse/dirt/rinse reduced the pain to bearable.

Coughs and harsh wheezing sounded close…very close. She launched backward, shoving against the bucket to spill the contents. No reason to give the intruder a way to get relief and then get even.

She rolled to her feet with her fingers fisted around the mop handle. Water sloshed from the tipping bucket, but the well house wall held it upright. The thief was ten feet away and closing too fast for her to attack the bucket again.

She sprinted for the cottage, figuring he wanted the bucket more than a confrontation. He didn't follow, but once he tamed his burning skin and eyes, revenge might be on his mind. Undeterred but more cautious, she returned to the yard to look for the scooter keys before he recovered.

Her fingers stiffly opened the leg pocket on her pants and fumbled for the light. Its narrow beam against weedy clumps of grass made the search tedious. With hardened heart, she faced the sounds of his cleansing and swept the ground with her light. The keys had to be close.

Dirt crunched under shoes of someone fast approaching from behind. She raised the mop handle and spun around, but not quick enough. The stick twisted easily out of her grip.

"Get inside." A solid hand to her back prodded her forcefully along.

The moment of surprise cost her a good five feet from her spot. "Bram?" She halted. "I have to find the scooter keys."

A string of unintelligible expletives came from the darkness.

Bram glanced toward the voice. "He's why you're not arguing with me on this. It's not safe out here."

"He's incapacitated."

"But enough of a threat you used pepper spray on him." Bram pushed her along again.

"He was going to steal the scooter. Without it, I can't hunt down Ian."

"Finding Taljaard is secondary to your protection."

"Fine. Protect me while I find the keys."

"Safety first. Keys later."

Suspicions rose, and she dug in her heels. "Wait. How did you get here?"

"Move now. We'll talk inside."

"Do you have a vehicle?"

He stopped and stared at her, as though incredulous she questioned his command. "Sure, I dropped in at the friendly rental agency on the way."

"Smart-ass. You had to get here some way." She attempted to twist away, but much to her chagrin, he countered, stepping in her way. "Did Mike's men bring you?"

"Mike who?"

She realized her slip. For their protection, the men purposefully hadn't been introduced. "How did you escape?"

"They let me go. Evidently, not because you asked them nicely." The lamp sitting on the porch highlighted irritation on his face.

"Look, I can't risk that thief will find the scooter keys. So unless you have transportation, I'm hunting for them."

Bram glanced toward the dark side yard, where water splashed. "Listen to me, *bokkie*. Your encounter with that guy has left you high-strung. You're not thinking straight. Once I tuck you safely inside, I'll come back out and look around." He pushed her toward the cottage.

"Two of us working together are safer than one."

"You're not going to win this one. Inside." He tossed the mop stick onto the porch and clamped his hand around her wrist that had been exposed to the pepper spray. Nerves along her traumatized skin lit up. An anguished yelp escaped.

He stepped onto the front porch and tugged her toward the door.

"Damn it, let go!" She twisted away and chopped her other hand at his wrist clamping onto hers. He easily caught her arm.

A solid body thrust past her from behind and slammed into Bram. A brief flash of light skin said the attacker wasn't the pepper-sprayed thief. Bram's hold broke, and together the men fell through the open door into the cottage.

Recognition clicked.

"Ian!" she shouted as the door slammed behind them and a resounding clank indicated the inside latch had fallen into place, leaving her alone outside on the porch.

Off balance, she stepped onto the mop handle and stumbled along the porch, accidentally kicking the lantern. It smashed against the side of Mike's cottage. The ceramic base shattered, flinging kerosene across the wood planking.

"Holy crap."

Flames erupted and dashed along the fuel path, setting the porch on fire.

CHAPTER NINE

An odd rage filled Ian. This stranger had dragged Joni toward the cottage, leaving her shrieking in pain. Whoever he was, a brief lesson in civility, Ian's style, wouldn't hurt. He grabbed the man behind his knees and flipped him to the cottage floor. Controlling one of the man's legs, Ian landed hard across his upper chest and went for a choke hold.

Joni's attacker expected the move. He deflected Ian's arms and shifted his body behind Ian, attempting to latch his legs around Ian's torso. Damn, if the guy wasn't attempting his own choke.

Second nature had Ian countering even as he assessed his opponent's skill level. Ian twisted out of the man's grasp. This bastard had grappled before.

The man rolled free to his feet and leaped over the coffee table, landing on the far side and snatching up a flashlight. "You and I need to talk."

"Like you were talking to Joni?" Ian followed, ducking the light swung at him. A side table screeched as their bodies shoved it aside. Ian struck in close and knocked the light away.

Again, the man broke free of Ian's hold and backed toward the door. "On the other hand, I've been curious as to how capable a man you really are." The umbrella bin clanked as the man snatched up a cane.

"Quite capable." Ian grabbed a rolled magazine and moved in. Joni's attacker swung wild, allowing Ian inside and able to strike the guy's neck, arm, and gut in a flurry of strikes. Amid grunts, the cane clattered across the floor.

Strong hands shoved Ian, and the guy maneuvered away. He rolled over the back of the couch to the opposite side near the kitchen. A smirk flickered across his face.

"You finding something *fokken* funny about this, asshole?" Who the hell was he? How had he reached Joni first?

The man grabbed an empty soda can on the counter and ripped it in two. In each hand, he wielded ragged aluminum.

Warnings flashed through Ian's mind, but images of Joni clogged his logic. *Bury your damn emotions and assess your enemy.* Barely a minute had passed in their fight. Both men stood close, gauging each another and looking for the perfect moment to strike.

Banging sounded on the door. "Fire!"

Surprised, the man glanced toward the sound. In seconds, Ian divested him of the jagged metal and had him shrieking in pain.

Joni's mind had taken several seconds to recognize Ian as the person who'd tackled Bram. For a man typically cool under fire, it had been a foolish move. Kagona could have been waiting in the cottage.

Horrified at how quickly the fuel ignited, she grabbed Mike's zebra-striped cactus pot and emptied the sandy soil onto the kerosene spill. The smothered portion of fire whooshed out. The cactus tumbled across the wood planks to untouched flames. Dear God, the plant sizzled.

Acrid black smoke brought on a coughing fit. Not giving up,

she grabbed the campfire plant and dumped the contents on the remaining fire. She kicked soil over the flames and then added handfuls of dirt scraped from the backyard.

The last of the flames sputtered out. Her lungs ached from the smoke, and her eyes, still sensitive from the spray, watered. Adrenaline pumped. She'd nearly burned down Mike's house. He had so little left in life—destroying his home would be an unfair blow.

She yanked on the cottage latch, to no avail. Beneath her feet, flames popped up through the cracks in the planking, not in just one place, but in a half dozen. A flash of heat warmed her skin. Crap. Dried leaves and brush under the porch had ignited.

"Fire!" She pounded on the door before dancing between flames off the porch. She snatched up the mop handle Bram had dropped and ran for the water bucket. A shadow bending over the bucket morphed from a clump to a standing threat. Light from the kitchen window highlighted something in his hand. The crowbar he'd used to pry the window open. Couldn't anything in life be easy?

She gripped her makeshift staff in both hands. "I don't care if you're a thief, but I need that water…now."

The intruder didn't answer. He merely knelt back over the bucket, keeping the crowbar in his hand. The spray had defeated him. All he wanted was relief, and she wanted the water that gave it to him. Only one effective weapon remained in her arsenal. Diplomacy.

"If you go now, you can have the scooter. I'll leave the keys in the yard where you dropped them. If you stay another minute, those men inside will make quick work of you." She pointed toward the cottage.

He slowly stood again, as though contemplating her offer. He squinted in her direction. Commotion sounded in the background. She looked back to see Ian running toward them. He rushed past her.

She swung back toward the thief. He'd disappeared.

Ian reached the bucket. "Who was that?" He broke off the padlock on the well house and wrenched the little door open.

"A local who wanted my scooter."

"Sure he's not with Kagona?"

"I'm not sure of anything at the moment. What are you doing?"

"I have to get the pump running." He shoved the bucket at her.

She lugged it to the porch and found fire creeping up the door. Bram snatched the bucket from her hands and pitched the water on it. Those flames died, but more had spread across the porch. He tossed the bucket back to her and beat down the flames with the crocheted blanket from the couch.

This fire required more than a one-man bucket brigade. With growing fear the firefighting was not proceeding in their favor, she ran back to the well. Ian had the shed opened and the pump motor on, but no water came out of the spigot. Profanities flew. He turned off the motor and grabbed the bucket from her.

"I told Mike he needed a new pump. This one is shot." He refilled the bucket from a large water barrel inside the shed. "Equipment leaks like a sieve. I have to prime the bloody thing."

"How long?"

"Probably too long." He handed the full bucket back before picking up a watering can. "Do the best you can."

By the time she returned to the porch, the fire had spread. They required a line of buckets coming one after the other. Without a word, Bram snatched the bucket and doused flames before tossing it back to her.

She dashed to the well house and sank the bucket into the barrel. Ian blew into a hose-like pipe and then used the watering can to fill it with water. She made another run and he was doing the same thing when she returned.

He attached the pipe to a pump and tightened a clamp. "Grab that hose and fasten it to the spigot out there."

The hose unrolled as she lifted it. By the time she screwed the connector onto the brass fitting, Ian had the motor running. He grabbed the nozzle end and ran with it toward the cottage.

She followed, making sure the hose didn't tangle.

Fire snaked up the white siding and nibbled at the beams supporting the metal roof. Ian started high and worked down. He extinguished one hot spot while another grew larger. Eventually he handed off the hose to Bram. They spoke, but the crackling fire made their words unintelligible. Ian tore around the side of the house.

Bram soaked the blanket, and she took over trying to beat out flames. It didn't take long to see the task was hopeless. Flames had sprung up at the pitch under the roof and were winning the battle.

The pump went silent and Bram retreated, pulling her with him.

"What are you doing?"

"We're done, Joni. There's nothing more we can do." His hold around her waist didn't falter.

"We can't let Mike's house burn." Defeat surged through her, taking a chunk of her spirit with it.

Ian returned with something wrapped in a thin blanket under his arm and her day pack over his shoulder. Her caught her elbow and pulled her away from the cottage. "We have to go."

"We can't quit."

"We're not quitting. There're more important battles to fight. We have to take what we can and leave. The neighbors will be arriving soon. And the man who ran off could bring back his friends or Kagona's police."

The next minutes passed in a daze. Light from the burning cottage made it easy to find the lost keys. She retrieved the scooter from its hiding place while Ian and Bram collected equipment from a camouflaged ground safe near the well. They spoke little to each other, but whatever had passed in the cottage must have resolved her relationship to them both.

Some time in the many trips to the SUV that Ian and Mad Mike had driven on her last venture here, they loaded the little scooter. Ian then plopped Joni in the front seat, instructing her to wait. Lights appeared in the distance. A motorcycle roared to life nearby and took off down the road. Bram's transportation? Why hadn't he told her?

Ian slid into the driver's seat and headed in the same direction the cycle had disappeared. Behind her, a part of the cottage roof collapsed. Her triumphant return to find Ian and save Sipho's father had literally gone up in flames.

They rode in silence. Tension between them was palatable and bittersweet. She'd destroyed one more piece of Ian's life as well as Mike's. Ian had lost his ranch in Zimbabwe, his family had dispersed to other countries, and his father had become a wandering mercenary. Mike, and their friendship, had been his buoy in this slowly sinking country.

"I'm sorry, Ian. I came to help. Instead, I've drawn attention to us all."

"Doesn't matter. Mike wasn't safe here anymore." His voice rang hollow. He felt the loss. "Lemmon was foolish to send you."

"He didn't. I asked to come."

"Christ, Joni. That plays right into Kagona's game. He'd love to get his hands on you."

"I had to know if you were okay. The gunshots when we took off—"

"I created a diversion so Zamani could escape. Kagona's men were almost upon his position."

"So why didn't you contact Lemmon? Let him know you were alive?"

Ian didn't answer. Instead, his fingers tapped the steering wheel, persistent, almost irritated. He let out a breath. "Eventually I would have. I'll likely need his help getting Mukono released."

A sinking built in Joni's stomach. Had she imagined the possible connection they'd shared? Granted, a one-night stand after death-defying events wasn't unheard of, but... "How long would you have waited to make contact?"

Ian slapped his palm on the steering wheel. "You don't get it, do you. I feared he'd send you back. That's the last thing I needed."

Stunned, his words struck deep. She'd made mistakes on her first venture into his territory. Now, the novice had returned.

The dirt road beneath her vibrated and shook the truth loose. That void of loneliness, which he'd filled barely a week ago, opened up again, and she balked at letting it grow larger. "For Sipho's sake, suck up your pride and work with me. Maybe we can still save his father. Lemmon said they were making sure his name stayed in the forefront of the protests." Better to get the truth out up front before they had to depend on one another in battle. "To be honest, Ian, I couldn't stay away. And I don't mean from this crazy business or Zimbabwe—I mean from you."

His foot hit the brakes and brought the SUV to a quick to a stop in the middle of the empty dirt road. He reached out and slid a hand to each side of her face.

"You are the most stubborn, hardheaded woman I've ever met. You really don't get it. You've never left. You're always here...in my heart." Hard and raw, his kiss reached past all her doubts.

When he finally let her go, he placed his lips against her forehead and whispered, "And Kagona knows you are my Achilles' heel. He'd torture you to get to me."

"Then keep me out of his hands."

An exasperated breath brushed against her cheek. "Knowing you, Joni, that's not an easy assignment."

Ian stopped the SUV in a tree-sheltered area not far from the crossroads where Joni's workmate, calling himself Kriegler, had waited on a motorcycle. Ian's blood boiled at the way the guy had handled her—or was it because Ian had let his weakness for Joni show?

Kriegler followed them and parked behind the SUV, killing his engine. Joni appeared curious about his transportation.

Yeah, he had a few questions about the cycle, too. Ian tapped her leg. "Come with me." He headed back, still fighting the urge to break Kriegler's neck.

Joni must have sensed his intentions and beat him to the cycle. She stepped between them. "You men didn't have a proper introduction."

Kriegler rubbed at his chin. "I think we delivered right proper greetings."

Joni sighed. "It's a good thing Mike will never see the shambles you two left in his place. Ian, this is Bram Kriegler, a fellow helo pilot at the Taz project office, and my ego-driven escort into Zim. He claims to be looking for a few good stories to share at the pub."

Ian growled, but before either could comment, she continued.

"Bram, this is Ian Taljaard, who obviously exhibited great restraint not to tear your limbs from their sockets or slit your throat first and ask questions while you drowned in your own blood." She stepped out from between them. "Now, how about shaking hands? It's highly likely we will be working together."

Over Kriegler's dead body. Ian easily imagined the possibility. Too many questions remained unanswered, including why Lemmon would send someone from an office compromised by a mole.

Ian extended his hand. "I'll take the keys to the cycle."

Kriegler's arms remained relaxed at his side. "Only if you give me the ones to your SUV."

"Stop it." Joni slid between them again.

Joni's refereeing had to end, for her own safety, and because her abbreviated height didn't block him from still being eye to eye with Kriegler. The night did little, though, to illuminate the expression on the man's face. Ian made sure his read of distrust.

"Before you get too eager to protect your office mate, Joni, you might ask how he came in possession of this bike."

She faced Kriegler. "Actually, I was curious about that."

"Mike's men lent it to me to follow you."

"You didn't even know Mike's name until I mentioned it back at the cottage."

Ian took out his phone. "That cycle is Mike's baby. A friend is refurbishing it for him. He might lend you a bike, but it wouldn't be Mike's." He punched up a number.

"Don't bother calling." An exasperated breath slipped from Kriegler. "I *borrowed* the motorcycle."

"You stole it?" Pissed, Joni walked to the opposite side of the bike from Kriegler. Wise move. "How did you get away?"

"Your friends locked me in their cold cellar and sat down for dinner. Lemmon told me not to let you out of my sight."

"Until I got on the train."

"You know how things changed."

"I don't," Ian said. He'd exchanged his phone for a knife, making sure what little starlight existed reflected off the blade. Kriegler had escaped not from simple friends of Mike's, but well-seasoned operatives. "How about explaining what happened on the train and how you found Joni at Mike's cottage?"

This questioning wasted time, but Ian refused to go farther

and expose his network. He slid his knife into a special pocket and maneuvered closer to Joni.

She started to say something, but Ian pulled her in against him. He wanted to judge her silent reactions to Kriegler's story. Surprisingly, Kriegler delivered a concise and quick rendition of events…of course the later part had no rebuttal witness available.

The tale made Ian's decision easy. "Hand over the keys and go wait by my vehicle."

Kriegler shrugged and did as instructed.

Ian gave Joni the cycle keys. "Driven one of these before?"

"Almost bought one once, but decided it might be too dangerous to ride. Silly of me, considering the mundane life I live." He liked her sarcasm. "You probably ride better than I do," she added. "I can drive your vehicle."

"Your buddy and I are riding together. We need bonding time. How close did his story match the truth?"

"He glossed over a few key points."

"Only a few?" Her muscles had gone taut so often he'd lost count.

"I saw him leave something behind for the man in gray at the falls. I couldn't tell what. He also had a train ticket when he followed me onboard. I'm guessing he bought it while he waited for food inside the Vic hotel next to the station."

"Are you positive?"

"I checked his pack when he left our berth for the bathroom."

"Nice move, but don't try it again. From now on, he won't let his guard down, even around a friend like you. Anything else seem unusual?"

"Yeah, Lemmon did send him. I called when Bram showed up at the airport. I just can't figure out why."

And neither could Ian.

"I brought several things to communicate with Lemmon. Maybe he'll have some answers."

"Until then, follow me. If I divert, you'd better be on my arse without question. It means trouble ahead." He mounted Mike's bike.

She dug out a pocket light, flicking it to a red filter, making it easy for him to give her a quick run-through of the bike's operation. When he dismounted and she took the seat, her light flashed across his shirt hanging loose at the waist.

"What happened, Ian? Did Bram do that?"

A damp patch of blood shone on his lower shirt. His bandage had leaked again.

She picked up on his hesitation. "Your diversion to save Zamani. Dear God, Kagona shot you."

"It went through. The doc added a few stitches. I must have popped one wrestling with Kriegler."

"And the doc didn't report you to Kagona?"

"He's a friend."

"I've heard that before."

He deserved that. He'd made a few mistakes, and his friends were paying dearly for them. "He's taking care of someone special to me."

"We're not going anywhere until you get stitched up again." She squeezed his hand and held on. "Why did you take on Bram, anyway? Your showing up would have been enough to stop him."

"Hell if I know. I didn't feel like conversation."

"Promise me you won't feel that way again."

"Lemmon sent your office mate for a reason. Until I figure it out, no promises." He stepped away, but she didn't let him go.

"Hey. I heard about Chief Zwide. Is that the friend the doc is treating?"

He nodded but said nothing. He couldn't.

"I'm really sorry," she whispered.

"Yeah…so am I."

He squeezed back, then let go and walked away. Guilt tugged at his heart.

Ian had no compunction about handcuffing Kriegler and putting a jacket over his head. If he wanted to stick with Joni, then he'd play by Ian's rules. And rule number one was if Kriegler wanted to live, he had to obey him implicitly.

CHAPTER TEN

Joni drifted off to sleep, but approaching footsteps, soft ones, awakened her. Alerted but not alarmed, she stretched her stiff body on the luxurious bed hung with mosquito netting. A kerosene lamp on a bedside table cast a creamy glow and created moving shadows on white linen curtains ruffling in a light breeze.

She wiggled her fingers and found the burning from the pepper spray had subsided and left no apparent skin damage. Dirt and soot that had spread across her clothing and stuck under her shredded nails had been washed away in a shower. Her hand-washed pants and shirt hung in a corner, drying.

On the bedside table lay the photo from Mike's she'd rescued. Again she looked at the woman about the same age as her mother. She smiled at the thought. Mike had found love. Was it so wrong to want the same for Ian or even herself?

As romantic as this safari resort room might be, romance was the farthest thing from everyone's minds. Spread out on a couch and floor were the remnants of Mike's arms stash and items Bram carried in his pack. To her surprise, Lemmon had sent along extra toys she'd been unable to carry in hers.

Ian slipped into the room. "Did you get some sleep?"

Dressed in a T-shirt and spare pants, she leaned up on propped pillows. "I showered, then went through everything. Somewhere after that, I lay back on the bed. That's all I remember."

"Good. Tonight may be all the sleep you have for a few days."

She noticed he'd showered and wore a clean shirt.

"Someone attended to your wound."

"Stitched up and a fresh bandage. It's healing well. The medic here is good." He leaned over and kissed Joni on top her head. "But her hands are cold."

She couldn't help but smile. "How's Bram?"

"Tucked in for the night. Don't worry, he won't be showing up uninvited."

"He's going to be unhappy."

"Pissed as hell, but I need sleep." He noted the photo in her hand. "What's that?"

"I picked it up at Mike's. I'm guessing she's someone special to him."

A boyish grin blossomed. "Crikey, I nearly got killed looking for that in his burning house. He made me promise to retrieve two things if he could never come home again. That was one of them. I thought it lost."

"Who is she?"

Ian snuggled up next to her, an arm bent under his head. He slipped the photo from her fingers.

"Miss Janey. At least that's what I called her. She died when I was ten." His eyes softened, and he swallowed hard. "Mike has never been the same since." He handed back the photo. "Keep it safe. That's his favorite picture of her."

Determined to make sure the treasure landed in Mike's hands, she would tuck it in a zippered pocket in the morning. "You said two things. What did you retrieve from his place?"

Ian pointed at a long object still wrapped in a blanket and tied with a belt. He swung his legs off the bed and got up. "Maybe I should demonstrate."

She rolled to her side and propped her head up on a hand.

He exposed a prosthesis. Mike had lost his foot back in the seventies.

"Mike's backup?"

"One he uses in special circumstances." A knifepoint sprang out of the toe.

"Quite special." She lay back while he rewrapped the leg. "How did I ever end up with such strange friends?"

Ian sat on the bed and leaned over her. "I've asked myself that question ever since you dropped out the sky and into my life."

"Landed, to be more precise. Safely. You were the one who rather led me into trouble, if I remember correctly."

He lowered his head closer and brushed his nose against hers. "I'd gladly lead you into trouble any day."

"You already are."

His kiss brought a rush of memories, terrors, and thrills. Tantalizing, yet deadly, all pushing her to flee. But she wanted more of him, like they'd shared during their rescue of Sipho or in a dark barn days ago. She trusted him to trust her. Let her be his captain and he her ground warrior. Or let them be partners in crime…at least preventing it.

Her mind pushed away the work demands that hung over them and let her body succumb to the moment. Ian relaxed against her, working magic with his touch. With a sigh, he unexpectedly pulled away and lightly planted a kiss on her nose.

"Keep those thoughts. We'll find time for us, but you asked to be awakened at your check-in time for Lemmon." He gave her an affectionate pat. "I'd say you're fully aroused."

"Lemmon has lousy timing."

Ian handed her an electronic tablet she'd brought in her pack, which she connected to a larger antenna. She initialized a special app for scrambled and secure communications.

Ian propped the tablet on the table. He slipped an earbud from the headphones connected to the tablet in her ear and one in his. From his shirt pocket, he fished out Sipho's red braid. He'd discovered it on her earlier and wanted to know when Sipho had given it to her.

She folded her fingers around his hand. "We'll get his father back."

Lemmon's voice came through clearly, but the video feed remained blank. Lemmon likely had a clear view of them whether they enabled the video or not.

Ian, who had expressed no love lost for Lemmon, skipped the greetings. "I'd like an update on Sipho."

"The boy is well, as Miss Bell will attest."

Ian looked to Joni, and she nodded confirmation. "He's okay. I called him before I left."

"Since Ms. Bell left, we've made progress on the new account information he provided about Chitima."

Ian tensed. "Need I remind you my godson has a fragile autistic psyche. If you—"

"Relax, Mr. Taljaard. We haven't touched the boy. Miss Bell is the one who extracted the information."

Joni rested her hand on his. "*Extracted* isn't quite correct. He offered it up on the flight back to South Africa."

Lemmon chuckled. "Apparently, you two haven't had time to catch up. Have events been demanding there?"

"Joni's been busy burning down Mike's place."

"I'm not sure where that fits into our plans."

"It doesn't," Joni snipped. "Honestly, we haven't had time to bring each other up-to-date on events."

"I'd offer twenty-four hours to let you compare notes, but I'm afraid our timetable is quite urgent."

"I'm more than willing to assist with your problem." Ian crossed his arms. "But as usual, I expect something in return. My leads on Mukono have gone cold. I'm hoping to use recent events to pressure Kagona into moving his captive, but I still have to develop a plan to free Mukono when I find him."

"Have faith, Mr. Taljaard. We've already taken into consideration your problem and are working on it."

"In that case, what new information did Sipho provide that is so critical?"

"His father uncovered an account in the Ministry of Mines and Mining Development that wasn't tied to any particular industry. Since Zimbabwe President Tangwerai controls the mining sector, and the newly elected opposition party handles the financial sector, distrust is ramping up between the two ministries. That's part of the reason diamond-mining tax revenue has not been showing up in the government's coffers. Everyone wants their piece of the pie."

"The bottom line is?"

Paper shuffled on Lemmon's end. "This latest account we've investigated showed a payout eighteen months ago to the Uranium Mining Corporation of China."

"That's no surprise. The Chinese have been going back and forth on whether the Kanyemba area holds enough high-quality reserves to mine. Except why would Zimbabwe be paying China to mine uranium? Shouldn't it be the other way around?"

"Excellent question. Zimbabwe lacks resources to pay for a nuclear power program, thus no need to process uranium ore. China could legally mine the uranium, but they tend to pay for mining rights with weaponry or loans to Zim to support infrastructure. Our analysts are broaching several theories, all of which they'd like confirmed on the ground."

"Why the rush?"

"Because the money trail doesn't end there. Two days ago money was transferred *into* the account. The transfer came from a bank in Lebanon."

"Lebanon?" World financial markets were not Joni's forte. "Any idea who sent the money?"

"Lebanese banks have an international reputation for withstanding world crises but are also known for doing business with anyone in the Middle East. It could be Egypt, Hezbollah, Iran, Syria, the Palestinians, or possibly ISIL. Our analysts believe the money is a payment."

Ian nodded. "And that means something either has been received by the payer or is close to being shipped."

The implications left Joni unsettled. "So you're saying money is going into Zim from the Middle East and out to some Chinese uranium company. Great. It appears someone is playing secret games."

"And don't forget, Miss Bell, Mukono, via Taljaard, had already passed along information on another account. A portion of those funds went to Mozambique, whose port provides a straight shot to Pakistan and Iran, and a slide up the Red Sea to Egypt and the Middle East."

"And for landlocked Zim, the easiest path to the sea," Ian added. "Something is shipping out and Kagona is worried about covering it up." He fidgeted, which succeeded in yanking out her connected earbud.

She snatched the fugitive bud and stuck it back in her ear. "So you're seeking confirmation of who is involved with the mining in Kanyemba."

"Exactly." Lemmon sounded anxious to gain intelligence to paint a clearer picture of what Mukono's money trail suggested. "Both the South Africans and the Americans want to know what is being shipped and where it is going."

"Color me uneducated, but what are we looking for? Train cars full of unprocessed ore, crushed aggregate, or what?"

"There are no trains in the Kanyemba area," Ian said. "Anything mined would have to go by truck."

"For that reason, we believe they will refine it to an easily transportable state."

"Like what?" She feared the answer might be something hot to handle.

"Yellowcake, an unenriched uranium. Obtaining it is a simple enough process and can be done on-site. Ore is crushed and leached with chemicals. The resulting powdery product is about seventy percent or so uranium. Don't worry—exposure will not leave you glowing in the dark."

"Sounds ominous. I presume you want to make sure this doesn't end up in the hands of the wrong people."

"We've been remiss in checking in on our Zim friends and their ever-changing claims concerning their uranium deposits. Whatever you find, I'll immediately pass along to our nuclear experts."

Ian dropped his earbud and retrieved two small objects from the couch. "If product is being shipped, I'm guessing you want us to tag it."

"Looks like you've discovered the tools to carry that out."

"Uranium mining isn't exactly on my specialty list," she said. Irritation rose that Lemmon hadn't used an hour of time to brief her on mining before she left. Surely he must have done some speculating on what Zimbabwe might be up to. "How can we assess how far along they are? I'm not sure I'll even know what I'm seeing."

"You might find Mr. Kriegler of use."

"Bram? Pray tell he doesn't have a degree in nuclear engineering."

"I'm surprised how little you know about your colleagues, Ms. Bell. I thought pilots bragged about their past assignments."

"It's not the first topic on my mind when relaxing over a beer." Joni clenched her fists. Had Lemmon manipulated her once again?

"Kriegler used to transport officials for one of the largest mining companies in Africa. They included him on several facilities tours. An expert, no, but he may be able to make sense of what you see."

"How convenient. Perhaps you should forward Bram's résumé and I can see what else I'm missing."

"Eventually, but at the moment we're still trying to clear up a few inconsistencies in it."

"Christ." Ian let out an exasperated huff. "That's a red flag considering the leaks in Joni's office. Why did you send him along?"

"Don't be so quick to speak. Your own background has peculiar gaps."

Joni cast Ian an askew glance. Gaps? More than one? What else hadn't Ian revealed to her about his life? "Does Bram know that's why you sent him?"

"It won't take him long to figure it out. I fully expected he'd stick with you once in the country. He isn't the type to kiss and run."

"Let me guess. You made that decision based upon his personality profile."

"You are starting to astound me with your insight. Be sure he wears that watch of his. You might say it'll help me keep track of him, if necessary. Well, we've taken up the allotted amount of time for this connection. Good luck."

A light on the screen turned red. "We'll need it." She disconnected the earphones and dropped back on the bed. "How are we going to get to the Kanyemba mining area unnoticed? Usually they're in the middle of nowhere."

"In this case it is, but I've been working on the problem."

"You knew about this?"

"Not exactly. The CIO hauled in an Africa News Beacon reporter. I believe he uncovered something in the northern part of the country important enough Kagona risked messing with the media. That means he's desperate."

"So how is that going to help us?"

"I met with another reporter from the Beacon today…" He looked at his watch. "Damn, make that yesterday. They've found the reporter's videographer somewhere up north. Zamani is following the rescue crew. He's actually caught up with their vehicle. They're headed toward Mkanga Bridge and he is accompanying them."

"That's a bit brazen."

"Not at all. People are foolish to drive back roads in a single vehicle. It's easy to get stuck, particularly at the start of the rainy season. Caravans are what we do."

"So are we driving?"

"Not enough time. I've some contacts to make, but I've an idea on how to get us close."

"Ian, don't shut me out on the plans. I came back this time to find you, but also to be a part of Mukono's rescue. For Sipho." And for herself.

"You'll know as soon as I work something out." He wrapped her in his arms. "Think you can handle Kriegler?"

"Depends on what you have in mind."

"Any way you can." He slowly stepped her back toward the bed. "Except the way you handle me."

"And how is that, Mr. Taljaard? It's been so long I've forgotten." Her hair slid across an eye.

"It's hard to get used to you as a brunette." Ian swept the lock back. "But I'm willing to give it a try."

"Trying might not be good enough."

"You'll be the final judge."

She tugged him downward, but he resisted, much to her chagrin.

"I've some work to do, to see the bulk of Mike's stash gets in the right hands. I won't be long. We'll be up early." He lifted her against his body. "I'll need help getting to sleep." His lips brushed along her cheek, her neck, and lingered over her mouth. "Turn the lamp out. Slip into…a lot less, and warm the sheets."

He gently set her on the bed, and with a soft kiss to her forehead, disappeared as quietly as he'd arrived.

CHAPTER ELEVEN

The twin props of the King Air 90 hummed around Joni as they flew above Zimbabwe, heading north. The agricultural areas around Harare morphed into thinly settled hills and eventually into a fractured, rocky landscape etched by rivulets cutting through bedrock on their journey to the Zambezi. Some lands below were treed while others displayed twisted stratigraphy in a geologist's paradise. Roads were few, dirt, and far between.

A single charter pilot flew up front while the others rode behind him in seats facing each other. Ian sat across from her, his chair tilted back, legs stretched out and intertwined with hers, and a well-seasoned bush hat over his eyes. He'd sent his newer hat with Sipho, and that fact likely left Ian content with wearing his older one.

Bram sat across the aisle against the window and watched the landscape below. He picked up on her scrutiny.

"You worried about what lies ahead?" He indicated snoozing Ian. "He's not."

"He's good at catching naps when he can. He didn't sleep much last night."

"I'll bet." Damned if Bram didn't grin.

"Jealous?" came from underneath Ian's hat.

"Why should I be? I'm officially her beau today." He scooped up Joni's hand. "Right, *bokkie*?"

Ian pushed his hat back and sat up. "Don't overplay your part."

"You could have let me play the guide."

"I prefer to live." Ian checked out the window. "We're almost there."

"Nothing much out there. I haven't seen a paved road for ages."

"There aren't any in this region."

Bram frowned. "How about runways?"

"A few dirt ones. The runway nearest the mining district is in the best shape."

"Is that where we're landing?"

"Nope. We're putting down about twenty-five miles to the north. It's used by tourists ending their canoe trips on the Zambezi."

"Why so far if these roads are bad at best?"

Ian studied Bram.

Lemmon had sent him along fully aware a possible traitor might be involved in their investigation. Feeding him information of any kind contained risks. Already a suspicious Ian had divested Bram of any means of communication.

"The airstrip near Kanyemba is known for being protected." Ian glanced at Joni and back at Bram. "When activity is ongoing, campsites are often adjacent the runway."

"You're assuming the mine is active."

"It's not been on my radar for a while, but I did my homework this morning. Our pilot indicated his company has run quite a few people in and out over the last year. Some for hunting safaris at a nearby camp, but mostly government people and foreigners. He never spoke to any so has no idea of their nationalities. He's seen a military chopper parked next to the runway, too. Mentioned when he flies in, he has to maintain a specific flight path."

Joni sat forward and grabbed a camera she had stowed under her seat. "Sounds like someone doesn't want flyovers. Think the pilot could make a map of his flight path? We could cross those areas off our search list."

"He showed me on a topo map. I've a pretty good idea where to look first."

Bram shook his head, appearing unconvinced. "If the Chinese are mining up here, wouldn't that be obvious?"

"They've been exploring this region for years. Seven years ago, they improved the dirt roads to allow exploration drill rigs access."

Joni tilted the camera to inspect the lens. "So the local tribes became used to seeing big equipment move around."

"Yes, but the Chinese exploration permits ran out a few years ago. Yet, last night I talked with a friend who runs birding safaris in this region. He's seen recent evidence of roads being smoothed out."

"Are the Chinese back?" She pulled out a small cleaning cloth from a pocket on her day pack.

"It's possible they never left."

Bram pointed at the camera. "You've cleaned the lens twice."

"Missed some dust." The action steadied her nerves. She'd rather be flying. She looked to Ian. "With better roads, do you think the people here will be protective of a mining project?"

"Hard to say. Improvements are mostly in the mining region, which is in a state-designated safari and wilderness district. Without an impact study, no one on the outside knows what damage is being done."

She replaced the lens cap and folded up the strap. "I'm guessing as long as the Chinese are willing to wheel and deal with the government, that's not a big concern."

"About eighty percent of foreign investments here are Chinese. Although, if they're actually mining, I think a lot of people in this country would be interested in hearing about it."

"The film crew from the Beacon?"

Bram looked confused. "The Africa News Beacon? What happened to them?"

"They ran into trouble. Highly likely they were following the story and stuck their noses in where they weren't wanted."

"How are we going to drive around without being accosted like them?"

"It's a rather isolated area." Ian pulled out a birding book from the pack sitting next to him. "But just in case, start reading up on your favorite tweeters. We're on the hunt for an African Pitta."

Bram crossed his arms. "If we're a bit more careful than the film crew, then it's doubtful we'll run into anybody."

"I guarantee our arrival by air will be noticed. I'm guessing even this far north of the region, they'll want to make sure no more reporters arrive."

"So what's our transportation once we get on the ground?" Joni asked.

"Zamani is meeting us there."

"Who's Zamani?" Bram asked.

"A friend who helps me out on occasion."

"Does he live up there?"

"He accompanied a Beacon rescue team up to the Mkanga Bridge to pick up their stranded videographer. The reporter with him went missing."

"A reporter doesn't usually simply disappear. Any idea what happen to him?"

"Neither the videographer nor the rescue team were saying much. They're understandably scared, and should be." Ian looked at Bram, obviously deciding what to say in front of him. "The CIO hauled the reporter into a police camp outside Harare."

Bram leaned forward, suddenly interested in their conversation. "And you learned this bit of trivia how?"

"I was there, watching."

"Gutsy, sitting on Kagona's doorstep, when he wants you dead. I'd ask why, but I assume you won't tell me. Your hospitality has been less than agreeable."

"You were cozy enough last night."

"I don't plan on sleeping in a lion cage again."

"Then don't give me a reason to put you in one." Admittedly, Ian had picked a secure place to leave Bram for the night. "At least you got a hot shower this morning."

"Because Joni refused to be near me. Claimed I smelled a bit gamey." Bram reached out and settled a hand on her leg. "That would be awkward for a happy couple on safari."

Ian smirked at Bram's attempt to get a rise from him. "Hygiene is important in the wild. Stay downwind of the enemy…unless you're ready to do battle."

Joni brushed off Bram's hand and shook her head at the two men struggling for dominance. She'd not pegged the affable Bram as an alpha type, at least not until now. Call it a suspicious nature, but Bram's posturing hinted of distraction from his actual goal. Would he threaten their assignment or promote its success?

Joni watched as the plane dropped lower and the twisted rock landscape came closer. Their pilot, separated by a narrow partition, leaned his head through the gap. "Touchdown in five."

Rock, rattle, and roll best described the landing, and set Ian's mind and body in high gear. They'd accomplished the easy part. Now the true tests lay ahead.

With no buildings, no taxiway, and nothing but a dirt strip in the middle of nowhere, the plane turned and taxied back on the runway to the end where it had touched down. Dust hung in the air.

Zamani drove up to meet the plane. His Land Rover had a tire attached to the back and an extra on top along with a jerrican of fuel and a winch on the front end. They didn't have the luxury of a caravan.

Unloading the plane went swiftly. Ian and Kriegler grabbed larger packs laden with tents, food, and paraphernalia from the Kriegler's day pack they'd left behind, while Joni collected the camera equipment and her day pack with a collection of surveillance necessities. The pilot left them with several additional boxes before he ran up the engines and took off.

They loaded the two larger packs in Rover before Joni, with her day pack and camera, and Kriegler climbed into the rear passenger seats.

Ian caught Zamani behind the vehicle. "What did you find out?"

"The cameraman heard I was going to Kanyemba to pick up a canoe safari. He said I will pass his 4x4. Asked if I could repair a hole in gas tank and find someone to drive vehicle to Harare."

"Did you find it?"

"*Yebo.* About ten kilometers from mining region. Looks like someone shot the tank, took his jerricans, and told him to push off. He made it partway to Mkanga Bridge."

"Can you fix the vehicle?"

"No faith, *mngane.* Gum and duct tape cure many evils…for short term."

"Good, we could use a backup."

"I hid it well, but did not fill the gas. Hid and locked a jerrican inside."

Ian patted Zamani on the shoulder and settled into the front passenger seat. Something haunted him about the Africa News Beacon crew. Mining deals had been on-again, off-again in the area for years. The Chinese had been coring and sending the samples home. They scouted and worked the wilderness with impunity, without environmental restrictions, and knowing after their financial and armament assistance to Zimbabwe, the leaders wouldn't dare shut them down.

No one would be surprised if the Chinese started mining. Kagona wouldn't risk arresting a reporter from a foreign news agency to cover up an anticipated event. The politicians would simply emphasize the value to the country of such a lucrative mining arrangement.

So what story was the reporter chasing? What was Kagona hiding?

Zamani drove along a narrow trail to where the airport road intersected with a substantial dirt road. A small metal-roofed house marked the intersection. As expected, a local man in worn pants and loose-hanging shirt waved them over.

Kriegler slid a possessive arm across the back of the seat behind Joni's head. The right move, but it irked Ian all the same.

Zamani hopped out and dragged down the three boxes he'd set on the bonnet for the short trip from the runway. He chatted with the man and shrugged before coming around to Ian's open window.

"He wants your guide license."

Ian dug out a license—one borrowed from a friend who looked similar—and handed it over. Using his own license was impossible since he'd become a hunted man. He doubted this local would give it much scrutiny. Rather, the man wanted to ensure Ian would hand over a toll for his safari clients' use of the airport.

Ian hid money in his palm until the request came. Even then, he had his fingers on the license before he relinquished the toll. With business complete, Zamani set them on the road toward the Dande safari district and the Kanyemba uranium region.

"Business must be slow around here." Joni broke the heavy silence after a good ten minutes.

"That was the easy part. It'll get harder from here." Ian shifted his attention to Zamani. "Did you see any evidence someone is mining the Kanyemba uranium?"

"The road between Mkanga Bridge and the mining area is much improved. I saw no trucks on road, though."

"A mining operation would have to move ore to a processing facility. That means construction at some point. Construction and mines require a lot of workers. Where are they housing everyone? They can't all be camping out."

"Maybe it's a small mine."

"It needs to be productive enough to return an investment."

"I did encounter a roadblock. Military."

"Out here?" The news disturbed Ian. The military rarely bothered with local problems. "Maneuvers or guarding something?"

"They did not say much. Wanted papers to prove I headed to collect a safari group."

"You had something appropriate to show them?"

"Always when I travel up here."

Ian looked over his shoulder at Kriegler, curious as to his thoughts. The newcomer watched brush and trees going by outside the window, as though ignoring their conversation. Ian didn't buy his indifference for a moment.

Joni caught his scrutiny. "Any idea exactly where to look for this mine?"

"We're not sure there even is one yet. But years ago I scouted the region with a group of geologists prospecting for a Canadian company. A lucrative summer job. All I had to do was keep them alive." He found the memories refreshing. "Wasn't easy."

"I can relate to that." A quirky, rather nostalgic smile graced her face.

Yep, keeping Joni alive had proved quite a challenge during Sipho's rescue. She'd tripped a booby trap and nearly been killed. The simple reminder revived new fears.

"How long ago were the Canadians here?" she asked.

"About ten years."

"Practically yesterday. Hope you have a good memory. So what's the plan?"

For a moment, he considered keeping the details private, but this was her mission as much as his. "Stops along the way to recon. As soon as we find evidence of something going on, then we go on foot. Lemmon wants a report. We'll do our best to give him all the necessary facts."

"How far away are we?"

Zamani answered. "On this road with stops, perhaps an hour out."

Joni rose and bent over the seat, holding on as the Land Rover jostled her back and forth. While her backside presented a nice view, his interest lay in her actions. She grabbed the camera sitting on her day pack and a lens that dwarfed it. She handed the equipment over to Kriegler, who mounted the lens. Next she extracted high-powered binoculars before settling back in her seat.

Ian had inspected everything in her day pack before they redistributed the equipment between them all and repacked this morning. Lemmon had sent a useful assortment of toys. "You came well prepared for bird watching."

"I'd like to see if the vultures are circling or if they're simply a gaggle of geese," she replied.

The truck jostled back and forth as they crossed a rough patch. Joni had tasted the danger of what might lie ahead, and yet faced it with humor. Lemmon had sent her back for a reason— one stronger than merely establishing contact with him, and if his hunch was right, one that included Kriegler. The thought left Ian contemplating the truth. If he didn't figure out why fast, she could be a sacrificial lamb for Lemmon's true intentions.

Five minutes later, Kriegler tapped Zamani on the shoulder. "Pull over."

Ian glanced back. Kriegler had his window down and camera aimed at something outside. Ian signaled Zamani to stop.

Underneath a tree beside the road, two large birds with ebony feathers and long black beaks enjoyed the shade. Bright red surrounded their eyes and throats as they focused on their gawkers.

Kriegler fired off a succession of shots from the camera. He clicked back through a few. "Good enough. Since we're on a bird-watching expedition, I figure I should have a few on the camera."

Ian shrugged. "Not a bad idea." Kriegler seemed to be thinking about their cover…a point in his favor.

"Might help if I knew what they were."

"Southern ground hornbills."

"Common? Rare?"

Ian tilted his head at the hornbills disappearing around the tree. "We're lucky to see them. Not uncommon, but declining."

Kriegler smirked. "And I thought hunter-guide types focused only on big game."

Smart-ass. "Survival depends on being aware of all *animals* in the environment." Kriegler caught his subtle warning but maintained a stoic facade.

"In about five kilometers is a hill." Zamani pointed to the east. "With a short climb, we can see several kilometers down the road."

"Perfect. We'll use the stop to prepare for eventualities."

Zamani sighed and looked over at Ian. "I miss days when we take trips with clients or for fun. I always fish better than you."

"The hell you did. A damn tiger fish almost pulled you overboard on our last trip. If I hadn't dropped my pole to save your hide, you'd have been croc lunch."

A sandy, dry stream cut across the road. Zamani slowed to work down the uneven bank into the creek and back up the other side.

Once at the hill, Joni duct-taped satellite phones and other necessities that they didn't want easily discovered under the seats. Kriegler watched the trees and brush for birds. Ian and Zamani hiked up the hill with Joni's binoculars.

Three kilometers of road stretched before them, although hills, dips, brush, and trees blocked large portions of it. Zamani tapped Ian on the shoulder and pointed at the farthest stretch.

Ian swung the binoculars in the direction. "Let's get out of here."

"You have a plan?"

"You should know by now, I always have a plan."

Scrub snatched at Ian's khakis as his boots slid over scree, grass, and dry leaves in his haste to get back to the Rover. From the sound of it, Zamani was steps behind.

Joni hid behind a large boulder nestled against a towering tree. A truck slowed as it neared their vehicle. Two men rode in the cab and two, dressed in fatigues and carrying what looked like AK-47s, sat in the open bed. While Ian had decided the dust cloud seen in the distance likely belonged to Dande area rangers, these markings and dress were clearly military.

The binoculars offered a clear view of Ian, who had been leaning against the front fender of the Rover. He stretched to a stand. His wide-brimmed hat, khaki pants, and shirt had the look of a typical guide.

Zamani sat in the vehicle, while Bram stood a good distance away and used the camera to follow something in the upper branches of a thicket.

The men in back hopped down and quickly chose positions in front and rear of the Rover. The driver emerged with the swagger of a man in charge. Bram noted their arrival but ignored the actions, staying engaged with his photography.

Ian spoke with the men, showed them paperwork, but it didn't stop the last man in the cab from sticking his nose into the Rover and opening up the back. He poked around at their packs. From Ian's gestures toward Bram while he talked with the leader, it was clear Ian was giving them the birding cover. The man going through the vehicle stuck his hands up with four fingers. They wanted to know where the fourth man had gone.

The guards instantly brought their weapons to bear on Ian and Bram. Bram lowered his camera around his neck and with empty hands, spread out and visible, turned toward the men. This was Joni's cue to go into action.

The slightest crunch of dried leaves sounded behind her. What had Ian said about wildlife in this area? Not many lions. Lots of buffalo, bushpigs, antelope-type creatures, and then smaller animals. She prayed for the smaller.

She held the binoculars at her midsection and very slowly turned. *Be careful what you wish for.* Three sets of rounded black ears twitched at the slow breath she released. The wild dogs spaced out and moved closer. Their black snouts wiggled, taking in her scent.

"Hey, guys. You don't want trouble."

Their ears twitched, but they made no retreat.

She avoided direct eye contact with any of them, instead focusing on the white tail tip on one's caramel-and-black coat. Men's voices sounded in the distance on the other side of the boulder. A dog readjusted his ears to listen.

"That's right. You don't want to attract their attention. They carry big guns."

The dogs didn't move. A tough audience, or did she represent an easy meal?

The brush rustled behind the dogs. Another snout appeared, then another set of dark eyes. Two more dogs emerged off to the right and another off to the left. How big was a pack?

It hardly mattered. A pack could take down a big animal. One or two could probably finish her off. Even though Ian was close by, he couldn't get here fast enough to do any good.

The first shout from the hillside froze all the men. The panic in

Joni's voice nearly pierced Ian's control. He rushed for the Rover and the rifle riding between the seats. Guns leveled in his direction.

"My client's in trouble." He calmed enough for it to sink in that Joni acted, not panicked. She'd shouted for a reason, and he'd play along.

The head man signaled weapons to be lowered.

Ian grabbed his rifle and ran for the bush.

Ahead, a hasty rustle sounded, and Joni staggered out from around a boulder fronting on thick brush up the slope. Binoculars swung around her neck and she tugged wildly on her pants zipper.

He exhaled a silent yet relieved laugh.

She caught sight of the men staring agape at her. With a surprised look and hasty turn of her back, she stuffed her shirt into her pants.

Chuckles arose among the new arrivals.

Looking wild-eyed and unsettled, she worked her way down toward Ian. Proud of her memorable show, a grin spread across his face. He fought the urge to sweep her into a hug but planned to whisper a *well played* when she brushed past. His words went undelivered.

Kriegler stepped in at the last minute and swept her into his arms. "You gave me a scare, *bokkie*. What was all the shouting about?"

"Wild dogs. A pack of them." She spoke loud enough for all to hear and then leveled a distrustful frown at Ian. "You didn't mention they traveled these parts."

Her words floated past Ian. He focused on the location of Kriegler's hands—one tightly gripping her waist and the other sliding up and down her back in mock comfort. As Kriegler's fingers rose again along her spine, Ian's ire spiked. He slipped the strap over his arm and shouldered the rifle. "You didn't ask."

He walked back toward the men. Joni had pulled off a better

show than expected. So why the irritation? The answer swept into his mind, but he shoved it away. No time for personal problems. He had cooperated with all the men's requests, now he wanted information.

"Sorry." He stopped near the leader. "But I hadn't a chance to explain that my other client required a stop for necessities."

"As witnessed. How many days do you stay in Dande?"

"Three or four depending on whether we catch sight of a Pitta."

"Not an easy bird to find." The man scratched at a chin in need of a razor. "Last birders found Pitta down by Mkanga Bridge. Good place to focus efforts."

Sure, and stay out of the places he'd like hunters and birders to avoid. "Thanks, we'll check it out. I don't usually see military in these parts. Any problems we should watch for?"

"Poachers, as usual."

"No surprise. Good day to you."

Poaching had been a problem in this region for ages. Thankfully the remote location had prevented the full-scale onslaught common in other parts of Zimbabwe. The most effective solution recently had been the safari owners operating hunting concessions in Dande. They'd formed a coalition with the local farmers and villagers and paid bounties for snares and removal of poachers' hunting dogs. Local villagers who were apprehended poaching frequently became employees of the coalition, giving the poor an income.

A slowdown in the wildlife decline showed the coalition worked. But to date, the military hadn't bothered with the problem. Considering the political environment, Ian doubted that policy had changed. No, these men had an agenda other than poaching.

The men piled back into their vehicle and continued up the road.

"Think they'll be back?" Joni asked.

"Assuredly." With a new threat bringing unease, he stowed his rifle and signaled everyone to load up. "That's why we need to close in on our destination and cut to the back roads. Going will be tougher, but I'm hoping the *bird* sightings will improve."

Once underway, Kriegler handed over his camera to Joni. "I caught at least five new birds. No idea what they are or that I could find so many in such a short time."

"Did the men check out your camera?"

"Mr. In Charge wandered over, so I showed him the hornbills and a few others. Nice show, by the way, *bokkie*. You had me convinced."

"You should've been."

A delayed fright stilled Ian. He twisted to look back. "Bloody hell, the wild dogs were real."

"All six—at least, that's all I could see in the underbrush."

"Amazing. Next time, don't run from a threat. They might consider that a challenge."

"Ha. I'd already learned that lesson from you." She winked at him. "I asked them nicely to *push off*, as you say. Then suggested strongly that they find something better to eat. Eventually they backed off. Once they'd melted back into the jesse, I let out a shout and put on the show you requested."

"Nice work, but it's the last time I let you go off by yourself without a weapon."

Kriegler shrugged. "I've never heard reports in Africa of adult humans being eaten by wild dogs."

Finding it hard not to chuckle at the image of her sweet-talking the dogs, Ian settled back in the seat. "With Joni, there's always a first time."

CHAPTER TWELVE

In a clean T-shirt and panties, Joni settled on top of a sleeping bag and crossed her tired legs. Ian had allowed a bit of water to sponge sweat off her face and neck. The weather had been warm but not oppressive, and the night had cooled into the low seventies. Zamani had dropped them off about six hours ago. Since then, they'd scouted three valleys in the Zambezi River watershed.

In the last valley, they'd caught sight of their objective—a large swath of cleared land containing buildings and equipment. She and Bram had wanted to move closer tonight and check it out, but Ian squashed the idea. He wanted time for daylight reconnaissance, and the sun driving toward the horizon pushed them to make camp and eat. Ian chose the site and Bram helped him create a circle of thorny thicket around their tents to keep out nocturnal hunters.

Ian crept into the small tent on hands and knees. He zipped the tent flap to keep out incessant insects. One reason why bug repellent had become her new best friend. He removed his boots, swearing softly about a pebble in his shoe. With practiced ease, he shed his clothes in the tight space and stretched out on top his sleeping bag close to her.

"Bram all tucked in for the night?" She wished for better light to see the man in mere T-shirt and briefs next to her.

"No place for him to go. I'll hear him if he takes a step outside the tent."

"How so?"

"I spread dry twigs."

"You're devious," she whispered. "Of course, he'll likely hear us as well."

"I'm counting on you to keep the pertinent things quiet." He leaned over and kissed her on top of her head…a sign he meant to keep distance between them. After last night, her body wanted more—hell, she wanted more. Her heart ached with the fear their time together might be short. Ian showed no signs of giving up on his life here, and honestly, this was where he thrived…unencumbered.

He slid his arm under her neck and cuddled her head onto his shoulder. "I don't know where tomorrow will take us, but I have something I need to share with you."

"Those gaps in your past Lemmon mentioned?"

His chest vibrated with a breathy chuckle. "No. I have a message for Mukono. I'd like to give it to him, but if I can't, I need you to pass it along."

"That sounds morose." She pushed up to an elbow and looked upon him in the darkness. "What are you planning, Ian?"

"Nothing more than we all are. I'm just hedging my bets. I don't want Mukono to believe we've forgotten him. Think of it as the first one of us to reach him. Are you game?"

"How hard can it be?"

Quietly Ian let off a string of unfamiliar words and clicks.

"That's not fair. I only know a few Ndebele words."

He reached up and pulled her close. His warm body, tantalizing and distracting, made her desire anything but talk. His mouth brushed her ear. "I was speaking Xhosa. A common language in southern Africa, but one Kagona doesn't speak."

She leaned up, pressing her fingertips into his chest. "Is knowing that supposed to make it easier?"

"Only more fun."

"Challenge accepted." Her hands slid from his warmth and she sat back, folding her legs in tight. "No promises, but I'll give it my best."

Ian sat across from her and pressed her hands between his. "We'll start with the hard part first. The three clicking sounds. Get those down and the rest is easy."

"Nothing is ever easy with you, but I'm not one to go down without a fight."

He reached around and slid her closer until her knees rested on his thighs. "You make teaching tough." His voice sounded tight and hoarse, and it made her shudder with anticipation. She wanted more than talk and so did he.

Slowly he drew a deep breath. "The first click is like you were urging a horse to trot. Your tongue goes to the side of your mouth. Tsk-tsk-tsk. It's the sound for X."

"Do I have to spell, too?"

"Is that asking too much?"

"Slave driver." She poked him in the abs. With her tongue slid to the side, she tried the sound. It didn't quite mimic the one he'd made. They continued back and forth. When she'd semimastered one style of click, he moved to the next.

At one of her efforts, Ian burst into quiet laughter.

Frustrated, she shoved him over. He lay on the sleeping bag doing his best to silence his chortles. Eventually, he sat up again. "My apologies. Your struggles remind me of when Nomathemba taught me."

They both quieted at the mention of her name. Mukono's wife and Ian's childhood friend had played a huge part in building Ian's love for Zimbabwe. Only weeks ago, she had tragically been ripped from them at the hands of Kagona.

"Let's get this done, Ian. I'm ready."

For the next hour, they practiced the sounds and then mixed them into the greeting he wanted her to share. While she had no idea what it truly meant, she broke down the parts into key words and attached cues to enhance her memory. The sentences came quickly, not so much the words with the clicking sounds.

At last, Ian leaned forward and gave her a joyful squeeze. "I think you've got it so he'll understand."

"I don't want to be the one to deliver it, but if it's important to you I will."

He pulled her into his arms. She sat with her back against his chest and he nestled his chin onto her shoulder so his mouth rested near an ear. "One last thing. This message is personal. Don't extend it where anyone can record it."

"Why did Nomathemba teach you Xhosa?"

"I don't know. Kids' stuff. The challenge. We didn't have video games."

"But why Xhosa?"

"It's a lot like Ndebele. Many in her tribe speak it. Minister Mukono fell in love with Nomathemba while she was helping him learn the language. Even though he's Shona, he had a great respect for Nelson Mandela. He came from Xhosa roots. Mukono studied Mandela's life and wanted to learn the language. He later had a chance to meet Mandela."

"I'm guessing they spoke in Xhosa." Discussions of überachievers exposed her insecurities. "Look, there's no guarantee I won't mess up the message."

"You've learned it well enough. Besides, I suspect you're going to mentally practice. This greeting could go a long way to giving Mukono hope."

"If I meet him before you, it'll likely be in Kagona's prison. What will I have to hang onto for hope?"

"Me." He lay back and rolled her on top of him. His hands slid up under her T-shirt and tugged it off. He coaxed her face down to his. "I'll never leave you in Kagona's clutches. Ever."

The offering of his heated kiss sealed the promise.

The sun shone high in the sky where a few clouds threatened to build. Heat ate through Bram's shirt as he lay belly down across a rock ledge covered in gravelly dirt. Joni stretched out on one side and his new best friend, Taljaard, on the other.

The guy stuck close, except for his foray this morning to recon the mine facility below and locate this vantage for their surveillance. He'd taken a bow for stealth and left his rifle behind for Joni, with detailed instructions to shoot only as a last defense. Ian's sideways glance seemed to include Bram on the list of possible targets.

From their position on a hillside overlooking a wide valley below, they examined the elusive mine. After a long night trapped in his tent with nocturnal hunters prowling outside and likely devouring each other, his eyes blurred from lack of sleep.

Taljaard appeared to have slept soundly. Who wouldn't with Joni to tell him bedtime stories? Bram had listened to their laugher and low voices for an hour. Then silence…yeah, not the sleeping kind. Lucky bastard.

"Are we going to watch, wait, and photograph forever?"

Taljaard handed over the high-powered binoculars. "Recon is the easy part. Getting Mukono out of Kagona's prison will be the challenge. Take a good look through these, then pass them on to Joni. I want everyone to check out the fencing, buildings, their entrances and exits, and anything else that will help in our assessment of the target. Let's send some photos off to Lemmon."

Bram shrugged. "He probably has better pictures than we can capture. The Americans have satellites."

"You're assuming Lemmon has enough pull and money to redirect one. If he resorted to sending you and Joni to assist me, I sincerely doubt that. What you two brought in your day packs will provide better intel than a satellite." Taljaard scooted back from their ledge and, once out of sight of anyone below, stood. "If I had my druthers, we'd watch for at least a day or two. Pick up patrols and their patterns."

"I believe Lemmon mentioned we were under a time crunch."

Taljaard ignored him. He gathered up a bow and aimed at a target he'd fashioned an hour ago when Bram had taken a nature break. Mr. Safari's action had sent an unspoken message: if Bram tried to wander off he'd be hunted down.

He passed the high-powered binoculars to Joni before shoving back from the edge. He stood near Taljaard. "We have to get down there. Confirm what they're mining."

"Are all Afrikaners in such a hurry?" In a move staged to unsettle, Taljaard raised the fancy bow, drew, and fired in a swift blur. The bow proved amazingly silent. The arrow penetrated the makeshift target next to a tiny cluster of berries at the center and disappeared.

Show-off. "If we hit trouble, you may need that." With a gun, Bram would have made a decent attempt at stripping Taljaard's orange fletching while the arrow flew.

"That's a practice arrow. I'm more accurate with quality ones."

"A gun is easier to conceal and faster."

"It's also a hell of a lot louder."

"When are we planning a close-up recon of the plant to figure out what's going on?"

Taljaard nocked another practice arrow and fired. "Tonight, when I'm more confident I'm not sending Joni into an ambush."

"I'm going in with her."

"If you plan to live, you'd better make sure she comes back. I'll be directing the op on comm. Calling out threats. That reminds me. I'm assigning names. I'm Ingwe. Joni, you're Chopper."

"Hey, I fly helicopters, too," Bram pointed out, finding this name game irritating at best. "My call sign is Skate."

"I'm tagging you Impisi."

From behind the binoculars, Joni snickered.

Fokken great. This is what he endured, operating unwanted in somebody else's territory. Bram's ego handled the slight. "You don't like me much, do you?"

"Nothing personal. I didn't envision Joni returning to Zim with someone in tow. You can keep Skate under one condition."

"Sounds ominous."

Taljaard shrugged nonchalantly. "See that bunch of berries on the target?"

"I don't plan to set them on my head like an apple."

"Nah. Too dangerous. Simply stretch your arm out and dangle them from your fingers."

"Only if I get a turn." He found an ounce of pleasure in calling Taljaard's bluff. "Always wanted to give a bow a try."

"Sure. If I miss. Don't fret. I promise to use a decent arrow."

"Impisi sounds better already. Dare I ask what it means?"

"It's Ndebele for hyena."

Bram raised a brow. Clearly neither trusted the other. If the situation were reversed, he'd take the same stance. "What about Ingwe?"

"Leopard," Joni answered.

In a breath, Taljaard dispatched another arrow. This one exploded the berries and disappeared into the thicket. A more serious, perhaps nostalgic look settled on Taljaard's face. "A friend used to call me Ingwe." He put away his bow and slipped into the brush to find his arrows.

Bram chose the opportunity to reposition himself next to Joni, the safer of his bush companions. "Anything happening down there?"

A fine sheen of moisture played along her neck, exposed by the cloth band holding back her dark hair. If he'd met her on any street, the last thing he'd imagine was this slim wisp of a woman confidently handling a helo with the ease of a 4x4.

Her finger triggered the shutter. "A few people have walked between buildings, but that's about it. I'm too far away to tell much about them." She handed over the binoculars and picked up the camera. "Same for these photos. Good for setting and general overview, but we need something closer."

"And it's about time you provide it." Taljaard appeared, as though he carted a radar that indicated Bram was studying Joni too closely. Taljaard crept out silently beside her on the ledge. A lizard warming in his place scurried away. He touched her shoulder in a way that offered encouragement in her activity. Yeah, the leopard was smitten.

"You ready to run if it's noticed?" she said.

"I'm counting on you to make sure it's not."

Joni looked hard at Taljaard, a slow smile blossoming. Damn, if she didn't thrive on a challenge. "Just settle back and catch forty winks. I'll wake you when I'm done."

She handed him the camera and left the men to warm their bellies on the ledge. Bram heard rustling behind him as she prepared a small drone for launch.

He'd spent the morning with her digging through their packs for pieces disguised in various ways to pass through security. Their typical banter between workmates and friends had resurfaced. Several times he'd caught the slight rise at the edges of her lips as good memories passed through her thoughts. Being around Taljaard had relaxed her wary edge. She counted on him for protection. For her own good, she should be more cautious, like her damn Tarzan.

A soft buzzing sounded behind him. Lemmon's drone had a quieter signature than anything on the open market. A result of the Americans' DARPA and their advanced research? The drone leaped to a swift takeoff and disappeared high into the sky.

Joni settled between him and Taljaard with the tablet hooked onto the controller. Live video displayed the thicket and grasses as the drone swept down the valley to where the facility lay.

Eventually metal buildings, tanks, pipes, and funky rows of upright cylinders inside the fenced complex came into view. Two corrugated-steel warehouses, one big and one small, sat on the end of the compound closest to their position.

Joni switched to a hover. "What do you think? Those look like evaporation ponds on the far side. And, if I'm not mistaken, spread out in that cleared area are wellheads. Placed in an interesting configuration, too. Look. There's one in the middle and others arranged around it. From the pumps attached, they look active. But doing what? Is Lemmon sure this is uranium mining? Is the mine underground? There's no open pit. No evidence of a shaft. No tailing piles either, for that matter."

Bram had underestimated Joni's knowledge base. "I've seen this before. It's in situ leach mining. They inject nasty stuff down wells. It eats the uranium out of the rock and then the solution is pumped up via other wells. No tailings. No pit. Little evidence."

"Humph." Taljaard grumbled, "Maybe this type of mining is intentional for that very reason."

"Possibly." Bram followed as Joni repositioned the drone. He pointed at the screen. "I'm assuming this larger metal building processes and dries the product, while the smaller one next to it is a lab or storage. That long metal-roofed structure has what appears to be power cables coming from it."

Joni nodded in agreement. "Running all this equipment requires a dedicated power station. And if this mine is what you say, then they have to keep those wells running twenty-four hours to maintain a pressure gradient and make sure the solution flows toward the removal well."

Bloody amazing. Joni would know if Bram's report on the mine wasn't accurate. Lemmon must be laughing his head off. "Maybe I should've let *you* tell us what's down there. Now that I think about it, you've never mentioned what you studied at university, *bokkie*."

"Civil engineering. I wish now I'd taken the mining elective."

Taljaard snickered. "Never underestimate a woman, Kriegler."

"No worries on that front. I learn from my mistakes."

Joni pointed at the screen. "Any idea what these smaller sheds are used for?"

Bram leaned close enough her hair brushed against his jaw. Fieldwork resulted in closer quarters than flight briefing rooms, passing in the halls, or a pint with friends. "Those two huge tanks might hold the liquid injected, or be part of the ion exchange that takes place, or it could be where they store the stuff pumped up. Your guess is as good as mine."

Taljaard kept his focus on the target with the binoculars. "I don't see any military guards below. Do you see any evidence?"

"Not yet."

"Keep hunting. Those men we encountered on the road were keeping check on visitors to this area. From the look of this complex, it's taken a while to build. Any guesses as to why the military is so judiciously guarding this now?"

Bram methodically checked the complex and saw only a few men out and about. "Most mining companies hire their own security. The Chinese already have platinum, copper, and diamond mines in Zim. At those their security is tighter than hell. If they're doing the mining, they don't need the military. My guess—the military is Kagona's contribution to the mix."

"No doubt. He's clearing out the riffraff so he can make his move."

The drone moved to a new angle. "I can drop in closer," Joni said to Taljaard. "Only three minutes to recall."

"Keep it high. I don't want to risk it being seen."

"I've spotted two outside cameras." Joni indicated a shadow at the far edge of the complex. She had a surprising eye for detail. "One on the gate and one that sweeps back and forth across the equipment area."

Someone moved at the far corner of the screen. "There are a

few workers down there. We'll need a closer look if we want to discover their nationality."

"That's the plan." Taljaard looked over at them. "I'll take the daytime shift. You and Joni will go in after dark. Careful. There may or may not be monitors inside."

"Recall time," Joni called softly as the drone headed home.

Bram switched to the camera with its high-powered lens. Men stirred not far up the valley at a cluster of four large military tents laid out on a flattened platform of dirt. Each tent could easily hold ten men with decent cots or beds. Five men left the trailers and walked toward the mine. He snapped several shots.

Taljaard lowered the binoculars. "This looks like a pretty small operation compared to a normal mine. Any idea how many people it takes to keep it running?"

"Not my thing, but it's small compared to an open pit or underground operation. And this one looks new."

"With the complexity and secretive nature, I doubt they're hiring locals for grunt-level positions." Taljaard pointed at the tents. "No way to tell if those are full or not."

The drone dropped into a quick landing. The tiny propellers hushed their whir. Joni unhooked the camera, set up an enhanced antenna, and began transferring the data to her satellite phone. Once done, she disassembled the drone into individual pieces and repacked it into her day pack.

Joni slid in between them again. "Did either of you notice the covered area on the far side of that bigger building? There's a raised platform under it, like a loading dock. Looks like fifty-five-gallon drums. Stacked two deep. Could they have product ready to ship?"

A chill ran through Bram. Again Joni proved her observation and assessment skills. "Not much we can do about that."

"Except track it," Taljaard added. "And that's exactly what you guys can set up tonight."

A vibration cut through the air in a regular pattern familiar to Bram's ears. He rolled to his back for a better view.

"Take cover," Taljaard commanded. He scooped up his power bow. Joni grabbed the rifle and headed for the nearest brush, where they'd secured their packs.

Taljaard prodded Bram along. No problem—he would secure Ian's trust when he and Joni pulled off a successful on-site recon later. Bram picked up the pace and hid fully from overhead view. Taljaard crouched down, settling in next to Joni.

A military chopper flew over them. "An Alouette III," Bram passed to the others. "Flown by the Air Force of Zimbabwe. This one is missing a designation identifier."

Joni and Taljaard looked at each other.

"I take it you two have had some experience with this particular chopper?"

"It's Kagona's." Joni frowned, looking worried.

After she returned home from her last mission, successful but bruised and battered, he'd expected she'd take this one in stride. Obviously he'd missed out on pertinent details of what she'd been through.

Sensing his thoughts, she added, "I left it on the lawn of the Victoria Hotel a few days ago."

"Christ, *bokkie*. You stole his chopper?" In a few days, she'd accomplished more to curry hate from the CIO chief than Taljaard had in years. Kagona would get even, and it wouldn't be pretty.

The Alouette circled the valley before heading toward a small strip they had scouted about five miles away.

Taljaard gave her a light hug. He said something Bram couldn't hear that brought a smiling grimace to her face. They had a camaraderie he envied, but hoping they would share it with him was a moot point. By tomorrow they'd both hate his guts for different reasons.

CHAPTER THIRTEEN

In what was becoming her least favorite position, Joni lay on her stomach next to Bram and watched as Ian crept closer to the mine entrance road. The chopper's arrival heralded an opportunity to collect critical intel, which forced them to act quickly in broad daylight. Among the team, Ian possessed the necessary skills to complete such a task.

An itch found her scratching her forearm. She'd done a better job today of tucking her clothing in tight after picking up bites from hungry insects yesterday. Permanent scrapes marred her elbows caused from propping up the camera and binoculars. Bruises dotted her knees from pebbles stabbing into them.

Mentally she didn't fare much better. A knot weighed heavily in her stomach. Fear. Fear something would happen and she'd lose Ian, or that she'd never have the chance to say the good-bye destined to come. Hell, it was more likely she feared screwing up or that Lemmon would undermine her again.

At least this time Ian had been open and straight with her about his plans. He'd tossed on a gillie suit made from an old flight suit. Camouflage paint covered the front, including the knee and elbow pads. The back had been enhanced with hanging cloth scraps to fit in with the thorny brush and golden grasses.

Netting with which to secure natural elements to mask his head shape hung from his hat. He'd moved slowly downslope, sometimes creeping, other times crawling on his belly. On the way, he had added grasses, leaves, and twigs and blended in so well, he became harder to track.

She glanced at her watch. Ian had a long way to go and not much time. Speed was not his friend, but a necessity.

A trail of dust rose through distant trees. More than expected from these roads. The helicopter's occupants must be arriving on one hell of a big truck.

"About a mile out." She spoke to Ian via their comm. She'd positioned the push-to-talk trigger on her finger. "No visual yet."

She refocused on the slope below and how it flattened near the base of the wide valley. Around the mine area, a large swath of ground had been cleared. Mostly grasses and a few scraggly patches of brush had grown back. Could Ian work close enough to see and hear the men without being spotted?

Ten minutes earlier a group of five workers had walked from their living quarters to the mine. They pushed the gates wide and left them open for the approaching vehicle. A man had come from a smaller building she and Bram decided must be a lab. A changing of shifts or a welcome for visitors?

She swung the binoculars back toward the upper valley. Crap. That one big dust cloud actually represented two vehicles. Visions of a truckload of soldiers spreading out across the valley left her mouth dry and adrenaline pumping.

"Two vehicles approaching." A minute later a flatbed carrying a dull red shipping container rumbled into sight. About thirty seconds after that, a second one appeared. "Eighteen-wheeler container trucks."

"Roger."

Bram observed through the camera, snapping a few photos. "Someone is arriving to pick up a load."

"Or drop one off. Those drums we saw might be empty for all we know."

"Well, *bokkie*, if your man doesn't get himself nabbed, we may get a chance to find out tonight. Unless those trucks arriving cart them away before then."

"Pessimist."

He aimed the camera, and it whirred as the first truck approached the gates. "Actually, the two trucks might be a lucky break."

"Lucky?"

"Yeah, look at the location where the gates open. It's not a large parking area. One truck can easily swing around and back in for loading. Two in there would get tight. Cross your fingers the second one parks at the entrance. Then if the dignitaries arrive, they'll have to park outside and walk in." Bram grinned, rather proud of his analysis. "You catching all this, Ingwe?"

"Optimist," Ian answered.

Admittedly, Bram had thoroughly assessed the layout and situation with the trucks. The second one did park on the road near the entrance, blocking passage. After the first truck loaded, the second could pull inside far enough the first truck could get out. The question remained as to when loading would commence and how long it would take. If before dark, they'd have no chance to tag the containers.

Joni attempted to locate Ian below them without success.

"He's good." Bram, using the camera, evidently struggled with the same problem.

"But not perfect. Crawling around must be hell on his wound." The minute it slipped out, she realized the mistake in revealing Ian's weakness.

Bram stared hard at her. "Are you telling me he's been injured?"

"I've said enough."

"Since I'm sticking my neck out, I've a right to know about the condition of our team."

Too late to retract her slip. "The big man winged him. It was almost healed until your tussle at Mike's house ripped open a few of the stitches."

"Left side?" An odd look crossed his face, but he was right about the location.

"None of your damn business."

"Don't get your *broekies* in a knot."

"You two done discussing my health?" Ian said in a low voice. "Buckle down. We've work to do. I won't be saying much for a while."

Joni had inadvertently held down her push-to-talk trigger on comm. Yep, her leadership skills were shining through to everyone, including Bram, who'd likely report her failures or turn them into a laughable tale at the pub.

Another small trail of dust caught her eye. A 4x4 appeared on the road curving into the valley. The visitors from the chopper. "Our helo friends are here." Minutes later the vehicle stopped behind the second container truck, like Bram had predicted.

The dark-skinned driver emerged and opened a rear door for two men with lighter complexions and relatively short dark hair. On the far side of the vehicle, the fourth man wore a wide-brimmed hat blocking his head and face. Distance made determining their race or country of origin a mere guessing game. They walked up the side of the container truck in full view. Hopefully, Ian perched somewhere with a clear sightline.

The man in the hat rounded the vehicle and strode behind the group. Black, tall, and broader than the others, he strolled with cocky confidence. His swagger and bearing seemed eerily familiar.

"Kagona." Her palms sweat. The binoculars became slippery to hold.

Bram leaned close enough his shoulder touched hers, as though adding support. "Which one?"

"Last man."

He snapped photos, then covered the lens and set the camera down. "Mind if I borrow those?"

She handed over the high-powered binoculars but couldn't take her eyes off the men who'd passed the chain-link fence and entered the mine yard. They eventually entered one of the larger metal buildings.

A small forklift moved into the yard and disappeared toward the area where the barrels were stored. She glimpsed it lifting a barrel locked in a circular attachment on the end of narrow forks. "How long it will take to load the truck container?"

"If it's yellowcake, it will take a while. They have special Kevlar straps inside that must be used to secure the drums. I've watched them do it but wasn't thinking much about it at the time. All I wanted was a chance to drive a forklift."

"Guys and their toys." Still uncomfortable with Bram's knowledge of mining, she kept her eyes on the scene below. "Can you see Ingwe down there?"

"I lost sight of him a while ago."

"He has to be near the road and those vehicles to hear a conversation. He has no way to amplify voices."

Methodically Bram shifted the binoculars. A minute later, he gave a guffaw. "Damn man has guts."

He handed her the binoculars back and directed her to follow a lump of ground inching toward a narrow, ten-foot stretch of scraggly low bushes not a hundred feet from the dirt roadway.

She closed her eyes, not wanting to accept the exposure Ian risked. Tension seeped through her, changing her focus into a bundle of nerves. She fingered the tiny pebble she'd found in her boot this morning and secured in her shirt pocket. The very pebble Ian had dropped in her shoe after it had plagued him last night.

The afternoon progressed another hour, and the heat had forced them to follow what little shade a measly overhanging tree offered. She and Bram changed positions several times and traded the binoculars and camera back and forth. Ian had to be roasting so covered up and yet so exposed.

At last, movement came from the processing plant.

"Men are exiting the building. You alive down there?" she asked.

"Yebo."

"They're watching the barrels being loaded. Can't see how full the container truck is."

Bram positioned the camera once again. His actions displayed proficiency at shooting. Yet at this distance, details were marginal.

"Driver walking the men past the gate. Headed toward the 4x4." Kagona brought up the rear of the entourage. The driver opened the passenger door for the two dignitaries. They paused and spoke with one another.

Kagona approached them, shaking his head.

"Something is going on. Kagona and the men seemed to be disagreeing about something." Whatever Kagona said, the men ignored. He backed away.

"Kagona is unhappy. Lit up a cigarette. Leaning on the vehicle hood."

One visitor reached inside the vehicle and brought out folded cloth. He handed part of it to his companion. The men looked around, pointing toward various places away from the road. They settled on a few clumps of bushes holding on tenaciously to life in the relatively barren area near the mine.

"Crap." Her mouth went dry. "Two visitors headed your way. Some kind of cloth in their hands." The closer they came to Ian's position, the more her insides tensed. "They stopped," she whispered to Bram. "Edge of grass."

One man pulled out his phone and held it before them. She

looked questioningly at Bram. He nodded and drew an arrow in the gravelly dirt of their perch and topped it with an N. Cardinal directions. She understood what, but not why.

The men maneuvered so that they faced the grass and meager bushes, yet lined up with a direction on the phone. They shook out long pieces of cloth and spread them on the ground. They knelt and, hands by their sides, prayed.

So did she…for about five minutes. They were close enough to Ian on the other side of a bush that his mike picked up their soft and often mumbled words. She recorded them on her phone.

The men rose and folded their cloths. Instead of leaving, they spoke to one another in low voices. Their accents and language, lighter than the guttural sounds of Arabic, struck no familiar chord. Surely Lemmon or one of his analysts would recognize it.

In the midst of their conversation, Kagona's name came out. The tone didn't sound flattering. Sweat trickled down her face. Ian hadn't breathed deeply for so long she feared he might have passed out from heat exhaustion. One pulled out cigarettes.

His friend waved away an offer. "Haram," he admonished the man offering…to no avail as his companion lit up the forbidden vice.

The hot sun eventually drove the men back to the 4x4. Kagona crushed out his cigarette and piled in with the others. The vehicle pulled away.

Joni followed its progress until out of sight. "You alive down there?"

"Yep. And we have our answer. They're Iranian."

Ian's slow, meticulous retreat gave him time to evaluate the fencing, buildings, and routines of the few men he'd seen inside the mining compound. The stench of his lightweight gillie suit had grown familiar. By the time he reached shade and decent cover to retreat on his feet without being seen, his clothing had become soaked.

Covered in sweat but feeling euphoric, he arrived at their overlook, taking Joni and Kriegler by surprise.

Joni heard him first and clambered to her feet. "Oh, my God, look what the cat dragged in."

"Must have been a big cat." Kriegler snickered. "Think I'll go check for a Pitta bird." He wandered off into the bush without his camera.

Ian divested himself of the gillie suit. His T-shirt had soaked clear through and curly hair had matted to his head.

Joni hugged him, sweat, stench, and all. Her welcome-back kiss was delivered with the right touch of hunger and teasing. He wished they were back at the lodge. To the victor the spoils. If working with Joni continued with such rewards, he'd go into battle more often.

He planted a slew of hungry kisses and cursed Kriegler's addition to their crew. The thought of a little open-air recreation made him bloody hard.

She pushed down gently on his encompassing arms and stepped back. Okay, so he'd gotten a little enthusiastic. A smirk kinked up her cheek. "I'm not sure Lemmon had that in his mission planning."

"He had it underlined in red."

At her frown, he recognized his mistake. "Crikey, Joni. The man's a spy. He uses everybody to his advantage." He reached out to her, but she shifted and caught his hands in hers.

"Working with you seems harder than I remember. Last time when we went after Sipho, well, maybe I was too busy surviving, or maybe—"

"We weren't lovers then. Yeah, I'm feeling it, too. It's hard to let you out of my sight. We have to get past it and trust each other. I'm not taking any more chances than I did before I met you."

"I am." She stroked a thumb across the top of his hand. "I've confidence in my movements flying up there, but not so much down here on the ground."

"You did great today calling out foes. It takes practice and training. We'll work on it."

"There's nothing I could have done if they'd seen you."

"You wouldn't need to do anything. That's my job."

Joni didn't appear convinced, even though she knew he carried a knife on his leg, another at his side, and more tricks up his sleeves than he could count. An impression arose he'd messed up somewhere, but he couldn't put his finger on how.

"This so-called job promises to get you killed, Ian. You can't even sleep in your house at night. It's been taken away from you."

"I wish I could change that, but I can't. Zimbabwe is where I live. I'm home every night I sleep on its soil."

"A home is a place with family and pets. People and things you love. A place you can look out your door over a land where you feel at peace."

Her words struck deep. He loved the beauty and people of this country, but it had become less of a home every day, as being near his friends grew more difficult. "Maybe it's my nature, Joni, but peace may be something I never find. I'm sorry if that disappoints you."

She smiled in a sad sort of way. "You'll never disappoint me. You're one of bravest, most giving men I've ever met. I guess I care enough about you to wish you happiness." She bent over and collected the binoculars, wrapping the strap about them. "Have you ever considered joining your family in South Africa?"

He folded his arms, wary of where this conversation was headed. "Did my uncle put you up to asking that when you dropped Sipho off with him?"

"Actually, your mother. She thinks it's time for you to live life, not expend it."

His mother and Zamani prescribed to a similar philosophy concerning his life. "She's lonely without my father."

"I don't think that's—"

"My father wasn't at the reserve when you were there, was he?"

"No."

"Point made."

"For your mother to still love him after all these years, he must be a decent man. Consider what he taught you."

Odd how his first thoughts returned to childhood. "When we had the ranch, I worked along with him like any son. But our free time wasn't spent playing football or fishing, it was learning survival, fighting techniques, and how to hunt…not only animals, but men. It was about his desires, not mine. And in the end, those drove him to be irresponsible."

"He comes to see her and sends money home. He's taking care of her."

"And you see that as a viable relationship?" He picked up his gillie suit and threw it over a bush to dry. "Is that how you'd like us to be?"

She cradled the binoculars tight against her body. "I'm not judging your parents, but I won't live like your mother, either. When I decide to spend my life with someone, that's exactly what I have in mind. Spending my life with him."

"My father doesn't have to be gone. He's not fighting for his country. He's a mercenary because it's in his blood."

"That's his decision. His choice."

"A poor one."

"Says the man who has no real home and is wanted by the country he is trying to save."

"At least I believe in something. What kind of man would I be to any woman if I gave up my ideals?"

"So why did you ask me to come back?"

"Christ, Joni." Her circular logic drove him crazy. He

grasped her arms so he could read the emotion playing in her eyes. "Because against my better judgment, I want you in my life. I did then, and I still do. It's just—my body and mind seem to be conflicting with one another on the timing." He'd entered into unknown territory hotter than lying in the dirt in full sun.

Her eyes hardened, with exactly which emotion he couldn't tell. "Maybe we need to set our feelings aside until this mission is over. Once Sipho's father is free, then we can figure out where we fit in."

She took the binoculars and headed for shade. A chill filled the air and left him reflecting on how quickly the victor could suffer defeat.

CHAPTER FOURTEEN

Evening came too quickly, but Joni wanted confirmation of the barrels' contents, clues to where they were headed, and to tag the containers for Lemmon. Once done, she and Ian could move on to figuring out how to get Sipho's father out of Kagona's hands. After that…well, time would tell. So why did she feel as if she'd been trampled by a rhino?

With a black cap pulled to her brows, black pants, and a lightweight black jacket over her tan shirt, she followed directions to their entry point, which Ian had scouted. Bram, dressed the same, but with liberal use of camo paint, crept along next to her, carefully watching their backs for unfriendly nocturnal creatures. He'd be the guide of the interior layout once they got inside.

Ian moved to a closer position to direct them from outside the fence and watch for workers and bad guys.

"Another twenty meters down to the fence." His voice sounded reassuring and clear in her ears. "The camera should be on a pole dead ahead along the fence."

"I see it."

"Parallel the fence toward the far corner near the building." They had figured, with the layout of the buildings and the camera position, that location put them on camera for a millisecond, and likely out of any motion sensor range. The security appeared more for maintenance reasons to spot problems at the plant than actual security from intruders. The surrounding fence kept out unwanted creatures rather than determined humans.

Bram used cutters to snip links up from the ground and then over to make an upside-down L. He pulled the fence back to expose a square hole large enough for them to crawl through.

Even though her pulse raced, calm focused her mind. She scrambled inside and hid in shadow, waiting for Bram to join her. The workers had locked up the gates after switching trucks. The first one, now loaded, sat outside the big gates, ready to take off down the dirt road. The other was backed into the loading dock.

The small forklift had been working madly. Whether they had finished loading or not wasn't clear. The operators had left through a smaller gate and returned to the tents. From the smell wafting down the valley, dinner was served. Whether a night crew still worked inside or planned to return after dinner, she had no means to determine. Eyes and ears open.

Bram tapped her shoulder and pointed toward a door into the corrugated steel building she leaned against. Step one—confirm what was in the drums. He led the way. They cracked the door open and listened, worried it might be alarmed. No sound.

Once inside, she checked the jamb for any contact points indicating an alarm setup. She shook her head at Bram and they moved on.

Light was low in the cavernous room. Reddish-brown steel beams stretched across the roof with smaller beams lain across them to hold up a corrugated white roof and sides. Huge silver pipes ran from giant tanks in various directions. Metal walkways with pipe railings connected the tops of the tanks and allowed for servicing.

"What are we looking at?" she whispered.

"Final drying stage." He pointed at a huge tanklike piece of equipment. Nearby a line of barrels sat on a long track of thin rollers. A single barrel had been positioned underneath an enclosed triangular hopper designed to drop product into it. Hoses and flex pipes attached to an odd setup that kept the drum top sealed and the product and its dust trapped.

"How can we see what's inside?"

"No need." Bram shifted closer to the drum and punched at something on the watch Lemmon had sent along. Numbers swiftly rolled past.

A Geiger counter. "Should we be standing this close?" she asked.

"At this level, an hour exposure is equivalent to radiation from a four-hour flight."

"So we'll live. At least we can be pretty sure what's in there." She moved toward the unsealed barrels on the assembly line while Bram headed toward an office door across the processing room. He'd search out whatever shipping information he could find.

He paused to listen at the door before opening it. She peeked in the other open barrels lined up on the rollers. Empty. Evidently once filled, they were sealed and hauled outside for loading.

"Bogey crossing from outbuilding headed for a back door." Ian sounded calm. "Five seconds."

Joni looked toward the office. Bram had no time to escape and nothing close enough to the office to conceal himself. Time moved in increments as her mind came up with only one feasible action.

"Listen for my signal," she whispered to Bram over comm.

She took cover. A door opened and footsteps shuffled across the floor. Legs and feet, with covers over the shoes, walked behind a tank that sat knee-high off the floor.

She ducked down as a man headed across the processing room for the office. Once past her position, she mentally counted, *three, two, one*.

With force, she pitched Ian's pebble to an upper metal walkway. It clanked against the slats before dropping and ricocheting off one of the tanks. The shuffling stopped. Hunkered down, she had no way to see if the ploy worked.

A minute crept past. Then another. The slightest sound of someone nearby reached her ears. She tucked her body tight, leaving nothing but black exposed. Someone moved near the barrel where she hid.

"*Dà lǎo shǔ,*" the man muttered, then turned away. She heard the office door shut.

"Clear," Bram said over her comm.

A thankful heart ramped down to normal speed. She slipped back to the door they'd entered and rejoined with Bram. "Did you hear that?"

"You mean the Chinese?"

"What do you think he said?"

"Rats." Bram obviously guessed, but he likely guessed right.

"What did you find in the office?"

"Food wrappers and personal dosimeters. I didn't stop to see if any of them were glowing."

His attempt at levity relieved the tension from their close encounter. "Come on. We have to tag those containers."

"No go on the door you came in," Ian voiced. "Three men returning from dinner. They'll be heading in the small gate."

She pointed to the door the guy had just entered. They'd be on camera if they stepped into the light, but they had no choice. She slipped out, noting light hit across the building right above her head. She blocked the door to prevent Bram from exiting.

"Come out low."

Bram followed, crouching.

"Stay put," Ian called.

The gate clanked as the workers entered. She and Bram held position, waiting.

"One disappeared inside. Second on the loading dock. Third coming down side of building." And would pass the end where Bram crouched and she had plastered herself against the wall. They slid as far as possible away from the door and still kept in shadow.

A man walked past the building and entered the place they had deemed the lab.

"Okay, move."

They stayed in the shadow along the side and worked back toward the front corner of the building. She peered around but couldn't see the man on the loading dock.

"Chopper, wait for my signal, then go out the way you came in."

"Roger."

The man out on the dock came around the truck and went to the big front gates. An identity badge or perhaps one of those dosimeters flapped on his shirt. He swung open one side and then the other. Were they actually going to drive these questionable roads in the dark?

Hell, yes. Kagona worked in secrecy. No better time to move than when every other smart person in these parts was tucked in for the night.

The driver climbed into the cab. A light shone on his face and clearly highlighted his Asian heritage. So who was mining? The Chinese or the Iranians, or the Chinese for the Iranians on Zimbabwean soil?

Note to self. Get a scorecard.

After a minute that seemed like ten, the truck engine roared to life. The truck rolled slowly through the gate and kissed the backside of the other truck outside. The driver left the engine idling and climbed out. He shut the big gates and headed inside the processing building.

"Go, Chopper."

She dashed for the opening Bram had cut.

"Put distance between you and the fence, then cut around to the front. Keep far enough out from the mine lights. I'll work you back toward the trucks."

So many things ran through her mind. *Don't get stuck going through the fence. Stay light on your feet.* She slid through.

"Impisi, go."

Joni ran on, figuring Bram would catch up quickly.

"Hard part is behind you," Ian encouraged her, and his voice provided comfort and confidence. "Follow the road in to the trucks."

Energized, she smiled through her heavy breathing as she skirted along in the shadows. "Let's get this done and go home."

Ian scanned the mine through night-vision binoculars from his close-in position. Joni had conquered her nerves and saved Kriegler's hide inside. How, he'd have to get the details later, but his heart had nearly stopped during those minutes of silence.

He'd initially considered sending Kriegler in alone. Yeah, for a microsecond, until a little devil on his shoulder reminded him not to trust the guy. Joni wanted to take charge and he had to give her a chance to lead. That's what she needed as a perfectly capable member of this team. Hell, she always had been.

Ian wished he had Mad Mike along again to keep her out of trouble. At least Kriegler had done his part. He and Joni understood the mine workings. Both of them going in made sense. Ian's strength lay in coordinating the dance to keep foe and friend separated.

Joni approached the trucks.

"Tag the truck closest to the gate first before the men become active again," he directed. "Impisi, take the second one."

They'd decided to place the tags on the tops, out of notice to anyone working or walking around the containers. To keep out of sight, Joni climbed up behind the cab. Her height, or lack of it, created a few extra steps.

Kriegler appeared and boosted her foot to propel her up. "Thanks for the rescue, *bokkie*. I owe you one." He then headed to the second truck.

Ian's attention remained trained on Joni and the mine past her.

"Done," she announced, and started to slide off the top.

Bloody hell. "Stay on top. Lie flat. Find cover, Impisi."

"Right behind you." He had climbed atop the container and flattened himself on the roof well behind Ian. "If I'd known you'd be here, I'd left the tag with you."

Ian had chosen this closer and shadowed vantage when his first choice hadn't offered a high enough clearance to see past obstacles.

The driver who had pulled out the truck earlier and another man appeared in the plant door that had swung open. They walked out the small gate and headed toward the trucks.

"Looks like we're about to go for a ride. Stay tight, Chopper. Once clear, we'll find a place to get off."

The driver of Ian's truck hopped in the cab and started it up. The other driver walked around Joni's perch. Mr. Safety shone a flashlight, checking tires and the rear door seals. Joni remained prone on the roof. Mr. Safety approached the other driver's window. He spoke loudly over the diesel's rumble. Whatever was said resulted in him walking away and back through the gate.

What the hell?

The driver of Ian's truck released his brakes and shifted into gear. "Come on, Chopper, now. Jump to our truck." No way was he leaving her behind.

She moved fast, making a leap from the container to the cab

top. With no time to perfectly judge the ever-widening distance, she lunged for the back of Ian's truck. Her boots thunked into the doors.

Ian shoved his head and shoulders over the edge of the container. Joni had grasped one hand around a vertical pole that fastened the doors to the top and bottom frame. The other hand fought for a decent hold.

He reached out to snatch it, but she slipped. "Hang on." She was too far down for him to reach and pull up.

Her other hand caught a door latch. Her feet swung not far off the ground.

"There's a metal bumper by your feet."

She struggled to secure a foothold, but succeeded. The uneven road shook the truck. It hit a bump and clanged hard, knocking off her foot that had found a hold and nearly tossing him off the container.

"I'm coming down to get you."

A loud noise echoed in the night. Both he and Joni looked up. The chop of air was unmistakable. A helo. Had Kagona's group never left?

A spotlight shone on the truck back at the mine.

Time had run out. He secured a good hold on the top edge and shoved his body forward. Something jammed against his foot and his body didn't budge. He tried to wrench his foot free. The truck jolted hard again.

"Ian!" Joni cried out.

Her hands still gripped the pole, but she'd become engulfed in a dust cloud stirred up by the wheels. Again, he attempted to kick his foot loose and not take his eyes off her. The spotlight moved toward their truck. "Hang on. I'm stuck. Damn it, Impisi, help me. Help her."

His foot wouldn't release. Kriegler didn't respond. The chopper blades reverberated through the air.

He pushed up to look at his feet. Somewhere in the darkness

he saw a white band around a boot. The truck went over a rough patch.

Joni screamed.

He launched his body forward. His foot still held. He reached out for her. Feet away, he watched her hand lose its grip on the pole.

"No," he yelled.

Her body tumbled to the dirt. The helicopter spotlight approached and caught her in its brilliance. She rose to her knees, holding her arm above her eyes to block the light and look toward him as their truck disappeared around a bend.

He struggled to get off, to no avail.

He twisted around. The pressure on his foot released. He leaned up. Kriegler sat with his boots jammed in the grooves of the metal for traction and stared at him. He held a piece of Kevlar strapping. Ian followed it to a loop tight around his boot.

"Fucking son of a bitch. You know what Kagona will do to her." He jerked his foot hard, but Kriegler held onto the strap.

"I know exactly what he'll do, and there's no way in bloody hell you can stop it."

The truck kept moving as if oblivious to the men atop it. Ian tackled Kriegler with a rage so primal the sick bastard stood no chance of survival.

CHAPTER FIFTEEN

The dazed woman stared in the direction the truck disappeared from sight. Her protector had failed…left her behind. A pity, but hardly mattered. In minutes, the truck on which Taljaard rode would be stopped, and he dragged away. A long night loomed. Kagona reveled in the thought.

His men shone several strong lights around the area. One highlighted the dust-covered woman. They pulled her to a stand and roughly yanked her arms back before cuffing her wrists. Unlike their last encounter, her face had little camo paint. Instead dust and scrapes accented bright, intense eyes.

One man patted her down, starting at the legs covered in a black nylon pants. His man pocketed an ankle knife, a mini flashlight, a second knife on her belt, and Mace. He unzipped a light black jacket, shoving it back off her shoulders and revealing a tan buttoned shirt beneath.

The jacket caught at her bound wrists and flapped against her hips in the disturbed air created by the spinning rotors nearby. Bell showed little reaction. No acknowledgment of those around her nor frantic scans to determine her captors. She had no doubt. His man removed an earpiece, and the communications unit hung around her neck.

A master hunter, he had stripped the bandage supporting his jaw that accented a past failure and now circled his hapless prey like a lion salivating with expectation of a kill. How long should he stalk before figuratively digging his teeth into her neck and crushing the life from her body—a payback for Taljaard's stranglehold that had dislocated his jaw? Did she know the pain of nearly suffocating or a bone slowly broken?

Kagona drank in each nuance of his success. Wary eyes followed his movement. She held her chin proud, but it failed to hide anguish playing on her face. So many games he planned to play at her expense. No reason to delay the fun.

He nodded at his right-hand man, Chaipa, who signaled the men to take her to the chopper. Without ceremony, they tossed her inside. She landed on a shoulder, facedown on the metal floor, but uttered nothing more than a grunt.

Kagona sat facing the rear, his feet kicking Bell's legs aside to make room. For a tall man of solid physique, the Alouette helicopter offered little space for maneuvering. That condition promised an up close and personal encounter ahead. Good. Nothing like the feel of a victim's sweat.

He slipped on a headset and watched his captive attempt to pull her legs beneath her. Foolish woman. Chaipa settled in along the back bulkhead and planted a boot in her back. He shoved her down, negating the few inches she'd achieved.

The engine whine grew in intensity until the wheels lifted off. He discovered his fingers squeezing tight against the seat. A glance toward Chaipa caught him calmly looking out the window at the activity below. A touch of insecurity shamed Kagona, through no fault of his own. He'd been in a fucking crash due to a pilot's incompetence at night. It still haunted him.

His current pilots lacked the skills of the men who'd piloted his craft years ago when he first took over field operations at the CIO. Back then, South Africa trained Zimbabwean aviation units, ensuring they developed first-rate skills.

Voices in his headphones—Chaipa speaking with the pilot—distracted his uncomfortable musing. Once at a decent altitude, they'd interrogate their passenger. Only this time Kagona had a different objective. The pilot, who flew frequent missions for the CIO, required no further instructions.

"Do you remember the day we flew the two dissidents from Bulawayo to Harare?" Kagona spoke to Chaipa in English through a clenched jaw.

Shadows from dim light in the chopper created a ghoulish face as Chaipa tipped his head and grinned at him. "Hard to forget. The smell of raw fear leaves a lasting memory. I believe you offered one man a chance to tell everything about the other?"

"You indeed have a good memory."

"How high up were we? Five hundred feet?"

"Three hundred when I helped him take that first step. No surprise the second man was more than willing to tell us about his network before we landed. Want to play again and see if this one cooperates?" Kagona shoved the toe of his boot into Bell's side.

A groan came from his captive at the unexpected contact. That simple response sent a cheap thrill through his veins. He had to control his eagerness to make her suffer for the sins of her partner. His jaw still ached thanks to Taljaard.

Chaipa plucked out a black hood held in a net pocket by the seat. In a swift motion, he swept it over Bell's head. She struggled as he tightened the cord around her neck to hold it taut. He then strapped a wide, padded gunner belt around her midriff and secured it with heavy Velcro and metal closures. In a final preparation, he fastened a sturdy snap hook connected to a long strap on the belt back to a bolt inset on the floor near the door.

Kagona slipped into a safety harnesses and anchored it. No reason to find himself airborne if the ride got rough. Time to get his hands dirty.

With fists full of the woman's clothes, he pulled her up onto his lap. The moment she attempted to get footing, he locked his arms around her neck. Power surged through him at the meager leverage required to shut off her air. She thrashed against his body. He increased the pressure on her throat. Too much and the airway would crush. The movement stopped and he let up. Allowing her to fall unconscious would rob him of the right to see her suffer.

He slid a hand along her shirt. Her chest rose and fell with desperate breaths. Heat emanated through the cotton cloth. Thrilling. Power over life and death hardened his body.

He pressed his mouth against her shrouded head. "Don't count on friends to save you. No one can reach you up here."

His chest vibrated in laughter against her warm body. He grabbed onto a breast through her shirt. Her gasps for air pressed it against his hand.

"I'm afraid I'm changing the rules on our game." He nodded at Chaipa who slid open the side door exposing the passenger bay.

Her movement froze. Fear set in with reality.

"As a helicopter pilot, you are aware of what that rush of air means."

Big in trouble but small in stature, she offered little resistance against his well-conditioned body. He lifted her past him to the open door. The toes of her boots hung over the edge of the chopper floor. She tried to scoot her heels back, but he set his boot behind hers.

A stiff wind flapped the hood against her face and tugged at his light jacket. His fingers gripped the back of her safety belt. With her hands cuffed behind her, balance became a dangerous issue. Slowly he loosened his hold until he lightly grasped the strap attached to the safety belt. She swayed precariously at the edge.

Chaipa slid over, placing him opposite Kagona.

"Are you finding it hard to keep your balance, Miss Bell?" He pushed her sideways and she staggered her heels along the lip of the door. Chaipa shoved her back toward him. She fought to stay upright and inside.

Kagona caught part of her jacket still wedged around her wrists. "Are you surprised I know your real name? You once claimed to be Canadian. Now South African. I know those are both lies. I know everything about you." He shoved her again toward Chaipa, who sent her back toward Kagona. Her balance gone, she tipped out the door. A tug on the strap to her belt brought her back.

He planted a hand flat against her back and caught her body's shudder. "Is it my touch or the taste of death that scares you?"

She stiffened but said nothing.

"It's easy to be brave when you believe I won't kill you. I'm afraid that is not the case. I don't need you to make Taljaard talk. I want something more from you than information."

He slid his hand up the inside of her leg and stopped at her crotch. "Wouldn't it be easy if that was my only desire."

She made no effort to pull away.

"It's not. I cannot tolerate weakness in my men, and they should not tolerate it from me. Days ago you stole this very helo in front of me…in front of my men. Only your death by my hand can recover my dignity."

He lifted his boot and kicked one of her feet out over the edge. Frantically, she leaned back to compensate, but he pushed her back straight. She fell sideways onto him and half rolled out of the door.

He caught her arm and stopped the fall, letting her legs dangle into space. "Sorry, Miss Bell. Your exit must be clean. Dramatic." With a strong tug, he brought her to a stand. This time he faced her toward the open door and placed himself behind her, pressing against her petite body. Her heart raced and so did his.

"You can save yourself." He stroked the hood, wishing to feel her hair beneath his palm or see the sweat run down the neck he could so easily crush. "Drop to your knees. Beg me to let you live."

She shook her head and leaned back into him. Her boot kicked back at his shin.

"Good try." Her attempted distraction added more drama to his tale. "But you will be making the trip down by yourself."

He grabbed the wrist of her fist clamping onto his jacket and wrenched it back. A miserable scream of pain heartened his soul. "I'm afraid the only one dying today is you. Think about Taljaard on the way down."

With two hands on her back, he shoved her free of the chopper.

The snap hook secured to the floor clinked tight. A strange sense of lightness, euphoria nudged him into uncontrolled laughter. Oh, the sweet scent of fear.

Chaipa lay across the floor. Kagona leaned out over the seat to watch Bell swing just below the wheels. "Bring her up. We've more fun ahead and not much time."

The two men pulled her back into the chopper and sat her on the edge of the door. Kagona tugged at the cord holding her hood and pulled it off. The wind whipped hair about her ashen face. He lifted her chin and turned her face so she looked back over her shoulder at him, sitting once again in a seat.

"In the brief second you believed death waited, what did you think about?"

A wildness had replaced the pride and wary glances evident after her capture. But oddly, she held her wicked, lying tongue.

His games had taken their toll. "I couldn't let you die without watching your face. Seeing the regret of dying alone with people enjoying your demise. I'll relish describing every moment to Taljaard. He risked everything to save you...and failed."

She craned her neck as he reached down by her butt and unclipped a snap hook from a floor bolt. He waved it up high to make sure she saw the safety strap attached to it.

"This time there is no coming back." He tucked it onto a cuffed palm behind her back and curled her fingers tightly around it.

"Taljaard will be a man easy to break once he hears how you died."

Still looking over her shoulder, her gaze locked onto his, with eyes narrowed and pure hate shooting through.

Perfect. With a smug grin, he positioned a boot on her back and shoved.

CHAPTER SIXTEEN

Ian carried a pack on his back and limped on the ankle he'd injured in the fight with Kriegler and escape off the container truck. At least the traitor suffered a few injuries of his own from blows Ian had inflicted. When Kagona's men saw Kriegler's battered state, not a one ventured into the bush after Ian.

Zamani hiked next to him with Ian's rifle over his shoulder, a pack on his back and Ian's power bow strapped to it. He'd watched the action go sour from their surveillance ledge and quickly secured their equipment, leaving only the tents behind in their vehicle.

The reminder pissed Ian off. "That son of a bitch Kriegler wasted no time leading Kagona's men to our Rover."

"The vehicle was compromised. Better to have it found quickly than have Kagona's men scouring the area to find it. I even left a key in spare tire like the team agreed upon. No reason to make it hard for Kriegler to find."

"Great." Pain shot up Ian's leg with an awkward step on uneven ground. "So he gets an easy ride out of the backwoods and time to lick his wounds while we're left with a five-kilometer hike."

"Better now that the Rover is gone. No one is watching the roads."

"The right move, but that doesn't make it any easier to accept. At least our lack of trust in Kriegler paid off." Ian had purposefully had kept secret his knowledge of the reporter's 4x4 Zamani had stashed.

The walking stick Zamani had fashioned helped carry Ian's weight. Ian didn't deserve friends of his caliber. Zamani represented true Zimbabweans—a friendly, kind, and giving people. Proud of their heritage, their country and its beauty, and tired of leaders who robbed and milked their constituents of every dollar, few of which trickled back down to the public.

Tortured thoughts of what Joni must be suffering created pictures in his mind. Kagona would try mind games first before getting physical. Did Kriegler care enough about her to mitigate the torture Kagona had in mind?

With Kriegler's betrayal, Ian now understood Joni's state of mind on her trip to rescue Sipho. Lemmon had fed her a bunch of crap. Now he'd screwed both Ian and Joni. He'd gladly squeeze the life from Lemmon, Kriegler, and Kagona given the slightest chance.

"How much farther?" Ian sounded like a damn kid, but his ankle needed relief and every part of his body ached.

"Another kilometer. I'll hurry ahead and drive back for you." Zamani slipped the rifle over Ian's shoulder. "Blood draws predators."

And Ian had enough on him to attract a pride. He bemoaned his poor state and its impediment in rescuing Joni, but disgust drove him on. He'd suspected Kriegler had more talents than he portended. The day he'd torn the soda can in half at Mike's place nearly gave him away. It was an old trick...and an effective one. He'd covered up his mistake by letting Ian take him down easily. Devious bastard. His grappling techniques were damn good.

Zamani made better time, but Ian arrived where the reporter's 4x4 was hidden just as Zamani finished refueling.

"Where to, *mngane*?"

"Back toward Karoi. By that time, I should have a good idea of where Kriegler is headed in our Rover."

"How?"

"By doing what I'm good at—tracking."

Ian feverishly longed to fight his way inside whatever CIO complex detained Joni. The odds pointed to the foolishness of such a tactic. Instead, once he pinned down her location, he'd employ another option, one he'd never have chosen but now was thrust upon him. One satisfying, but still damn risky for her.

As much as he'd like to find another way, this scenario offered the only real hope, and it would give him another chance to face off against Kriegler. He'd found satisfaction letting his knuckles plow into the man's flesh.

His friend grinned. "I assume you have a plan."

"Like I said once before, I always have a plan, Zamani."

Sweat dripped off her chin to a floor so filthy rings of dirt formed around the drops. A sheen of moisture covered exposed skin. Her tongue had swollen and dried into muck. Exhaustion wrapped Joni's mind, leaving coherent thought difficult at best. Her spirit had bottomed out.

Kagona's game had taken its toll. The first fall out of the helo had taken years off her life. Then he'd handed her the hook. Made her believe it belonged to her safety belt. The second fall. She winced at the memory.

Chains wrapped Joni's legs and arms and were secured to a metal chair set in the middle of a hot, windowless room. Kagona had left her to stew. How long had she been here? Hours? Days? Time had become immeasurable. How long were the short nods into sleep? The hours of fighting emotions and contemplating the unknowns made it impossible to judge.

Don't count on friends to save you threaded through her head again and again, followed by a mocking laughter that chilled her soul. If she hadn't truly hated before, Kagona had opened a whole new emotion in her.

Where was he now? Hunting Ian, waiting to drag him in and then torture her to learn about his contacts in the country? What about Bram? Had he survived?

If Kagona expected this wait to drive fear into her, the ploy failed. The fall from the truck had battered her body, and her captors' rough handling had created too many sore places to count. She'd so feared physical torture under Kagona's hand, the reality was anticlimactic. Why bother with the physical when he'd destroyed her mentally?

Refusing to speak once captured, she'd tried to distance her mind from reality and focus on anything but the words coming from his mouth. Yet fingers of fear had crept tighter around her as the inevitability of death approached. Oddly, before Kagona shoved her free the second time, the only picture in her mind had been of an arrow flying from Ian's bow into Kagona's heart. A desire so strong, she believed it a truth as she fell from the chopper.

A shocked mind had left her body limp the second time they hauled her up. Once they dragged her into this room, she accepted the odds were high she'd never come out alive.

Evil like these men had no remorse, only insatiable need. It was a battle beyond her control. Ian had commanded her in their last moments together to hang on. She seized the hope that he, Bram, Lemmon, or someone on the outside would work to set her free. But would it be in time?

Ian knew how to hide in the wild. He and Bram could escape Kagona's men. Bram had proved more than helpful. Unusually so. Lemmon's instinct on his usefulness had proven well placed. She'd even considered Bram might work for South African intelligence.

Hope rose, taking her spirits with it. She'd gone through mock prisoner-of-war camps in military flight training. She understood what to expect. Only this wasn't war and Kagona's vendetta was personal.

Still, her mind returned to the positives. Ian and Bram could have escaped. They had stashed their packs with supplies and Zamani had a vehicle waiting to collect them.

As adrenaline wore off from the capture, exhaustion took it place. The institution-white walls displayed a few dark smears. Blood? The floors had a layer of dust and markings where fluids had splattered on the floor. The thought nearly added her retch to the decor.

The door rattled. A tiny window cut in it had a metal shield that opened from the outside. Someone peered in and then promptly shut it.

Guess it wasn't quite dinnertime. She'd pass anyway. The ambience spoiled her appetite. The edges of her mouth quirked up at the spirit rising inside. Kagona hadn't destroyed her…yet.

On a small table with one chair across the room, her light jacket had been stretched out and the nonlethal things from her pockets and on her person lain out. Lemmon wouldn't be happy about the loss of more equipment. She could only hope the tagging devices they'd put on the containers weren't found.

Up in a corner near the ceiling, a video camera watched her every move.

Maybe Kagona wouldn't come back. Maybe his underlings would attempt to drag information from her. She had nothing to tell them. Ian had been with her. Surely Kagona had seen him. What more could she reveal?

Oh, right. The stuff about his friends…at least those left standing. Was Chief Zwide even alive?

At least one positive presented itself. The likelihood of finding Mukono increased. Focusing on the memorized greeting from Ian offered a distraction. If Kagona arranged a long stay in his prison, perhaps someone could teach her the whole Xhosa language.

A clinking sounded. Slowly the door swung open and Kagona strolled in. Not the grand, gloating entrance she expected after his games in the chopper.

One of men started to shut the door, but Kagona signaled for it to be left ajar. "Seems warm in here"—he glanced over to her—"wouldn't you agree?"

She saved energy and didn't answer, choosing to examine the splotches on the tiles further.

He adjusted the light to a dim glow in the room. "Better." He brushed his hands together. "A worthy night of excitement. I see you didn't suffer badly from your falls."

A nasty reply sailed through her head but stopped before exiting her mouth. The last shove from the helo had knocked her head on something hard and metal. The rest was a blur until they hauled her into this hellhole.

Kagona walked slowly around the room. "I have good news for you."

Her focus remained elsewhere at his poor feint. There was no good news for anyone sitting in a CIO interrogation room.

"Come now, Miss Bell, we can have a civilized conversation. I'm a fair man. I'll not hold any truth from you."

His hypocrisy raised a quirk of her lip.

"I can see you want to know what happened to Taljaard. He did try to save you. Sad for him that he failed. A boon for me."

A surge of emotion threatened. She shoved Ian's image away and focused on Lemmon.

Kagona sighed, impatient at her silence. "Look at me and I'll give you a straight answer about Taljaard. It's not necessary to be afraid. He's not dead."

She fought the urge to look toward Kagona and lost. Any news about Ian, even lies, became a vital need.

"Ah, see, my face isn't so unpleasant to look at. Now I will be honest with you. I do not have Taljaard in custody."

A mental knife gouged her insides. Kagona had killed him.

He laughed at her reaction. "Don't attempt to guess the truth. I promised not to lie. He is still alive, although barely. By the time my men stopped the truck you fell from, Taljaard had disappeared."

She tamped down rising faith that Ian had survived. Kagona wanted her up, so she'd fall harder. He easily read the signs she couldn't hide—a straightened back and hope-filled eyes. She made a lousy spy.

"You've seen how isolated the region is near the plant. Deadly creatures roam the night looking for weak and easy prey. The bad news is I'm afraid he's been injured…quite severely, from the reports."

He paused to study the impact of his words. Encouraged by her surfacing optimism, he looked smug.

"His chances of survival are slim."

Talk of Ian, no matter how dire, gave her strength. Strength to know Kagona had not defeated her spirit or ability to think.

He read the emotions in her eyes even though purposefully focused away from him. "Come now, you divulge nothing by speaking. Conversation simply feeds my ego. You had no trouble lying to me during your interrogation last week."

Speaking then had been easy and necessary to provide time and a distraction during Sipho's rescue. Her detainment now had much the same requirement. Waste time until while she waited for rescue.

Kagona paced, perhaps frustrated or simply playing to her weakness…Ian. "I'll be disappointed if my men find him dead in the morning. I had planned to interrogate him. He'd never withstand seeing you tortured. He'd tell me what I want to save you. Allow me to clean out all those who support his type. They work cross-purposes to the government's efforts to help the people."

She swallowed hard. "Your government has laws and judges. Or are those only for people you don't beat to death?"

Chief Zwide's crime was nothing more than being a friend.

"I give you honesty and you insult me."

"You misjudge Taljaard. He will never stop until you're gone."

"I'm afraid he is the one who is likely gone. I, too, am saddened by the prospect. I rather enjoyed having an enemy to hunt."

"Your men are lying. Covering up their incompetence." While fear threatened to take hold, she pictured Ian. He'd come back from worse circumstances. This time he wasn't alone. He had help.

She held her head steady.

Kagona started that demeaning, self-aggrandizing chuckle. "The determination in your eyes. You have such trust, such faith in your fellow man. You can't let go of your belief in Taljaard. Let me offer you a piece of advice." His levity quickly changed to callousness. "Don't wait too long to deal with the information you have. Do not sacrifice for him. He's not coming. The longer you wait, the less food, freedom, or peace your information will grant you."

"Peace?"

He shrugged, as if his point was obvious. "My men are hard to control around female prisoners."

She'd expected he'd stoop low enough to use such a threat.

He slowly rounded her chair, seemingly unconcerned at her lack of cooperation. His fingers stroked her head. "I liked you better with red hair. A rare color here."

She forced her mind to retreat and disassociate from her body. Kagona could try his best, but she'd persevere.

He stopped before her and brought close his face full of contempt. "You believe I have no means to get what I want from you, just like you believe Taljaard is alive and well. Your faith has been misplaced. You will give up everything." He paused and straightened. "Just not to me."

Puzzled, an uneasy pit opened inside her, one she feared was about to swallow her budding spirit.

The interrogation room door behind Kagona creaked farther open. He stepped aside.

Bright light outlined a tall figure. The man slipped in and leaned against the wall.

Recognition and disbelief slammed into her. "Bram?"

He wore no restraints, and a name tag was clipped onto his dust-covered shirt. He hadn't changed from their outing, still dressed in night field clothes. She strove to grasp all the implications. Bram and Ian weren't together. Bloody cuts covered Bram's face, still streaked with camo paint.

Bram offered her a tight smile. Not mocking, not arrogant, if anything almost sad. "Hey, *bokkie*. Is Mr. Kagona treating you right?"

His words punched air from her lungs. Being stoic or stubborn or tough was physically impossible with her heart torn apart by betrayal. "Ian?" she whispered.

"In a lot worse shape than me. I'm afraid they'll find what's left of him in the morning. You never should have told me about his injury."

Failure screamed in her face. Failure to make this mission a success. Failure to protect the man she loved. Yes, damn it. *Loved*.

Kagona grinned and walked to the door. "I'll leave you two alone."

"Wait." The word croaked out of her throat. "How do you know this traitor?"

"One of his first jobs was piloting my helicopter. You might say we've kept in touch." Chuckling, Kagona left her behind, as devastated as if she was being staked out for crocs at dinnertime.

The splotches on the floor took on new meaning. What devastation had those prisoners suffered? Bram crossed his arms and remained silent, waiting for her to speak.

He'd get nothing. No more people like Chief Zwide would suffer because Kagona learned their names from her lips. Yet, questions piled up. Words longed to push past her lips and attack Bram.

His patience outlasted hers.

"I take it people back home don't know about your history with Kagona?" she finally said.

"I've been careful to cover it up." He moved closer.

She willed her head up and looked him in the eyes. If anything they appeared apologetic for what lay ahead. The truth wasn't hard to guess. "I'm not going home, am I?"

"That all depends on you, *bokkie*. Cooperate with us and maybe we can work something out."

"Cooperate how?"

"You've details on Taljaard's network."

"Go to hell."

"I'm afraid that's where you are sitting now." Bram reached down and cupped her chin. His touch burned through her. "A few more hours in this heat and you'll change your mind."

She jerked her chin free. "Don't count on it."

"The choice is yours. If you don't talk to me, I can guarantee you'll tell Kagona everything he wants to know."

With that, Bram left the interrogation room, not bothering to cast a parting glance behind him.

His departure left her gloriously alone to wallow in heat and silence. Damn him. Ian had to be alive. That he and Bram had battled was apparent from Bram's battered face. Ian had exceptional fighting skills. He'd be able to protect his injury. Wouldn't he?

She shoved back doubts and focused on analyzing the new dynamics Bram's betrayal cast. At whatever cost, he and Kagona must be stopped. She merely had to figure out which of the two evils offered the best chance for her survival…and their demise.

CHAPTER SEVENTEEN

Bram looked back at Joni before a guard shut the interrogation room door. She'd met his expectations and hadn't talked. No surprise. As a former military pilot, she'd settle in first and attempt to gauge the situation. He simply had to break down that process and had already made progress on that front. The normal prisoner didn't expect their comrade to betray them.

He found Kagona in a makeshift office with attached bunk room in this secret, out-of-the-way confinement center in a town well northeast of Harare—a new addition since Bram's early days of flying for the CIO. He'd been young, eager to fly anything, and the cushy job of flying for a powerful man had its attraction.

But what he'd witnessed over the year left him jaded. Life sucked for the poor and powerless, and trust among the races, tribes, and even comrades proved nonexistent. He moved on to another job in South Africa before he became a statistic in a political power struggle.

He grabbed a seat in a cheap armchair while Kagona poured himself a drink. American whiskey. By habit, he didn't offer Bram any. Kagona had never allowed him to drink in his presence. He wanted him sober to fly at a moment's notice.

Ice cubes rattled as Kagona sat on a corner of an old desk. "You surprise me, Kriegler."

"Really. I thought you'd figured me out years ago."

"I was surprised you'd chance escorting Miss Bell into Zimbabwe. A gutsy move, and one that is proving fruitful."

"Why not? She's the key to drawing out Taljaard. I thought it best to hand her over personally after the, um, problem with Mukono's son."

"I can resolve that matter if you locate where they're hiding him."

Bram shrugged, finding this game of verbal barbs a refreshing challenge. "You asked a lot in a few days. You're lucky I caught wind of Bell's return to Zimbabwe. She honestly believed I came to make it harder for you to detect her entry into the country. Besides, the best way to ensure a payday is to show up personally."

"Money owns your soul."

"Maybe, but I'm patient. Saving it for a nice retirement. Now you, on the other hand, I'd say you're more a power seeker who likes money."

With an irritable grunt, Kagona finished half of what was in his glass. Distrust read in the steady eyes that gauged Bram's every movement. Bram had to watch his back while in unfamiliar territory. People, politics, and events had changed over the years.

He drummed his fingers on the armrest. "I'm not your pilot anymore. How about a fucking beer?"

Kagona indicated a small fridge in the corner of the room.

Inside, Bram retrieved a can of South African beer and noted a number of cold water bottles. He popped the beer lid. "Cheers."

"So what happened back at the mine?"

Bram guzzled a good portion of the drink and then wiped his mouth with the back of his hand. "You tell me." He took his seat again. "I alerted you to the perfect time to sweep up both Bell and Taljaard."

"Your brash attitude hasn't changed." Kagona's fist tightened about the glass. "But don't lay the blame on my men. You're the fighter, and yet he got the better of you."

"I didn't see your men running off into the bush to bring him back. I beat the hell out of Taljaard before he fell off the truck. Reopened an injury from when you shot him."

Kagona stopped middrink. "Me?"

"Or one of your men. The day Bell escaped with the kid."

A grin crossed the asshole's face. "I'd prefer Taljaard's body in my morgue, but I suspect at sunrise, my men will find what's left of him up at Kanyemba." He rose and walked around his desk to a laptop. He set his drink aside and poked away at the keys. With a long glance at Bram, he dramatically hit a key. "Payment is in your account."

"I'll be sure to double-check."

"No doubt." Kagona refilled his glass and then sat in the desk chair and propped his feet up. "Learn anything new from the woman?"

"Too soon to press. I told them to let her sweat for a while. I'll come offering cool water when I return."

"Rather callous feelings for a woman in your office."

"We were friends."

"Ah, but not lovers."

"Workplace romance is frowned upon."

"Yet it must sting when she shows up in Zim and falls for Taljaard."

"Are you my personal shrink? She'll soon accept the truth about his demise and realize the gravity of her situation." Bram let cool beer slid down his parched throat. "Once we finish here and I've scrounged up food, I'll pay her a visit again. I've learned a lot about her vulnerabilities after spending time with her and Taljaard.”

“She’s a pilot. Is she CIA?”

“American, yes. CIA, I doubt. Although the American handling her likely is. He showed up at our project looking for someone to send for Mukono’s kid. He hinted our funding might dry up if we didn’t cooperate. I volunteered, but they required someone smaller to handle the load on the craft.”

“A missed opportunity for easy money. She cost you.”

“She cost us all. The joke is, she didn’t want to fly into Zimbabwe. Actually, her words to the handler were *it’s a stupid idea*.”

“Miss Bell will regret she crossed our border. Again.”

“This time she volunteered.”

“Taljaard?” Kagona shook his head at the foolishness.

“Well, this problem is fixed.” Bram spread his palms. “Any more you want me to solve? I’ve noticed trouble brewing in the capital.”

Kagona savored a taste of whiskey, likely considering Bram’s angle for bringing up the street protests. “I doubt you’ve a magic formula in your pocket to stop protesters before the African Union conference. There will be international press coverage.”

“Don’t underestimate me. One of the things protesters are calling for is the release of Minister Mukono. That’s who Bell came to help Taljaard save. They’re also demanding news on a reporter you snatched.”

Kagona glanced sharply in his direction. “I’m starting to believe you are too observant. We picked him up not far from the mine site.”

“Had he discovered the shipment planned for Iran?”

A blank slate slid over Kagona’s features. He slid his feet from their perch to the floor and sat tall. “You know too much.”

Bram laughed. He had to tread carefully. “I see your trust in me hasn't wavered. I was with Taljaard, remember? He's good at what he does. Got close when your Iranian entourage was praying. You're lucky he didn't have time to report it to anyone."

"The damn reporter overheard two Iranian officials at a hotel, complaining about the rough roads on a trip up north. He realized they were discussing work, not pleasure, and investigated. His photos were damning and, with a shipment ready to go out, poorly timed for us."

"Is he tied to Mukono?"

"Not likely. Mukono audited the Ministry of Mines. We believe he discovered the buried uranium mining accounts but doubt he knew what purpose they served. I'd been watching him since he started a campaign to reduce corruption by officials. Feared he'd ask South Africa or the West for help researching the accounts."

"Why not pay him off?"

"Tried, but his wife had softened him. Left me no choice but to have him and his family disappear until I could assess what he'd done."

"That didn't go well. Taljaard ended up with Mukono's son."

Kagona snorted. "Mukono won't talk, and his wife, whom I'd planned to use as leverage, died. I've no way to know the extent of his damage."

"Is that why you haven't made him disappear permanently?"

"If this first shipment goes without mishap, I'll assume our secret is safe. Then I will have no further need for the minister."

Bram rose and paced. "If news leaks of the Iranians' involvement with the mining, Western countries will attempt to stop the shipments. They'll reinstate sanctions on Zim for helping the Iranians run afoul of the nuclear treaty. The Zimbabwean economy is already in the toilet. That will flush it for sure."

"You have a way with words, Kriegler."

"I see other opportunities for you in this mess. You'll need plausible deniability. At this point, the only people who know about your plans with Iran are dead or in your cells."

"Assuming Mukono's information stays locked in his son's head."

"That's why you need a contingency plan. Sooner or later people will notice Kanyemba is being mined anyway. Play up the Chinese angle. They've been toying with the possibility of mining Zim's uranium for years. Claim they are mining it for power generation."

Kagona lit up a cigarette and followed Bram's arguments. "And then if the Iranian connection is discovered?"

"You've already made Mukono your scapegoat. Expand on it. The government can claim it allowed the Chinese to mine, but Mukono had unofficially worked a deal allowing Iran to buy uranium from the Chinese. Announce you are investigating and not ready to release details, so can't comment on Mukono's whereabouts. You've already hinted to the public you are investigating millions in tax revenue he stole—add in the Iran deal and make it a billion."

Kagona looked unconvinced. "People would demand to hear his side of the story."

Bram paused a reasonable amount of time to make his well-conceived idea sound fresh. Kagona preferred to be the mastermind of his plans. "What if you claim Mukono's political cronies managed to get him released from jail and out of the country? What if he supposedly fled somewhere unreachable, where no one had access to see him?"

"You mean like Iran? I could convince the Iranians it would be in their best interest to keep Mukono detained after their egregious error with the reporter." Kagona's forehead crinkled as the possibilities ran their course. "They would recognize the sensitivity of the situation. Photos could be taken of Mukono to prove to the public he is alive, out of the country, and spending the money he stole."

"Go a step farther. Take clandestine photos of his escape from Zimbabwe with him walking onto a plane. Hell, for the final punch, add a woman on his arm."

A wicked grin surfaced on Kagona's face as he warmed to the idea. "For those who believe he's responsible for his wife's death, that would add to the rumors. We have the perfect woman sitting in my interrogation room. People tend to be suspicious of one fact, but pile them on, and a lie becomes a believable truth."

"Have your Iranian inspectors already left the country?" Bram had done his homework before walking into this room and knew the answer.

"About four hours ago."

"Commercial?"

"The Iranians chartered a flight."

"What type aircraft?"

Kagona studied him suspiciously.

"I'm trying to figure out their speed and if they'll have to make a fuel stop. I might be able to catch them."

"A charter picked them up in Harare. Big turboprop, I believe. I didn't see them off, but the one prefers jet airliners and dreaded the noisy trip ahead."

"Good. The likelihood is they'll refuel in Djibouti." Bram checked his watch. "If so, they should be arriving anytime. Once refueled, they could easily be redirected to come back and pick up Mukono and Bell."

"Of what use is Bell to them?"

"American spies are a valuable commodity these days." Bram worried at Kagona's reluctance to let go of her. "When do the African Union representatives start arriving?"

"In forty-eight hours."

Bram finished his beer and crushed the can. "If we made the exchange at sunrise, does that give you enough time?"

"My men can quickly spread rumors and photos among protesters."

"There's no guarantee the opposition will curtail their activity."

"Leave that to my operatives. This story will be gold in their hands." Kagona snuffed out his cigarette. "You always were inventive in those days you flew for me…and good. I rather miss your level of flying skills. Remind me why I ever let you go?"

"You regretfully stated you could never trust a white man. I'm assuming you still don't. As long as you pay me well, I don't really care." Bram headed for the office door.

"Handle the aircraft for me. Get clearances and whatever is needed to bring the plane back. The dignitaries won't be happy, but explain the necessity to make the shipment go undetected."

Bram turned back. "Is Mukono close enough to be brought here by early morning?"

"He's here."

"My help will cost you."

"I'm sure it will."

Success or failure now rested in Bram's hands. He walked out, knowing he'd have to tread carefully. Push Kagona too far and he'd push back. The only holes in his plan lay with Joni.

With this accelerated timeline to remove her and Mukono from the country in the morning, Kagona would seek to extract every last detail from her on Taljaard's network…and that couldn't happen. No one, and he meant no one, would lay hands on Joni but him.

Ian checked his rifle for the fifth time. He'd cleaned, oiled, and checked ammo—of which he had a limited supply. Every shot counted. A prolonged firefight would be out of the question. Joni had one chance. His action had to be quick, clean, and concise.

He let off several calming breaths. Putting Joni on the line skewed his focus. She was held a few kilometers away in an isolated and secretive CIO compound. The thought of her with Kagona tore him apart. She'd survived the sadist's death threats and torture during their last encounter. He'd try different tactics this time.

Ian closed his mind off from thinking about how Kagona would go about destroying her. What about Kriegler? Would he change the dynamics? For better or worse?

Before he could carry out her rescue, he had to regain the ability to disassociate his feelings. His aim had to be perfect or Kagona would win.

The thought of Kriegler going down in the action gave him a certain sense of satisfaction, just short of the euphoria he would experience seeing Kagona breathe his last breath. In the guise of helping his people, the man had been responsible for a string of inhumane deaths and maimings. His end would be payback for Chief Zwide.

"You are not one to seek revenge, *mngane*."

Were Ian's thoughts so obvious? "I won't kill any man without justification. However, Kagona has deserved to die for years."

"Don't sacrifice your soul."

"What if it were your wife?"

"I pray every day she remains removed from my actions." Zamani fidgeted, reading Ian's unbalanced emotions and not feeling successful with the events of the last day, but willing to stick with him nonetheless. "I can be at your side in case events do not go like planned."

"A means of escape is as important for both of us if things go to hell. That's our typical setup. Changing it now isn't wise."

Ian understood Zamani's wish to support him. As a black native African, Zamani frequently took the lead position on operations and Ian covered his backside. But this action would be different. In deference to Zamani's wife, Ian had promised to keep him out of the line of fire, and if possible off Kagona's radar. With Joni in trouble, that promise gained a certain relevance.

"We need to rest before the action starts." Ian opened the back door to the reporter's 4x4 and climbed in. Zamani took the front and stretched out the best he could.

Joni's satellite phone vibrated. He recognized the number…an expected call, one he had to treat with care. He swallowed hard, repeating the word *control* a dozen times.

He sat up and clicked it on. *"Yebo."*

"All is set for five a.m.," Lemmon said.

"Any news?"

"Isn't that enough?"

"You know fucking well it's not."

"Don't miss, Mr. Taljaard. Lives are depending on it."

He dropped the phone to the floor and sat quietly for a moment. He knew how Atlas must have felt. Reluctantly, he stretched out and pulled his hat over his face, but sleep had no place to settle in his head.

CHAPTER EIGHTEEN

Metal sliding then slamming shut brought her head up. She must have dozed off. Dreaming about being lost in the Sahara. Disoriented, she squinted in the light to assess her location. Kagona's interrogation room.

Her shirt stuck to her chest. A string of hair glued to her face partially blocked one eye. How much time had passed?

Her tongue felt thick, her face leathery with salt and sweat. Her legs had lost feeling and her shoulders ached at the strain of the chains.

Bram had never returned. At least his familiarity had promised some hope. Some fair treatment. Yet he'd left her here. Hot. Alone. Suffering.

He wanted information from her. To rat on those who helped Ian. Had Bram killed him? Her eyes stung. How could a friend do this? Why? Her heart ached.

A fan overhead started to spin slowly. It made the lights flicker as the blades passed beneath them.

The door opened. Two men walked into the room. Could one be Bram?

The unfamiliar voices mocked and teased. One poured water

over her head. Salt burned her eyes as the water washed sweat into them.

The chains rattled. A weight lifted from her shoulders as the heavy links tinkled like cascading water to the floor. The dirty floor.

She raised her free hands to her face and brushed back her wet hair. The chains at her feet dropped next. Two of Kagona's men pulled her up onto wobbly legs and gladly caught her when she collapsed. They laughed and groped.

One skidded the chair out of the way. The other held her up. Her legs went from wobbly to stiff. With a laugh, her support danced across the floor with her. She stumbled and he caught her, then the other man swept her up. The motion destroyed any attempt to gain equilibrium. Her body felt small, a rag doll for their play.

She caught sight of the open door. A breath of cool air wafted through it. When one released her, she spun from his grasp and stumbled for freedom. An arm stretched across the threshold, blocking her way out.

A hand grabbed her shirt, pulling her back and turning her toward him. "You must learn to cooperate. Tell us about Taljaard and you will be free."

"Go to hell."

The guard grabbed the front of her shirt and used it to lift her toward a wall. She hit hard, knocking breath from her lungs. "You are one going to hell."

Their stark cajoling created a nightmare atmosphere. The door slammed. The guard released her and she slid to a corner. At least she could protect her back. The men moved forward to box her in the corner.

She kicked out at the first one to reach for her. Half-ass energy sent her foot barely brushing against the man's leg. He growled in delight and pulled her off balance. She landed hard on the floor.

Realizing her vulnerable position, she rolled to her side and worked to a stand. They let her rise while circling and leaving her to guess when one might attack. A foot shuffled behind her. She glanced over her shoulder. The man in front grabbed for her. She swung out at him, but the man behind grabbed her arm and twisted it behind her back.

The second man stepped forward, ripping the buttons on her blouse.

"Bastard." She fired a knee up, and this one landed.

Bram left the communications room in the satellite CIO complex. No one had looked over his shoulders as he tracked the aircraft of the Iranian officials who had left earlier in the day. He started with the computer and could guarantee every keystroke was monitored. Kagona didn't trust him. Fair enough. He didn't trust Kagona, either.

His preparations had then moved to phone calls, where lazy bureaucrats made his task both easy and difficult. Only time would tell. Kagona wanted a landing site capable of handling an aircraft big enough to fly out a crew and four passengers, yet isolated enough so only his version of the "escape" surfaced.

Bram made the final calls on his cell. He stopped long enough to set a rendezvous time at a nearby dirt strip. No going back now. The finale for Joni and Mukono had been set in motion.

He leaned back against the wall, and with a heavy heart thought about what lay ahead. How in the hell had his life become so convoluted, so cold, and—as he'd come to realize—so empty?

That emptiness drew him back toward Joni. He had to stay near her, even if that meant he prolonged her interrogation. Better him than Kagona or his men. His drive to protect her rather surprised him and made him better understand Taljaard's obsession.

Kagona's aide stopped him in the hall and told him where to find a room and shower. The man seemed interested in small talk. Bram wanted to move on and get through this night. He broke away and headed toward the interrogation room.

A door slammed up ahead. He didn't care for the implications. His footsteps quickened. A woman's swearing filtered into the hall. His worst fear of her in Kagona's hands raged.

He burst into the room and smashed the first guard against the wall. A second later, he drew a knife to the neck of the one holding Joni.

"Let her go."

The man shot a fearful glance toward the doorway. Bram checked for further threats.

Kagona leveled a gun, not at his men, but at Bram. "It appears we have a standoff."

"These *maaifoedie* had no permission for playtime with my prisoner."

"Out," Kagona commanded his men. The one with the knife at his throat waited for Bram to lower his weapon before gladly vacating the room.

Bram slid the knife back into its waist holder. Kagona had set this up. The timing was too perfect. "Is this a typical interrogation method in your shop?"

Kagona holstered his weapon. "I'm an impatient man. Simply encouraging Miss Bell to loosen her tongue."

"You don't trust my methods?"

"Quite the opposite. I read your intentions clearly. If you wish to carry out her interrogation tonight, it will cost you."

Touché. Kagona used his words against him.

Joni found support against the wall, hands fisted protectively at the front of her ripped shirt. Her face glowed red and jaw clenched, radiating anger mixed with uncertainty.

Bram's affinity for her had betrayed him. Not totally

unexpected. "Consider us even. I've arranged everything for five."

He wanted to comfort her but knew better than to show further weakness in front of Kagona. Instead, Bram headed out, stopping in the doorway. "I'm going for a shower. Have her sent to my quarters."

He strode away, hating what he had to do yet, but finding it necessary to keep a promise to one person he might someday call a friend.

Various emotions had come and gone. Fear had long disappeared. It gained her little and was ineffective in understanding what was happening. Mental scorecards had been rendered useless, as the players switched sides and their motivations became impossible to track.

She'd become a tool, a storehouse of wanted secrets, and an object of obsession…or maybe these men simply played mind tricks. All she wanted was to sleep, to hide from reality for a few hours, and to recoup her senses.

A single guard hustled her along a corridor, her hands cuffed behind her back. At least her legs had regained blood flow and held her up. Exhaustion waned with cooler temperatures outside the interrogation room, but the need for water and the unknown expectations wore on her stamina.

No exit appeared down this corridor or the last. The containment facility appeared compact, though, as she'd passed a familiar landmark seen on her entry. Likely this building was a satellite location to hold prisoners and run CIO operations in this part of Zimbabwe, wherever that might be. The remote location bode well for a rescue. Ian had taken on an entire complex full of bad guys in Vic Falls and survived. He could do it again.

Only he had no idea where she'd been taken and might be too injured to help. Given time, he would find out. That meant she had to hold on, outlast Kagona and Bram and their plots until Ian could save her.

His words—*I'll never leave you in Kagona's clutches. Ever*—echoed in her mind. Hell, her heart and head were a mess.

At least Ian's promise also gave *him* a reason to live, to survive. *Live for me, Ian.* A selfish epitaph, but if anyone had the capability to save both of them, it was Ian. And what about his friend Zamani? Did he get away? Neither Kagona nor Bram had mentioned him. Why? Was Bram waiting to dig more information about him from her?

She had to stop his plans. Take any advantage shown.

The guard dragged her into an empty room with a metal bedstead, a sheet-covered mattress, a chair, and a small basin in the corner. He released a cuff on one hand. She kicked her bare heel back toward his knee and launched an elbow up at his chin. It never landed.

He kept hold of the cuff chain and jerked her attached arm up and back. A second later her face bit into the stiff sheet covering the mattress. Her shoulder screamed for release. She couldn't breathe.

"Next time I break your arm." He held her there for several seconds to bring home his point. Then he yanked her cuffed wrist and looped it around the fattest pole on the metal bedstead. A knee to her back kept her in place as he manipulated her other wrist near enough to clamp the free cuff.

He left and closed the door. No bolt slid into place.

Desperately, she brought her feet up and examined the metal frame of the headboard. With both hands grasped to the frame, she shook it to determine weakness. Nothing gave. The ends of the crossbars were securely inserted and welded into the main floor posts. With time she could work those loose. But how much did she have?

Revert to training instead of panic. She examined the cuffs.

Single lock. Escape was possible. She'd taken challenges with military friends, going for the shortest time to free oneself from handcuffs. Only once had she had to buy the beer. That was a night out with some Special Forces buddies. All she needed was a small piece of metal.

"Forget it" came from behind her. Bram, in a black T-shirt and loose pants, flipped a lock on the closed door.

That simple act gave her hope. They'd brought her to a room, not a cell. Their mistake. At some point Bram would fall asleep.

His wet hair indicated he had indeed gone to shower. A small white towel lay over his shoulder, and he held an unopened water bottle covered in condensation. Cold. Likely a ploy to gain her cooperation. She licked her parched lips anyway.

He crossed to a small sink and let the hot water run until satisfied before wetting the end of the towel. He swung a small chair around a foot from the bed and sat backward. She settled back against the metal and tucked her dirty feet up. They'd removed her boots and socks in the interrogation room.

For a minute, they studied one another. His bruised face had been shaven clean. A butterfly bandage held together a cut above his eye. A part of his lower lip had swollen. Satisfaction welled. Ian had landed the blows.

"Ian will kill you."

"He already tried." Bram tossed the warm towel into her hands. "Clean up those cuts and scrapes and I'll see what I can do to touch them up." He pulled an antiseptic tube from a pocket and flicked it onto the bed.

She sucked water from the towel before cleaning her face, hands, and whatever parts of her arms she could reach. When the towel turned brown, he took it from her and washed it out before giving it back again.

Questions came to mind, but none seemed to matter except one. "Why, Bram?"

"We all have reasons for what we do. I can't expect you to understand." He tugged off his T-shirt.

She froze. That fear she'd proclaimed conquered raised its ugly head.

He scooted the chair to the back corner of the room and used the shirt to cover a small camera mounted near the ceiling. As he dragged the chair back and faced her again, everything she thought she knew about him became uncertain.

The solid form facing her indicated his free time wasn't spent downing beers with his bar buddies like he bragged. Had his baggy flight suit hidden his physique, or had she not looked past his affable, full of life, and at times jokester facade? So much didn't make sense.

"Covering up your crime?" Her pretended indifference came off shaky.

"Kagona would find a way to use it against me. On the other hand, I can't silence the mike. It's sensitive enough to pick up your breathing."

She slowly wiped down her neck and parts of her arms within reach, ignoring Bram while collecting her senses. So many cues, clues, and innuendos floated about. Her mind wearied attempting to grasp them. A sorry state, for understanding their meanings meant control of the situation. "When you came along with me, I sensed something wasn't right. Yet believing a friend would deceive is…hard. I should have trusted my instincts."

He stood and plucked the towel from her hands. The bed dipped as he sat beside her.

She turned her face away, unable to look at him. Disgust ran rampant through her mind and body.

He dabbed at her scrapes and wiped places on her arms she had missed. Locked into place and unable to withdraw them, she closed her eyes. Her stomach churned.

The wet towel turned cold and raised goose bumps on her

skin. He wiped down her filthy feet before he tossed the towel aside. Neither spoke as he applied ointment and bandaged a cut.

When done, he collected the water bottle from near the sink. He turned his chair so it faced her and set the bottle on the seat. He leaned his hands onto the chair back. "We need to talk, Joni."

"I liked it better when you called me *bokkie*."

"Somehow that doesn't work anymore."

"What do you want from me?"

"Information."

"You're out of luck. I told you I don't know anything."

"You will survive this night, but you have to trust me."

"Trust? I'm chained to your bed. You've betrayed us all." She turned her face into her arm. "Sure, I trust you."

"For every answer you give me, a drink from the bottle is yours."

"I'm not thirsty."

"For every answer you refuse, I get a piece of clothing. Your choice."

"You're no better than those men back there."

"Do you work for the CIA?"

"Are you hoping Kagona will think your achievements grander than they are?"

"Come on, Joni, this isn't a game."

"Life is a game."

He came around and grabbed her ankles, pulling her legs straight. She kicked out, but his hands fisted onto her pant legs and pulled them off. The simple action left her shattered.

How could she be so vulnerable? No response surfaced as shock reverberated through her.

"It's a simple question, Joni."

She curled up at the head of the bed. "And you know the answer."

"I want to hear it from you."

"I'm not CIA."

"You came here for them."

"I came here to find Ian. I needed to know he was alive." She avoided the direct answer Kagona likely wanted on record.

Bram gave an easy smile. "See, that wasn't so bad."

She breathed deep at the momentary reprieve.

Success drove Bram on. "Taljaard has many friends here. Ones that help him. Tell me about them."

Time was her friend. Draw out the night. Give Ian time. "You promised water for an answer. Are you going back on your word?"

He snatched up the bottle. "I'm a man of my word."

"Wait. How do I know you haven't put something in it?"

"Ye of little faith." He held it close. The seal snapped as he twisted the lid. He held it out. She folded her hands over his and the bottle, planning to get as much down as possible before he snatched it away. She achieved several good gulps before he took it.

He set the bottle back on the chair. The refreshing water revealed the extent of her dehydration. She needed more. If he wanted answers, she'd give him an inventive array.

As though he understood her plan and sought to defeat it, he reached into a pocket and pulled out a paper. "This was discovered on you." The paper turned in his fingers.

Her spirit sank. Mike's photo. "It has nothing to do with Ian."

"No? Who is in the picture?"

"It's not important."

"Fine." He pulled a lighter from his pocket. "No need to hang onto it." A flame flicked to life.

Panic flared. She'd destroyed so much belonging to Mike. "Wait." She paused to collect her thoughts. "You're a son of a bitch."

"I've been called worse."

No reason not to give him the truth. "I took it from Mike's place."

"Who is it, Joni?"

"His wife."

"See, it's not so hard to tell the truth." He brought the bottle to her and this time let her drink more. "Now, about Taljaard's friends."

"You'll be disappointed. I know very little."

"Humor me. Start with your first trip to Zimbabwe."

She delayed, thinking how to make the lies sound feasible.

"You have few pieces of clothing left. Don't hesitate long."

After a deep breath, she started. "Down south, there was a farmhouse. No one was home, but we picked up supplies there."

Time stretched out. Ten minutes, twenty, and more. By then, the water had long disappeared. It became easier to ramble about the weather, the animals they'd encountered, the countryside, and she gave up a fake name Ian had once used at a roadblock.

Ian, sweet, Ian. Trouble eased in his arms. He'd be so proud of her lies.

She felt rather giddy with her success at draining the bottle and still coming up with distracting facts. A thousand more fairy tales to share played in her head.

She rubbed her eyes. Strange, the room had darkened. When had Bram turned out the light? "Are you still here?"

"I'm here." Oddly his voice sounded familiar, yet far away.

"Ian?" No, she was here with Bram. But why? What was wrong with her? Somewhere a little warning flared. "The water?"

"I couldn't risk you trying to escape while I slept." He'd moved closer and sat again on the bed.

Shudders racked her body. "Please, Bram. No."

"You told me what I needed, Joni. Now listen to me." She feared he'd demand a kiss, but instead he brought his face against hers, placing his mouth near her ear. "Listen carefully to me. I promise, I'll never leave you in Kagona's clutches. Ever."

His whispered breath left chills on her skin. She'd heard that claim before. So many promises never kept. From people she loved…and now from someone she had believed a friend. A tear rolled down her cheek.

Bram stretched out next to her and drew her back against his hard body. "It's best if you remember little of tonight, *bokkie*," he whispered against her hair.

The chill dissipated against his warmth, but the cold in her soul remained. Time. She'd run out of time. *I'm sorry, Ian.*

CHAPTER NINETEEN

Joni awoke to light in the room. Bram sat on the chair next to the bed and shook her shoulder. Fully dressed, he had a loose jacket over his shirt. She could see a hint of his black T-shirt at his neck beneath it all. A glance up caught the exposed camera.

"It's time to go, Joni." His soft voice offered an unwanted comfort. Commands to her arms and legs failed.

He slid a sock onto her foot. Then grabbed a boot and worked it on. He tied it tight before swinging both her booted feet to the floor.

He sat her up. Her brain, squeezed tight in her skull, screamed hangover. She screwed her eyes shut, praying the pain would pass.

Bram wrapped her fingers around a water bottle. "Drink up. Fluids will help."

Memory of tainted water played in her head, but the context remained fuzzy. "No." She let go.

Bram caught the bottle and handed it back. "It's not spiked, Joni. I need you awake. You're going to meet Mukono."

Nothing in the room seemed in focus. "Sipho's father?"

"Yes."

"Where?" At that moment, she recognized her pants had

been put on and a T-shirt had been placed under her torn blouse. "You dressed me?"

"I'm getting you out of Kagona's hands like I promised."

She held up her hands—without cuffs on them. Red and purple circles marred her wrists. Some of the last hours returned, but the rest...

"What happened last night?" Her voice cracked like her shattered insides.

"You fell asleep."

He pulled Joni to a stand and wrapped an arm around her waist for support. A flicker of him tugging off her clothes rose from memory. Her body went rigid; she felt cold against him. She pushed away, but he held her tight.

"Let me go." With slow, awkward strikes, she beat a fist against his chest. Each strike carried little strength, but the aggression buoyed her spirit. Oddly, Bram didn't stop the blows.

Footsteps of multiple people sounded in the corridor.

"Someday, I hope you'll understand." He let her go but stood nearby.

Kagona walked in followed by two men. "Cuff her." He gave her a quick once-over. "Brush her hair. She can't look like shit."

His comment left her wondering why it mattered. Someone handed Bram a brush. As though he understood her turmoil at his touch, he quickly got the job done.

Kagona examined her overall state and appeared satisfied. "Today I will grant your wish to meet Minister Mukono. Bring her."

She stumbled at a push from the guard who'd cuffed her. Bram caught and righted her. Once out the door, he took one side and the guard the other. They half carried her down the corridor.

With every step, her head cleared a bit more. While the night was a blank, she remembered much of what brought her to Kagona's lair. The mine, the trucks, Ian's hand stretching out for hers, yet unable to reach her. Why hadn't he been able to move?

The questions drained her energy. Nonetheless, she raised her chin. She'd get through this. Hope hadn't been lost. No one had mentioned Ian. He'd promised he'd never leave her with Kagona...*ever*.

For a moment, her mind grew confused. She'd taken Ian's words to heart, but her memory put the words to Bram's voice. Damn drugs.

At the end of a second corridor, they stopped. They pushed her up against the wall to wait. For what?

Kagona pulled Bram apart from the others. Bram spoke on a handheld radio and glanced at his watch several times. Snippets of aviationspeak filtered through. He spoke to an aircraft...one in range.

Shuffling and footsteps approached down the same corridor she'd just trod. Two guards escorted a man in cuffs with a chain between his legs. His hollow cheeks, drawn face, and tall but thin build weren't familiar. Yet, the closer he came, the more he resembled the photo of a robust Mukono that Lemmon had shown her in a briefing.

Her foggy mind reviewed the greeting Ian had taught her. She clicked her tongue in practice and focused. The pounding in her head made the effort a strain. Yet, with Kagona distracted, this was her best chance.

The men stopped Mukono feet away. He studied her, likely curious as to the reason for a woman's presence. The feeling was mutual. Why had Kagona brought them together, especially when Bram had promised he would take her from Kagona's lair?

With effort, she overcame doubts and worked up a smile. The delivery of the greeting came out shaky, but she made it through without badly messing up and then added, "Your son is safe."

Mukono's eyes rounded in surprise before he smiled. "*Ndiphilile*. Thank you."

Kagona heard her speaking to Mukono. "Keep them silent."

A guard answered him in a tribal language. It brought Kagona rushing toward her. His hand pinned her to the wall at the throat.

"You dare speak Xhosa behind my back." He signaled a guard, who stood down the hall, to join them. She guessed he spoke the language. "Repeat what you said."

The pressure made it hard to get words out. "I gave him a greeting."

"Repeat it." He raised a hand to hit her, but she didn't flinch.

Mukono spoke to Kagona in Xhosa. Some words sounded familiar, but he'd changed the greeting. He ended with English. "At last I have the honor of your meeting. May your spirits stay high."

"Is that all?"

"She told me my son is safe." Mukono wished to keep something in her message secret. Perhaps Ian had wanted him to know he worked on his release and gave him hope. Whatever the message, Mukono had gained a victory over Kagona. He carried his chin a little higher, and his tired eyes had a renewed sparkle.

The guard who spoke Xhosa nodded at Kagona. He released her. If he had intended to gain key information about Taljaard's compatriots or plans, he'd failed.

"Where are we going?"

Kagona faced her. "I believe Mr. Kriegler promised you'd be free of me today. He is keeping his promise."

"I don't understand."

"You will."

Kagona signaled a guard, who made a call. A door beeped, and Kagona pushed it open.

Outside, two vehicles waited—a van and the Land Rover Zamani had used to pick them up at the dirt strip and take them to the Kanyemba mine. If Kagona had the Rover, Ian and Zamani would have trouble getting away from the desolate mine area.

Time. Everything would take time. Was Bram transporting them somewhere new? If it was to an awaiting plane, it might be time she and Mukono didn't have.

Bram caught her consternation from afar but offered no hints as to the plan. Kagona's guards herded her and Mukono into the van. She sat in the third seat behind Mukono with a scowling guard. At least it wasn't one who'd attacked her last night. Kagona's flunky sat next to Mukono, and Kagona took the front with a driver. They drove off. Bram followed in the Rover with another guard.

A mere hint of the eventual sunrise dimmed the night stars. A window, rolled down, brought the smell of dust and a freshly turned field. In the distance, hills made an undulating dark outline against the sky. Eventually, the van turned off tar onto a dirt road.

Again she attempted to reconstruct more about what had happened last night. She'd been accosted in the interrogation room. Bram had stopped the attack. His anger had surprised her. He'd been willing to kill to protect her. Or had all that been an act? He'd wanted her for himself.

Nausea swirled inside, and the bumpy road they had turned onto didn't help. She remembered being cuffed to his bed. Her mind went to Ian, fearing he would never understand. Bram had taken something from her she could never get back…a loss she struggled to define.

She shifted to look behind her at the Rover. What had happened after he climbed in bed beside her? She fought to recall, but nothing solid formed. He'd promised to rescue her from Kagona. Was she being traded to the Americans like spies from the past?

Hope was a funny thing. It sprang up at the bleakest moment, making the fatal blows more potent when hope dimmed and blacked out. She wasn't an important spy in the scheme of things. Simply a puppet who believed she led a mission. Laughable.

Even though the sun had not risen, light gleamed from behind the hills. A plane droned in the distance, growing closer. The van drove onto a raised, flat area, one that appeared suspiciously like a dirt and grass strip.

The vehicles stopped. Kagona picked up an AK-47 and oversaw the guards as they brought out the prisoners. The action struck her as odd. Why hadn't he brought more men?

A suspected answer reared that ugly fear again. He wanted to limit the witnesses to what was about to happen. If Ian had been killed, then Kagona might well have decided to get rid of all those involved.

A plane circled the field, likely checking out the site before landing. A guard unlocked Mukono's cuffs but left the leg chains attached. He retrieved a suit jacket from the van and slipped it on Mukono. The jacket fit large on his thin body.

Bram parked away from the group, and a guard who had ridden with him strolled over to Kagona. Bram walked out into the open area away from the others. A radio crackled. He grabbed a handful of dried grass and tossed it into the air. A good breeze whisked it away.

He was getting winds for a plane about to land. Seconds later he signaled to Kagona. Five minutes.

Kagona's driver appeared with a camera hanging from a strap on his shoulder. Did he plan to document whatever happened here? But why the plane? To take her and Mukono somewhere? Alive or dead?

A clear picture failed to materialize. Bram had adamantly promised he'd remove her from Kagona's prison. How?

Kagona had handed off the AK-47 to one of the guards. All together they made a small group. Three guards, one driver, and Kagona. He must be damn sure Ian wasn't going to show.

She scanned the horizon, aware that if he were out there, she'd never see him. Call it silly, but that damn hope of rescue

Ian had instilled in her wouldn't fade. She touched her lips thinking how he'd sealed that promise.

Funny, Bram had made the same promise.

The drone of a plane echoed through the cool predawn air. The sun, hidden behind the hills, offered a halo of light to the new day. The shadow of an aircraft cut across it.

The sun crested the hills, and a minute later a high-winged turboprop came into view and touched down. Dirt flared up under the big wheels that made landing on unimproved strips possible. The props changed pitch to slow the craft, throwing up more dust and dirt.

The aircraft taxied toward them. Bram used glow sticks to direct them where to stop. The pilots feathered the engine on the loading side and kept the other one running.

Kagona turned toward Mukono. "I've made an arrangement for you to be taken out of Zimbabwe. Don't come back."

"I make no promises."

"But I will. Your life is the price of appearing in Zimbabwe again." Kagona faced Joni. "The same goes for you, Miss Bell. Although my men would be pleased at your return."

"What reward are you getting for us?"

Kagona laughed. "Every man has a price." A guard came up behind her and removed her cuffs and Mukono's leg chain. He signaled them toward the aircraft as a hatch in the fuselage opened and a few steps dropped down.

Nothing about the scene made sense. Bram shifted beside Kagona, and no one escorted them to the plane. Kagona's driver actually stayed the closest, snapping photos as they neared the aircraft, with Kagona and Bram behind him. In this poor light, photos wouldn't come out well. Perhaps that was the plan. Was this some kind of setup?

Mukono turned back to Kagona. "Nomathemba's spirit is yet to be settled. I will come back to assure she will forever watch over her tribe."

"Do not expect Zimbabwe to wait."

A pilot stuck his head out and signaled toward her and Mukono. They walked together, but her lack of trust in Kagona meant a steady look over her shoulder. Mukono deferred to her loading first.

"Wait, Miss Bell," Kagona called out.

She hesitated. The pilot signaled Mukono to board the aircraft. A little unsteadily, he climbed the stairs.

Kagona approached, stopping only steps away. Bram, looking worried, followed. Kagona spoke over the engine's burr. "One last thing, Miss Bell. Did Mr. Kriegler tell you where this plane is headed?"

Uneasy, she shook her head.

"Do you speak Farsi?"

Her attention shifted to Bram, whose emotionless face revealed he knew the truth. The reality left her agape. Iran? Once on their soil, she had no way home. No one would ever know where she'd gone. People didn't walk out of Iranian prisons. Ever.

Ever ran through her head.

"Get on board, Joni. The risks staying here are greater." Unreadable emotion rippled across his features.

"It's a death sentence either way."

"Go."

All the little details started to mesh in her head. *Ever. Ever?* Both Ian and Bram had used it. He wanted her on the plane. Ian wanted her on the plane. She grabbed the cording on the hatch stairs for balance and stepped onto the first step.

Kagona's hand grabbed onto her shirt and pulled her back. One arm bent tight around her neck, the other pressed the cold metal of a gun into her temple. Kagona swiveled her body toward Bram. "I'm afraid she stays with me."

Joni kicked back at Kagona's shin and contacted. He didn't flinch, but his arm cutting off her air tightened. Breath became near impossible to take.

Kagona's guards raised their weapons and motioned for Bram to back away.

He took a few steps back and held his hands out from his body so as not to tempt anyone to shoot. "This is not a great lesson to teach your men."

"You are wrong, Mr. Kriegler. These, my most loyal men, have witnessed a well-executed plan that you and I constructed. And you have been paid well." Kagona purposefully moved so Joni thrashed in his arms. "I believe it a folly to waste a perfect resource. You had your fun with Miss Bell, now it's my turn. After a few more days, I suspect I'll have everything I need to clean out dissenters."

An odd thud sounded as a rifle shot rang out from far away. Bram collapsed to the dirt, unmoving. A red spot blossomed on his jacket.

No longed to explode from her throat but was blocked by Kagona's hold. Surprise and fear swept across the guards' faces. Kagona swung her around to face the direction of the shot. She dug her nails into his arm and tossed her head back, but he countered every trick.

Pandemonium broke out. A bullet hit the dirt by the feet of a guard. The plane hatch behind her hastily closed up.

"Find him," Kagona yelled. He grabbed her by the waist and dragged her toward the van.

The pilots spun up the second engine and started to taxi.

No one had any idea the location of the shooter. Had one of Kagona's men taken out Bram? Then why were they running? Or was it Ian? The driver, with the camera instead of a weapon, crouched low and dashed for cover.

She lifted her feet to become dead weight, but her size compared to Kagona's made it easy to carry her along. A shot landed near his feet. Ian must be afraid of hurting her. He didn't miss. Two men fired into a nearby knoll and brush while running for cover.

Kagona kept his weapon pressed against her head. "She's dead, Taljaard, if you don't stop."

A bullet blew out a window in the van.

Don't let them take me.

Kagona shoved her into the van's backseat and climbed in after her. His men quickly followed. Frantic. Fear permeated the air. Not something she'd ever seen with Ian.

"Get out of here." Wheels spun as the driver floored the accelerator. The uneven road and high speed jolted and tossed them about. "I want Taljaard found, Chaipa. He's in our fucking territory."

"Yes, sir. Once clear, I'll call for support."

A bullet plunked into the engine but failed to stop the van. Yet the effort gave her a measure of satisfaction. Ian never quit.

Kagona crouched on the floor while she sat on the seat, head tucked down and staring at a man whose chest rose and fell in fury. Score one for the good guys.

Her victorious mind-set died as the vision of Bram hitting the ground replayed in her head. Confusion kept her from putting all the pieces together. More visions of last night had come back when she'd approached the plane. Bram had repeated the same sentiment as Ian before her memory failed. Why? What did he hope to achieve? How did he know the exact words unless Ian told him?

Odd as it seemed, she'd believed he and Ian had planned a rescue. If so, why would Ian kill Bram? Because the smooth talker was a bastard through and through. Her desire to believe Bram had good in him had blinded her to the deadly truth…until too late.

Harsh memories blocked out the good times in South Africa. Bram's smile, his laughter, and constant ribbing had disguised the evil greed that lurked beneath. No matter his loyalties or horrors of his deeds, she refused to hate him, but his death would haunt her…forever.

The van rattled on the washboard road and tipped precariously taking a turn. She snapped on a seat belt, both relieved and disheartened the gunfire had ceased.

In the unseen distance, aircraft engines ran up for takeoff. Eventually the plane rose into the sky, carrying Mukono to Iran.

A weight took hold of her heart. She and Ian had failed Sipho. His father was gone. Set point to the bad guys, or was this the match?

She straightened and stared ahead at the dirt road. Giving up was not in her genes. As long as Ian was alive, a rally of hope flickered in her mind.

CHAPTER TWENTY

"**D**amn it to hell, Z," Ian yelled into his comm. "Nothing went as planned. Kagona grabbed Joni."

"Where is she now?"

He collected his weapon and ammo and took off running. "With Kagona and his goons in a van headed your way."

"Do you have a plan, *mngane*?"

"Hell, no." Loss totally overwhelmed his mind. He'd failed again.

"Good, because I do."

"Don't do anything stupid. Your wife won't forgive me." Yet down deep he wanted—no, needed—someone, anyone to do whatever it took to stop Kagona. Selfish? Hell, yes.

Sounds of an engine started.

"This fucking plan had too many holes, too many unknowns." Ian caught sight of Kriegler laid out ahead. "I'm going to tear apart the man who came up with it."

He dropped his weapon and gear and stooped by Kriegler. Ian snatched up his feet and dragged him a good five meters, leaving a blood trail. He dropped the feet.

"You can get your bloody arse up now."

Kriegler looked up. "So why in the hell did you drag me along? Thought someone was watching?"

"Kagona will think I loaded you into a vehicle. Hid evidence of your murder. Don't worry, I'll leave tire tracks."

"As long as they're not across my body." Kriegler scrambled to his feet. "We have to get Joni back."

"Because you screwed up."

"You try winning Kagona's trust. That word isn't in his vocabulary." Kriegler rubbed at his chest. "That charge packed a punch."

"Give me the keys, then grab the equipment."

Kriegler tossed them over. Ian picked up his rifle and ran for the Rover. He had one vision in mind—killing Kagona.

The vehicle had barely started and Kriegler collected when a thud and grunting sounded over the comm, followed by shattering glass and the crunching of metal in the background.

"Z. What was that?"

Dreaded silence punched hard. Ian swung the Rover around toward where he'd dragged Kriegler and then floored the accelerator. He took the turns fast, tossing Kriegler around, but heard no complaint. A lump rose in Ian's throat. Ahead a mash-up of Kagona's van and the reporter's 4x4 came into view.

"Dear God, Z. How did you expect to survive this?" Ian likely spoke to himself. At no answer, Ian became convinced. How could his life fall apart so quickly?

He screeched to a halt next to Kagona's crunched van. Kriegler beat him out. They looked past the dead driver, his feet dangling inside and the rest of his body hanging out the shattered windshield. About twenty feet from the van lay a guard's body.

"Back passenger side," he yelled to Kriegler. Ian hardly recalled prying open the bent door, with Kriegler pulling alongside him.

Joni sat secured in a backseat, eyes closed and head drooped.

Blood in her hair indicated a wound on her scalp. He felt for a pulse. Relief swept through him.

"Breathing." He snapped off her belt and lifted her into his arms.

Kriegler crawled in and checked the other men, who'd been tossed about. "This one's gone." He moved to the next, Kagona's number one. "This one will live to see another day." He collected their weapons.

"Think they called for reinforcements?"

"Your luck isn't that good, Taljaard. I'd count on it. So far this day's gone to hell."

"Then we'd better damn well build a stairway to heaven, because I'm getting Joni out of this mess." Ian laid her out on the backseat of the Rover. She groaned, but he didn't have time for consolation.

"You're driving, Impisi. Don't leave without me. And keep your eyes out for Kagona. He wasn't in the van."

"Where are you going?"

"To find a friend." Ian tore back to what was left of the 4x4.

He'd asked too much of his friends here in Zim. They'd all suffered over the years, but now Chief Zwide had been beaten and Zamani sacrificed. Had Kagona taken him? Was he trapped in the wreckage alive?

Frantic, he pawed through twisted remnants, tossing out their equipment packs and weapons as he went. Breathing sounded in his comm.

"Damn it, Z, where are you?" He uncovered Mad Mike's prosthesis and tossed it out.

Guilt rode Ian's back. Was his friend pinned underneath this mess?

In the small space between the steep embankments rising above the scene and the road, Kriegler squeezed the Rover past the wreck. "Come on, Ingwe. We can't wait."

"Don't leave me, *mngane*," came a winded voice in his ears.

"I'm not leaving till I find you." Urgency, combined with the fear of loss, drove Ian on.

Kriegler got out and started tossing their equipment into the Rover. "He's not in there."

Ian ignored him. He found his bow, but no sign of his friend.

"No. I mean he's not in the truck." Kriegler tossed in the day pack. "He's out here."

Ian followed where Kriegler pointed. Zamani staggered down the embankment where the 4x4 had rolled down in front of the van.

Ian clambered out of the wreckage and bear-hugged his friend. "I was imagining you smashed in that carnage."

"You think I'm crazy? That van was loaded with men and guns."

"I owe you…big. I'm figuring out what, or rather who's important to me."

"You son of a bitch," Joni yelled behind him.

Ian whirled in time to witness her wielding his hunting knife and lunging at Kriegler. Whether she'd successfully struck already was impossible to determine with the fake blood staining his clothing.

Kriegler deflected her strike and backed away. "Settle down, *bokkie*. You're safe."

"None of us will be safe as long as you're alive." Unsteady, her steps wobbled. She fisted the handle. Determination read in her clenched jaw, and an irrational fury glazed her eyes. "You hurt Ian. You used me. I had closure with you dead."

Kriegler, who easily could have stopped her, simply kept outdistancing her efforts. In a dramatic lunge, she raised the handle and literally fell toward him. Ian caught her knife-wielding hand and swept her up before she hit the dirt. He disarmed her, tossing the knife to Kriegler.

"Settle down, Joni. You're free of Kagona. He's gone." Ian held her tight as she struggled in his arms. Seeing the results of Lemmon's stellar plan tore him apart.

"You don't understand. Bram hurt us all."

"Kriegler's on our side." He brushed a hand along her hair, whispering calming words, wishing he could take away the pain of the last hours.

"The bastard." She buried her face in his chest, mumbling a string of curse words, which became quieter with each outburst.

"I agree with your sentiment. But it's going to take that bastard's help for us to escape." He fought his own desire to know what had transpired but had to bring Joni down to earth first.

Feeling her shiver with anger, he kissed the top of her head and fought his own fury. What had Kriegler done to her? Her incoherence showed all the marks of a person drugged and trying to find her bearing again. He and Kriegler required one-on-one time. Weapons not required.

"Load up, everybody. Time is precious."

He secured a simmering Joni in the backseat behind the front passenger. That position would keep her from suddenly deciding to strangle Kriegler while he drove. The time for her to recover was anybody's guess, and that fact added to the complexity of the team's predicament.

Ian settled into the backseat behind the driver. Kriegler tossed in the last things from the wreck before loading into the driver's seat. He glanced cautiously at Joni, who ignored him.

Zamani had disappeared. Bloody hell, Ian was losing his grip on this group. "Where are you this time?"

"Collecting something, *mngane*."

In a trance, Joni stared out the window at the wreck, ignoring them both. Her chest still heaved from exertion. On that same chest lay a shirt with the buttons ripped open and a strange T-shirt underneath. He crushed his fist so hard his knuckles cracked.

"You realize our comm is compromised," she said softly. "Kagona has mine and is probably listening to everything we say."

Kriegler started the vehicle. "His men are sloppy. Seems they didn't notice the comm missing this morning." He handed her unit back to Ian.

Vehemence hovered below the surface with her glare at Kriegler. How in the hell would they work together to escape the country?

Ian lifted her hand and placed the earpiece in it. "Whether you believe it or not, he's one of us." He slipped the base comm unit around her neck.

Joni tugged at Ian's shirt and pulled up the side. Delicately she touched his bandage. Dirty and dust covered, it had held up well in the tussle with Kriegler.

"Hey, I'm okay. Relax." He squeezed her hand. Kriegler had avoided going for his injury, and Ian had used that small advantage. He'd had nearly broken Kriegler's arm before the traitor convinced him they were on the same side. "Z, we'll all be joining Kagona for breakfast if you don't get your arse in here."

Conflicting emotions—relief, anger, hurt, and definitely confusion—ran rampant on Joni's face. Ian watched her grappling with questions in silence. Her gaze traveled from him to Kriegler, who turned off the engine, and back again.

"How did you find me?"

"That watch attached to Kriegler's arm."

Her forehead crinkled as she attempted to weave the details into some sensible explanation. "What happened back at the plane?"

"Besides bad planning?"

"Please, Ian. I need this straight."

He hated to reveal that Lemmon had used her for his games again. "Lemmon and Kriegler brainstormed a god-awful idea to get Mukono out."

She stared, speechless, for several moments. "When did you learn about their plan?"

"Not soon enough. And that's my fault. I recognized early on your work buddy wasn't quite what he claimed. Only I failed to put the pieces together."

"We got Mukono out," Kriegler defended.

"He's on a plane to Iran." Joni's wavering pitch indicated emotions still threatened to break loose. "How is that better?"

Kriegler let out a long breath as though hesitant to add any further fuel to the fire burning inside her. "He's headed to South Africa. I'm hoping it will take Kagona a little while to figure that out. Hardly matters. Mukono will soon be across the border."

"You tricked Kagona?"

"Afraid so, *bokkie*. The good guys were flying that plane. Once he figures it out, he'll exchange my name for yours on his hit list."

"That's why you wanted me on the plane. Why not simply tell me?"

"I told you Kagona could hear everything said or whispered in that room. I also couldn't risk he had another camera somewhere."

"What room?" Ian looked between them as a pit of fear opened inside. Cameras and recordings were standard in every interrogation room. She'd expect that. Kriegler needn't remind her.

Joni pressed against her temples. Zulu drums likely pounded in her head. "What's done is done. I came here to prove I could run ops. Lemmon took that plan out of my hands."

"If it's any consolation," Kriegler added, "no one ever knows the score in these games. If there had been another way, believe me, I'd have taken it. We spent two days running scenarios, and this was the only one that had even a small chance. If I'd told you, you'd have given me away to Kagona."

"You'd no way to predict that." Her voice cracked. She rubbed absently at raw wrists, as though they had all plotted against her.

"I'm honestly sorry, Joni."

"Christ." Ian read the truth. Whatever happened in interrogation, she'd been devastated at Kriegler's betrayal. Even now, the fear she showed was palpable…and that scared him. "What the hell happened last night?"

She leaned against the door as though securing her own little corner of the world, and again found something outside on which to focus her attention. "Doesn't matter. Bram's right. It worked."

"You matter to me." He longed to reach out and touch her, but all the signals screamed *stay away*. Something had gone wrong, very wrong, regardless of Kriegler's promise to protect her. Ian prayed with time he could help her get past the damage.

Kriegler gripped the steering wheel hard. "What happened was one hell of a brave performance. One that allowed Kagona to trust a plan he and I created. Because of Joni, Mukono is free."

Joni glanced down at her shaking hands and then directly at Ian. "Why did you shoot…pretend to shoot Bram?"

"With Kriegler down, we anticipated Kagona and his men would abandon him in their haste to save themselves. That part worked as planned. Then Kriegler and I would have loaded onto the plane with you and Mukono and flown away. By the time Kagona got the guts and men to return, the plane would be out of the country."

"Except Kagona hung onto me."

Ian slid a hand around hers and held it tight. "I wasn't leaving you behind."

Kriegler cleared his throat, sounding uncomfortable. "Neither was I," he said quietly. "I owe you."

"Damn right you do." Ian's buried tension flared. He squeezed the edge of Kriegler's seat, but would have preferred to crush the man's shoulder instead. "I should have left you in that lion's cage."

"Sorry, Taljaard, but there was no other way for this to work. We couldn't tell you. Either of you."

"I'm the country expert, yet you didn't even attempt to brainstorm with me. Instead you played me and risked Joni."

"You hadn't reestablished contact with Lemmon. Time became critical. Besides, would you have let Kagona take her?"

"Bloody hell, no."

"Then Lemmon rightly pegged your profile. He declared you'd die first."

"Damn right. The odds of her coming out unharmed or even alive were abysmal. You're a piss-poor friend to have allowed it."

"Kagona would've picked up Joni without me there to protect her."

"Protect?"

Zamani climbed into the front passenger seat. "Hate to interrupt a good discussion, but we must go."

"You suddenly in a hurry?" Ian snapped. Kriegler started the vehicle and they tore down the road, leaving behind a mess for the CIO to find.

Zamani shifted around to face Joni. "Apologies for the accident. I had to plan fast."

"No complaints. Only thanks." She swallowed hard. "It's a small price to pay not to end up in Kagona's hands again."

"Any idea what happened to him?" Ian asked no one in particular.

Joni frowned as though retrieving a foggy memory. "He crawled over me and out the front window."

Zamani nodded in agreement. "I saw him limp down the road past the wreck. Never stopped to help his men. You should have shot him." Zamani's description spoke volumes about the moral ethics of their enemy. Kagona had none.

"Wasn't in the plan." Ian squeezed his fists tight. "Although I was tempted to rewrite it. Hopefully I won't regret my decision. As soon as he's able to contact someone, he'll send choppers to look for us."

Kriegler looked back via the rearview mirror. "That'll take time. The nearest flyable one is at Thornhill Air Base in Gweru. And before you ask, I checked when I arranged for Mukono's flight."

"I'm not doubting your loyalty. Just your methods."

"Fair enough. So where are we headed?"

"Kagona won't know if I'm escaping back to home territory or fleeing the country. The border at Chirundu is an hour and a half away, and our best chance. Unfortunately, it's also the most obvious direction. The odds are iffy no matter where we go."

"The border it is then." Kriegler sported a solemn face. Joni's outburst had scared him, as it should. His grand idea had costs that weren't pretty. Using people never turned out well for anybody.

Hypocrisy raised its ugly head within Ian. Hell, he used his friends to meet lofty goals. "We're dropping Zamani off first. I can't afford to have him implicated in this mess."

Zamani raised his brows in surprise at Ian's pronouncement.

"Isn't that a moot point?" Kriegler glanced over at Zamani. "I drove your vehicle from Kanyemba to Kagona's CIO hideout. I'm sure he has the number plate on this vehicle. They will trace it back to you."

"Not so easy. Ian acquired our Rover under unique circumstances. No record to me."

"What about the vehicle you crashed back there?"

"The Beacon reporter's. It may take them a while to figure that out." Zamani grinned at Ian. "I can help you get out of Zim."

"Forget it. You've a family and you're my anchor here. Besides, there is one person I fear more than Kagona."

"Who is that?"

"Your wife."

"She will miss you sorely. But I have a plan."

"You're making me look bad."

"My specialty is backup. When you have no plan, I do. This one will help get me home and you and Joni out of Zim." He pulled out what he'd hidden under his shirt.

Ian, well aware of what the main road in this area represented, nodded. "Always thinking ahead. Must be why we've survived together for so long. That gives me an idea, too. If we're going to do the obvious, we'll need more than one diversion."

"Best you wait till I leave to discuss. I will need a quick stop before the Harare-Chirundu highway."

Ian tapped Kriegler on the shoulder. "Did you catch that?"

"Yep. A quick stop coming up."

Ian hunted through one of the packs for a multipurpose tool and a phone. "Be careful, Zamani. Kagona will be out in force looking for us."

"That is exactly what I hope, *mngane*. It's the only way my part of the plan will work."

CHAPTER TWENTY-ONE

A multiaxle truck hauling vegetables from Zambia passed them heading toward the capital, Harare. The sound and motion brought Joni out of her hypnotic stare at the dusty roadside along the paved highway. Sometime after they'd dropped off Zamani, she had conked out. Eventually a drone of male voices discussing options had awakened her, but she refrained from joining in until assessing memories and recent events to gain a footing on reality.

Her head and shoulder hurt but clarity had returned—not so desirable since she repeatedly relived the moment Zamani's vehicle launched in front of Kagona's van. After the impact, all had gone quiet until Kagona had wriggled past her. Inner whispers had urged her to bolt, but knowing Kagona lurked left her rooted in place. The rest was blank until she felt herself being carried and placed on a car seat. When Ian spoke, relief had flushed through her.

Then she'd heard a voice that riled deep anger, and, though she hated to admit it, fear. Confusion and consternation had sent questions barreling through her. Fearing Ian was at risk, the vulnerability she'd experienced exploded into action. She had attacked Bram.

Laughable. She'd succeeded in making a further fool of herself. Seeing Bram raised insecurities she had no idea existed. Damn him, whether friend or foe.

Ian worked on something from their packs. "Who owns your arse?" he asked Bram. "CIA or South African intelligence?"

"That's a good question. Lately I haven't been so sure."

"You owe me more than that. Not that I'll believe you, anyway."

"I'm former South African National Intelligence Agency. I'd been playing Kagona off and on over the years since I quit flying for him. The NIA liked having an inside track into their neighbor, even though I only occasionally touched base with Kagona."

"When did you leave the NIA?"

"When country politics regrouped it and others into one new alphabet soup and political parties started spying on each other. Still, people came to me for little jobs."

That Bram was a spy for hire who had worked as a double agent at times for South Africa gave her little empathy for him. He played nasty games and left destruction in his wake. The night with him reigned dark in her memories.

She stared at a wad of bloody gauze in her hand. Sometime during the drive, she'd pressed it against a gash on her scalp.

Ian smiled at her. "Are you ready to join the discussion?"

"How long did I doze?"

"It's been forty minutes since we dropped off Zamani. Feel better?"

"Everything hurts. But that hasn't stopped me before." More likely Bram's drug still ran through her system, but she held back mentioning that fact. Ian had greater concerns getting them out of Zim. "What happened while I was out?"

"We made contact with Lemmon. He knows we're heading to the border."

"Can he help us?"

"The Americans can't officially get involved."

"A little late for that. I'm an American."

"Technically, you came in as a South African."

"That's BS. Can't he or won't he help us?"

"Likely both. But he promised to *find* us help. We're waiting for contact again."

"What about the South Africans?"

"They have Mukono so aren't going to further antagonize their neighbor."

"I'd laugh if my head didn't hurt so much. When it comes to no man left behind, the military takes it to heart, while the CIA stabs you in it."

"I don't see you as one to give up hope," Ian added with an encouraging smile.

"Actually, I'm becoming more of an optimist around you. No matter what Kagona wanted me to believe, I knew you were alive." She fiddled with the gauze before sticking it in a pocket. "We'll get out of this. I don't like to lose."

"The battle will be a tough one. You ready?"

"Since yesterday." She licked dry lips. "Do you have any water?"

Ian dug a container out of his pack and extended it toward her. Her fingers hovered near it for a second before wrapping around it.

"You okay?"

"Yeah." She opened the lid and took several swigs. "Any news on Kagona?"

"I'm sure his men are out there. Kriegler's been scanning for police transmissions, but in these hills we aren't picking up much. Makuti is ahead. It's a small town, but has a few communication antennae, so our luck might change."

"How far to Makuti?"

"About five miles. It's the next step in our plan. Ready for a quick review?"

She gave a partial nod, careful not to aggravate any unknown injury.

Ian went through the steps he'd formulated with Zamani and the part she would play.

Her part sounded simple enough and gave her something to focus on besides the man who wanted her dead. "I can handle this little piece of action, but I look like I've been run over by an elephant. Mind if I borrow your hat? I'd prefer not to scare children and grown men."

"All you have to do is smile." He handed over his safari hat.

Bram pulled the Rover over and they played musical seats. Joni drove. Ian sat up front, and Bram changed into an extra shirt of Ian's and then hid out in the backseat. Another mile down the road, Ian instructed her to pull over where another paved road broke off and ran southwest.

"Is that the road to Kariba?" she asked.

"*Yebo.* The only other tarred road in this region. It leads to a border crossing via the Kariba Dam on the Zambezi River."

"The one that backs up Lake Kariba?"

"One of the largest man-made lakes in the world."

"Won't a critical structure that will be rolling in security?"

"It poses the same problem as the bridges at Chirundu. Neither crossing is passable for us. However, since we've made it to this juncture, Kagona will have to consider two avenues of escape we could take."

"Chirundu is closer. Why might he believe we'd consider Lake Kariba?"

"Boats, lots of them, and a shared lake with Zambia. With more locations for us to cross, the more spread out his men will be. All that works in our favor."

"Let's get going." Bram grabbed a pack and slipped out of the Rover. The tension inside the vehicle lightened.

Joni drove a thousand feet on the Chirundu road before turning into the only petrol station with fuel until the border. It sat up on a slight hill along the road. Across from it, a dirt turnout had several long-haul trucks parked.

"I've seen a lot of trucks, but not many private vehicles. This Rover stands out. Is that going to be a problem?" she asked.

"Possibly. The Chirundu highway is a truck corridor that runs south through Zimbabwe to the docks in Durban, South Africa, and north to the Congo and Tanzania. With fuel scarce, tourists travel by aircraft or boat. That reduces travel by personal vehicle. If Kagona plays his cards right, the Rover will be easy to spot."

"What about checkpoints? We haven't hit any yet."

"There are fewer in this remote area. But I've been watching for them nonetheless. I expect it's only a matter of time until we run into Kagona and the CIO. That's why we're changing things up."

"And why we're stopping for gas when we don't really need it?"

"Exactly."

Kagona glared at the med tech removing pieces of glass from his hand. A cut on his leg ached after being stitched. His chief operative, Chaipa, paced the command center, his neck wrapped in a brace, waiting for answers, for news, for any fucking information on where Taljaard and the woman had gone.

"Have you found where they dumped Kriegler's body? That might give us an idea to the direction they fled. I want the rifle. A match will seal Taljaard's fate as a killer."

"We have discovered several bullets, but not the one that killed Kriegler. It may be in the body."

"Give me one piece of positive news." He gestured with his hands, to the consternation of the med tech.

"The borders are sealed. All vehicles and trucks are being checked. A helicopter is on the way. It's bringing a special operator and equipment we were using to observe protesters in the capital. Thirty minutes ETA."

"No traffic leaves the country until they are found."

The radio in Chaipa's hand lit up. He glanced over at his boss as a report came in. "Kriegler's Rover has been spotted right where you expected."

"Are they positive?"

"It matches the license plate on the vehicle Kriegler drove in from Kanyemba."

"Excellent. Taljaard likely doesn't realize we have video of the vehicle when it sat out front of our facility."

Chaipa asked for confirmation of the people inside. "What do you want to do? They report no one in the vehicle. The people must have gone inside a restaurant."

"I'm surprised Taljaard would risk going inside and leaving his weapons behind. Keep the uniformed men out of sight. Send in someone to get a description of the occupants. But whatever happens, don't let that vehicle leave."

The technician dabbed antiseptic on Kagona's hand before wrapping gauze tape around his hand and fingers.

"Fool. I need my fingers free." A brief tug-of-war ensued until the technician released the tape. Kagona worked it around like a boxing wrap. He extended his hand for the technician to cut the tape. Encounters with Taljaard had proved damaging. His jaw still ached from their encounter last week near Bulawayo, and the yellowing from the bruise had yet to disappear.

Next time he met Taljaard face-to-face, his enemy would not walk away.

"Sir, a witness says a man and woman exited the Rover after it parked. The men are in position to take Taljaard when they return to their vehicle. There is no escape."

"Excellent. Tell them to leave a radio channel open. I want to hear everything that happens."

Ian had watched Joni go inside to pay for petrol. He smelled fuel, so despite difficulties in obtaining it, this station had some available. Another vehicle sat nearby. Two of its occupants waited for the single occupied toilet.

Ian hated to lose sight of Joni, but nature called and they had no time to waste. He strolled around back, all senses on alert for anything out of place. A funny niggling made him wish he'd come armed.

A few birds scattered out of nearby brush as he approached. He watered a dry hole.

"You there, Ingwe?" came over his comm.

"Can't a man piss in peace?"

"All set. About half a klick from your location."

"Perfect." Ian kicked dirt over the wet spot.

Behind him, he heard a motorcycle arrive near the pumps and then quickly leave. An expected arrival? Hopefully Joni had been quick about loading up on a few liters. They had to hit the road fast.

He peered round the building. Joni talked to a white man in khaki and green, displaying all the swagger of a professional hunter. From all appearances, he had prey in his sights.

Joni's voice floated over. "There I was all settled for the night, wrapped in mosquito netting, the gal next to me chatting away. Our guide whispered for her to hush. Not this gal. She started giggling. Next thing I know, this spotted catlike thing with a Mohawk down its back barreled out of the jesse and landed on me. I yelled. It snarled, and I launched it into the air. It landed back on me and took off. In my haste to scurry out the netting and find a flashlight, I destroyed most everything I had on. My safari mates laughed for an hour."

She had the civet story down pat. Damn event had happened to his father, wherever the wayward man might be. Not a bad way to explain away her tattered appearance, but unnecessary. Unexpected emotion pressed his lips tight. It seemed like a year instead of days ago when he'd shared the tale with her in a musty barn on a dark night. He shoved away memories. Focus had to be on the present.

He'd expected a safari guide with time on his hands to show up for the arranged meeting. Instead this PH had arrived. He must have decided to make extra money on the way to pick up clients. The dirtbag stepped closer into Joni's personal space. If he knew the trouble she offered, he'd run. Time to put a stop to his stalking and set him to work.

Ian stepped out from behind the building and strolled toward Joni, whistling a whimsical ditty. He stepped between her and the hunter and opened the Rover door.

The man appeared surprised. Good. That's the reaction Ian required. "I strongly suggest you push off to where you're headed." Another truck pulled up across the road from the station. Things were getting crowded.

Ian aimed a strained smile at Joni. "You coming, poppet?"

Joni gave the PH a friendly nod and climbed in. "Poppet?"

Ian gunned the Rover's engine and turned around, heading to a shortcut out of the parking lot that picked up the side road to Lake Kariba. Out of sight of the station, he swung back around so the vehicle could easily access the highway to Chirundu and stopped.

"Grab your day pack and glean the car of everything that shows we were here." He patted the back of the Rover. "Zamani is going to miss this."

Joni loaded up, burdened with a day pack and rifle. "I hope we don't need any of this stuff. I'm planning on being out the country before dark."

"Contingencies." Ian fastened his bow to a pack and slid it on his back. For years he'd forgone killing anyone. Not his method of operating, but that didn't mean he wasn't fully prepared to do so if cornered. Kagona wanted them dead.

The professional hunter appeared on foot and strolled toward them.

"Joni, take that path a short ways and I'll catch up with you. Both of us standing out here isn't smart."

She headed out with the gear, sounding like a parade of elephants.

The hunter picked up his pace and stopped a safe distance from Ian. "You're a bit touchy for someone doing you a favor."

"Part of the deal was to follow directions and meet over here, not ogle my client."

"Client, is it?"

Smart-ass. "If you don't want the job. I'll find someone else." Ian had spread the notice of a vehicle ferry needed among guide and hunting friends.

"Nothing illegal with that Rover, is there?"

"Nope. A news crew had me recover it up past the Mkanga Bridge. I'm headed to Lake Kariba, but they wanted it dropped at Chirundu. I'm on a schedule and can't do both."

"What was a reporter doing up there?"

"Ask him. Here's the number to call when you get there. You know how to find Mundana Point Fishing Lodge?"

"No problem."

"The reporter said not to bother them until your feet hit the dirt. He's following a story but has arranged for someone to collect the Rover."

"Right. He's likely out tiger fishing."

"He'll tell you where to leave the keys. Don't be late. He wants it in an hour."

"It'll likely take double that. What about payment?"

"He pays well. You might even see more if you deliver on time." Ian dug out a hundred bucks. Not a bad wage for a few hours' drive.

The man eagerly took it. "You said you recovered it. What was wrong with this thing, anyway?"

"Picked up a hole in the gas tank." Ian realized he'd used the story behind the reporter's destroyed 4x4. Might as well stick to the lie. "Has a temporary fix, but it got us here. There's an extra jerrican onboard in case you run low."

"Good to know." The guy shook Ian's hand.

"Thanks for helping me out." Ian walked after Joni. From a secure vantage, he watched as the Rover, the vehicle of many adventures, passed the gas station and disappeared down the road to Chirundu.

Kagona listened to the live reports.

"The man is walking toward the Land Rover. No woman in sight."

"Wait for her to appear," he instructed. "I want them both." He glanced at Chaipa, who looked over the shoulder of a computer tech. "What's taking so long with a visual? I want to see what is happening."

"A live feed is coming any moment, sir."

"Female suspect has been spotted. Go. Go."

"We have the feed." Kagona looked past Chaipa to a screen.

The parking lot of a Chicken Inn displayed on a screen. A white Rover sat in the foreground. Nearby two people lay facedown on the dirt parking area and were being handcuffed by the police.

The truth glared at Kagona. The vehicle might be white and a Land Rover, but the make and model were not the vehicle that Kriegler had driven. The man looked nothing like Taljaard, and while he couldn't see the woman's face, he surmised she wasn't Joni Bell.

"Fools. They're not the suspects. Get me a visual on the license."

A policeman who manipulated the video hustled to the Rover. The plates matched Kriegler's vehicle.

Kagona frowned at Chaipa. "A diversion. They attached Kriegler's plates to a vehicle going toward Harare. That means they are headed to the border at Chirundu."

"Or Kariba."

"Time is of the essence. They'll take the shortest route and are using a stolen plate or driving without one."

"The 4x4 we rammed had no number plate. Perhaps they removed it. There's no report yet, on the vehicle registration."

"Then get one." Had incompetence reached his inner circle?

Chaipa grabbed up a desk phone.

Kagona paced, putting himself in Taljaard's mind. How would he carry out an escape? Several scenarios came to mind, including using a motorcycle. He ordered an officer to check the town for any reports of stolen vehicles, in particular a motorcycle. The woman was small and could fit on a cycle with Taljaard.

Another fifteen minutes ticked past before Chaipa snatched up a piece of notepaper he'd been scribbling notes on and turned toward Kagona. He looked unhappy, and not at all excited about passing along the news. "The vehicle is registered to the Africa News Beacon reporter we imprisoned."

Kagona swept paper files off a desk. Loose papers floated in the air and slid across the floor. "Find me Taljaard." He waved his injured hands. "I want everyone on the lookout for the reporter's number plate on a white Land Rover. This trick will not give Taljaard the time he hopes. Inform me when the helicopter arrives. It's taking me to the border."

He strode out of the room, heading for his office to pick up a personal weapon and make sure he could manipulate it with his damaged hands.

CHAPTER TWENTY-TWO

Ian caught up to Joni on a worn path that wove along the road to Lake Kariba. A very long hike and one he had no intention of making. "I'll take the rifle."

She cast him a doubtful look but gladly handed over his rifle and hat. "I hope the tradeoff for extra time makes it worth giving up fast transportation. You realize the hunter could simply drive the Rover to the nearest police station and turn us in."

"Yep, but it's back that way." He pointed in the opposite direction from where they had stopped. "Kagona will have the Rover in his hands sooner or later with or without us in it. I'd prefer we be somewhere else by then."

He directed her to cross the road when cleared of traffic and people on foot, then hustled her back toward the highway they had driven in on.

"How much time do you think we'll gain?"

"An hour if we're lucky. Kagona likely has found the first diversion by now."

"How much farther to the border?" Her toe struck a rock and she stumbled but caught herself. The drug she'd been given had worn off, but residual effects still lingered. It would help to know what had been administered, but at this point, he'd nothing to help reverse the effects.

He slowed down and stayed close. "Forty-five minutes, maybe an hour. Use it to prep for the escape. Do you know how to use everything I saw in those day packs?"

"More or less. I wish I knew more, but we'll have to make do with less."

"Figure that Kagona will have the border crossing shut down, and speedboats out on the river."

"What's the fun if he makes it too easy?"

He waited for her to smirk or wink or give some signal she'd put the night behind her, but it didn't show. Something weighed on her mind. He wanted to blame the drug, but he'd sensed a distance between them since her rescue and the confrontation with Kriegler.

More had happened during her capture than either she or Kriegler had admitted. Until he discovered what, helping her heal would be difficult.

"Sounds like our team is ready for action." He shot her a reassuring smile, then triggered his comm switch. "Impisi. We're on our way. Ten minutes out."

He picked up the pace, leading the way and contemplating how to ask the questions he could no longer leave unanswered.

When the trail widened enough they could walk side by side, he let her catch up. "I have to ask. Are you okay working with Kriegler?"

That confident edge she'd spouted a minute ago disappeared. "I'll have time to reflect on things later. For now, I'm good to go."

"You pale every time his name is mentioned or he even glances your way. You can hate him later for being an asshole. But until we're safe, accept I have your back."

"It's going to take time, Ian."

"Care to tell me how those buttons got ripped?"

Her chin rose and steps quickened. Dry grass and weeds crunched under her feet. He kept pace and waited.

"Two of Kagona's men."

"Did they—"

"No. Bram stopped them. Nearly sliced one's throat."

Relief swelled within. The fear she'd been raped had haunted his thoughts since he'd seen her. "I almost killed Kriegler up in Kanyemba. Fucking bastard kept me from pulling you onto the truck. He'd no right to risk you. I had only moments to make decisions, but he promised me he'd not let Kagona's men touch you. He swore he'd do whatever it took to keep you safe."

She walked in silence again. The distance between them grew, or rather spread into a gulf of what she and Kriegler had experienced and what he had been left to guess had happened. Damn Afrikaner. What he couldn't get from Joni, he'd extract from the hyena. The question remained—if Kriegler had saved her from Kagona's men, why the negative reaction between them?

"Why did you check my bandage?"

"Bram told Kagona he'd opened your wound where Kagona shot you. I see he lied." The fact seemed to leave her emotions fighting with the different faces of Kriegler. "Kagona was quite pleased you'd been hit."

"I'm sure he was. Was Kriegler present for your interrogation?"

She hesitated. "Some of it." Her words caught and that familiar tormented look whitewashed her face.

"I have to know details to protect my Zim friends, Joni. Did Kagona learn anything from the interrogation?"

"No" came out with vehemence.

"What did he ask?"

"He played games with my head. I'd have told you anything important."

"It's my business to understand the interrogation process. It will help if you can remember what transpired."

From the taut muscles in her neck and jaw, and the flit of her eyes while her memory played back events, he knew she remembered.

"Kagona played the good cop." She took a long breath and many steps. "Told me you were alive. Of course, he added you were left dying as fodder for night prowlers."

"So who played the bad cop?"

She didn't answer.

"Christ. I'll kill him myself. What did Kriegler ask?"

"He wanted to know about you. Your friends. What I'd done while in the country."

"What did you tell him?"

"Trivial things. Your friends are safe."

"I need to know exactly. Kagona records everything."

"I made stuff up."

"Did he ask about locations? About people we encountered? About transportation? Give me more details, Joni."

She stopped dead and faced him. "I don't remember. There. Are you happy?"

"Because Kagona drugged you?"

Her eyes widened. "I should've known you'd figure it out."

"It wasn't hard. When you attacked Kriegler, your eyes were still dilated, your movements uncoordinated, and your inhibitions, well, rather lacking. You didn't need to hide it from me."

Indecision played in her eyes. Indecision at what?

"Any idea what Kagona gave you?"

"I'm sorry, I didn't mean to slow us down." She started walking again.

Panic rose. She avoided the question. Had Kagona administered the drug before Kriegler arrived or had Kriegler, the bad cop, allowed it to happen? Hell, what if he'd administered it? Did this have something to do with the room Kriegler had mentioned? One besides an interrogation room?

The suspected truth filled his head and he wanted to roar. *That son of a bitch. I'll kill him.* He grabbed Joni's arm, abruptly halting her. His mouth opened to question her, but nothing came out. What could he say? Where should he start?

A stricken look engulfed her. Moisture filled her eyes, and she stiffened under his touch. "Please, don't ask more, Ian."

Heartbroken at the damage done, he released her and let her walk away. Not far along the highway, they reached Kriegler and a truck parked on a dirt pull off. Ian watched her approach and Kriegler step out from behind the truck. She gave him wide berth and rounded the cab to stay out of sight of the road.

The pack on his back weighed a ton. He'd been outmaneuvered and unable to protect Joni. Her conquering hero had failed.

Bloody hell, he couldn't think straight. She didn't want or need to be conquered. She looked at him to be a partner, one to work in unison with her, one to watch her back. Her faith in him had dwindled...hell, shriveled.

He wanted the old Joni back, the one driven to succeed with wit and humor, and that fact left him filled with guilt. Kagona, Kriegler, and Lemmon had stolen from them both. The loss inside left him angry and wanting answers, but not from the tattered psyche that walked away from him. They both had rebuilding to accomplish, and it started now, with their survival.

With a tainted aura, Joni climbed into a canvas-sided truck, bypassing Bram's extended helpful hand. The soft sides allowed for easy loading by forklifts and provided access and a decent hiding place for three fugitives on the lam.

She took a good look at what lay inside. "Farm equipment?"

"Headed to Zambia. Some farmers run out of Zimbabwe rebuilt there."

Recent events underscored the farmers' need to move to safer pastures. She held back a canvas flap behind the cab as Bram jumped down and handed up their equipment. She tossed the two big packs with food and survival gear against a crate marked *generator*.

Bram climbed back aboard, pocketed his earpiece for the break, and found a place under a tractor to stretch his legs out.

Ian finished up with the driver, paying part of a bribe to allow them onboard. Oddly, he told the driver to leave the cab door unlocked before joining her and Bram. Ian secured the canvas flap as the truck pulled onto the road.

The sudden darkness, even though not complete, wrapped a vicious cold around her. She sensed Bram moving closer. *Are you still here?* echoed in her head. *I'm here.*

Ian had yet to be seated when a frantic desire to see her surroundings sent her pushing past him. She felt around on the floor behind him for her day pack. Her hands lighted on stiff nylon. She grabbed the shoulder strap on the bag and yanked it to her, squatting back in the space she'd claimed.

Light, where was the damn light? Inside the pack, her fingers delved into every nook, hunting, straining to find her small flashlight. Her fingers encircled a cool metal of a cylinder. A breath of relief slipped out. A weak but welcome light brightened the dim space.

The thin beam caught Bram still in the place he'd settled, staring at her with his mouth slightly agape. He cast a quick glance toward Ian, whose face looked grim as he huddled close enough his knees touched hers. Not sure why, she pulled her legs in tight and wrapped her arms around them.

Ian's face blanked. "You okay?"

"Fine." Dear God, was she? Being in this confined area in the dark had left her scrambling around like a madwoman.

Darkness had never bothered her before. Damn Bram and his flawed plan. He'd played on her weaknesses back in that room and used them to his end.

Ian reached out toward her, then stopped. Confusion or concern was written in the bunched lines of his forehead. His jaw tightened. He wanted to know what she couldn't tell him. Heavy emptiness blocked all emotions. What hadn't been lost in the helicopter had been destroyed with Bram. Learning the truth had done little to bring it back.

A firm hand gripped her shoulder. "We're going to get out of here alive, Joni. But it means keeping your head in the game." The grip on her shoulder loosened and slid lightly down her arm to the hand clutching the little torch. "Relax. I'm not going anywhere without you." His eyes softened with pleading concern. "We'll get through this."

She longed for it to be so simple, but nothing in her head made sense, so expecting her heart to follow was near impossible. What if he learned the truth about the interrogation? What would he think of her?

He let go of her hand. "Time is tight. Go through your pack and arrange it so anything important is within an easy reach." He placed an energy bar in her hand. "Eat. No excuses. We have a hike ahead." He ripped open the wrapper.

As though on autopilot, she lifted the bar and took a bite.

"Now where do we stand?" Ian looked over at Bram, who had his equipment out.

Bram pointed out the scanner. "It paid to be sitting here under one of Makuti's antennae. Picked up a police frequency. Kagona caught onto the merry-go-round Zamani played with the vehicle number plates. A 4x4 he tagged with the Rover's plate was discovered heading toward Harare. They've determined you and Joni were not the occupants."

As Bram spoke her name, it pulled her to focus on his words and the discussion.

"How about our vehicle?" Ian asked.

"Right before you arrived, I picked up a broadcast to look for a white Land Rover bearing the reporter's number plate. Someone must have noticed it missing from the wreck. The 4x4's vehicle identification number likely led them to the reporter's registration." Bram gave a smug smile at Ian. "Rather ironic he is sitting in their jail and yet helping us escape."

"I'm sure that fact isn't lost on Kagona."

"You'd better hope your guy ferrying the Rover drives fast. Once the police stop by the gas station, they'll be on his tail."

Ian checked his watch. "All we need is time."

He dug out a satellite phone and made a call, no doubt to Lemmon. Her fearless CIA leader had created this debacle and again fooled her into doing his bidding. *Heartless* jumped to mind when she pictured his lying eyes. Her fists clenched at the sound of his voice on speaker.

The narrowing of Ian's eyes indicated he also had issues with Lemmon. Likely deadly ones. "Tell us you have help stationed at the border."

"I've arranged for a boat and chopper on the Zambian side."

"Mike?"

"He said you'd know the frequency. How you work with him is up to you, but he can't cross the border, so don't tempt him. Use the sat phone to touch base with the boat." Lemmon rattled off the number and Ian tapped it into a phone database. "The boat captain won't cross until you signal. He knows the area well."

"Good. I'll tell him where to meet us when we get closer."

"Don't expect a speedboat."

"Damn." Ian switched hands with the phone. "That means we'll need a diversion."

"Your team will have to pull that off. How far out are you?"

"About forty till drop-off and another fifteen to reach the river."

"Good luck. I'll be listening in." Lemmon hung up.

She started when Ian set a hand on her knee. Worry edged his eyes, surely wondering if she had it together enough to handle what lay ahead.

He opened a mini tablet and brought up a map of the border. "This is what we have to contend with." He pointed out the few houses in the area they would have to skirt as well as the location where Kagona might land if he came in by helicopter. "The fishing camps where boats are available are here. I can guarantee he'll have them watched."

"Couldn't the two of you incapacitate a few men if Lemmon's captain doesn't come through?"

Ian and Bram glanced at one another, then Ian shook his head. "It is better to avoid rather than engage if possible. Once we're spotted or the men don't report in, the location will be overrun with Kagona's men."

Ideas floated around in her head. She formulated a few ways to play games with Kagona. For the next ten minutes they tossed around possible scenarios. They devised a basic plan, with options depending on Kagona's moves. Ian assigned Bram communications and gave him the radio frequency Mad Mike used for contingencies.

"I'm monitoring several channels Kagona's pilot might be using," Bram said. "Advance notice if he closes in will give us an edge."

"I remember the frequency his pilot had dialed in on his radio last week," Joni added. Her mood lifted a bit at the memory of her prior success.

"You *are* a dangerous woman, *bokkie*."

Ian tucked his feet beneath him. "You've no idea just how dangerous messing with her can be." He and Bram stared at one another for a few seconds, while Ian made sure his subtle message sank in. He'd gone into protector mode.

"I can take care of myself around you two, but I might need a little help with Kagona."

Ian shifted closer and dropped to a knee. "We're going to make it across the Zambezi. You saved my arse last time. I fully expect you'll do it again." He leaned in and kissed her forehead…gently and without expectations. She had closed herself off to him, and he struggled with the results. So did she.

He nudged up her chin in his endearing way. His hand adjusted the earpiece on her comm unit and untangled the wires around her neck that held the unit at her chest. Once straightened, he tucked it all back under her loose shirt.

"I'll be riding shotgun so the driver knows where to stop." He moved to the canvas side panel on the truck. "I'll give you a two-minute warning when we approach our drop-off."

In a precarious move while the truck rumbled along, Ian swung out onto the cab and pulled open the door before slipping inside.

CHAPTER TWENTY-THREE

Bram found relief in Taljaard's departure. Since Joni's rescue, the tension between them had escalated. For good reason. If Taljaard ever learned the methods he'd used in Joni's interrogation, he'd be lucky to live.

He battened down the loose canvas side. His eyes readjusted to the dim light to find Joni rubbing her palms along her pant legs. Her hands sweat. She feared being alone with him.

He settled in with the scanner, not knowing how to carry on a conversation with a woman who had tried to kill him an hour earlier—for justifiable reasons. He figured the less they said to one another the better. He stretched out and propped his head on Taljaard's pack.

The foot attached to the fake leg Taljaard had stuffed into the pack stuck out and hung above Bram's head. Irritated at the strange nuances of the safari king, he reached up.

"I wouldn't," Joni started, but he shoved the foot back. A blade sprang out between his fingerstips, which narrowly escaped an extreme manicure.

"…touch that," she finished.

He carefully moved his hand away, then tested the blade. *Fokken* sharp. "Where'd Taljaard get this thing?"

"From Mad Mike's."

"I see why you call him that." Bram played around with the prosthesis and reinserted the blade into the toe. This time he cautiously turned the foot so it faced another direction.

"How much battery do you have left?" She indicated his scanner. Her all-business attitude didn't hide the uneasiness behind her words.

"I recharged while I waited for you and Taljaard to arrive. A solar recharger, in case you're wondering." Even with his hands settled behind his head and doing his best to relax, his conscience refused to let him off so easy. He sat up and faced Joni. "I'm not sure where to start, but we need to talk."

"There's little you can say to take away what happened."

"I did what I did to protect you."

She snorted and looked away.

He didn't do well with female emotions. "Consider me a jackass, sicko, or whatever, but I had to make a real pervert believe my actions were legit."

"I was chained to your bed. You ripped my damn clothes off."

"Technically only your pants."

"Asshole." She pressed her lips together…hard. From inside her day pack, she tugged out the contents. "You drugged me…after I'd cooperated. Each step I take still feels out of focus."

"The only way to ensure your safety was in my arms."

She raised her chin. Her jaw wavered, face twitched, but her stare focused on him with a steely glare.

"Joni, that is all that happened. I held you. I shielded you."

"Did you dress me?" She shoved something into a side pocket.

"If I hadn't, Kagona or his men would have enjoyed the process."

He trod on shaky ground that showed no signs of firming up

any time soon. "I'm sorry about the interrogation. I have to admit the stories about your adventures in Zim were entertaining. I gave you plenty of room to waste time. The more the drug took effect, the giddier you became. I still imagine Kagona's men scouring the stories for useful details."

No sign of relief showed in her features. He swallowed hard. Her innocence had ripped him apart. Making light of the situation only highlighted what a cold asshole he'd become.

He tried and failed to smile. "If someone I loved was in Kagona's hands and Taljaard had a chance to protect her, I'd expect him to do the same. I wouldn't like it. I might even want to draw and quarter him, but the bottom line is she would come out alive. In the scheme of things, that's all that bloody hell matters."

Her head tilted and she studied him, but said nothing.

"I can't expect us to be friends again, *bokkie*, but I owe you the truth."

"What happened after you lay next to me, Bram? I...I remember you drawing me against your body."

"You were shivering...disoriented. I brought you close until the drug kicked fully in."

"And then?"

"I pulled a sheet up over us and spent the next hours holding you tight. You slept and I tried. It's hard to destroy someone's faith and have a clear conscience to fall asleep. I'm not sure I'll find any until I drop unconscious from exhaustion."

She played with the light propped between them, swirling her finger mindlessly around it. "I want to believe you...but it's not so simple."

God, he'd struck so damn deep. A notch to add to his already heavily marred, soulless belt. Life sucked. Of all the people who had slipped under his skin, she'd been one of the few to honestly share her friendship.

"You've lied to me from the start," she added.

"Is that a surprise? Your actions on the train indicated you already mistrusted my actions."

"Don't feed me that shit. At that point, I didn't trust anyone. You played me long before that. Convinced me with a big act to fly in and rescue Mukono's kid. I'm talking about the person I worked with day in and day out. The one who welcomed me home with a hug and noticed my injuries. The über-friendly Afrikaner always looking to share a beer. Was that an act? Who or what is the real you, Bram?"

He empathized with her feelings. They both lived on shifting sand, searching for a rock where they could find footing. She had believed her job in South Africa a solid place to steady her life. He'd just rolled that rock from under her feet. "At least accept that what you suffered allowed Sipho's father to go free."

"One right doesn't make all the wrongs disappear."

He wished it did.

She repacked her day pack, leaving out the drone tablet. She turned it on and swiped at something on the screen. Slowly at first, then faster and faster. She clicked it off, as though she'd came to a decision. With hesitation, her mouth opened. He waited for whatever played on her mind to come out.

"When…when Kagona took me away in the Alouette." She drew a deep breath and looked away. The truck bounced over a patch of rough road, and it jostled her back and forth like a rag doll. With shoulders drooped forward, she shook her head and tossed the tablet back into the pack. A hard swallow and shallow eyes accompanied a blank expression.

Bram hung his head, riddled with guilt.

"Joni, I made mistakes. Obviously grand ones. I deserve whatever you hand out." He reached into his pocket and pulled out a piece of a photo. "I'm aware this isn't the first time you've been screwed by the system. Lemmon gave me something for you. A sort of apology, I suspect. It's been trimmed down." He handed over a photo of another boy she'd rescued years ago in Colombia. She'd been led to believe he died.

She pressed her lips tight and held the photo near the light. Fine lines crinkled around her mouth. Not exactly a smile, but at least a sign of hope.

"How do I know when this was taken?" Her voice sounded tight and hoarse.

"There's a date stamp on the back. Thus the awkward shape."

She flipped it over. Her eyes closed and a breath slipped out in a slow sigh. "He's alive."

"Lemmon's suffered his own guilt trip. Told me you went above and beyond the call of duty to save this kid. His men never gave up on you. They were hampered by politics, but your military buddies refused to quit. It was Lemmon's decision to send them in on the day you were rescued. About a month, I heard. That's a hell of a long time to survive with a frantic kid in a jungle that belonged to the enemy. You're made of tough stuff, Joni. Don't let me or anyone else destroy you."

She stared at the teen's photo as though it might disappear any second. Awkward silence came as her chin rose and her eyes stared into the shadowy depths of the laden truck. Light gleamed off moisture in her eyes.

The photo disappeared into a leg pocket, and eventually her hollow gaze shifted to him. "This token doesn't mean I'll trust you again."

"I can accept that. The only person worth yours is Mr. Trustworthy riding in the cab. Stick with him. Considering the pain riddling my body, he's willing to kill or die for you. I should be so lucky to find someone with such conviction."

"You reap what you sow."

Yeah, and he'd sown enough seeds of discord with friends to start a revolution. Figuring he'd done enough damage for one day, he settled back against a pack.

She retrieved the tablet and set about going through the drone functions. He closed his eyes, hoping for a reprieve from his guilt. Instead, his skin prickled with unease. He peeked out through half-closed lids.

Joni had frozen with the tablet poised in her hand. "How long have you been working with Lemmon?"

For someone whose brain had been addled by drugs, she put the facts together quickly. Should he give her the truth and further destroy her confidence, or lie and achieve…what? "I met him a few months before you joined the project office."

"I see." Her eyes had narrowed in doubt. "Because you worked on Taz?"

"Pfft. Hell if I know for sure. Seems he knew more about me than I did. You Americans are scary." His levity brought no ease to her scowl. "Your CIA was looking for people who had past ties to various leaders and intelligence organizations in African countries. Guess I was on the list. Evidently Lemmon was switching venues from South America to Africa. He had a few small jobs for me that related to the overall stability of Africa. Some in conjunction with South African intelligence, others not."

"Your shark diving vacation this year?"

"Yeah, that. A real thrill diving with the great whites. You should give it a try. A great stress reliever."

The glare shooting his way indicated she wanted the truth.

"I wasn't diving. And that's all I can tell you."

A video from Kanyemba played on the small screen. She watched, seemingly accepting of his answers. "After Colombia, I got out of the military. A friend told me about the project office job in South Africa flying Taz. How many other pilots applied for it?"

"It's not that simple. The Americans offered funding for Taz to keep the project alive. We figured with Special Forces toys in demand, they wanted a piece of the action. Part of the deal was assigning an American helicopter test pilot. They recommended you. Obergen was thrilled at bringing such a talented pilot into his project."

"Were there any other recommendations?"

"Come on, *bokkie*. Don't torture yourself."

"I need the truth."

He leaned up on an elbow. "No. At first I thought you were one of Lemmon's operatives, but I never noticed any absences to account for it. Before your first mission into Zimbabwe, Lemmon admitted your job was payback for the Colombian rescue you pulled off. As much as you hate him, he watched out for you."

"Until he used me again. My whole career has been a sham of manipulation."

"It wasn't like that. Lemmon had been building off my connection to Kagona for a while. When we heard about Mukono's son, time was of the essence."

"So whose idea was it to send me to get him?"

"Both of ours. If I'd ever imagined you would've ended up in Kagona's hands on that mission, I'd never have let you go."

"That didn't seem to bother you this time. You delivered me to him."

"Knowing I'd be at your side. I'm not proud of how it turned out. Lemmon and I let desperation overrule reality. We'd run out of time."

"So I became the easy solution."

"Your capture became the key to gaining Mukono's release. I figured I'd be along for the ride and could control the situation. I lost sight of the fact that you weren't a trained operative."

"I'm growing tired of people pointing out my shortcomings."

"Don't worry, mine are extensive enough to fill a book."

"If I'd been trained, would you have told me the plan up front?"

He hesitated. "Lemmon controlled those details."

"So, the answer is no."

He laid his head back on the pack again, closed his eyes, and tried to ignore all his mistakes. Within minutes, he sensed Joni hovering close. He forced himself not to move but opened his eyes.

Her hand hovered near his face. She hesitated when he looked into her eyes, then she reached past him and retrieved something from a pocket on Ian's pack. He'd hoped for some touch of forgiveness, but accepted that at least for now, she'd moved on to survival.

CHAPTER TWENTY-FOUR

Kagona's shirt flapped wildly in a hurricane of rotor wash as the military helicopter landed in a weedy open space near the CIO compound. He turned his back and shielded his eyes from dust and debris. A good twenty meters away, Chaipa stood with a hand over one ear and a phone over the other. Efficient, thorough, and of a like mind on country politics, his number-one man spoke to headquarters, receiving the latest updates.

Chaipa finished his conversation and headed toward him. His slim, drawn face gave no hint as to the news. Over the years Kagona had watched him the driven youth rise through the ranks, efficiently carrying out his orders in a timely, concise, and, if necessary, ruthless fashion, making him the perfect candidate to bring under Kagona's tutelage. Maturity had seasoned Chaipa into an operative who anticipated the moves necessary to stay ahead of their adversaries—those who threatened the stability of the country and those supporting political opponents inside the CIO.

Kagona signaled an officer armed with an AK-47 standing nearby to head toward the chopper. Once the man moved out of earshot, Kagona focused on Chaipa, not solely for the latest on

Taljaard, but for more pressing private concerns. "What's the latest on Chitima? Have the trucks reached the border?"

"The containers are in Mutare being loaded onto a train as we speak."

Taljaard had failed to rally enemies within the county to stop the yellowcake shipment. Victory dangled before Kagona, although new threats would rise after the train moved outside Zimbabwe. It wasn't yet time to reach for the golden ring. "What about our *despachante*?"

"He will forward all customs and shipping documents necessary to our Mozambique contacts. They have indicated radioactive sensors at the port are going down for unexpected maintenance."

"And the payments for their assistance?"

"Partials were distributed. The remaining bribes will be delivered after the shipment leaves port."

"Excellent. How long to the port once the train leaves our border?"

"Fourteen hours."

"With Taljaard on the run, there is little he can do to stop it." He patted Chaipa's shoulder, contemplating how future payments from Iran would give a welcome boost to their candidate, the president's chief opponent, in the upcoming elections. Careful manipulation had ensured only a select few knew of the Iranian deal. It was unfortunate that a portion of the money went to the current president. A necessity to keep the deal quiet.

"I can guess what you are thinking," Chaipa said. "Does President Tangwerai suspect you support his opposition?"

"If he does, any attempts to remove me from my position would leave him vulnerable. I know every dirty secret about him." That knowledge left a warm feeling in Kagona's gut. "This is a good day for us. It'll be perfect when we rid ourselves of Taljaard."

Chaipa nodded agreement, although no excitement eased tension lines on his face. He glanced toward the chopper, ready to move out.

Kagona extended a hand to stop him. "What's the word on Taljaard?"

"They've stopped a white Land Rover with the reporter's number plate. A solo driver. They're checking him out."

"Where?"

"Outside Chirundu. Taljaard sent us on a wild chase east toward Harare, while he went west toward the Chirundu border crossing."

"Taljaard is playing games, and may still be doing so if we discover the driver isn't him."

"You give the man too much credit. We have him, and we have the vehicle identification number. Our people are checking both out. Taljaard couldn't register a vehicle without us knowing about it. That means someone else had to use their own identification. Soon we will arrest the person assisting Taljaard."

The turn of events pleased Kagona, but Taljaard had proven resilient over the years. "Never assume facts. But if it is Taljaard, the killing of Kriegler will be the undoing of his network. White men have no business interfering in an African's playground. When they start killing one another, people take notice." He started toward the chopper. "If we're lucky, his assassination of a South African will break the protesters' spirits."

The men ducked their heads and moved under the rotor.

Kagona stopped at the open hatch. "Search for Taljaard's woman. She can't be far away. He's too much of a hero to leave her behind."

"And if the driver isn't him?" Chaipa had begun to see the gaps in the easy capture of the Rover.

"Assume he'll be on foot or have secured other transportation. But be assured, Taljaard is headed toward the

Zambezi River and an escape to Zambia." Kagona climbed into the helo, taking the rear-facing front seat.

A junior operative who had flown in on the helo sat across from Kagona. His baby-fresh face looked barely twenty. He clutched a stiff, sport-size satchel on his lap. Technology had its benefits, but the younger generation relied too heavily on it.

The officer with the AK-47 sat on the far back side with Chaipa in the center next to the young agent. Chaipa directed the pilot to head toward Chirundu before picking up the conversation where they had stopped.

"Taljaard and the woman will require a boat or aircraft to cross the Zambezi. A chopper could easily snatch them up and be gone."

For a pro at evasion like Taljaard, escaping Zimbabwe posed little problem. "There's a dirt strip near both Chirundu and Lake Kariba. Have officials watch for the Adventure Tours helicopter. Taljaard used it effectively at Victoria Falls last week. It may be staged on the Zambian side of the border waiting for his signal."

"I've sent men across the border into Zambia near both border crossings. I also placed armed men at each of the dirt landing strips." A sly smile quirked an edge of Chaipa's mouth. "A Bell helicopter would make a swift craft for CIO use."

"As I'd hoped when we had hands on it in Victoria Falls. What I don't like is how Taljaard is dividing our resources. He has proven a complex quarry. Expect nothing less now." Kagona donned a headset, which pressed against his sore jaw and did little to soften the buffeting noise as the helo lifted off and headed toward the Zambezi River.

"Patching through a message from Chirundu police," the pilot announced.

Chaipa ordered the dispatcher to report.

"The driver we stopped outside Chirundu is a professional hunter." His name rang unfamiliar.

"You are sure it isn't Ian Taljaard?" Chaipa asked.

"Yes, sir. An identity photo confirms this."

Kagona's agitation grew with every word. Another decoy. Taljaard wouldn't separate from the woman. "How did the hunter get the vehicle?"

"From a guide at Makuti. The man asked him to ferry it to Chirundu and deliver it to a Beacon reporter."

Rage filled Kagona. Taljaard mocked him. Rubbed in the fact he knew of CIO movements and the arrest of the reporter. "Show the driver a photo of Taljaard. Get a positive ID of the guide in Makuti." Kagona struggled to form a picture of what the traitor was planning. "How long ago did the hunter leave Makuti?"

"Forty minutes."

"Did he see where the guide was going? Was he with anyone? Was there another vehicle?" A dozen questions came to mind.

"The guide and a woman headed off on foot down Lake Kariba road. They carried packs."

With surprise, Chaipa looked at Kagona. "Would he try to survive in the bush?"

"It's Taljaard's specialty, but his injury will slow him down, as will the woman."

"Where was the hunter to leave the Land Rover in Chirundu?" Chaipa asked the dispatcher.

"Mundana Point Fishing Lodge."

Kagona had fished there many times. He understood his prey's motivation. "Taljaard picked a camp within a few kilometers of the bridges and highway. He wanted the vehicle to be found if we missed it on the road. He is counting on it drawing scrutiny."

"And our concentration of manpower to Chirundu," Chaipa added. "He's likely headed toward Lake Kariba. Should we focus our forces there?"

Kagona considered the necessary actions before answering

both Chaipa and the dispatcher. "I don't want him to reach the lake. There are a hundred boats he could steal. Have police start from Kariba and work toward Makuti, where Taljaard was last seen. Stop every vehicle. Have police in Makuti start from the turn off the Chirundu highway and drive toward Kariba. Don't quit until you find them."

The dispatcher signed off, leaving Kagona to put the pieces of Taljaard's puzzle together.

"Do we change our heading to Kariba?"

"We can't let Taljaard spook us into irrational moves. The damn traitor isn't invincible. We'll find him." Kagona sorted facts in his mind. "We've given him plenty of time to enact his plan. All we have to do is figure it out."

"Perhaps you give him too much credit. He fled after failing to stop Mukono from flying away. How much of a plan could he have made?"

"I've never known him not to have backup. He'd obtained the reporter's vehicle, and you claimed the army shot a hole in its gas tank near Kanyemba. How did that happen? How did he track us to the airfield?"

Chaipa's features blanked with the realization errors made with the reporter and his vehicle rested on his shoulders. "He must have followed Kriegler and our operatives when they drove back to the CIO compound. But why didn't Kriegler tell us about the extra vehicle?"

"Because Taljaard didn't trust him. You're beginning to see how quickly he thinks, and in unexpected ways. He'd have planned a way out after rescuing Bell."

A flash of doubt flickered in Chaipa's eyes. He saw the van crash at the airport as an act of desperation. His face still bore a swollen cheek and a bandage across a cut, but he had abandoned the brace around his neck. "We still must make a decision. Do we fly along the road to Kariba and help search for him? Or head to the Mundana Point Fishing Lodge in Chirundu?"

Kagona pointed at the satchel the junior operative carried. "Are you proficient with that?"

"Most proficient. I have logged over forty hours in the last two weeks in Harare."

"Perfect. You will have a chance to prove your worth."

CHAPTER TWENTY-FIVE

The son of a bitch ripped Joni's clothes off. Anger grabbed Ian so firmly his stomach cramped and mind threatened to melt down. He'd gotten the answers he'd sought, but at what cost? The pictures in his head threatened to tear him apart.

His capability for unfettered situational awareness dropped to zero. He'd be lucky to get them—or more precisely, Joni—out alive. Kriegler wasn't going anywhere except to hell.

He'd given a two-minute warning to Joni and Kriegler in back. The big lorry pulled to the side of the road and Ian jumped out. Kriegler hopped from the back a second later. Ian fought an all-encompassing urge to launch an uppercut at his unsuspecting chin.

Joni caught his hostile glare and tossed him the day pack. "I take it asking the truck to drop us farther down the road was out of the question?"

"Not unless you wanted to be dropped off at the police station."

"Here is fine." She handed down the rest of equipment. "I'm no stranger to hiking."

He liked hearing a little snark in her voice. The old Joni didn't let fear or bad odds slow her down. Still, something bugged him about her discussion with Kriegler. She'd left something unsaid.

Against his base desires, Ian took a subtler tact to let Kriegler know where he stood with him. He caught Joni as she jumped to the ground. Making sure his motion didn't go unnoticed, Ian pulled out the comm unit hanging around her neck and switched her voice-activated mike back to push-to-talk mode.

For a tough guy, he swore Kriegler whitened. The weasel slipped on his comm earbud and hefted a pack onto his back.

Joni stiffened and snatched the unit from Ian's hand. "I hope you heard what you wanted."

"I do what it takes when friends' lives are at stake." He secured the side canvas cover back onto the truck.

"Fine. Live with the consequences." She slipped on her day pack and shouldered his rifle.

"Wait out of sight. We're crossing the road."

Without a word, she stalked after Kriegler.

Bloody hell, he'd done a fricking *fine* job of making his stance perfectly clear. Behind the daggers in her eyes, he'd seen deep hurt. Could he screw up any worse? Yeah, sure. Just give him time.

He donned his gear and caught up with Kriegler and Joni. The lorry joggled back onto the asphalt and rounded the long curve toward the immigration and customs facility a few kilometers away.

"He didn't waste time," Kriegler said. He glanced over at Ian with the same grim look Joni wore. "You must have paid him too well."

Damn critics. "Come on. We're heading to the river." He made sure the road was clear before signaling them across.

"How far?" Joni asked.

"On a good day, with no cares about people seeing us…ten minutes along a nearby dirt road."

"On a bad day?"

"Double that. We have to avoid a shantytown that sits along that road, plus we're not in top form."

"Can we beat Kagona across?"

"His men are already on the river. But we'll deal with that problem when we get there."

He set a grueling pace, ignoring his damn ankle, which had swollen again. Kriegler, who could easily dog his heels, stayed back and corralled Joni between them—whether to help the team or to keep a safe distance from a man who wanted to kill him was unclear. It hardly mattered. Ian had to focus on other parameters.

He skirted an area where several lorries parked and women from the shantytown serviced drivers for a few dollars. He headed toward a rocky knoll covered in scraggly jesse and buffalo thorn. Sunlight cooked his head and face. He looked back to make sure Joni, with her fair skin, had donned his hat. The wide brim shaded nearly to her chin and covered a good part of her neck, which was exposed with her hair tucked up. She eyed him curiously and swatted at ferocious tsetse flies, but said nothing.

He snatched an extra cap hooked to his pack and used the pause to dig out his satellite phone. He activated a path programmed during the lorry ride. With winding animal trails in directions the team didn't want to go, a wrong turn could cost them time.

Contrary to heading toward the water, they gained twenty meters in elevation and passed above and behind the shantytown below. The thicket offered safe passage even if it slowed their progress and increased exposure to the sun and a few houses on an opposing hill. Shade waited below, where trees gathered along the river shore.

Kriegler retrieved the radio scanner. "Time to see what the kids are up to in the local playground." He plugged in an earphone. Satisfaction blossomed immediately. "Bingo. This elevation is giving us a clear signal from the Chirundu police station."

Ian kept them moving while Kriegler, who attached the radio to the outside of his pack, reported.

"Local authorities are heading downstream of the Chirundu bridges to Mundana Point Fishing Lodge. Isn't that the hunter's drop-off point for your Rover?"

"*Yebo.* It's several kilometers from our position."

"It means they have your vehicle."

"Zamani is going to miss that Rover."

"He claimed it can't be traced back to him. Does it point to other compatriots?"

"Just one." Revenge, however slight, tasted sweet. "Wish I could see his face when he finds out."

Joni peered through a break in the thicket toward the Zambezi. "Too bad we aren't in position to cross the river. Their discovery of the vehicle is a perfect diversion for us."

"It is what it is."

Kriegler touched his earpiece. "Hey, sounds like the border is effectively shut down. That line of trucks along the highway will be backing up. Think our driver will report us?"

"Doubt it. He'd have to forfeit the money and delay his delivery."

"What about the police?"

"I suspect in the next few minutes, they will put men on foot and offer a reward to any locals who spot us. A good reason to get off this hillside, in the thicket, and under the trees near the river." Joni's breathing sounded labored as Ian picked up the pace, yet she matched him step for step.

Kriegler answered his sat phone, spoke for a minute and passed on the message. "Our captain is in the boat, waiting to launch. Confirmed the speedboats hightailed it downstream. He wants to talk to you."

"Handle it, Kriegler. I'm not slowing us down."

Kriegler spoke to the captain again. "He's not giving up. Said to tell you he caught a tiger fish this morning while waiting for you."

What the hell? Ian had fished this stretch of the Zambezi dozens of times with tourists. Fishermen had a one in ten chance of landing the fierce buggers once they took the bait. Personally, the bloody things cost him more tackle and lures than the effort rewarded. Unlike his dad, who had fisherman's luck. Yeah, the wayward dad who hadn't bothered to show up for a promised fishing trip two years ago. Too busy off fighting his own battles to satisfy his need for action. Ian had tired of the promises.

He stopped and turned toward Kriegler, who tossed the phone up. Ian pressed on and brought it to his ear. "You picked a damn fine time to walk back into my life."

"Don't be such a prick, son. I'm trying to save your youthful arse."

For a good twenty paces, Ian found nothing to say. He'd buried emotions the call threatened to unleash.

"Whatever diversion you used," his father continued, not fazed by the silence, "it worked…at least for the moment. Now is a good time for me to launch."

"We're a good ten minutes out. If you come now, you'll pinpoint our location."

"I can come partway. Hide behind the little island in the Zambezi. You know the one. Then I can be across to your position in a minute."

"I'm not going to argue. This is my op. My call. Trust me on this, Dad."

No reply left Ian suspecting his father had broken communications. Damn, if guilt didn't fill him and flow into the big hole inside called family.

"I do trust you, son. Holding on my end. Waiting your signal."

Ian swallowed hard and stopped. Meves's starlings, the only birds making noise in the heat of the day, let off harsh calls. He tossed the phone back to Kriegler.

Joni raised inquisitive brows. "Dad? Mr. Irresponsible?"

The memory of his disagreement with her over his family added to his burdened conscience. Was he really that much different from his own father? Could he give up a life of action for someone he loved? Bloody life-is-a-bitch hell, did he even know how to love someone?

"This way." He corrected course.

Ian found himself constantly glancing back at Joni, worried about how she was enduring what had become an oppressively hot, humid day. Her face had reddened and become streaked in dusty sweat. At the first opportunity for cover, she had to hydrate. Those drugs wouldn't have totally flushed from her system.

"I'll let you know if I need to stop." She brushed away insects going after the sweat on her neck.

"We've passed the shantytown and don't have much farther to go. Once we're down the hillside and under the trees, we'll pause for a water break."

A minute later the footsteps behind him stopped. He turned and saw Joni with her head tilted, listening. "We're being followed."

He was aware of what made the rustling sounds around them. An irritation more than a threat, but anything that slowed them down could prove deadly. "I suggest we keep moving."

They headed downhill toward the river and towering trees lining its banks. As the ground flattened onto an upper level of the flood plain, the bush thinned. A crunching under Ian's boots brought him to a halt at the edge of an open field partially covered in animal tracks hardened into a mud substrate. The roughened ground promised risky passage for his ankle. At least the rejuvenating rain of the season had yet to tangle the fresh undergrowth into impassable, thorny masses.

Joni picked up a circular seedpod that had floated down from a tree. "What are these?"

"Trouble."

Her lips thinned into a dangerous look demanding not to be patronized.

"Elephant cookies," he added.

"And I'm guessing that's not a good thing."

"A lot of animals eat them. We don't have time to stay around and find out which ones. Once we reach the trees, we'll cut back north to a decent pickup point for the boat."

Slow, crushing steps came toward their position. Bloody bad timing.

"Incoming," Kriegler called.

It took a second for Ian to realize what Kriegler meant. The beat of distant rotors reverberated in the air.

"Follow me. Stay close. We have more than one visitor to contend with. And for God's sake, do whatever I tell you."

The open space proved deceptive. Elephants and buffalo had torn up the mud substrate in the dry season, and a recent damp day had served to stir up the mud again. Elephant-size depressions, footprints, and rough dried mud made every step with a pack difficult. Joni danced over dung piles mixed in.

Midway across the space, five elephants strolled out of the thicket into the open.

Ian signaled the team to stop. Kriegler was slow to get the message and took several steps past him. Enough that it startled the elephants.

All except a large bull with daunting tusks halted. He took several steps, stopped and eyed the team. He turned back toward his herd of cows and encouraged them to head off toward the shade trees.

Ian didn't move. A sixth sense told him this guy wasn't through. "Kriegler, work your way behind me. Joni, pass up my rifle."

With slow movements, Joni slipped it into Ian's outstretched hand. "Won't your bow work?" she whispered.

"Yes, but it wouldn't bring him down instantly. Stay close behind me and don't panic at anything he does. Movement only encourages him to charge."

"Great."

Time acted against them. The elephants, although capable of fast speeds, moved slowly. Meanwhile, the chopper grew swiftly louder.

As soon as the other elephants had safely trotted away, the bull faced them again, standing proud and observing them down the length of his long tusks. His trunk sniffed the air.

"Sorry for interrupting your travel, *mngane*." Ian's words brought the bull's full concentration on him. "Push off, now. Go join the others." A shot to save their lives from a raging bull would bring Kagona and his colleagues down on them.

The bull's large ears flapped to cool his body. Mud and bits of debris stuck to the bull's back. With a sudden burst of speed, he charged forward. After a few body lengths, he stopped and trumpeted his irritation.

To their credit, neither Joni nor Kriegler moved.

The beat of a chopper moved closer. All were frozen in place…watching the bull and his large eyes staring them down. The bull glanced toward the rest of his group, then cautiously followed. He picked up speed as he went, but kept constant vigilance on the team's location. The thicket near the trees finally swallowed his giant gray form.

"Move it," Ian commanded. They scrambled for the nearest clump of thicket. Grunts and groans sounded with their jolting steps, but they made questionable cover.

The helicopter closed in overhead.

"Everyone down." Ian yanked down some branches of thorny brush and held them over their huddled bodies and camo-colored packs.

Kriegler checked the chopper as it went over. "It's Kagona's Alouette. Why isn't he down in Kariba?"

"Because he's thinking like I am. This is the shortest path to safety. He's not going to add to his failures. I made a mistake believing he would."

"Don't sell yourself short, Taljaard. It took guts to follow on the tail of your Land Rover. Every security person in Chirundu is likely aware you're on the run, and yet you strolled right up to their doorstep."

"Obviously it didn't work."

"Something must have worked. We made it this far."

Ian eyed Kriegler. "Sucking up won't make me less inclined to kill you when I have the chance."

"I meant every word."

The chopper made a cursory pass over the area, then headed upstream toward Lake Kariba for several kilometers. They scampered for the trees. Minutes later it returned along the river and headed north past the Chirundu bridges to where popular fish camps hugged the river.

"Ready to call for the boat?" Kriegler asked.

"As soon as the chopper lands."

Another five minutes passed until the Alouette put down close enough they could hear it land.

Kriegler didn't look happy. "Sounds barely north of the Chirundu road where we stopped. Why didn't Kagona circle the helo longer? Staying in the air, he could have tied us down until ground forces could move in on foot."

"Because he isn't sure we're here."

"Then why didn't he land farther downstream at the dirt strip nearer the Mundana Point Fish Camp?"

Regardless of his jaded feelings toward Kriegler, Ian had reached the same disturbing conclusion. "Kagona is hedging his bets by coming here, and likely directing the hunt for us in Kariba from afar. Since he didn't land near the camp, I'm guessing he knows it's a false lead. He's suffered enough misdirection for one day."

He handed Kriegler his rifle, then released his bow from the tabs attaching it to his pack.

Kriegler shouldered the rifle. "From my days working for him, I learned Kagona only takes bold steps if he minimizes risk. He must have something to tip winning in his favor. Your escapades have put too many dents in his reputation."

"If he discovers you're still alive, it will add one more."

Kriegler brought out the satellite phone to call the boat.

"Wait." Joni reached out and touched his wrist before quickly withdrawing from it.

Ian recognized she sensed something wrong. "What is it?"

"It's what Bram said about minimizing risk. I've a hunch what Kagona has in mind to keep a step ahead of us. Sending the boat now could be risky."

"Can we work around it?"

"I've an idea, but we need to be close to the pickup point and ready to cross the river. It's risky."

"All the better." Ian handed her a water bottle.

A grateful gleam flickered in her eyes. Somewhere in the night she'd suffered a loss of confidence. This trial helped the strong woman to resurface. A satisfied feeling flushed through him. Joni had kept her head, assessed the problem, and now created a plan, regardless of the poor odds.

She refused to give up on the team and survival. Maybe, just maybe, she wouldn't give up on him.

CHAPTER TWENTY-SIX

From a few hundred feet above the Zambezi River, Kagona had methodically searched for signs of Taljaard along a stretch of the river several kilometers up and downstream from the border town of Chirundu. Two bridges crossed between Zimbabwe and Zambia there, but at the moment, traffic headed in only one direction—into the country.

His men had at least done something right.

"We've cut off an easy exit for Taljaard." Chaipa had reached the same conclusion.

"Don't be too overconfident. The river narrows along several reaches. Dirt roads run to the water on both banks, making it easy for a quick boat crossing and getaway. Perfect conditions for Taljaard."

"How do you know he won't get the woman out and stay behind to take revenge on you."

Kagona shook his head and grimaced as his jaw throbbed. "He and I are different. He has one goal in mind…escape. He'll waste no effort seeking vengeance."

"He killed Kriegler."

"Kriegler was a traitor, who would still be free to ply his

trade if Taljaard hadn't killed him. Speaking of our old friend, any word on where Taljaard dumped the body?"

"No reports, but finding him hasn't been our immediate focus."

"Everything matters when Taljaard is involved. Find the body."

The Alouette had landed on uneven ground in an opening about two hundred meters through thicket and trees from the Zambezi River. The engine spun down in a cacophony of descending pitch, heightening his urge to surprise the agitator who believed he'd fooled his enemy.

Kagona longed for a one-on-one with Taljaard as payback for a dislocated jaw. No matter how many decoys Taljaard dangled, everything in Kagona's mind pointed to Chirundu. The closest border crossing to where the plane with Minister Mukono took off was Chirundu. Taljaard and Bell hid out nearby.

No argument or assumptions could change Kagona's assessment. Their capture was simply a matter of time. The task of grounding Taljaard in place, and preventing his crossing the river while Kagona tightened the noose, was assigned to the junior officer.

Although small, Chirundu had the reputation for being a godforsaken border town. More transients than locals filled the streets. Truckers passing through waited, often for a day or more, in long queues to cross the border. Prostitutes came in from surrounding villages or the nearest towns to service truckers. Add to that tourists crossing from Zambia into Zimbabwe planning to fish, camp, and safari. New faces of all nationalities and people carrying packs raised little notice and would likely not be reported.

But Kagona and Chaipa had experience with the traitor. They knew Taljaard's modus operandi.

The junior officer climbed out, taking his oversize satchel with him. Kagona and Chaipa followed, the latter carrying a field radio. Behind him, he ordered the pilot and armed guard to stay with the helicopter. Kagona had been burned once when Miss Bell stole his Alouette. She wouldn't have a chance to repeat the event.

A line of thicket blocked his view of the river. He walked along the brush until a break opened. Several meters later, he emerged onto a maintained lawn spotted with numerous shade trees, creating a cooling canopy of green. A fish camp with a main building and a half dozen large tents spread out across the lawn.

Closer to Chirundu than the camp Taljaard had chosen for the delivery of the Rover, Kagona selected this central place near the highway and bridges for a command center. Reports had come in from police and CIO officers. No sign of Taljaard had been discovered in Makuti, on the road to Lake Kariba, or in Chirundu. Impatience filled Kagona. He wanted news. Good news.

The radio Chaipa carried sprang to life. Disjointed reports came in. No one had crossed the Kariba Dam in the last hour. Officers had been dispatched to the closest roads with boat access to Lake Kariba. No reports of missing boats had surfaced.

Kagona fought back frustration. Facts were needed to develop a picture of the plan Taljaard enacted. He lit a cigarette.

By the time he'd taken three drags, hope came across the airwaves. A red helicopter had been spotted on the Zambian side of Lake Kariba. CIO officers sent to check it out arrived too late. The helicopter had taken off and disappeared.

He looked over his shoulder back to Chaipa. "That could be the Adventure Tours craft."

"Perhaps we should be headed to Kariba."

"It's an enticement to draw us away from here." Kagona held steadfast to his assessment of Taljaard's tactics. "Have faith, Chaipa. Chirundu is the quickest route to Zambia. Taljaard wants Bell out of the country. He wouldn't fuck around in the bush or take the longer drive to Kariba."

"Why would he send the Rover to where he planned to escape?"

"Because he's willing to take risks, rather like I am. That's why we've survived for so long. Taljaard wants me to believe I've been fooled again and retrain my focus on Lake Kariba."

"More clues are pointing there."

"Taljaard weaves a tapestry of deception. He either kept well ahead or behind his Rover in another vehicle and likely is on foot somewhere near Chirundu, biding his time before crossing the Zambezi."

"And if you're wrong?"

"I'm not."

Chaipa appeared skeptical of the news. "It would be too soon for the helo to have collected Taljaard off the lake."

"He might be fast, but without an aircraft, the time is too short to have dropped the Rover with the hunter and made it onto the lake."

"The helicopter might be positioning to pluck him off a boat or pick him up onshore."

"I want updates on where that helicopter is at all times." Kagona knew the radar in this region had deteriorated. Upgrades provided by the Chinese had yet to become functional and likely wouldn't until the Chinese completed a new air base near the diamond district. Tracking a low-flying helicopter along the border would be hit-and-miss, if not impossible. "Find out if it was the helicopter Taljaard used last week." He dropped his cigarette butt and ground it into the dirt.

Kagona walked across a tree-shaded lawn toward a steep embankment with a three-meter drop to the water. A wood deck set up with tables and chairs overlooked the Zambezi River. Campers' tents and the lodge building sat back with a view of the water. A set of steps took fishermen down to a floating dock. He spotted a speedboat and fishing pontoon tied up below.

Chaipa had the satellite phone to his ear again and walked

away from the others. Once in a position to ensure privacy, he partially turned so no one could approach him unexpectedly.

The junior officer crouched in a spot on the lawn with a large gap in the canopy above. He opened his satchel. Inside laid the shiny black body of a small drone. As much as youth depended on technology, Kagona feared the intricacies promised trouble.

"How quickly can that be airborne?"

"Fast, sir." He assembled the parts.

"How long does the battery last?"

"About twenty minutes. Then I'll have to change it."

"How many backups do you have?"

"Four."

Kagona wished for additional drones and a good number more batteries to maintain a constant presence in the sky. Without revealing the crisis concerning Chitima known only to a handful, he'd been lucky to get one drone away from those monitoring the Harare protests.

True to his word, the officer had the drone ready to launch in a few minutes. It whirred to life and bolted into the air, hanging like a giant spider ready to leap onto its target. Kagona nodded at the young man. The drone rose swiftly, sending a live video feed of both banks of the river and the nearby bridges to the control tablet.

The video had surprising clarity, even when light reflected off the water. To the south, elephants wandered along the edge of a shaded lawn near an old fish camp.

"Target the narrower stretches of the river. They'd make for the quickest escape across the river. Go several kilometers each side of the bridges. Watch for boats on either side that could pick Taljaard up, or boats docked on our shore that they could steal. Taljaard and the woman are adept at fieldwork. Check out anything suspicious."

"Yes, sir." The officer lowered the drone's elevation for a closer view of the ground. "North or south first?"

"Your choice. My guess is they are close and waiting to cross the Zambezi. They'll be hiding beneath the tree canopy."

Chaipa walked over, not looking happy. He signaled Kagona to join him away from the drone operator.

"What is it?"

"The vehicle identification has been traced on the Land Rover we stopped in Chirundu." Chaipa paused, looking unsure as whether to continue.

"I don't have time for indecision. Who has been aiding Taljaard?"

Chaipa cleared his throat. "*We* have. The vehicle is registered to the CIO. It disappeared three years ago."

Snags and holes left Joni's shirt looking like swiss cheese by the time they emerged from a thorny thicket at the edge of the trees lining the Zambezi. Regardless of easier paths to travel where cottages and old fish camps lay along the river, Ian had woven them in and out of bush until they approached their destination.

A distant but recognizable buzz reached Joni's ears. "Take cover." The direction seemed hard to pinpoint with the tree canopy overhead.

Bram shielded himself near a spiky tree trunk. "From what?"

"A drone."

He looked up. "I feel like Big Brother is watching."

"He is. Head to that tree." Ian pointed at a huge one with grayish bark and made up of three separate emerging trunks, each large enough to hide a man. They tossed the camouflage packs under a nearby bush.

The canopy shielded them from up high, but the bush beneath had been cleared to the river for a cottage they'd passed. A low-flying drone could see under the canopy. Ian's reason for keeping to the thickets became clear.

"I can't tell if the sound is coming off the river or from inland."

"Doesn't matter." Ian loosened a large creeper hanging from the tree. "We're going up. Kriegler first."

Bram, with long, strong arms, made climbing look easy. "I hate that the bad guys are going high-tech these days."

"Kagona's been using drones to monitor the protests in Harare." Ian handed up his bow. "We can only hope he doesn't have more than one."

Movement caught her eye out over the river. "Ian, go up. Quick."

She snatched Ian's hat off her head and dived into a cleft between two parts of the trunk. Ian disappeared. Above her, he and Bram stretched out along a main limb as wide as their bodies and blended into the greenery.

The drone maneuvered closer to the tree line along the shore and slowed. Her position offered protection from that vantage, but the cleft left her exposed on the inland side. She tried to shift to a better position, but the day pack still on her back blocked movement. She flattened and stuffed Ian's hat into her waistband.

A remote handler manipulating the drone under the canopy with numerous unseen obstacles was nothing short of suicide for the little machine. Their detection depended on the skill of the controller and how well the team blended into their surroundings.

The drone came into view of one eye. She avoided looking directly at the machine and its camera. Time in the wilds with Ian last week taught her how animal brains pick up eyes of predators watching them. That included humans, who use the same primitive survival mechanism. A human worked the controls and studied the live video. She picked a spot below its landing feet to track it.

The drone hovered along the river shore, waiting…watching.

The whirling carbon propellers disturbed a heron wading below. With a broad flap of its wings, it launched into the air, disturbing nearby storks. The drone rose to avoid the birds. It continued to rise.

Relief slipped out. She listened for its retreat, but the whir grew louder. She triggered her comm. "It's overhead. Coming toward the inland side."

She retreated from her position enough to slip off the day pack and hide it in the cleft. Careful to not move too quickly, she slipped around the trunk to the side facing the river. The tree, positioned at the edge of a copse and slightly out from the others, increased her exposure. The propellers burred ominously close. Sheltered for the moment, she realized if the drone shifted, it could view nearly two-thirds of the uneven trunk.

"Raise your arms overhead," Ian whispered.

She snaked her hands up along her body and stuck them up overhead.

The drone dropped low not far outside the umbrella of branches. Its whir left her shaking. It skidded sideways just above a nearby thicket. The trunk, with its odd shape, wrapped around her on that side. The other side offered no such protection.

As though reading her thoughts, the drone moved.

So did Ian. Two strong hands grasped around her wrists and slid her up along the trunk. Once her feet settled on a solid branch, Bram and Ian released their holds. Ian tugged Joni back with him against the trunk. They froze, huddled together, praying the act of repositioning the drone forced the operator to focus on obstacles and not their movement.

Ian's encircling hold revealed the rapid pounding of his heart beneath her ear. His fingers squeezed reassurance, but his arms held on as though afraid she'd be torn from his grasp. He didn't fear his capture. He dreaded hers.

Her lungs strained for air she refused to draw. The starlings had ceased calling and cicadas dropped silent. The buzz of the drone sawed into her nerves.

Minutes that seemed like hours passed before the drone rose and left. Joni waited to speak until her ears no longer detected the buzz. "Sounds like it headed upriver toward Lake Kariba."

"It won't get far. If those are the ones the CIO has been flying over the protest in Harare, their batteries last only fifteen to twenty minutes. It wasted time here."

She leaned back from his chest, but he held on. "Think he detected us?"

"No way to know until the patrol boats arrive."

And Kagona takes me away. Distorted memories flashed in her mind. The small scar cut through Kagona's eyebrow. The slow-motion beat of the Alouette rotor keeping them aloft. The gleam of wild power in the bastard's eyes as he tucked the safety hook into her fingers. And his euphoric satisfaction when he placed a boot to her backside and shoved. Shudders racked her body.

Ian hugged her tight. "Don't give up on me, Joni."

Her body wanted to stay wrapped in security, but her mind fully recognized the futility. She lifted her head. "I know what he'd do to all of us. I can't let that happen."

Ian's shoulders relaxed. With tender familiarity, he brushed clumps of leaf mold out of her hair. Something warred behind his stormy blue eyes, and she doubted it had anything to do with the drone.

"We're not going down without a fight. Kagona will not win this round." He kissed her forehead and moved to another branch. "Stay put till the drone passes again. I'm going to take a quick look at the landscape." With that, he left her propped against the trunk and headed higher in the tree.

Bram watched him go, looking wary of where he stood with Ian.

Ian made it almost to the top of the tallest tree in the grove.

Her concerns he might be spotted eased. His placement and clothes offered decent camouflage. He'd done this before.

A faint sound reached her ears, one that would have been drowned out by the river, cicadas, and buzzing insects if she hadn't been waiting to hear it. She waited until it passed before swiping at ants marching across her pant leg.

Ian rejoined them. "We're at a decent location to rendezvous with the boat. There's a small island for him to shelter from approaching boats once we get rid of that drone. I could see at least one speedboat still hanging around the bridges. What we need is a rock-solid distraction to send them elsewhere." Ian touched her arm, telegraphing strength and camaraderie between them. "You're the drone expert."

"Expert, no. Decent operator, maybe." If he realized her lack of expertise, he'd risk the crocs and swim across the Zambezi. "Drones and I have a turbulent history." Rhino dung left fragrant failure on her mind. But the current price of failure had inched higher than humiliation. This time it meant death.

"We can't cross the river with one watching. If spotted, I guarantee Kagona, with every speedboat in Chirundu at his disposal, will stop us before we reach Zambia."

"I agree." Bram straddled the big branch. "Lemmon had confidence you'd know what to do with drones. So do I. How about telling us how to defeat that thing without giving away our position?"

"Theory and experience are two different animals." Her heart rate had barely quieted, but her mind functioned clearly. No part of Lemmon's plan had gone perfectly from the start. Ian, Bram, and she had all made mistakes, and yet success had happened. Sipho's father had been freed and they'd uncovered Chitima. A sweet finale would be getting everyone out alive.

She looked over to Ian, crouching on the massive branch. "If Kagona is scouting out places he thinks we'd use to cross, then he has a lot of river to cover. We can use his search to plan a distraction. How long do you need to get the boat across and back again?"

"It's not a speedboat, so maybe ten minutes under perfect conditions."

"And if not-so-perfect ones?"

"Hell if I know." A curious smile rose at the corners of his mouth. "What do you have in mind?"

"You remember that risky ploy I mentioned earlier? I think I've another angle on it that will add to our success. Something I've never tried, but I discovered the parts I need to pull it off in Bram's day pack."

Bram risked staring right at her. "You're damn good at pulling things together, *bokkie*. I've seen it every time you take to the sky. Tell me what to do and I'm in."

Ian rose and balanced on the branch. "Me, too."

"I'll need to assemble the drone while someone gets me the GPS coordinates for a spot well to the north. A place that looks good for a crossing but is out of sight of our stretch, and gives the rescue boat time to cross both ways."

A satisfied smirk thinned Ian's mouth. "I know just the place."

"Good. I owe Kagona a taste of his own twisted medicine."

"Poison, I hope." Ian snapped a stick he played with in his fingers.

The details solidified in her mind. Risky, with low odds of success, but at this point they had little to lose. "You guys up for a little spoofing?"

Bram grabbed onto the creeper. "Beats hanging out in this tree like a bunch of baboons."

As if on cue, the defamed creatures barked in a nearby tree. Loud screams and thrashing answered from a thicket.

Ian set a hand against the trunk over her head. "They've been following us since we crossed the road. Not sure why, but it's a good reason to collect our stuff."

Bram made the ground, so Ian held out the creeper for her. She rappelled down the tree with the vine in hand and boots on the trunk. Not sure why, once down, she saluted up at Ian. As the team leader in his territory, he'd chosen to rely on her, when hours early she'd displayed less than stellar mental control. A mistake or confidence well placed? Good thing the boys didn't know about the rhino midden.

Ian yanked hard on the creeper and gained a little more give. He swung down like Tarzan, minus the echoing yodel, grinning all the way. His landing protected an ankle he'd favored all day but neglected to mention, highlighting his indomitable spirit. Unintentionally, his silence and fortitude reminded her of the cost of failure.

CHAPTER TWENTY-SEVEN

President Jacob Tangwerai eyed with curiosity, and a touch of trepidation, Mozambique's ambassador to Zimbabwe. The request for an emergency meeting had come directly from the president of Mozambique and claimed dire consequences if denied. The ambassador refused a drink and showed no inclination for discussion of polite frivolities.

They sat across from one another like sober men contemplating a doomsday event. No interpreter accompanied the ambassador, but his English was as good as his Portuguese, although both heavily accented by his tribal tongue.

"Ambassador Chimoio, I have opened my schedule to accommodate the curious request from your president. Please explain the reason for this visit."

"Very well, President Tangwerai. Our country has received notification of a questionable shipment headed toward our border and the port of Beira. We are hoping this report is false but are taking extra precautions to ensure the transport is stopped."

Shock coursed through Jacob's system, but he maintained a neutral expression. "Our friendly relations with Mozambique assure many shipments go through your ports. We do our best to police the contents and stop smugglers and thieves."

Chimoio leaned forward. "Yellowcake of this quantity is not likely handled by smugglers."

"Surely your report is mistaken." Jacob worked hard to portray surprise with a touch of indignation. "Such a shipment must be registered with appropriate international authorities. And while Zimbabwe has profitable uranium deposits, there is no program as of yet for processing the ore. Even if we did, a shipment out of the country is within our right."

"We do not argue your rights, but shipments to Iran would break international treaties."

"Vicious rumors."

"Are they?" From a flat satchel on his lap the ambassador removed a paper-size photo. It showed a fenced area with large tanks, several metal warehouse buildings, and what appeared to be wellheads.

Jacob had seen photos of the complex. Not from this higher angle, but ones with similar details to recognize this one came from the uranium complex.

"This could be anywhere in Africa and shows no connection to the Iranians."

"No, but this one does." Chimoio presented a second photo of two men near the complex.

Jacob look carefully and noted the men not only knelt—they prayed. "Fabricated. What credible source supposedly has your president's ear?"

The ambassador sat back. "Former Zimbabwean finance minister Edward Mukono, who served under your administration."

"Impossible." Or was it? According to the CIO, he was on a plane to Iran.

"Our president received a phone call from the president of South Africa. He has spoken with Finance Minister Mukono. He claims to have been imprisoned by your Central Intelligence Organization."

"More vicious rumors. The man stole millions from Zimbabwe. We temporarily held him while we investigated the thefts. Recently his political friends illegally released him and he fled the country." At least that was the story Kagona claimed to be releasing. An update with the CIO was in order.

"I've been told he has documentation of the funds dealing with the uranium."

"Zimbabwe has its political enemies. Someone is building a case of misinformation."

"What about the missing Africa News Beacon reporter? Protesters in this very city claim he uncovered evidence of the mining and then disappeared, supposedly into your jails."

Jacob feared his features no longer hid the rage building inside him. Someone had leaked inside knowledge held tightly by the CIO. "I'm afraid you have me at a loss. I'm not aware we have imprisoned this reporter."

"Whatever you know or don't know at this point does not matter. Minister Mukono also forwarded his knowledge to the Americans. If any unsanctioned yellowcake crosses the Mozambique border, they will levy heavy sanctions against us and withdraw much needed funding. Our unemployment is over twenty percent. Our coffers are dependent on American generosity. Sanctions are something we cannot risk."

"And what do you propose I do to ease Mozambique's concerns, Mr. Chimoio?"

"You must decide for your country. But I pass along a message from my president. Inspectors are looking for your shipment. If it enters our country, we will expose it. However, we wish to be good neighbors and continue to provide Zimbabwe a port for trade. If the yellowcake stays within your borders, knowledge of this act will remain mere rumor, at least from Mozambique."

Chimoio stood and waited until Jacob rose. "Thank you for the timely audience, President Tangwerai." He gave a polite nod of his head.

Jacob motioned him out before turning back to his desk and contemplating the next course of action. Fatal mistakes had been made. Time to glean the details and cover up.

Twenty minutes had passed. Twenty wasted minutes. No sightings of Taljaard or Bell or the red helicopter. No river crossings had gone unchallenged. They had not escaped.

The drone had uncovered elephants munching thicket, impalas drinking at a small pool, baboons playing in trees, locals strolling near the shantytown and Chirundu, pale tourists at a fish camp, and boats loitering along both sides of the river. But no Taljaard or Bell.

"Every minute this drone is on the ground, Taljaard is free to move."

"It's a two-minute turnaround, sir." The junior officer knelt in the hot sun, changing the drone battery. "There is a lot of land to search out there, but I won't quit until we have him."

"Taljaard is a pro. Don't become overconfident with this drone. Its role is to shut down his movement. Feet on the ground will find him."

Twice the operative had caught movement that uncovered nothing. While providing decent aerial views, close-up details lacked clarity. Taljaard understood camouflage. He'd use it.

The officer ran back to collect his controller and work from the shade.

Kagona followed, checking his watch. "Every minute goes to the enemy. Your next battery swap will be faster."

"Yes, sir." The young man wiped beaded sweat off his dark forehead. A single tap to an icon launched the drone into the sky. "I'll do a high overview first. Make sure no one has moved on the Zambezi."

On the small screen, treetops came into view, then the fish camp, then water, and finally the entire width of the river and the two bridges upstream.

No wakes rolled across the Zambezi's surface except from patrol boats, one returning near the bridges and the others to the north near the Mundana Point Fishing Lodge.

"Head downstream."

The drone dropped toward the river. A green bar shortened as the battery slowly discharged. Kagona picked up a second tablet receiving flight video. He brought up the one from the last flight and played it, skipping ahead and replaying various parts. "Where are you hiding, Taljaard?"

Kagona switched his focus toward Chaipa, who'd wandered off to contact headquarters again. Reports from Kariba were five minutes late.

From a distance, Chaipa caught Kagona's scrutiny. Something in his protégé's expression made Kagona believe he'd been the topic of discussion. Chaipa shifted away. The phone disappeared from his ear. After several seconds, he spoke again to someone.

A dropped call? Trouble getting answers? Perhaps Kagona relied too greatly on Chaipa to handle communications. Overreliance allowed corruption room to operate. He'd been on the phone longer than seemed necessary to gain updates unless there had been a break. Body language killed that possibility.

No time today to act on harbored suspicions. After Taljaard was secured, Kagona would have the calls traced. Find out what contacts Chaipa nurtured. Never ever underestimate anyone, even your friends.

The drone officer worked quietly, offering no alarms.

Kagona peered at the battery health on the controller. "How much longer until it must head home?"

"Six minutes."

From the tracking map, he saw the drone had worked three kilometers downstream. The controller had a five-kilometer range. Fruitless time ticked past.

"One minute until I bring it home for battery change."

"Stretch it out." Kagona had no will to play it safe.

"Sir, we could risk losing the drone."

"I've faith in your skills."

Chaipa strolled over, his expression too bland to ascertain his mood. "Taljaard seems to have vanished."

Kagona straightened. "He's hunkered down, waiting."

"There's plenty of bush for him to hide. I ordered trailing dogs to Makuti. But we have no object for him to scent on."

"We don't need his. I have Miss Bell's jacket with us."

Chaipa grinned and pulled out his phone. He stepped away to pass on the information.

"Mr. Kagona." The drone operator's voice wavered with fear. "We have a problem."

Kagona looked at the control screen. The video flickered. Faded in and out.

The operative tensed. "If the drone loses my signal, it will automatically land. That could put it in the river."

"Bring it in over the land."

"I already have, sir." Treetops flew by as the drone dropped in elevation. The video blanked in and out.

"Look." Both Kagona and the operative shouted at the same moment.

Someone moved—limped, to be more accurate. A white man in typical khaki wear with a pack on his back and a rifle over his shoulder. He wore a safari hat. Taljaard's signature.

"Stay on that man."

"I'm trying. The drone isn't responding to my signals."

The video streaked and grew grainy. Nothing but trees appeared for several seconds. Then the man appeared and pointed up toward the drone. He looked back toward someone.

The video faded, parts pixelated, but a woman appeared with a controller in hand.

"Bell." Satisfaction played on her face as she looked up at them and punched something on her controller.

The video went blank.

The operative pressed at the home button and garnered no response. "She's jammed our drone, sir. Without a signal, it will go down."

"Can you get their GPS position off the video?"

The operative replayed the video to where Taljaard appeared. He marked it and then enlarged the map to fit the screen.

Chaipa had the local police on radio and issued coordinates for them to raid. Boat motors roared on the river. A boat on the water near the bridges headed north, and others pulled out from the shore and followed.

Kagona stabbed a finger in the operative's chest. "Have a police 4x4 pick you up. I want that fucking drone found."

He waved Chaipa toward the shore and beat him to the wood stairs leading down to the dock. The boat had keys aboard and full fuel. Kagona eased the throttle back and edged them into the river before pushing in full power.

The horsepower beneath him electrified every bone. Choking the life from Taljaard promised a sweeter thrill.

Chaipa tapped him on the shoulder, looking confused, because they were headed in the opposite direction as everyone else. "Where the hell are we going?"

"Watch, and I'll show you how to catch Taljaard."

Glints of light reflected off the Zambezi as Ian scanned the river through binoculars from high in his perch atop the tree. Kriegler's police scanner lit up with calls to head three kilometers north of Chirundu. In spite of the odds stacked against her, Joni's ploy had succeeded in misdirecting the enemy. Euphoria rose.

Below, Kriegler radioed Ian's dad to get his butt on the river. Damn awkward time for a family reunion. Joni switched out the drone battery.

The faraway purr of a boat engine grabbed his attention. The pitch was higher than he expected from a pontoon boat. He shifted the binoculars downstream toward the bridges.

"Bloody hell." He hit his comm. "Kriegler, have our boat wait behind the island. We've company coming in fast. A single speedboat." He adjusted the binoculars. "Two men. Can't tell for sure, but I'm figuring it's Kagona."

"*Kak.* Why send his men one way and head another? Always was an unpredictable bastard, but he's not the type to run from a fight."

The truth sank in. "He's running to one. Knows me too well. Likely he's revisiting the spots the drone double-checked."

Below, Kriegler said something to Joni and handed over his radio and satellite phone. Ian looked down through the branches. Kriegler snatched Ian's hat and slipped on a pack.

Joni grabbed his arm, but he brushed her off.

"What the hell are you doing, Kriegler?"

"Making sure you and Joni make it across. Wait for Kagona to get out of the boat." He snatched up Ian's rifle. "This is your chance. Don't waste it."

"Hell, no, Kriegler. We stick together."

He didn't answer. Instead, Kriegler slipped off his comm unit and earpiece and ran off toward Chirundu.

Ian headed down, hampered by his ankle, while Kriegler angled toward the shore. Joni rummaged around in the remaining big pack and pulled out a semiauto taken from the accident. She checked the chamber for brass before sticking it in her back waistband.

"Forget it, Joni."

She glanced up the tree at him, then took off after Kriegler.

Fucking great. Did no one on this team listen to him, or did they all want to get themselves killed?

Ian hit the ground, a string of cusswords accompanying the pain. He snatched up his bow and hustled after Joni, staggering like a drunk and ignoring the screams shooting up his leg. While Kriegler attempted to be noticed, Joni at least kept to the thicket as well as possible. That slowed her progress enough she'd dropped well behind Kriegler's fast-moving position.

The direction of the boat engine shifted. They'd picked up on Kriegler's movement. In moments, Kagona would land. Joni had guts to run toward the man of her nightmares to save another who only compounded those fears. A lasting effect of the drug or a damn gutsy move by a brave woman?

Her attempts at stealth did well, but his trained ear made following easy and the bush with its natural traps meant he'd catch up quickly. With her guard down assessing Kagona's arrival, she'd headed into a thicket of buffalo thorn. The hooked thorns grabbed onto her clothes.

In haste, she peeled them away, ripping cloth when necessary. He set his bow down. The last thorn released as he closed in, still unnoticed. She'd taken two steps when he grabbed her arm. Much to his surprise, she pivoted, grabbed his shirt, and launched a knee to his groin. He chopped his hand high onto her upper thigh. The stun stopped the attack dead.

A grunt escaped before he covered her mouth.

She yanked his hand off. "Damn it, Ian" came out in a fierce whisper. "Let go. We have to save Bram."

"Sorry, but my ankle can't afford to chase you down again." He divested her of the gun and tucked it at his waist.

"You don't understand." She attempted to pull free. "Kagona has to be stopped."

"Kriegler is bent on saving you. By going after him, you're negating the risk he is taking."

"Bram can't take on Kagona by himself."

"Give him credit. I'm guessing he is quite proficient at evasion."

"But he plans to lead them away. That increases the chances he'll be caught."

"He knows the consequences." For some damn reason, his assessment left her frowning.

"There are only two men."

"For now. They'll call in reinforcements once they confirm it's Kriegler…or at least think it's me."

"It'll take time for them to arrive."

"Forget it." An urgent wildness gleamed in her eyes, not so different from when she'd attacked Bram. Kagona's presence had triggered bad memories, and Ian didn't like the results. "You're in no shape to deal with Kagona."

"If Bram dies without our help, it'll come back to haunt you every day of your life. We can't leave Kagona alive."

"We're not assassins, Joni. Your conscience couldn't live with that."

"My conscience can't live with leaving Bram at Kagona's mercy. I'm going after him."

"Hell, no. Your protection is primary."

She fisted his shirt. "There's no choice. This isn't about me. It's about Kagona and the people he's destroyed. He has to be stopped, for what he did to Chief Zwide and untold others. He'll play a deadly game in the helo with Bram. He did it to me."

He pulled her closer. "What happened with Kagona?"

"He and his aide…" She gritted her teeth, building strength to let the rest out. "They threw me out. Twice. The second time, Kagona disconnected my safety hook, then grinned as he shoved."

A deep burn built inside him as emotions contorted her face.

"I survived, Ian. For others in the past, it was their last step."

Mind games were Kagona's forte. But that he'd used the very instrument Joni loved to fly to enact his dirty deed made killing the bastard a justifiable task. Ian hugged her tight, wishing away the evil from her memories but knowing it futile.

"Please, Ian. Whatever Bram did to me, he doesn't deserve what Kagona will hand out. If that means killing Kagona, I will."

He stared into the tangled brush, as knotted and unforgiving as his insides. As much as Joni longed for Kagona's death, she'd no idea how to kill a man. Her only chance of success was to take him unaware, kill him before he knew he'd become a target. Impossible. Her untrained conscience would interfere and bring her face-to-face with the beast. Against a trained killer, she'd lose.

Ian released her. "The only way to catch Kagona is if I go. Taking you along would kill us both."

"You can hardly walk."

"I caught you, didn't I?" He scooped up his bow.

"I need to be a part of this, Ian."

"Bloody hell, you're the key part. Someone has to see to our rescue. The only person left is you. Guide my dad to the pickup point. If he putters along the shore, Kagona will see him. Worse, if no one meets him, he'll land to find us. We can't risk that. If you can't find us in two minutes, head to Zambia."

Uncertainty and assessment played behind eyes well aware every moment of indecision risked Bram's life. "I'll bring in the boat," she finally said.

"Also, see if you can raise Mad Mike. Tell him to get his peg leg up here. We'll need a speedy exit once we cross the Zambezi." Ian removed the knife from his ankle sheath and folded it into her hand. "If we fail and you get caught, Kagona will come close to you. Keep it hidden until the last second."

Her high-strung mood had calmed, but he guessed her mind was on the edge of slipping into chaos. She needed help and fast. Whether she had the strength to hold her emotions together and get the job done remained to be seen. Joni nodded, her lips pressed together, strong yet concerned. Not for her well-being…for his.

Guilt dogged his heels as he slid away into the thicket. He

wouldn't have left Kriegler behind, but would have made him wait until his dad had Joni safely on the boat. If that had been too late for Kriegler, so be it. Now perhaps the bastard had a decent chance to survive. But if something happened to Joni while she was alone, Kriegler would pay for it with his life.

CHAPTER TWENTY-EIGHT

Bram scrunched Taljaard's safari hat well down on his head. His build ran leaner than Ingwe, but their equal heights and nondescript khakis matched closely enough.

He pictured Taljaard and shook his head. *Leopard.* Fat chance. Lover boy had the strength of a gorilla.

New growth on thickets had blossomed since the first rain this week. With his reckless haste, hooks and thorns savagely clawed at his exposed forearms. Sounds of a boat engine grew louder. He cut closer to the shore. Breaths of exertion huffed out in a steady rhythm. He didn't slack.

Poorly secured, the rifle strap constantly slipped off his shoulder. The thicket ended ahead in an area exposed to the river. He sprinted across it, making sure to add a noticeable limp.

Mr. Gorilla had been favoring his foot since the rescue at the plane. His fall from the container truck during their fight had taken a toll. The injury had slowed him down, but not more than Joni in her less-than-stellar state.

Yeah, no one to blame for that debacle but himself. She would never suffer under Kagona again.

The boat cut toward the shoreline. His movement had been noticed. Thicket once again hid him, but he pressed on. Distance was his friend. The more between Joni and him, the better her chance of survival.

The boat engine idled. It must be pulling ashore. The enemy would soon be on foot. A second later the engine revved to life again and headed back downstream. Correction—the two men had split up. One behind him and another soon to be waiting ahead. Confirming his thoughts, within a minute, the engine noise died.

Would Kagona shoot first and claim the kill? No, the bastard liked to play with his food. Watch the fear and suffering on his captives' faces. Good. It wasted time. Time for Joni to escape. Time for him to live. Maybe, if he pegged Taljaard correctly, time for a rescue once Joni had cleared.

Evasion moves screamed inside his head. *Move inland to thicker cover. Take the men out one at a time.* The rescue boat required a safe distance from Kagona's speedboat. That he could give Joni. His boots pounded against the sun-hardened silts, but he made no effort to be silent.

Shade from tall trees swept over him, offering relief from the heat, but it reduced the sun-loving thicket. Ahead, only trunks of well-spaced trees offered screening from the hunters. A flash of movement brought the rifle off his shoulder.

"I suggest you drop that, Taljaard."

A bullet hit the ground near his feet. No doubt the shooter had better aim.

He dropped the rifle. The game had begun.

"Now the pack. Let it fall."

Bram unclipped the clasp around his chest and waist, then worked the straps off his shoulders. It dropped with a thud behind him.

"Step forward."

He complied with one small step, keeping the rifle within reach.

"A few more. I'm aware of your skills at marksmanship."

Kak, *is Taljaard the best at everything?* Bram took several more steps forward.

Kagona's flunky, Chaipa, stepped out from behind a trunk. The nine-millimeter in his hand made any charge at this distance impossible.

A look of surprise flashed across Chaipa's face.

"Take your hat off."

Bram reached up.

Behind him, thicket rustled and dried tree litter crunched under boots that ran toward them. Not Taljaard's silent style. The footsteps stopped. His enemies boxed him in.

"Keep it slow and your hands raised."

He grinned at the nerves apparent on Chaipa. Surprises made the CIO flunky nervous. Bram shoved the hat back off his head. It dropped to the ground.

Behind him, Kagona breathed heavily from exertion. He drank too much. "Not sure how you fooled my drone, but your tricks are over, Taljaard. Turn around."

Chaipa stepped sideways out of the line of fire, wisely assessing the damage Bram's identity would strike on Kagona. Dead men did tell lies.

Bram dropped his hands to the top of his head and turned. The shock on Kagona's face perhaps offered the last moment of pleasure in Bram's life.

The merciless sun beat down on Ian's exposed head. Damn Kriegler for running off with his hat. Sweat cascaded down his neck, and his soaked shirt stuck to his back. Insignificant annoyances compared to the pain shooting up his leg with every contact of his foot against uneven ground. Angry purple skin from the ankle injury swelled out around the top of his boot. He had loosened his laces slightly to allow for blood flow.

Without a cumbersome pack, he followed Kagona's

deafening path. Ian pictured Kagona's ugly mug framed in his rifle scope back at the landing strip. He'd itched to squeeze the trigger and see the heartless killer drop.

In a shady open area ahead, men spoke. He paused, remaining concealed in a mahogany thicket. He dropped to his hands and knees and crawled for better positioning.

Flies buzzed wildly, aiming for open cuts and scrapes on his arms. Pain lanced a knee. He bit off a string of oaths. Spines from a puncture vine capable of flattening a tire pierced his khakis. His hand shook as he yanked his skewered pants away from his skin. Pulling the barbs out brought fresh blood with it. Ian carefully moved on, avoiding the barb field, until the men ahead became visible.

Kagona stood with his back to Ian and arm bent behind his back. A defining ragged scar ran down his forearm. Bandaged fingers encircled the grip of a semiauto tucked in a waist holster. Satisfaction buoyed Ian's spirit. Kagona also had suffered through this ordeal.

The identification brought no fear, no loathing, and oddly, no emotion whatsoever. Ian longed to hate the CIO chief for what he'd done to Joni, to so many he loved. Yet, hate didn't rise. Only determination that Kagona must never be allowed to inflict his will on another. He would die here, and Ian accepted he could live with the consequences.

Beyond Kagona, Kriegler faced an armed Chaipa. Kagona had brought along his number-one man. A sick son of a bitch who had learned all too well from his mentor. The lack of lower-ranking manpower indicated these men didn't want witnesses. Whatever came of this encounter would be their version.

Ian's safari hat lay on the ground along with his pack and rifle. Kriegler stood unarmed. Favorable odds for the enemy.

Kagona drew his sidearm as Kriegler turned toward him. Ian nocked an arrow and waited. His dad required time to get Joni to safety.

In a sudden move, Kagona aimed the weapon at Kriegler's head. Stoic as ever, Kriegler let a satisfied quirk edge his mouth. Cocky ass.

"I should have known better than to trust you, Kriegler. How long have you and Taljaard worked together?"

"Never have."

"You are now."

"The Americans offered a deal I couldn't refuse."

"All these years, I considered you smart enough to know when risk outweighed gain. You've let money become your master."

Kriegler tilted his head. "Not much different than you."

"Where is Taljaard?"

"By now, in Zambia."

"Impossible."

"Quite possible with the decoys I created. You fell for most all of them. Honestly, since no one was looking for me, I didn't expect to get caught."

"Liar. I saw him. Not faring well."

"You saw him on your drone video. Preplanned and recorded. I tried to copy his performance. Did a believable job of appearing injured. Had Chaipa fooled for a minute."

Kagona looked at Chaipa, who snorted in disgust but remained silent, not sure where Kriegler and his accusations might lead.

Kriegler continued talking. "I hate to deliver bad news. Taljaard is in prime shape. Why do you think he evaded your men so easily?"

Kagona visibly seethed. "I shot him last week near Bulawayo."

"I can't remember if you heard that from me or Miss Bell. Either way, we lied. He wasn't wounded."

"Your excuses are thin. We saw Bell, too."

"Ah, yes. I quite liked when she looked up at the drone. That wasn't her only performance. She did an admirable job during interrogation. Revealed very little about Taljaard. Not that she knew much to tell. To be perfectly honest, she really doesn't know much about him. Their relationship was all an act. My idea."

Ian used the time to assess how to take out the men. Chaipa first or Kagona? Would the surprise allow him to get off two arrows before either responded?

"On your knees," Kagona commanded.

"An execution before interrogation? You're losing an opportunity to obtain useful intel."

Kagona motioned Kriegler down with his weapon. "You know my skills. Which knee are you willing to give up?"

Kriegler dropped to his knees, his hands still warming the top of his head. Kagona shifted closer to Kriegler.

Bad news. The men lay along the same trajectory—a problem for his powerful bow at this close range. Shoot Kagona, and the arrow could pass through and hit Kriegler.

Maybe that wasn't such a bad thing…

Bloody hell. As much as Kriegler deserved to suffer for his game with Joni, the Afrikaner played for time, leaving him to certain death. The guy had guts.

"You've changed, Kriegler. Softened over the years. Perhaps you and Bell are lovers. A risky move, putting her in my hands. I could have been the one fucking her instead of you."

Nightmare images rolled through Ian. He relaxed his arm and wiped away sweat dripping in his eyes. A single arrow would take out both men who'd abused Joni.

"I might yet have that chance," Kagona ranted on. "I think you're leading me away from her. She's close. Likely tending to Taljaard. I'll find her. Her interrogation promises to be productive."

"The only place you saw Bell was on the drone video. Notice the bad feed? Choppy…pixelated. My talents don't lie with editing."

"We saw her jam the drone."

"I'm afraid you have that part wrong. I hacked your drone's access ID. Then I changed the return-home protocol to simply land when the batteries ran low or it lost a signal. Once I completed the housekeeping unnoticed, I fed in fake video snips with Bell and Taljaard, spoofed the GPS coordinates, and then cut the signal. The drone shut down." Kriegler lifted his hands up off his head. "Can I put my arms down? It's hard to talk this way."

Kagona held his weapon steady on Kriegler's heart. "Chaipa, call in this position. I want Bell and Taljaard found."

Kriegler glared at Kagona. "How are you going to explain me…a colleague supposedly killed at your side hours ago?"

Ian cringed at the brash way Kriegler pushed his luck. Ian raised his bow, afraid Kriegler had run out of luck.

"I've no plans to bring you back. You're already dead and crocs will devour any contrary evidence."

"Kill me and you'll be left to discover for yourself the full extent of my damage to the CIO. My knowledge can prevent you from becoming a laughingstock back at headquarters."

"I believe there will be sufficient evidence in your pack. Is it filled with CIA equipment?"

"You'd be disappointed."

Kagona snorted. "Perhaps I'll prolong your life long enough for you to beg for death."

"You seem to be forgetting an important point." Kriegler sounded too calm for a man a bullet away from a short life. "I doubt either of you are drone experts. Did a junior operative run your aerial search? Does he have an explanation for what you saw on the video? He might wonder why you sent the police and your men one direction while you went another."

Kagona's head shifted toward Chaipa. Positive Kagona had reached his limit of endurance, Ian prepared to shoot.

"You must know about Mukono by now." Kriegler hastily offered real intel, likely figuring he'd pushed too far.

"He's on his way to Iran."

"More likely he's in South Africa, talking to the president."

Chaipa didn't flinch. His boss noticed.

Kagona shifted slightly as he took in the unexpected news. "Has headquarters heard from the plane with the Iranians?"

"No communication was expected, sir."

"Find out. I want confirmation of Mukono's location."

Chaipa didn't move. "Once we dispatch Kriegler."

As if on cue, a boat engine sounded close on the river. Kagona glanced toward the river and then back at Kriegler. "Taljaard's boat is coming. Our talk is over. At least I'll have the satisfaction of seeing you dead for good this time."

Kriegler's time had run out.

Ian willed Kagona to move, but the thug stayed in place.

"Your friends won't escape." Kagona raised his gun toward Kriegler's head.

A shot rang out before Ian let an arrow fly. Odd, how in those moments of disorganized terror, time slowed down, yet thought operated at a sprint. Those thoughts urged him to hesitate, unsure of the dynamics.

His ears determined the retort came from an unexpected direction.

Kriegler's eyes rounded in disbelief before he dropped to the ground.

Kagona collapsed to his knees and toppled to the side.

Kriegler rolled toward Ian's rifle. Chaipa's aim shifted toward him.

Ian fired.

His arrow hit Chaipa's shoulder and pinned him to the tree. Screams of agony filled the air. In seconds, Kriegler had forgone the rifle for a knife, which he held at Chaipa's throat.

The gun tumbled from the killer's hand below the impaled shoulder. "I wouldn't...have killed you."

"At least not until my trial for murdering your boss?"

On autopilot, Ian ran for the men, stopping at Kagona. Crimson had spread across the bastard's chest. His open eyes stared at nothing. No sympathy welled. No satisfaction at his enemy's death. As he glanced up at Chaipa, he understood why.

Chaipa's deadly aim had hit his boss in the heart. That action took a steady hand at this distance from someone not bothered by remorse at killing a friend or mentor. An easy task for a sociopath cleaning up his organization, and for one who stood to gain by stepping into Kagona's shoes. Had Ian's wish for Kagona's death only unleashed a younger version of his kind?

Ian secured Kagona's weapon before he reached down to check for life. His fingers confirmed what the frozen features on Kagona's face announced.

"Dead," he called out.

A noise cast Ian's attention toward the Zambezi. Assured of no threat, he joined Kriegler.

"Took your damn time, Taljaard."

"If I'd shot, the arrow might have penetrated Kagona and hit you."

"Are you saying you hesitated to shoot me?"

"Ironic, isn't it?"

Blood oozed from Chaipa's shoulder. He grimaced at Kriegler, who seethed inches from his face. "I have a message for your boss." Chaipa's words came out in heavy pants of pain.

Kriegler looked surprised. "My boss?"

Ian collected Chaipa's gun. The impaled killer shifted his eyes to focus on Ian. "Kriegler is a poor liar. You look like shit." The man grinned briefly before pain contorted his face. "I'm the one…who shot you in Bulawayo."

"Sorry, but Kriegler didn't lie about my health. I look battered and bloody, but not from your bullet. You missed. Another of your failures." No reason to give Kagona's protégé satisfaction.

Kriegler pressed the knife hard enough a speck of blood

arose at Chaipa's neck. "What do you want to tell my boss?"

"Tell him—" Chaipa tried to breathe but couldn't draw air without the knife sinking deeper. "Tell him Chitima has been stopped."

"Why should I believe you?"

"No choice. Mozambique ambassador came to president."

The actions over the last minutes came into focus. Chaipa had known about Mukono's freedom and Mozambique's demand. Considering Kagona's surprise at Mukono's rescue, it meant Chaipa had neglected to relay the news to his boss. Opportunity knocked and the student seized the moment to replace the teacher.

Kriegler relaxed the knife. "You know, Taljaard, if we leave this shit alive, he's going to blame Kagona's death on you."

Chaipa gasped down air.

Ian stepped closer to his pinned victim and patted him down. "I'll be blamed whether he's dead or alive." The man's radio, phone, and knife went into Ian's pockets. Next came his boots and socks. Damn smelly. "With this failure, he'll be lucky to survive the upcoming purge when there's a battle for new leadership."

"You'll do well to remember Chaipa Nandoro." Chaipa relaxed enough to show he believed his life was safe. Ian's reputation for avoiding useless slaughter preceded him.

"Your name, while one I won't forget, is irrelevant." Ian tied the laces together, then spun the boots and launched them onto a high branch. "What *is* important is that you will forget ours."

"Is that the price you're offering for my life?" The man's eyes laughed at the weakness in Ian's idealistic terms.

"Simple, isn't it? Forgotten names mean neither you nor your CIO and police friends will ever hunt us again."

"A man like you, Taljaard, is smart enough to see the holes in your offer."

"Holes perhaps. It all depends on your perspective." Ian

walked around Kagona's body. "You shot Kagona. That indicates you're the guy making a move to replace him. I wish you a long career."

Confusion flickered in Chaipa's arrogant eyes. Kriegler grinned with understanding.

Ian pointed to the river, and Chaipa's gaze followed. Joni stood onshore, pointing the camera from the drone at the men. "Bell got it all on video."

Chaipa's triumph faded to concern. His lips pressed together. No way for him to know how long she'd been recording.

Ian had no idea, either. It hardly mattered. Chaipa would be the last person to call his bluff. President Tangwerai had known whom to inform of the halted shipment. That meant he, too, was implicit in the affair and had likely ordered Kagona's execution.

"Where are the boat keys?"

Chaipa shivered in shock. "I will not make your escape easy."

Ian triggered his comm. "I'm hoping our boat isn't far behind. If we can't find the speedboat keys, we're going to need it."

"On its way." Joni's feminine voice cast a fresh breeze across the bloody scene.

Kriegler shouldered the pack and Ian's rifle before heading toward Kagona's boat.

Ian made one last stop by Chaipa. The arrowhead had passed through and embedded the broadhead into the tree trunk, effectively pinning Chaipa to it. With no remorse, Ian yanked Chaipa forward. His shoulder slid along the arrow shaft until the fletching passed through his wound and he fell free of the arrow. His screams sent loitering guinea fowl scattering.

Ian had no desire to leave behind evidence that might be traced. He ripped a piece of Chaipa's shirt not saturated in blood and wrapped it around the arrow shaft still stuck in the tree. A poor grip, but it mitigated the slick blood covering the shaft. He then stabbed a knife at the trunk near the arrow's broadhead and chipped away wood. The arrow worked loose.

He secured his knife, stepped past a moaning Chaipa curled up on the ground, and then grabbed his hat Kriegler had left behind. Satisfaction, not empathy, accompanied his steps toward the shore. His damn emotions mixed with testosterone and had stripped his brain of humane actions.

Humane? Hell, he should have put that arrow through Chaipa's heart.

So he wasn't perfect. Who the hell was?

With his hat on its rightful head and bow strap secure on his shoulder, Ian limped toward the river, carrying the arrow in one hand.

He caught up to Kriegler at the shore. A touch of pallor still accented the Afrikaner's face. "No keys in the boat," Kriegler said. "Give me some time and I can rig the ignition."

"Time is the one thing we don't have."

They slid down a steep bank, past roots and tall grass to a small pontoon boat pulling up. Joni stood near the water, a sight to ease a man's conscience. The boat idled, leaving a short gap of water between the shore and the boat. She hesitated to enter territory where crocs ruled.

"Move it, Joni. Either swim with crocs or the CIO. I know which evil I'm choosing."

Joyous water splashed around him as he waded knee-deep into the Zambezi. Before reaching the boat, he sent the arrow sailing out into the river. A quick dip of his hands in the water still left a filthy feel on his skin.

He tossed his bow onto the pontoon deck and turned around. Joni nearly walked on water in her haste to get to the boat. His hands cupped her slippery foot and launched her aboard. She secured the video camera and reached back for Kriegler's pack. In return, Kriegler boosted Ian onboard. Kriegler then shoved the boat adrift, and Ian pulled him aboard.

The three hunkered down on the boat, keeping a low profile to anyone watching along distant riverbanks. Ian stretched out against the second pack where Joni sat. His father must have loaded it and picked Joni up to bring her near their location.

Ian set a hand on her thigh, needing a warm human touch. "Took your time getting here."

She smiled. "I believe you ordered me to Zambia."

"Glad you follow orders so well."

The boat vibrated beneath them as the engine progressed from purring to a full-out roar. He reached up and tugged Joni down, not giving a rat's arse who witnessed the kisses he'd wanted to shower on her since she'd been torn from his grasp.

CHAPTER TWENTY-NINE

Joni sat on the deck with her back propped against Ian's chest. The wind whipped her hair and whisked away a lingering cloud of self-doubt and second-guessing. Not only had they all made it to the Zambezi alive, a boat swept them across the river. Though not a speedboat, the pontoon made good time.

Bram knelt nearby covered in dirt, leaves, and splattered blood. She hadn't arrived early enough to witness all that transpired, but in time to see that Ian had saved his life.

She shifted back and looked up at Ian. "At least Bram's ghost won't haunt you for life."

A funny vibration burred against her back. He was laughing. Quietly and rather contained, but clearly laughing.

"What's so funny?"

"I'm learning once a woman sets her mind to something, it's not worth arguing."

The radio scanner attached to a pack interrupted the brief moment of relief. Static, voices, and curt orders cut in and out.

"We've company." Bram pointed at two dots on the river headed their direction. "Speedboats."

Joni crouched, slipped the video camera into her pack and removed the binoculars. "How long to get across the river?"

she called out over the motor's burr to Ian's dad driving the boat.

"Five minutes at best, missy, but our boat is slugging along a bit slower than that."

Ian struggled to his feet and snatched the binoculars. "Get your butts to the stern. Weight over the engine keeps the blades in the water."

He dragged his pack across the deck to the starboard rail facing the speedboats. Bram tossed his pack next to Ian's, blocking an easy view of their position.

Ian signaled them to keep low while he focused on the boats. He canted his body slightly to one side, favoring his injured ankle. "It's going to be close, Dad."

"Doing my best."

The pontoon boat skimmed the water at a good speed. The Zambian shore grew closer, but so did the speedboats…and if they had snipers, the boats didn't have to catch them, only get close.

"You don't happen to have a sniper rifle, by any chance?" Bram asked Ian's dad, his mind arriving at the same conclusion as hers.

"I considered bringing weapons, but figured anything other than fishing gear might attract interest."

She peered over the canvas side. A bullet ripped through the awning overhead as the report echoed across the water. Sitting ducks on a boat with cloth sides almost made swimming ashore through crocs a viable alternative. Almost, but wouldn't happen. She'd dined at a croc dinner table before and found them messy eaters.

"Stay down, missy. They'll get better with practice."

A plunk placed a bullet in a pontoon.

"They're getting closer, Dad."

"Almost there, kiddies." He abruptly changed course. His hat flew off and dropped into the river. A bullet shattered the fiberglass driver's stand six inches from him.

Shit. Their opponents had honed their aim.

Rotor blades chopped the air. A sweet sound on any day…unless it belonged to Kagona's Alouette. A shudder racked her body. Damn emotions. The man was dead.

Ian gave her shoulder a reassuring squeeze. "It's Mike." The red Jet Ranger roared up the Zambian side of the Zambezi and swung onto the river, passing overhead. Mike dipped the rotor, creating a gale-force wind against the approaching boats.

Ian's dad waved his fist in the air and hooted.

Hair needled her eyes, making the scene all the more surreal. "The Zambians aren't going to be happy we're creating a border fiasco."

Bram peered up at Mike's chopper. "I don't think the CIO will be raising a stink."

Ian's dad pulled into a small spit along the shoreline with a ten-foot river-cut bluff. Both she and Ian reached for the big pack.

"Forget it." He secured his hold on the pack. "I'm injured, not incapacitated."

Not in a mood to argue his deteriorating condition, she hefted her day pack onto her shoulders. A few tweaks to the straps snugged it tight.

Ian slipped his bow strap over a shoulder. "When we hit shore, run for cover. That includes you, Dad."

"Right there with you, son. Hee-yaw, wouldn't have missed this for the moon." He did a quick and perfect job of grounding the boat.

"Go, go, go." Ian slid off the pontoon.

Bram, with the other pack and rifle, jumped off after her. "Move it, *bokkie*, or I'll be stepping on you. With no one around to notice, I wouldn't put it past the CIO to follow."

Ian's dad was the last to disembark and hung back with his son.

"Damn it, Dad. Get moving. This isn't the time to be heroic."

"Just bringing up the rear. Mad Mike didn't hunt me down for this gig for nothing."

Bram used his body and the pack to shield her from the boats. Shots, barely discernible over the helicopter, rang out over the water. She hit the steep climb. Sand and silty clay cascaded down with each step. For every few feet up, she slid one back.

Her hands clawed for added handholds in the dirt and roots. A solid shove from Bram below put her over the top. In a final scramble using hands and feet, she crouched down. Bram landed by her side and dumped his pack. She checked back for Ian, who'd reached the loose soil. His ankle made climbing the ten feet up nearly impossible.

Bram dropped the rifle beside her and slid back down. A bullet exploded dirt near her head. If Mike and his helo let up, they'd be easy pickings.

Ian's mobility on his ankle was running out. His dad came up under one arm and Bram the other. Together, the men climbed the river cut, suffering the same struggle with the loose soil.

She donned Bram's heavier pack and started inland along a cleared strip of clay Ian had declared a road, carrying the day pack with the drone in her hand and the rifle strapped over a shoulder.

Behind her, the men had crested to the flood plain. Bram tugged the second pack off Ian, donned it, and swept the bow strap over a shoulder. Ian and his dad set up for a three-legged race to wherever Mike landed the chopper.

The reassuring beat of the helo passed overhead as Mike backed off the river. The raised elevation, uneven land, and patches of thicket ahead offered a patchy screen from the river. She hustled along well ahead of the men and worked the day pack up a shoulder to free a hand for a radio call to Mike. "Where's the pickup point?"

Behind her, the rumble of speedboats retreated. The enemy returned to Zimbabwe. It wouldn't be long before they found Chaipa and discovered Kagona was dead.

"Negative on that, missy. Vehicle closing in on your position. About twenty seconds to find cover."

"Incoming Zambians," she warned Ian, the only one still wearing his comm unit. The men behind her had little chance to avoid detection at their location with sparse cover. She dived for the closest brush, hoping those in the arriving vehicle focused on Mike passing overhead.

A pickup rumbled past in a cloud of dust. No police or ranger markings on the vehicle, but the two men wore uniforms. The passenger held a weapon…one a lot more powerful than her rifle. If both in the vehicle had similar firepower, it meant two AK-47s against her rifle and a handgun. A hunting rifle was not her forte when it came to weapons.

Shouts came from near the river. A single shot rang out. A lump formed in her throat. *Focus, girl.* The new arrivals had used single fire. Likely short on ammo.

"Do we look like poachers?" Ian had left his comm unit open for her to hear.

AK-47s against a simple rifle meant using deadly force wasn't an option. She'd lose. These men also could be police doing their job. Shooting Zambian authorities for the team's escape would be criminal at best. On the other hand, ending up arrested and in their questionable legal system offered other deadly potentials…like a return to Zimbabwe.

Voices sounded in the background. The men claimed to be border control. The statement brought a smile to her face and likely to Ian's. Lemmon had done a thorough job briefing her on all the enforcement agencies in Zimbabwe and Zambia and their capabilities and deficiencies.

One of the men ordered Bram to drop the bow.

"Our weapons are for protection against animals." Ian stalled for time. He counted on her to take action. "Poachers are more likely to have AK-47s like yours."

She doubted the men picked up on his slight. Her hands shook as she emptied the contents of her day pack. With practiced precision, she attached the landing gear, the camera, then each propeller of the drone. The batteries were low, but a few minutes of flight time should be enough.

With the console in hand, she hit a button for auto launch, then took control of the drone.

The video below showed Bram standing a little apart from the other men. One of the uniformed men had a weapon on Ian and his father, and the other focused on Bram. Ian held his arms raised and spoke with the man covering him, all the while inching away from his father and closer to the gun wielder. His injury did nothing to stop him from assessing and positioning for action.

"Move away." A man signaled Bram back from a pack.

She hovered and waited, knowing the drone had only minutes of life.

The man stuck his arm deep into the pack. She dropped the drone to hover ten feet away and rotated the camera to look into his face. His chin tucked back and eyes grew large. He stumbled several steps back, yelling and pointing as he went. His partner glanced around, attempting to find from where the drone had come.

"Surprised we're watching you?" Ian brought his arms in closer. "Everything you're doing is being recorded. The government is tired of thugs like you robbing local people and businesses at the border crossing."

She shifted the drone toward the second man and selected a central point on his head to circle around. He spun and pointed his gun at the drone. She zoomed it higher.

Distraction anywhere near men who were trained fighters had only one consequence. By the time she stopped the circuit and rose high enough to encompass the entire scene below, Ian, his dad, and Bram had the two men on the ground. Ian and Bram hog-tied them, while Ian's dad flung their AK-47s over the bluff into the river.

With a grin, she signaled the drone home. "Mike, you're cleared to land."

Ian left the men tied loosely enough to free themselves with minimal effort. In his current mood, they were lucky to find him so charitable. With Kriegler at the helm of the worn pickup, they jolted down the marginal dirt road. About a quarter mile away, Mike settled the chopper onto a clear spot. He was one damn loyal mate, and his excursion here proved he truly had to be mad.

A sense of pride overwhelmed Ian at the sight of Joni up ahead. For someone with a wealth of problems to overcome in a long day, she'd slung her day pack over one shoulder, the rifle over the other, gripped a drone in one hand, and perched a foot up on a big pack.

Kriegler halted the truck next to her.

Ian leaned out the passenger window. "Looking a bit smug there, woman."

"Simply wondering what it's going to take to keep you boys outta trouble." She handed up the drone and day pack to Ian's dad in the truck bed before hefting in Bram's pack.

"Nice timing with that drone, missy." His dad reached out and tugged her into the back.

Less than a tooth-rattling minute later, they reached the helo. The sound of transportation to freedom pumped hope through his veins. He climbed from the cab with his bow on a shoulder in time for Joni to hand down the drone from the truck bed.

"To hell with this equipment." He steadied her jump from the truck bed and then jostled the drone aside to pull her close. "I want you in my arms, safe and alive."

"Bet you say that to all your teammates."

"Hope not," Kriegler cut in as he yanked a pack from the truck.

"Butt out." Ian released his hold and swept up her hand. He closed his fingers over hers, unsettled by how she'd changed his life in such a short time.

He hobbled beside her toward the chopper as his dad and Kriegler loaded the equipment. Mike's damn prosthesis fell from the pack opened by the poacher, a reminder of how crazy their last days had been. Kriegler hefted it into the storage hatch behind the backseats.

Joni stopped near the helo. Her fingers released their hold. Her gaze switched from him to the spinning rotors and back again. Fearing she planned to offer assistance, he hustled to set the drone inside the chopper and heft his body inside. Pride was a touchy thing, and his had been damaged enough for one day. An injury didn't shut him down—it only slowed his ability to act.

Kriegler climbed into the copilot seat and Ian's dad barreled into the back. Ian turned back, expecting Joni to bound inside next. Instead, she stood outside, frozen in place, and staring at him and his dad.

An odd chill encompassed him. He'd seen that expression before. She didn't stare, but rather looked through them as though seeing something or someone…terrifying.

Christ.

The *whop, whop* of the blades echoed overhead. As if on autopilot, her feet inched forward. She handed in the day pack and rifle. Her hand touched the floor of the cabin. The vibrations shook her hand and traveled through her body. Emotions on her face changed too fast to interpret. Ian and his father exchanged concerned glances.

Gone was the jubilation of escape. Instead, Joni rubbed at raw wrists…ones that Kagona had bound behind her back. Two men had been in the helicopter last night with her. Two stared back at her now.

She shuffled back in the dust. Disturbed air whipped her hair.

"Come on, *bokkie*," Kriegler yelled, not able to see her actions.

Ian slipped out of the helo. "Joni, you're safe." He inched toward her. "This is Mad Mike's chopper. He's flying the damn thing home." He reached out and gently cupped her cheeks. "I'm not leaving you behind." He slid his arms around her, comforting, both her and him. "Damn it, girl, I love you."

Kriegler, evidently sensing something amiss, appeared at his side. "You need help?"

The glaze over Joni's eyes retreated, leaving a frown and look of confusion. She glanced up at Ian and then over at Kriegler.

"I'm fine," she answered. "Nerves are just shot."

Ian set a hand to her back and urged her toward the copilot's door. "Joni's flying shotgun."

"Not smart." Kriegler stretched an arm across the cockpit door. "I don't think the drug has worn off."

Joni glared at him. "Move your ass, Bram."

Ian caught Kriegler's arm. "Trust Mike to keep an eye on her."

"Ian's right, son," Mike called out. "If you value what's important, don't cross this little lady."

"Too late. I'm already on her hit list." Kriegler relented and Joni climbed inside.

Ian shut the copilot door and stepped back. Joni donned a headset and fastened her harness in well-practiced motions. It gave him hope she'd find her home in the skies again. Being at the controls offered assurance she wasn't about to be shoved out the door.

Puzzled, Kriegler stared at him. "She's in no condition to be anywhere near controls."

"What's wrong? Afraid to take a few risks?" Ian leaned into Kriegler's personal space. "There's shit you don't understand, but I promise, soon enough you will."

Ignoring the roaring pain in his ankle, he pulled himself inside the chopper. Kriegler followed him in and shut the rear cabin door.

"All on board. Get this crate off the ground." Ian set his hands on Joni's shoulders from behind. "Help this gnarly son of a bitch in the pilot's seat fly us home." Ian winked over at Mad Mike. "The Zambian authorities won't be far behind."

"Didn't you just leave two of them in the dust?"

"Only poachers who claimed to be border patrol."

Joni looked up at him. A cocky grin spread across her face. "Except Zambia doesn't have one."

Her comment signaled she'd moved past the bad memories…at least for now. Mike had the chopper in the air and headed toward Mozambique, the closest border, by the time Ian's dad passed around high fives. Excitement ran rampant, but until they set foot on South African soil, none of them would be safe.

Ian settled a headset in place and keyed the comm. "Mike, I wasn't sure you'd arrive in time to rescue my arse."

"Me, either, but once I heard missy was heading back to Zimbabwe, I figured I should play close to the border. Saving your hide has cost me a damn fortune, though. Scrounging fuel in these parts is near impossible."

"What are you going to want from me this time?"

"My foot you're hauling around in that pack." Mike frowned back at Kriegler. "How come you're playing with my toys, anyway?"

"Don't look at me. It fell out of Ian's pack."

Mike cast Ian a suspicious look. "Dare I ask why you are hauling around my foot?"

Hell. He hadn't planned on pleading such stupidity so soon. "I…um…found Joni tidying up your place."

"Uh-oh. You two have any trouble with my traps to keep out unexpected visitors?"

"An absolutely charming little place." Joni came to the rescue. "I caught a quick snooze on your couch. Nibbled on cheese and crackers with a lovely lady in a photo."

Mike glanced over at her and then Ian, catching the guilty looks on their faces. "Something tells me I'm not going to like how this story ends."

"I told you to get that well pump fixed," Ian grumbled, doing his best to put off telling the truth.

"I'm sorry, Mike." Joni sounded genuinely apologetic. "I'd rather wait until you put me safely on the ground to explain, but I...I, ah...oh shit, I burned down your house."

Bloody great, did she have to be so honest? The burr of the rotor and engine droned over the verbal silence in the chopper. *Shock* best described what he could see of Mike's stiff body as they swept over sparsely inhabited country.

Ian couldn't let Joni take the blame alone. "Damn it, Mike. I fucked up. Your leg is the only thing we have to show for our rescue efforts."

"That"—Kriegler struggled to remove something from a pocket—"and what Joni saved." He produced the photo Mike had had sitting in his house for years. "A good-looking woman. Your wife?"

Mike plucked the photo from Kriegler's fingers. "Aw, now you've gone and done it, missy. The only thing I cared about in my place and you brought it back to me. I'd given up ever holding it again."

Ian folded his arms in mock disgust. "What about your damned foot? I risked my neck to rescue that thing."

"Don't need it. I'm thinking I ought to retire from these games. Fun times, but damned risky." Mike kissed the photo and lovingly slipped it into a pocket. He looked back at Ian's dad. "We've both had one last adventure and I've my lady back. Isn't it about time we go home to see yours?"

Ian's father locked Mike in a silent stare that passed a

thousand memories between them. "Yeah, I've squandered time with those I love long enough." He settled back in his seat. "Maybe these young people can learn from our mistakes. Must admit they work damn well together."

Kriegler glanced up at Joni and then Ian, whether for reassurance they included him in their team, or just to see if they'd broken into hysterics at the thought of their dysfunctional group as one. The small butterfly bandage over a cut on Kriegler's forehead hung loose. Bruises blossomed on his jaw and along his forearms. A black ring had formed under one eye. He'd paid a price in this debacle. They all had.

Ian loosened his bootlaces more but refused to totally remove the boot. Until home safely, movement was paramount. Dust covered his fingers. Underneath the layers of dirt ground into his clothes and skin, deeper wounds existed. He'd witnessed a calculated execution of his enemy by a man guilty of torturing Joni, and yet he'd let him live. Damned if he knew why.

Joni's outer appearance fared not much better than theirs, but unlike her inner wounds, the physical ones would heal quickly. In truth, she needed to be far away from him and Kriegler. Yet they were the only people who understood her suffering, and they all sat here together because they'd pushed one another to survive.

He'd give her room, let her call the shots, and stay close enough to carry her through the hard times. He knew how. He'd been there himself. Together they'd find healing, and if fortune shone, maybe a life together.

CHAPTER THIRTY

Hoedspruit Air Base, South Africa

Joni sat on a picnic bench underneath a thatch shade. The knoll where the Taz project office hid beneath the ground blocked a view of the runway. She poked at a tablet screen then shifted it so Ian, sitting next to her, could see. On-screen, Sipho's grin grew larger. "Ian! Miss Joni!"

Someone gently moved the boy back and a second face appeared on-screen—Minister Mukono. Other familiar voices sounded on the video feed. She picked out Mad Mike. After leaving her and Ian in Hoedspruit, he'd refueled his helicopter and then taken off with Ian's dad for an animal reserve farther west in South Africa, where Ian's mother and uncle lived. It was also the place where they'd secured Mukono's son from Kagona's reach.

"Hey, Sipho." She waved. "Looks like the animals at the ranch have been treating you well."

The next fifteen minutes slid by fast as Sipho chatted, Minister Mukono offered his gratitude at the rescue of him and his son, and Ian's mom sneaked in a plea for Ian to come see her soon. She also offered Joni a simple thank-you in words, but a greater unspoken message with the moisture welling up in her eyes.

Joni discovered the numbness, which had relegated her feelings to a locked place inside, rippling. She swallowed hard, holding back emotions fighting to surface. Of all the apologies, explanations, and logic used to help her inner wounds heal, seeing the fruits of her labor offered the greatest hope.

Both she and Ian had showered and tended their wounds, shielding the majority from the camera's view. Lemmon had asked—rather required—them to remain at the project office until debriefing. They'd chosen to sit outside without the constraints of the confining briefing rooms belowground. They said the last of their good-byes with a promise to contact family again soon.

As Sipho's grin disappeared from the screen, Ian reached an arm around her waist. "Manna for the spirit."

"You're good at that," she said.

"What?"

"Saying the right thing."

Her mind still had difficulty remembering life a week ago, when she'd flight tested Taz, and enjoyed an ordinary workplace environment. The memory left her yearning for those days of ignorance…before she learned Lemmon had rigged her hiring on the project, before he'd coerced her into rescuing Sipho, and before he'd destroyed her camaraderie and trust in a workplace friend.

Speak of the devil, Bram strolled in their direction, wearing a clean flight suit like the rest of them. He carried three cold beers. A peace offering?

"Relax." Ian had sensed her body tensing.

She'd have to work past the reaction to her workmate or search for a new job…one not selected by Mr. Lemmon. She clicked on a video to have an excuse not to look into Bram's eyes.

Ian shifted his leg from the bench where he'd propped his wrapped ankle and grabbed a crutch. "Nature calls."

"Coward." He left her alone to reconcile the best she could with Bram. An impossibility? Her emotions had developed their own life regardless of attempts to control them.

Bram settled at the table across from her and slid a beer over. "Have a chipper visit with the kid?"

"We caught them in the middle of a reunion. Mike had just landed with Ian's dad and they were celebrating."

"Has Taljaard heard from Zamani yet?"

"He's back home in Bulawayo. Safe."

Bram simply nodded and played with his beer, uncomfortable, but here because they both knew they had to settle things and move on.

She eyed him, not sure where to start. "I thought maybe you'd drowned in the shower."

"I had a brief chat with Obergen."

"The boss must have been curious as to why we arrived on Mike's chopper. At least I was supposedly on vacation, but you had claimed to be recovering from the flu."

"He's not happy that Lemmon shut down test operations by tying up the program pilots. In the future, he'll be wary of giving visiting dignitaries too much leeway."

"Lemmon hailing us heroes in front of him probably didn't help." The CIA ops officer had briefly shown his face when they landed.

"Rather added fuel to the fire."

She brushed her thumb at moisture building on the beer bottle. The last thing she felt like was a hero. They'd successfully extracted Minister Mukono from CIO prison and stopped, for at least a while, the further proliferation of nuclear material.

But heroes…not by any means.

The three of them had walked away from an assassination and allowed a new despicable man to assume power in the Zimbabwean CIO. Bram had deceived and broken trust between friends, and messed with her and Ian's heads and hearts. All of them had witnessed and partaken in the seedy side of mankind. Survivors fit more aptly, than heroes.

"You ready to talk with Lemmon?"

A subconscious need for distance brought her arms across her midriff. "I'd prefer to head home. Would have, but Lemmon absconded with the car keys from my desk."

"Don't lay the blame on him." Bram dangled a set of keys in his hand and made no effort to hand them over. "For your own peace of mind, you need to put this debrief behind you."

"And you don't believe I'm capable of making that decision?"

"At the moment, no. But you could have walked home."

Damn him. On any other day, she'd have headed out on foot, but that meant leaving an injured Ian at Lemmon's mercy. "Besides acknowledgment when we landed, Ian and Lemmon have never talked face-to-face."

A self-satisfied smile thinned his lips. "Their proper introduction promises to be sweet."

"You've already briefed Lemmon?"

"We spoke before my shower."

"Your version?"

"The only version I know, *bokkie*. You'll have yours."

"Are you expecting our stories to match?"

"I'm here to offer support. I told Lemmon I screwed up big-time. I also warned Obergen he was going to be without a pilot for a while."

"Why? Where are you going?"

"No place. You are. You've three weeks to forget about me, Lemmon, Kagona, and this whole damn thing. Get your head on straight and tame the inner beast making a yo-yo out of your emotions."

"No thanks to you."

"I'm not belittling what you're going through or my role. Ian and I have been where you are. Take the time. Obergen whined about the project schedule, but I told him if you didn't get the time, he'd be without us both in the future."

Her mind worked to wrap around his news. "Would you really walk away from flying Taz?"

He took a swig of beer as though wishing what he had to say could remain unspoken. "I'll do what's necessary for you to be happy flying here."

"There's no guarantee we'll be able to work together when I get back."

"I recognize that possibility, Joni. Whether you've accepted it or not, we successfully worked together before and during this fiasco. Your past indicated you'd hold together under Kagona's interrogation…and eventually mine. You actually exceeded my expectations. You didn't fail. If anything, you succeeded too well."

"I could've handled the truth and made your ploy work."

Bram gave no reply as Lemmon rounded the knoll and headed their way.

A rush of anger swelled. She grabbed the edge of the table to steady her nerves and let emotions subside. Lemmon had let her believe she had some semblance of control in the mission, yet hidden the truth. Bram had hidden the truth. The two had conspired to place her in the hands of the man of her nightmares.

Ian's strong hands gripped her taut shoulders from behind. "Some battles are worth fighting. Others are best left as history." His touch infused a safety net of trust. Just as his instincts had chosen the right moment to return, his promise to never leave her in Kagona's hands had carried her through bad times.

Her fingers released their grip on the table and settled on his hand. For a moment, she sat with him behind her, in spirit and form. Lemmon stopped across the table from them.

Ian's eyes narrowed. "You're the son of a bitch who helped me save my friends."

"And you're the bastard who pulled it off. I should thank you for getting my people out."

"I strongly considered leaving one behind." He glanced at Bram.

"But you didn't." Neither man put out a hand to shake.

"Perhaps I should have. I still can't guarantee one of you didn't betray our presence at Chief Zwide's kraal to Kagona the night Sipho was taken?"

The two men looked at one another, puzzled. "Can't blame that one on us," Bram said. "We wanted him out of the country as quickly as possible."

"Fair enough."

Ian's shoulders relaxed. He accepted that the Ndebele *sangoma* or someone in the kraal was responsible for Sipho's kidnapping and the trauma suffered by the chief. Joni squeezed his hand, offering her own comfort to Ian over the chief's unstable state.

A satisfied nod from Lemmon ran counter to the empty, exhausted looks of those around him. "You three have pulled off a mission my supervisors claimed impossible. The director has sent his congratulations. I fully expect messages from even higher up."

His words had no impact. Had she grown so cold, kudos didn't matter?

Ian sat once again and propped his leg up.

Lemmon settled next to Bram. "Might as well jump right in. I've been reviewing the political fallout from your actions. Across the border, cleanup and cover-up is well underway." He opened a leather valise and tugged out a small laptop. "Here's a report just filed by an Africa News Beacon reporter in Zimbabwe."

A face appeared on the small screen.

Ian snorted. "At least we know the poor bastard made it out of CIO confinement. I hope he never finds out what Zamani did to his vehicle."

Bram snickered. "I wonder if the CIO gave him his license plate back."

Deep inside a sense of satisfaction stirred. Add another win to their column. The reporter might have lost a 4x4, but he'd regained his freedom.

She focused on the report. *President Tangwerai announced today that authorities stopped an illegal shipment of yellowcake from leaving Zimbabwe. Unnamed sources say it was bound for Iran via Mozambique.*

"What will Zimbabwe do with the yellowcake?" Joni asked.

Lemmon paused the report. "The tagging devices you planted show it's already on its way back to the Kanyemba mine for storage. Several agencies will be keeping a close eye on the product and the mine." He restarted the video report.

An illegal mining deal between China, Iran, and officials within Zimbabwe has been uncovered. Chief of Operations Tinashe Kagona of the Central Intelligence Organization spearheaded the deal with other suspected government ministers but without President Jacob Tangwerai's authority. This was initially discovered by Finance Minister Edward Mukono, who was jailed by Chief Kagona to keep the knowledge of the deal secret. Politicians who learned of this abhorrent miscarriage of justice were able to attain a temporary release of Minister Mukono. In a move to ensure his safety, they attempted to take him to Zambia until the truth could be sorted out. In a tragic twist to this story, Chief Kagona was involved in a boating accident on the Zambezi River after shutting down border crossings and attempting to prevent Minister Mukono from leaving the country. His body has yet to be recovered.

"Smart." Ian tapped on the table. "The president laid all the blame on Kagona, and then Chaipa used Zambezi flatdogs to hide the fact he killed him."

"Flatdogs?" She stilled his fingers.

"Crocs, *bokkie*," Bram answered.

Lemmon glanced at the three of them. "Should I be surprised there is no mention of you?"

"I believe Chaipa is afraid of what we have on video." Ian squeezed her hand. "So what do China and Iran have to say about the news?"

"Iran denies the allegations, of course." Lemmon folded his hands on the table. "They claim it's a stunt by the US to unravel the nuclear deal. China said they have an economic relationship with Zimbabwe but had no idea that the product at one of their plants was being diverted to Iran."

Joni shook her head. "So everyone makes these absurd denials and life moves on. Case closed. Everybody is happy. I guess we can go home."

"Do you debrief all your flights with such abandon, Miss Bell?"

"Your plan had so many in-flight changes, I've no idea where to start evaluation or what to conclude. Except after several death-defying encounters, we completed the test and arrived home alive."

Lemmon shrugged. "Admittedly, timing forced much of the planning to take place behind the scenes. But you're a professional. You knew the risk of encountering Kagona was high and yet still chose to go."

"I understood that the possibility existed, not that your antics made it one hundred percent assured."

"Would you have gone if you'd known?"

Ian leaned toward Lemmon. "That's not a fair question. Joni isn't one of your operatives. She volunteered to do a mission no one else in your stable could handle."

"Her accomplishments make her far better than any who've worked for me. Are you perturbed she took those risks for you? Would you have established contact with Kriegler or any other agent I might have sent?"

"Play your mind games on someone else. You led Joni and

me to believe a mole existed in the Taz project office. You wanted me to trust only her. Accept the fact you fucked up on this one and got lucky in the end."

"No one can foresee all the consequences of a mission. I tasked Kriegler with creating a situation to effectively turn over Bell without you being taken at the same time. From what he's related, he screwed up the exchange, leading to your injury. You should consider he risked his life, too. We knew you wouldn't let Joni go without a fight. You could've easily killed Kriegler."

"Not so easily," Bram cut in.

Ian fisted his fingers beneath hers. "You're both doing an excellent job of reminding me why I should hand you your heads on a platter."

"Considering your affections for Miss Bell, I understand your mind-set."

"How could you have been so sure Kagona wouldn't kill her outright?"

"Kriegler convinced him she had a wealth of information about your network. From what Kriegler described, she sorely disappointed them but gave plentiful false leads to keep them busy."

"An amazing feat considering Kriegler drugged her so that she has little memory of revealing anything. Was that also part of your plan?"

"Lemmon's innocent of the deed." Bram looked apologetically at her. "A premature escape would have interfered with our plan."

He'd given her that excuse before and she didn't buy it then. "And you happened to have this drug in your back pocket?"

Bram and Lemmon exchanged a quick glance.

"That's what I thought." She rose and let her hands rest on the table. What was done was done. "I knew the risks. Like every mission in the military, when the wheels leave the ground, all hell can break loose. My job is, and was, to handle the unexpected. Perhaps I should be thankful what happened with Bram and Kagona was a surprise."

Ian lightly touched a hand. "They don't deserve your forgiveness."

"Forgiveness? Not a chance. But I owe Mr. Lemmon."

Lemmon tilted his head, obviously curious.

"I failed your field test. Defeated by a drone. Yet you sent me to Zimbabwe with a camera-ready drone, disassembled and well disguised. That worked perfectly for surveillance on the mine. But it was what Bram brought in his day pack that made me realize you had more faith in me than I imagined."

"Glad you knew what to do with that stuff, *bokkie*, because I sure didn't."

"That's what surprised me. At first I figured Bram had been trained on the advanced functions. But at the mine, I discovered he had no idea how to assemble the parts. Lemmon sent the drone modifications knowing I could use them."

"That should come as no surprise to you, Miss Bell, according to—"

"I know…my profile. After I was humiliated in that test, you knew I'd devour the operating manual. It suggested a dozen possible configurations to handle various threats. With Bram's extra equipment, you made it possible for me to set up the drone as repeater and make my signal stronger than the one from Kagona's operator. Hacking became possible. The rest was easy with these guys to help and software that did the work for me."

"From Kriegler's report, you accomplished a diversion without ending up in a dung pile."

She caught Bram quickly looking away. "You'd heard about the rhino midden?"

"Your, um, stunt was too spectacular not to make the rounds."

"Yet you trusted me to operate the drone?"

"I always had faith in your capabilities, *bokkie*. You failed to deceive the drone in training, but you did something the men around you respected. They're trained to hide in places no one would look. Yet they walked past you and didn't turn back until the drone operator radioed in your position. You taught them a lesson."

"Then why, after my capture by Kagona, did you and Ian look at me as a liability of your own making? You squabbled over blame for my condition. We should've worked as a team. Instead, we did our best to sabotage one another."

Bram shrugged. "Short of claiming to be an idiot, I'd say guilt clouded my judgment."

"She's right." Ian looked grimly at her. "When Kagona and Chaipa showed up on the river, the three of us should have taken them on together. Three against two were damn good odds considering our talents. Instead, Kriegler made a rash decision and I followed it with one as equally stupid."

"I demanded you go after him."

"We account for our own decisions. By the time Kriegler figured out his mistake, he was praying I'd show up and save his sorry arse." Ian shot Bram a smug look. "Then all hell broke loose. We were lucky you arrived and supplied us with the perfect squeeze to use on Chaipa. Your video is likely why he called off the boats."

Lemmon shut the laptop. "Before you head out of town, Miss Bell, I expect to receive your and Mr. Kriegler's written versions of what happened."

"I trust Bram can supply the details you need. I'll review the report with him after time off to clear my head."

Lemmon rose. "I'm afraid that won't be possible. Mr. Kriegler will be gone when you return. Didn't he tell you? He's leaving the project." With that, Lemmon stepped back. "I've matters to attend. We're finished for now." After his usual abbreviated dismissal, he strode away.

Stunned, Joni watched Bram read the label on the beer bottle as if it shared great truths. He hadn't planned to tell her. Just cover the time while she was off getting her head on straight, then be gone when she walked back into the project. He loved flying here. Was this his decision or Lemmon's?"

"It's my decision," he said, as though reading her thoughts.

Joni shoved to her feet. "Save my beer." She stalked away, heading to find their project office boss and for once control Bram's future like he'd controlled hers.

Bram rose to follow but stopped cold at the excruciating pain radiating from his wrist.

Taljaard had pinned it with his hand to the table. "You haven't finished your beer."

"Haven't we been beaten up enough for one week?"

"Just getting your attention." The gorilla released his viselike hold. "Joni has her own battles to fight. This one she'll win."

Bram shook out his wrist. "We both know what's best. My presence will keep triggering episodes like the one at the Mike's chopper. I'm man enough to recognize I'm the one to walk away."

"On the contrary, you're going to stay and fix your fucking mistake."

Bram raised his hands and rounded the table to face Taljaard. "I surrender. I'm guilty. I know I screwed up, but in the end, I did what I did to protect her."

"Too bad it's not that simple." Taljaard swung his foot off the bench and picked up his crutch. "Your plan had holes."

"What do you mean?"

"Do you think it's what you did to her that has her messed up? Give her more credit. You forgot one minor part of Kagona's interrogation methods."

Bram's insides hollowed with fear. What had he missed?

"Looking a bit white there, Kriegler. Have you figured out

what Joni left out during your tête-à-tête on the lorry ride? Notice she didn't account for all her time with Kagona?"

Bram ignored common sense and grabbed Ian's collar. "What the hell happened?"

"*When* is the appropriate question, and it might well haunt her every time she steps into a helicopter."

"The flight from Kanyemba?" Bram had heard rumors of Kagona's deadly antics using a chopper.

"*Yebo.* Not a nightmare I'd want to have." Taljaard wove an arm between Bram's hands holding his collar and leveraged them off.

Bram sat on the bench, feeling as though a buffalo had trampled his body. Horrific images of Joni's plight terrorized his mind.

Taljaard stabbed the end of his crutch into the grass. "She only told me because she was afraid you'd suffer the same plight. Next time you come up with a plan to manipulate people, think about the bloody consequences."

"Another reason I need to leave."

"On the contrary, you're going to do everything in your power to make sure she feels comfortable in a helo again. It's the one thing in life she loves."

"Wrong. It's what gives her confidence." Bram rose, knowing he required time to process this news. "You're the one thing she loves, Taljaard. Don't screw it up like I have." He stepped away.

"Not so fast, Kriegler. I've a few rules with Joni going forward."

"Are you planning to stay around to enforce them?"

"Whether she wants me or not. It's going to take a while for my urge to kill you to fade. If I ever catch you near her bed again, you're a dead man."

"It's not in the flight plan. Never has been. I've seen what my lifestyle can do to a woman."

"Joni's not just any woman."

"I realized that as we worked together. Scared the hell out of me. Why do you think I call her *bokkie*? Using her name was too personal."

"Did you use it the night of interrogation?"

"Get that shit out of your head. If you'd seen the tear roll down her cheek when I got close to her, you'd know her heart belonged to only one man."

Bram was disgusted with himself, with Lemmon, with the damn universe that left him torn apart because he'd failed to protect Joni. "I deserve whatever you hand out, Taljaard. I owe you for saving my arse with Chaipa. It doesn't matter what lies he spouted back there. He'd have killed me along with Kagona given the chance."

Taljaard stood, his face stern and jaw set with unwavering determination. "Consider us even, then. That piece of dung you called a plan at least freed Mukono."

Bram watched as Taljaard left, setting up a steady rhythm with his crutches and healthy foot. Joni appeared and settled in alongside him, but not before casting a triumphant smile in Bram's direction.

Evidently his plans had changed. He'd be staying at the project office.

Damn if that didn't lighten his guilt. He drew in a deep lungful of air and headed in the direction Lemmon had disappeared. They'd all been through hell. Maybe with time and healing they'd work their way back to humanity.

CHAPTER THIRTY-ONE

Gansbaai, South Africa

"She's busy right now." Ian spoke into his cell phone, surprised a signal reached them offshore. He was sorely tempted to end the call. A crewman stood on the raised part of the boat stern, whipping around a long rope with a football-size chunk of fish and a float on the end. Ian held up his phone and snapped a photo when the man launched the lure out across the water.

"No problem, you're the one I want to speak with," Lemmon answered.

"How did you get this number?"

"You thought buying a new phone would distance you from me?"

"I could hang up."

"You could, but I'd just keep calling, and likely at inopportune times."

"Like now?"

The crewman slowly dragged the rope toward the starboard side, where divers floated in a narrow cage attached to the boat's side. The open top allowed access and the bars extended well below the boat. Joni submerged.

"I gave you several unfettered days to relax, but I don't believe in wasting time. You'll need the rest of your vacation to consider my proposal."

"You don't have a proposal we'd be interested in. Joni's days of being your flunky are done." Anticipation ran high as the rest of the crew and Ian watched the deep water.

"I'm not calling about her."

His eyes rose to the horizon and the distant rock island covered in seals and white dung. "Exactly what do you have in mind?"

"What are your future plans, Mr. Taljaard? Your uncle's wildlife reserve is getting a bit crowded with family. Are you planning on working as a tour guide?"

"That's none of your business."

"A man needs to make a living. A decent living."

Damn right, but *living* was the key word. "If you're looking for mercenaries to fight your battles, my father retired, and it's not a life I want to live."

"Your talents are too great to be wasted on such adventures. I have something completely different in mind."

Curiosity, as well as a desire to do something worthwhile with his skills, urged him to hear Lemmon out. "I'm listening."

"Africa is a huge continent. I need educated eyes in countries where it's difficult for an American to venture."

"Shark!" a crewman called out. The one manning the rope drew the fish bait across the water toward the cage. A dark mass appeared under the surface, followed by a telltale fin. A twelve-foot great white angled off.

"I can think of better candidates than me."

"Oh, the job isn't so difficult. I'd give you a camera and send you around Africa to photograph animals and the countryside. On the way, you'd simply collect information. How hard could that be?"

"I'm waiting for the catch."

"A good number of the shots and observations will be from the air."

"Meaning Joni might be involved?"

"Possibly. And, on occasion, your other talents might be required for survival."

"Ah, now we're getting to the real details. I've seen the way you treat your people. Why should I expect anything less than subpar treatment from you?"

"On the contrary, expect to be well paid and equipped. Human resources are very valuable to us."

Another shark appeared as well as the first. Within seconds, four huge creatures checked out the bait. Ian hit the video button on his cell phone. The crewman tugged the lure directly at the cage. One shark lunged. The bait dragged over the cage above Joni. The shark's head with pointed snout and mouth open slammed into the cage inches from her.

"If I say no, will you promise to lose this number?"

"Only foolish men make promises. No rush on an answer. Enjoy the last two weeks of your vacation."

The line cut off. The sharks disappeared as quickly as they had arrived. A euphoric Joni rose to the surface shaking her fist in the air. A loud whoop followed. With help from a crewman, she climbed from the cage back into the boat. A broad grin revealed her odd choice of therapy was working. Personally, he was looking forward to serene wine country.

She tore off her mask and then shoved back the head covering on her wet suit. "Your turn. But be careful. Their bite is bigger than their bark."

That description rather reminded him of Lemmon. With water dripping off her nose and chin, she planted a kiss on his cheek. He wanted more, but patience had always been a virtue in dealing with animals, and this sexy one had more allure than any he'd ever encountered.

They each took several more turns in the cage, sometimes

together and other times alone to photograph the adventure for each other. By the time they made it back to shore, dined, and settled in for the night, he'd reached a decision.

He lay in bed on his back. A cool breeze wafted through a window open to an ocean view. Water running in the bathroom stopped. The light clicked off. Only a glow from a dim bedside lamp filled the space.

A goddess walked toward him. The thin white nightshirt she'd left unbuttoned floated away from her body with each step. Perfect visible breasts and what hid beneath tiny white lace panties begged to be fondled. Best of all, her relaxed face offered a teasing air as she slid onto the bed, tucking her knees beneath her.

Damn lucky bastard ran again and again through his head. He slid a hand up through her hair to the back of her head and pulled her in for a kiss. A long, hot, heavy one heated enough to start a *braai*.

She slipped her leg across him until she straddled his midsection. As if on autopilot, his brain shifted its thinking to one place. She broke away from the kiss and trailed a finger down his chest. *Holy crap.* Her knees tightened against his sides.

"I heard you got a call on the boat."

That was the last thing he'd expected her to say. "You're bringing this up now?"

"I'm curious."

"Me, too, but my curiosity involves what's hiding beneath those panties." He ran a hand up inside the shirt until he encountered a handful of soft breast.

"Once you tell me who called, you'll find out." She added emphasis by sliding herself and those frigging sexy panties along his abdomen.

He returned the favor by brushing a thumb across her breast. "If I give you an answer, then I want one in return."

"Seems fair, but no promises."

"Why is it so hard for people to keep promises these days?" He worked up to a sit, leaning back on several pillows behind him.

The heat generated between their bodies drove him crazy. He delivered light kisses around her mouth and wound his thumb into the panty strap along her hip in an attempt to swing the discussion back to a more carnal subject. "Can't we talk later?"

"I'll lose my advantage. Who called you on the boat? No one has the new number."

"The B and B in Stellenbosch does. They were checking on our arrival tomorrow." No remorse rose over his decision to wait until after vacation to mention Lemmon's proposal. He'd no desire to even consider the future for the next two weeks. Even more important, Joni needed to recover without Lemmon's shadow hanging over her.

Joni took his hand. His hope she'd touch those luscious lips to his fingertips ended when she entwined her fingers in his. "Stop protecting me."

"I'll do whatever it takes for you to heal."

"That will only come when I learn to accept Lemmon for what he is." She slipped off him to sit at his side.

"A jackass? This is your damn holiday." The day—hell, the week—had progressed so well. Until now.

"You've avoided every discussion of what will happen when it's over."

For good reason. He'd no freaking clue. "I was hoping you'd let me stick around."

"Hoping? What do *you* want, Ian?"

"Aren't you enough?" He slid an arm around her, but she didn't budge.

With a sigh, he let go and leaned back against the pillows. Her question triggered a truth he'd refused to face. "I can't tell you what I haven't figured out for myself. Right now, all I can think about is protecting you. I never want to see you hurt again."

"That isn't possible, is it?" Her eyes softened, and she stroked the back of his hand. "Not for you and me. We've been hurt before, and the way we live, it's likely to happen again. Are you going to blame yourself every time things go wrong?"

"Honestly, I don't know. But the last thing I want is to walk away. You're all that's right in my life. Don't you feel it?"

Her chin slowly dropped to her chest and took his heart with it.

"Joni?" Fear, stark and real, engulfed him. He wanted to reach out, coax her to look at him again, but he stilled. The next move for them both belonged to her. He'd go if she asked. The thought tore his insides out.

She raised her head and studied his eyes. "Twice this week I've dreamed you were violently wrenched from my side. My heart raced until I awoke and touched you." The soft glow of the lamp showed moist eyes. "I want you, Ian, here with me…but…"

Afraid of the doubts that threatened, he kissed away her next words. "No buts, Joni. We'll work it out."

"None of what happened to me was your fault," she said softly. "Be with me. Beside me. But don't suffocate me. If I'm going to heal, I have to learn how to face Lemmon and my inner demons."

He brushed dark hair back from her face. "You're asking different things. I'll always protect you. Can't do anything else, because that's what loving you means. But I'll give you the space you need. Or at least, I'll try." He snuggled her in close, and she molded against his chest. "Give me a chance." He kissed the top of her head.

"Only one?"

"That's all I need."

"Lemmon pegged your profile."

"And what's that?"

"The very thing I love about you, Ian. Overconfidence."

He chuckled, his heart again feeling safe. "So where do we go from here?"

"You tell me why Lemmon called."

"He offered me a job."

"And…?"

"And I said I wouldn't spoil our holiday thinking about it. I'm not ruling out anything he offers. I can't give up on this world, Joni. My passion is about improving life for others. If he can facilitate that, I'm willing to listen."

"There are safer ways to do it than his jobs."

"Perhaps. I'm aware he isn't the only game in town. However, there are jobs left undone because no one has the will or skills to do them. That's where I thrive. And in many ways, so do you. You're one of a kind."

She pressed a palm against his chest and sat up fully, letting her fingers brush slowly down his midsection. "A foolish woman would believe your flattery."

"You're not foolish. You know it's the truth." He reached out and slid his palms along the outsides of her arms—bare arms softened by a sweet-smelling lotion. "Now it's your turn to answer a question for me."

"Ask away. I've nothing to hide." She leaned in and teased his mouth with brushes of hers, nearly rendering his mind blank.

He reciprocated by pulling her in and stretching out with her at his side. With deliberate slow ease, he crawled fingers up her inner thigh. Her breath quickened in anticipation of his touch.

Perfect.

"What's the story behind the rhino midden?"

"Oh, hell, no." She rolled away, but he'd expected a reaction and quickly trapped her beneath him.

"That answer doesn't bode well for our new relationship." Her open shirt allowed his kisses to close in on a breast.

"However, I can be persuaded to coerce the information from you."

"Cocky bastard."

"If the role fits…" He shifted his weight to free an arm and caressed along smooth skin toward those white lace panties. He fingers slipped into the place likely to help achieve his answer. "So, about that midden."

Her mouth pressed into a tight line.

He smiled, perhaps rather wickedly. Coercion was his strength. In mere seconds, she arched under his touch.

She cupped his chin in her hands, bringing him to focus on her face. "There is only one detail you need to know about that day."

"I'm assuming it's the best one."

"It's the one that counts." She wrapped a leg over his thigh and rolled him over so she straddled him.

"If we run into trouble or the going gets tough, Mr. Taljaard, no matter how disgusting or unthinkable, I will do anything for you. Anything. Never forget that." Her gaze, honest yet seductive, looked through his eyes to his swelling heart as she leaned down for a kiss. "Ever."

Thank you for taking the time to read OFF THE CHART. *If you enjoyed the story, the greatest way to say thank you to an author and encourage them to write more in the series is to tell your friends and consider writing a review at any one of the major retailers. It is greatly appreciated.*

BOOKS AND NEWSLETTER

Authors love to get feedback, so stop by Sandy's website, or blog, True Airspeed, and make contact with her.

Website: www.sandyparksauthor.com
Blog: sandyparks.wordpress.com

If you would like to be informed of upcoming books, please sign up for Sandy's newsletter via the website. It's sent infrequently and will be fun as well as informative. Also look for future additions to the website, Pinterest, or blog with photos and information on locations, settings, or aircraft mentioned in the Taking Risks series.

Join me:
Facebook: Sandy Parks-Writer
Twitter: @SParksauthor
Pinterest: parks3353

Thanks for your support, and stay tuned. More books are coming.

If you enjoyed Sandy's writing, you might like to try her romantic thrillers in the Hawker Incorporated series, which starts with multiple award-winning *REPOSSESSED*.

Join Jet as her daring team repossess high-end aircraft from less-than-upstanding citizens around the world. The first chapter is included in the following pages. *REPOSSESSED* is available in e-book or print.

CHAPTER ONE

Santos Dumont Airport
Rio de Janeiro, Brazil

Gnawing apprehension spread through Jet as Maximilian Furst climbed up from the dark night onto his business plane and cast her a triumphant look. Behind him the door closed and the steward flipped the locking handle, securing the aircraft and effectively cutting off rescue if her true purpose were to be discovered.

The cushy leather seat beneath her offered little comfort. Minutes before coming onboard, she'd learned Furst had left a disloyal employee floating face down in a local lake. She drew a calming breath through a fake smile. Had she overestimated her ability to manipulate a powerful man—one who was proving far more dangerous and unpredictable than her boss portrayed?

Looking back, getting onto the Gulfstream 550 had been easy—maybe a bit too easy. Whatever the case, she had to keep a step ahead of Furst if she hoped to find the aircraft's landing site.

He leaned over her leather chair, using his rock-solid body as unspoken intimidation. Without a word, he picked up the ends to her seat belt and buckled her in. Her heartbeat didn't slow until the plane had taken off from the domestic airport and risen out of the haze into a clear night.

Jet controlled her fear by focusing on the sleek cabin. She related more to machines, particularly those with wings, than men.

"You have an impressive aircraft," she said, with the proper amount of awe to feed Furst's overblown ego. She could recite checklists and emergency boldface items for the fifty-million-dollar beauty that surrounded her, but she had to be careful not to reveal her flying expertise. "Will I be as impressed with your home?" Or wherever the plane might land and "magically" disappear.

Maximilian shifted in his seat to face her and tented his long, dark fingers. "After the excess of my party, you will like the peaceful place we are going."

"Peaceful? I see you more as the type who never rests." She pointed at a well-developed bicep on his arm, making sure not to touch or even hint at coming close enough to doing so. "Those don't come from lounging around."

"*Senhorita*, you flatter me. What is a strong body without a fit mind? My sanctuary awaits. It cleanses the body and soul of troubles."

"I find it hard to believe you have many troubles."

"A man without them has never been tested. Take this plane, for instance. The company and I have a financial disagreement to resolve. My legal sources have informed me impatient Americans have arrived to take it back. They are supposedly in Rio at this very moment."

Perceptive sources. She held back the gulp striving to launch down her throat.

Maximilian, his spicy cologne still potent after the long night, leaned forward and encouraged her to do the same. She worked out of her seat belt and rather reluctantly moved closer.

With her head near, he softly added, "You, *senhorita de verão*, are an American. I believe you have come to steal my plane."

Photo by Robert Vanelli,
Exposure Photographic Art Studio

Sandy's romantic thrillers are award winning. *Repossessed* collected a 2013 Kiss of Death Daphne du Maurier Mainstream Mystery/Suspense Award, a 2013 Maggie Award for Novel with Strong Romantic Element, and a HOLT Award of Merit.

Flying and science are evident themes in Sandy's manuscripts. She is a hydrogeologist by training, with an MS in geological sciences, and has completed additional graduate engineering course work. She has taught at a university, worked on a military project for the Air Force Flight Test Center, worked as a design engineer for a civil engineering firm, and done computer modeling and field studies as a hydrogeologic consultant. Keeping up with her two sons, she also learned how to fly and dive and survived sparring for fifteen years as a black belt in kenpo karate. She has studied in England and Italy, traveled to South Africa, Egypt, Asia, and South America, and still travels to places of interest all over the world so she can make her stories richer.